P9-DNO-156

JOHN CONNOLLY

THE REAPERS

Pocket Star Books
New York London Toronto Sydney

The sale of this book without its cover is unauthorized. If you purchased this book without a cover, you should be aware that it was reported to the publisher as "unsold and destroyed." Neither the author nor the publisher has received payment for the sale of this "stripped book."

Pocket Star Books
A Division of Simon & Schuster, Inc.
1230 Avenue of the Americas
New York, NY 10020

"Vision and Prayer" (excerpt) by Dylan Thomas, from *The Poems of Dylan Thomas*, copyright © 1946 by New Directions Publishing Corp. Reprinted by permission of New Directions Publishing Corp. "The Heaven of Animals" (excerpt) by James Dickey, from *The Whole Motion: Collected Poems*, © 1992 by James Dickey and reprinted by permission of Wesleyan University Press.

This book is a work of fiction. Names, characters, places, and incidents either are products of the author's imagination or are used fictitiously. Any resemblance to actual events or locales or persons, living or dead, is entirely coincidental.

Copyright © 2008 by John Connolly

All rights reserved, including the right to reproduce this book or portions thereof in any form whatsoever. For information, address Atria Books Subsidiary Rights Department, 1230 Avenue of the Americas, New York, NY 10020.

First Pocket Star Books paperback edition May 2009

POCKET STAR and colophon are registered trademarks of Simon & Schuster, Inc.

For information about special discounts for bulk purchases, please contact Simon & Schuster Special Sales at 1-866-506-1949 or business@simonandschuster.com.

The Simon & Schuster Speakers Bureau can bring authors to your live event. For more information or to book an event, contact the Simon & Schuster Speakers Bureau at 1-866-248-3049 or visit our website at www.simonspeakers.com.

Cover design by Carlos Beltran

Manufactured in the United States of America

10 9 8 7 6 5 4 3 2 1

ISBN-13: 978-1-4165-6953-4
ISBN-10: 1-4165-6953-7

For Kerry Hood,
without whom I would be very lost indeed,
even with a map.

PROLOGUE

All things are an exchange for fire, and fire for all things, as goods for gold and gold for goods.

—HERACLITUS (C. 535–475 B.C.)

SOMETIMES, LOUIS DREAMS OF the Burning Man. He comes to him when the night is at its deepest, when even the sounds of the city have faded, descending from symphonic crescendo to muted nocturne. Louis is not even sure if he is truly asleep when the Burning Man comes, because it seems to him that he wakes to the sound of his partner's slow breathing in the bed beside him, a smell in his nostrils that is familiar yet alien: it is the stink of charred meats allowed to rot, of human fats sizzling in an open flame. If it is a dream, then it is a waking dream, one that occurs in the netherworld between consciousness and absence.

The Burning Man had a name once, but Louis can no longer utter it. His name is not enough to encompass his identity; it is too narrow, too restrictive for what he has become to Louis. He does not think of him as "Errol," or "Mr. Rich," or even "Mr. Errol," which is how he had always addressed him when he was alive. He is now more than a name, much more.

Still, once he was Mr. Errol: all brawn and muscle, his skin the color of damp, fertile earth recently turned by the plow; gentle and patient for the most part, but with something simmering beneath his seemingly placid exterior, so that if you caught him unawares it was possible to glimpse it in his eyes before it slipped away, like some rare beast that has learned the importance of staying beyond the range of the hunters' guns, of the white men in the white suits.

For the hunters were always white.

There was a fire burning in Errol Rich, a rage at the world and its ways. He tried to keep it under control, for he understood that, if it emerged unchecked, there was the danger that it would consume all in its path, himself included. Perhaps it was an anger that would not have been alien to many of his brothers and sisters at that time: he was a black man trapped in the rhythms and rituals of a white man's world, in a town where he and those like him were not permitted to roam once dusk fell. Things were changing elsewhere, but not in this country, and not in this town. Change would come more slowly to this place. Maybe, in truth, it would never come at all, not entirely, but that would be for others to deal with, not Errol Rich. By the time certain people started talking aloud about rights without fear of reprisal, Errol Rich no longer existed, not in any form that those who once knew him could have recognized. His life had been extinguished years before, and in the moment of his dying he was transformed. Errol Rich passed from this earth, and in his place came the Burning Man, as though the fire inside had finally found a way to bloom forth in bright red and yellow, exploding from within to devour his flesh and consume his former consciousness, so that what was once a hidden part of him became all that he was. Others might have held the torch to him, or sprayed the gasoline that soaked and blinded him in his final moments as he was hanged from a tree, but Errol Rich was already burning, even then, even as he asked them to spare him from the agonies that were to come. He had always burned, and in that way, at least, he defeated the men who took his life.

And from the moment that he died, the Burning Man stalked Louis's dreams.

Louis remembers how it came to pass: an argument with whites. Somehow, that was often how it started. The whites made the rules, but the rules kept changing. They were fluid, defined by circumstance and necessity, not by words on paper. Later, Louis would reflect that what was strangest of all was the fact that the white men and women who ran the town would always deny that they were racist. *We don't hate the coloreds,* they would say, *we just all get along better when they keep themselves to themselves.* Or: *they're welcome in the town during the day, but we just don't think they should spend the night. It's for their own safety as much as ours.* Curious. It was as hard then as it was now to find anybody who would admit to being a racist. Even most racists, it seemed, were ashamed of their intolerance.

But there were also those who wore such an epithet as a badge of honor, and the town had its share of such people as well. It was said that the trouble started when a group of local men threw a heavy pitcher filled with urine through the cracked old windshield of Errol's truck, and Errol responded in kind. That temper of his, that fury that he kept bottled inside of him, had erupted, and he had tossed a length of two-by-four through the window of Little Tom's bar in reprisal. That had been enough for them to act against him, that and their fear of what he represented. He was a black man who spoke better than most of the white people in the town. He owned his own truck. He could fix things with his hands—radios, TVs, air conditioners, anything that had a current flowing through it—and he could fix them better and cheaper than anyone else, so that even those who wouldn't allow him to walk the town's streets at night were happy to let him into their homes to fix their appliances during the day, even if some of them didn't feel quite as comfortable in their living rooms afterward, although they weren't racists either. They just didn't like strangers in their home, particularly colored strangers. If they offered him water to slake his thirst, they were careful to present it to him in the cheap tin cup set aside for just such an eventuality, the cup from which no one else would drink, the cup kept with the cleaning products and the brushes, so that the water always had a faint chemical burn to it. There was talk that maybe he might soon be in a position to employ others like him, to train them and pass on his skills to them. And he was a good-looking man, too, a "nigger buck" as Little Tom had once described him, except that, when he said it, Little Tom had been cradling the hunting rifle that used to hang above his bar, and it was clear what being a buck implied in Little Tom's world.

So they hadn't needed much of an excuse to move against Errol Rich, but he had given them one nonetheless, and before the week was out, they had doused him in gasoline, hanged him from a tree, and set him alight.

And that was how Errol Rich became the Burning Man.

Errol Rich had a wife in a city a hundred miles to the north. He'd fathered a child with her, and once each month he would drive up to see them and make sure that they had what they needed. Errol Rich's wife had a job in a big hotel. Errol used to work in that hotel, too, as a handyman, but something had happened—that temper again, it was whispered—and he had to leave his wife and child and find work elsewhere. On those other weekend nights when he was not seeing to his family, Errol could be found drinking quietly in the little lean-to out in the swamps that served as a bar and social hub for the coloreds, tolerated by the local law as long as there was no trouble and no whoring, or none that was too obvious. Louis's momma would sometimes go there with her friends, even though Grandma Lucy didn't approve. There was music, and often Louis's momma and Errol Rich would dance together, but there was a sadness and a regret to their rhythms, as though this was now all that they had, and all that they would ever have. While others drank rotgut, or "jitter juice" as Grandma Lucy still called it, Louis's momma sipped on a soda and Errol stuck to beer. Just one or two, though. He never was much for drinking, he used to say, and he didn't like to smell it on others first thing in the morning, especially not on a working man, although he wasn't about to police another's pleasures, no sir.

On warm summer nights, when the air was filled with the burr of katydids, and mosquitoes, drawn by the heady mix of sweat and sugar, fed upon the men and women in the club, and the music was loud enough to shake dust from the ceiling, and the crowd was distracted by noise and scent and movement, Errol Rich and Louis's momma would perform their slow dance, unheeding of the rhythms that surrounded them, alive only to the beating of their own hearts, their bodies pressed so close that, in time, those beats came in unison and they were one together, their fingers intertwined, their palms moving damply, one upon the other.

And sometimes that was enough for them, and sometimes it was not.

Mr. Errol would always give Louis a quarter when their paths crossed. He would comment upon how tall Louis had grown, how well he looked, how proud his momma must be of him.

And Louis thought, although he could not say why, that Mr. Errol was proud of him, too.

On the night that Errol Rich died, Louis's Grandma Lucy, the matriarch of the house of women in which Louis grew up, fed Louis's mother bourbon and a dose of morphine to help her sleep. Louis's momma had been weeping all week, ever since she heard of what had passed between Errol and Little Tom. Later, Louis was told that she had gone over to Errol's place at noon that day, her sister in tow, and had pleaded with him to leave, but Errol wasn't going to run, not again. He told her that it would all work out. He said that he had gone to see Little Tom and had apologized for what he had done. He had paid over forty dollars that he could ill afford to cover the damage, and as compensation for Little Tom's trouble, and Little Tom had accepted the money gruffly and told Errol that what was done was done, and he forgave him his moment of ill temper. It had pained Errol to pay the money, but he wanted to stay where he was, to live and work with people whom he liked and respected. And loved. That was what he told Louis's mother, and that was what Louis's aunt told him, many years later. She described how Errol and Louis's momma had held hands as they spoke, and how she had walked outside for a breath of air to give them their privacy.

When Louis's momma eventually emerged from Errol's cabin, her face was very pale and her mouth was trembling. She knew what was coming, and Errol Rich knew it, too, no matter what Little Tom might say. She went home and cried so much that she lost her breath and blacked out on the kitchen table, and it was then that Grandma Lucy took it upon herself to give her a little something to ease her suffering, so Louis's momma had slept while the man she loved burned.

That night, the lean-to was closed, and the blacks who worked in the town left long before dusk came. They stayed in their houses and their shacks, their families close by, and nobody spoke. Mothers sat and kept vigil over their children as they slept, or held the hands of their menfolk over bare tables or seated by empty grates and cold stoves. They had felt it coming, like the heat before a storm, and they had fled, angry and ashamed at their powerlessness to intervene.

And so they had waited for the news of Errol Rich's leaving of this world.

On the night that Errol Rich died, Louis can remember waking to the sound of a woman's footsteps outside the little box room in which he slept. He can recall climbing from his bed, the boards warm beneath his bare feet, and walking to the open door of their cabin. He sees his grandmother on the porch, staring out into the darkness. He calls to her, but she does not answer. There is music playing, the voice of Bessie Smith. His grandmother always loved Bessie Smith.

Grandma Lucy, a shawl draped around her shoulders over her nightdress, steps down into the yard in her bare feet. Louis follows her. Now all is no longer dark. There is a light in the forest, a slow burning. It is shaped like a man, a man writhing in agony as the flames consume him. He walks through the forest, the leaves turning to black in his wake. Louis can smell the gasoline and the roasted flesh, can see the skin charring, can hear the hissing and popping of body fats. His grandmother reaches out a hand behind her, never taking her eyes from the Burning Man, and Louis places his palm against her palm, his fingers against her fingers, and as she tightens her grip upon him, his fear fades and he feels only grief for what this man is enduring. There is no anger. That will come later. For now, there is only an overwhelming sadness that falls upon him like a dark cloak. His grandmother whispers, and begins to weep. Louis weeps, too, and together they drown the flames, even as the Burning Man's mouth forms words that Louis cannot quite hear, as the fire dies and the image fades, until all that is left is the smell of him and an image seared upon Louis's retina like the aftermath of a photographic flash.

And now, as Louis lies in a bed far from the place in which he grew up, the one he loves sleeping soundly beside him, he smells gasoline and roasted meat, and sees again the Burning Man's lips move, and thinks that he understands part of what was said on that night so many years before.

Sorry. Tell her I am sorry.

Most of what follows is lost to him, wreathed in fire. Only two words stand out, and even now Louis is not certain if he interprets them correctly, if the movement of that lipless gap truly corresponds to what he believes was uttered, or to what he wants to believe.

Son.

My son.

There was a fire inside Errol Rich, and something of that fire transferred itself to the boy at the moment of Errol's death. It burns within him now, but where Errol Rich found a way to deny it, to temper its flames until at last, perhaps inevitably, it rose up and destroyed him, Louis has embraced it. He fuels it, and it, in turn, fuels him, but it is a delicate balance that he maintains. The fire needs to be fed if it is not to feed upon him instead, and the men he kills are the sacrifices that he offers to it. Errol Rich's fire was a deep, scorching red, but the flames inside Louis burn white and cold.

Son.

My son.

At night, Louis dreams of the Burning Man.

And, somewhere, the Burning Man dreams of him.

I

He will now be felled with my arrow,
as I am enraged at him, and gone are
his lives now, and indeed the earth shall
drink his blood.

—*SRIMAD VALMIKI RAMAYANA* (C. 500–100 B.C.)

CHAPTER ONE

THERE ARE SO MANY killings, so many victims, so many lives lost and ruined every day, that it can be hard to keep track of them all, hard to make the connections that might bring cases to a close. Some are obvious: the man who kills his girlfriend, then takes his own life, either out of remorse or because of his own inability to face the consequences of his actions; or the tit-for-tat murders of hoodlums, gangsters, drug dealers, each killing leading inexorably to another as the violence escalates. One death invites the next, extending a pale hand in greeting, grinning as the ax falls, the blade cuts. There is a chain of events that can easily be reconstructed, a clear trail for the law to follow.

But there are other killings that are harder to connect, the links between them obscured by great distances, by the passage of years, by the layering of this honeycomb world as time folds softly upon itself.

The honeycomb world does not hide secrets: it stores them. It is a repository of buried memories, of half-forgotten acts.

In the honeycomb world, everything is connected.

The St. Daniil sat on Brightwater Court, not far from the cavernous dinner clubs on Brighton Beach Avenue and Coney Island Avenue where couples of all ages danced to music in Russian, Spanish, and English, ate Russian food, shared vodka and wine, and watched stage shows that would not have been out of place in some of the more modest Reno hotels, or on a cruise ship, yet the St. Daniil was far enough away from them to render itself distinct in any number of ways. The building that it occupied overlooked the ocean, and the boardwalk with its principal trio of restaurants, the Volna, the Tatiana, and the Winter Garden, now screened to protect their patrons from the cool sea breeze and the stinging sands. Nearby was the Brighton playground, where, during the day, old men sat at stone tables playing cards while children cavorted nearby, the young and the not-so-young united together in the same space. New condos had sprung up to the east and west, part of the transformation that Brighton Beach had undergone in recent years.

But the St. Daniil belonged to an older dispensation, a different Brighton Beach, one occupied by the kind of businesses that made their money from those who were on nodding terms with poverty: check-cashing services that took 25 percent of every check cashed, then offered loans at a similar monthly rate to cover the shortfall; discount stores that sold cheap crockery with cracked glaze, and firetrap Christmas decorations all year round; former mom-and-pop grocery stores that were now run by the kind of men who looked like they might have the remains of mom and pop rotting in their cellars; laundromats frequented by men who smelt of the streets and who would routinely strip down to filthy shorts and sit, nearly naked, waiting for their clothes to wash before giving them a single desultory spin in the dryer (for every quarter counted) and then dress in the still-damp clothes, folding the rest into plastic garbage bags and venturing back onto the streets, their garments steaming slightly in the air; pawnshops that did a steady trade in redeemed and unredeemed items, for there was always someone willing to benefit from the misfortune of another; and storefronts with no name above the window and only a battered counter inside, the shadowy business conducted within of no interest to those who needed to be told its nature. Most of those places were gone now, relegated to side streets, to less desirable neighborhoods, pushed farther and farther back from the avenue and the sea, although those who needed their services would always know where to find them.

The St. Daniil remained, though. It endured. The St. Daniil was a club, although it was strictly private and had little in common with its glitzier counterparts on the avenue. Accessed through a steel-caged door, it occupied the basement of an old brownstone building surrounded by other brownstones of similar vintage although, while its neighbors had been cleaned up, the edifice occupied by the St. Daniil had not. It had once formed the main entrance to a larger complex, but changes to the internal structure of the buildings had isolated the St. Daniil between two significantly more attractive apartment blocks. The club's home now squatted in the middle of them like some poor relation that had muscled in on a family photo, unashamed of its ignominy.

Above the St. Daniil was a warren of small apartments, some big enough to be occupied by entire families, others small enough to accommodate only an individual, and one, at that, for whom space mattered less than privacy and anonymity. Nobody lived in those apartments now, not willingly. Some were used for storage: booze, cigarettes, electrical goods, assorted contraband. The rest acted as temporary quarters for young—sometimes very young—prostitutes and, when required, their clients. One or two of the rooms were marginally better furnished and maintained than others, and contained video cameras and recording equipment for the making of pornographic films.

Although it was known as the St. Daniil, the club did not have an official name. A plate beside the door read "Private Members Social Club" in English and Cyrillic, but it was not the kind of place where anyone went to be sociable. There was a bar there, but few lingered at it, and those who did stuck mostly to coffee and killed time while waiting for errands to run, vig to collect, bones to break. A TV above the bar showed pirated DVDs, old hockey games, sometimes porn or, late at night, when all business had been conducted, film of Russian troops in Chechnya engaging in reprisals against their enemies, real or perceived. Worn hemispherical vinyl booths lined the walls, with scuffed tables at their center, relics of a time when this really was a social club, a place where men could talk of the old country and share the newspapers that had arrived in the mail or in the suitcases of visitors and immigrants. The decor consisted mainly of framed copies of Soviet posters from the 1940s, bought for five bucks at RBC Video on Brighton Beach Avenue.

For a time, the police had kept watch on the club, but they had been unable to access it in order to plant a bug, and a wiretap on the phones had expired without anything useful being learned. Any business of consequence was, they suspected, now conducted on throwaway cellphones, the phones replaced religiously at the end of every week. Two raids by vice on the building through the doorway above the club had scored only a couple of johns and a handful of weary whores, few of whom had English and fewer of whom had papers. No pimps were ever apprehended, and the women, the cops knew, were easily replaced.

On those nights, the door to the St. Daniil had remained firmly closed, and when the cops finally gained entry to it they had found only a bored bartender and a pair of ancient, toothless Russians playing poker for matchsticks.

It was a mid-October evening. The light outside had long faded and only a single booth in the club was occupied. The man seated there was a Ukrainian known as the Priest. He had studied in an Orthodox seminary for three years before discovering his true vocation, which lay primarily in providing the kinds of services for which priests were usually required to offer forgiveness. The club's unofficial name was a testament to the Priest's brief flirtation with the religious life. The St. Daniil monastery was Moscow's oldest cloister, a stronghold of the Orthodox faith even during the worst excesses of the Communist era, when many of its priests had become martyrs and the remains of St.

Daniil himself had been smuggled to America in order to save them from harm.

Unlike many of those who worked for him, the Priest spoke English with hardly a trace of an accent. He had been part of the first influx of immigrants from the Soviet Union, working hard to learn the ways of this new world, and he could still recall a time when Brighton Beach had been nothing but old people living in rent-controlled apartments surrounded by little vacant houses falling into decay, a far cry from the days when this area was a beacon for immigrants and New Yorkers alike anxious to leave the crowded neighborhoods of Brownsville, East New York, and Manhattan's Lower East Side for space in which to live and the feel of sea air in their lungs. He prided himself on his sophistication. He read the *Times,* not the *Post.* He went to the theater. When he was in his realm, there was no porn on the TV, no poorly copied DVDs. Instead, it was tuned to BBC World, or sometimes CNN. He did not like Fox News. It looked inward, and he was a man who was always looking at the greater world outside. He drank tea during the day, and only compote, a fruit punch that tasted of plums, at night. He was an ambitious man, a prince who wished to become a king. He paid obeisance to the old men, the ones who had been imprisoned under Stalin, the ones whose fathers had created the criminal enterprise that had now reached its zenith in a land far from their own. But even as he bowed before them, the Priest looked for ways in which they might be undermined. He calculated the strength of potential rivals among his own generation and prepared his people for the inevitable bloodshed, sanctioned or unsanctioned, that would come. Recently, there had been some reversals. The mistakes might have been avoided, but he was not entirely to blame for them. Unfortunately, there were others who did not see it that way. Perhaps, he thought, the bloodshed would have to begin sooner than expected.

Today had been a bad day, another in a succession of bad days. There had been a problem with the restrooms that morning and the place still stank, even though the difficulty had apparently been solved once the drain people, from a firm trusted by the organization, got on the case. On another day, the Priest might well have left the club and gone elsewhere, but there was business to be conducted and loose ends to be tied, so he was prepared to put up with the lingering bad odor for as long as was necessary.

He flicked through some photographs on the table before him: undercover policemen, some of them probably Russian speakers. They were determined, if nothing else. He would have them identified to see if there was some way of putting pressure on them through their families. The police were drawing ever closer to him. After years of ineffectual moves against him, they had been given a break. Two of his men had died in Maine the previous winter, along with two intermediaries. Their deaths had exposed a small but lucrative part of the Priest's Boston operation: pornography and prostitution involving minors. He had been forced to cease providing both services, and the result had affected, in turn, the smuggling of women and children into the country, which meant that the inevitable attrition of his stable of whores, and the stables of others, could not be arrested. He was hemorrhaging money, and he did not like it. His comrades were suffering, too, and he knew that they blamed him. Now his club stank of excrement and it would only be a matter of time before the dead men were finally connected to him.

But word had reached him that there might be a solution to at least one of his problems. All of this had started because a private detective in Maine could not mind his own business. Killing him would not get rid of the police—it might even increase the pressure upon him for a time—but it would at least serve as a warning to his persecutors and to those who might be tempted to testify against him, as well as giving the Priest a little personal satisfaction along the way.

There was a shout from the doorway in Russian: "Boss, they are here."

• • •

One week earlier, a man had arrived at the offices of Big Earl's Cleaning & Drain Services, Inc., on Nostrand Avenue. He had not entered through the brightly carpeted, fragrant-smelling lobby. Instead, he had walked around the side of the building to the maintenance yard and waste-treatment area.

This area did not smell at all fragrant.

He entered the garage and climbed a flight of steps to a glass booth. Inside was a desk, a range of mismatched filing cabinets, and two cork boards covered with invoices, letters, and a pair of out-of-date calendars featuring women in a state of undress. Seated behind the desk was a tall, thin man in a white shirt offset by a green and yellow polyester tie. His hair was Grecian-formula brown, and he was fiddling compulsively with his pen, the sure sign of a smoker deprived, however temporarily, of his drug. He looked up as the door opened and the visitor entered. The new arrival was of below-average height, and dressed in a navy peacoat buttoned to the neck, a pair of torn, faded jeans, and bright red sneakers. He had a three-day growth of beard, but wore it in a manner that suggested he *always* had a three-day growth of beard. It looked almost cultivated, in an untidy way. "Shabby" was the word that came to mind.

"You trying to quit?" asked the visitor.

"Huh?"

"You trying to give up cigarettes?"

The man looked at the pen in his right hand as if almost surprised that there wasn't a cigarette there.

"Yeah, that's right. Wife's been at me to do it for years. The doc, too. Thought I'd give it a try."

"You should use those nicotine patches."

"Can't get them to light. What can I do for you?"

"Earl around?"

"Earl's dead."

The visitor looked shocked. "No way. When did he die?"

"Two months ago. Cancer of the lung." He coughed embarrasedly. "Kind of why I decided to give up. My name's Jerry Marley, Earl's brother. I came on board to help out when Earl got sick, and I'm still here. Earl a friend of yours?"

"An acquaintance."

"Well, guess he's gone to a better place now."

The visitor looked around the little office. Beyond the glass, two men in masks and coveralls were cleaning pipes and tools. He wrinkled his nose as the stink reached him.

"Hard to believe," said the visitor.

"Ain't it though. So, what can I do for you?"

"You unclog drains?"

"That's right."

"So if you know how to unclog them, then you must know how to clog them as well."

Jerry Marley looked momentarily puzzled, and then anger replaced puzzlement. He stood up. "You get the hell out of here before I call the cops. This is a business, dammit. I got no time for people trying to cause other people trouble."

"I hear your brother wasn't so particular about who he worked with."

"Hey, you keep your mouth shut about my brother."

"I don't mean that in a bad way. It was one of the things I liked about him. It made him useful."

"I don't give a shit. Get out of here, you—"

"Maybe I should introduce myself," said the visitor. "My name is Angel."

"I don't give a good goddamn what—" Marley stopped talking as he realized that he did, in fact, give a good goddamn. He sat down again.

"I guess Earl might have mentioned me."

Marley nodded. He looked a little paler than before. "You, and another fella."

"Oh, he's around somewhere. He's—" Angel searched for the right word. "—cleaner than I am. No offense meant, but his clothes cost more than mine. The smell, y'know, it gets in the fabric."

"I know," said Marley. He began to babble, but couldn't stop himself. "I don't notice it so much no more. My wife, she makes me take my clothes off in the garage before I come in the house. Have to shower straightaway. Even then, she says she can still smell it on me."

"Women," said Angel. "They're sensitive like that."

There was a brief silence. It was almost companionable, except that Jerry Marley's desire for a cigarette had suddenly increased beyond the capacity of any mortal man to resist.

"So," said Angel. "About those drains . . ."

Marley raised a hand to stop him. "Mind if I smoke?" he asked.

"I thought you were giving up," said Angel.

"So did I."

Angel shrugged. "I guess it must be a stressful job."

"Sometimes," said Marley.

"Well, I don't want to add to it."

"God forbid."

"But I do need a favor, and I'll do you a favor in return."

"Right. And what would that be?"

"Well, if you do me my favor, I won't come back again."

Jerry Marley thought about it for less than half a second.

"That seems fair," he said.

For a moment, Angel looked a little sad. He was hurt that everyone wanted to leap at that deal when it was offered.

Marley seemed to guess what he was thinking. "Nothing personal," he added, apologetically.

"No," said Angel, and Marley got the sense that the visitor was thinking of something else entirely. "It never is."

The two men who entered the Priest's den a week later were not what he had expected, but then the Priest had learned that nothing was ever quite as he might have expected it to be. The first was a black man dressed in a gray suit that looked as if it was being worn for the first time. His black patent leather shoes shone brightly, and a black silk tie was knotted perfectly at the collar of his spotlessly white shirt. He was clean shaven and exuded a faint scent of cloves and incense that was particularly appealing to the Priest under his current, excrementally tainted, circumstances.

Behind him was a smaller man, possibly of Hispanic origin, wearing an amiable smile that briefly distracted from the fact that his clothes had seen better days: no-name denims, last year's sneakers, and a padded jacket that was obviously of good quality but was more suited to someone two decades younger and two sizes larger.

"They're clean," said Vassily, once the two men had submitted, with apparent good grace, to a frisking. Vassily was deceptively compact and his features were gentle and delicate. He moved with speed and grace, and was one of the Priest's most trusted acolytes, another Ukrainian with brains and ambition, although not so much ambition that it might pose a threat to his employer.

The Priest gestured at a pair of chairs facing him across the table. The two men sat.

"Would you like a drink?" he asked them.

"Nothing for me," said the black man.

"I'll have a soda," said the other. "Coke. Make sure the glass isn't dirty."

The smile never left his face. He looked over his shoulder at the bartender and winked. The bartender merely scowled.

"Now, what can I do for you?" asked the Priest.

"It's more a matter of what we can do for you," said the small man.

The Priest shrugged. "Cleaning, maybe? Selling door-to-door?"

There was an appreciative laugh from his soldiers. There were three of them in all, plus the bartender. Two were seated at the bar, the ubiquitous coffee cups before them. Vassily was behind the men and to their right. The Priest thought that he looked uneasy. But then, Vassily always looked uneasy. He was a pessimist, or perhaps a realist; the Priest was never entirely sure which. He supposed that it was all a matter of perspective.

The small man's grin faded slightly.

"We're here about the paper."

"Paper? Are you looking for a route?"

There was more laughter.

"The paper on the detective, Parker. We hear you want him taken out. We'd prefer it if that wasn't the case."

The laughter stopped. The Priest had been informed that two men wanted to discuss the detective with him, so this opening gambit was not unexpected. Usually, the Priest would have left such discussions to Vassily, but this was not the usual situation, and these, he knew, were not usual men. He had been told that they merited a degree of respect, but this was the Priest's place, and he enjoyed goading them. He respected those who respected him, and the mere fact of the men's presence in his club irritated him. They were not pleading for the detective's life; they were trying to tell him how to run his business.

The bartender placed a Coke in front of the small man. He sipped it and scowled.

"It's warm," he said.

"Give him some ice," said the Priest.

The bartender nodded. One of the men seated at the bar leaned over and filled an empty glass with ice by scooping it through the ice bucket. He handed it to the bartender. The bartender dipped his fingers into the glass, retrieved two cubes, and dropped them into the Coke. The liquid splashed onto the small man's jeans.

"Hey," he said. "That's rude, man. And seriously fucking unhygienic, even in a place that smells as bad as this one."

"We know who you are," said the Priest.

"Excuse me?"

"I said, 'We know who you are.'"

"What does that mean?"

The priest pointed at the small untidy man. "You are Angel." The finger moved slightly to the left. "And you are named Louis. Your reputation precedes you, as I believe people say under these circumstances."

"Should we be flattered?"

"I think so."

Angel looked pleased. Now Louis spoke for the first time.

"You need to burn the paper," he said.

"Why would that be?" asked the Priest.

"The detective is off-limits."

"By whose authority?"

"Mine. Ours. Other people's."

"What other people?"

"If I said I didn't know, and you didn't want to know, would you believe me?"

"Possibly," said the Priest. "But he's caused me a lot of trouble. A message has to be sent."

"We were up there, too. You going to put a paper out on us?"

The Priest wagged his finger. "Now you *are* off-limits. We're all professionals. We know how these things work."

"Do we? I don't think we're in the same business."

"You flatter yourself."

"I'm flattering somebody."

If the Priest was offended, he didn't show it. He was, though, surprised at the men's willingness to antagonize him in turn when they were unarmed. He considered it both arrogant and unmannerly.

"There's nothing to discuss. There is no paper on the detective."

"What does that mean?"

"I cut my own lawn. I shine my own shoes. I don't send out for strangers to do what I can take care of for myself."

"That puts us at odds."

"Only if you let it." The Priest leaned forward. "Is that what you want?"

"We just want a quiet life."

The Priest laughed. "I think it would bore you. I know it would bore me." His fingers moved the photographs on the table, rearranging them.

"Friends of yours?" said Louis.

"Police."

"You go after the detective, and you're going to create more problems for yourself with them as well as us. They can be persistent. You don't need to give them any more reasons to breathe down your neck."

"So you want me to let the detective slide?" said the Priest. "You're concerned for me, concerned for my business, concerned about the police."

"That's right," said Louis. "We're concerned citizens."

"And what is the percentage for me?"

"We go away."

"That's it?"

"That's it."

The Priest's shoulders sagged theatrically. "Okay, then. Sure. For you, I let him slide."

Louis didn't move. Beside him, Angel grew tense.

"Just like that," said Louis.

"Just like that. I don't want trouble from men of your, uh, caliber. Maybe somewhere down the road, you might do me a favor in return."

"I don't think so, but it's a nice thought."

"So, you want a drink now?"

"No," said Louis. "I don't want a drink."

"Well, if that's the case, our discussions are over." The Priest leaned back in his seat and folded his hands over his small belly. As he did so, he raised the little finger of his left hand slightly. Behind Angel and Louis, Vassily's hand reached behind his back for the gun tucked into his belt. The two men at the bar stood, also reaching for their weapons.

"I told you he wouldn't agree," said Angel to Louis. "Even if he said so, he wouldn't agree."

Louis shot him a look of disdain. He picked up Angel's glass of soda, seemed about to take a sip from it, then reconsidered.

"You know what you are?" he said. "You a Monday morning quarterback."

And as he spoke, he moved. It was done with such fluidity, such grace, that Vassily, had he lived long enough, might almost have admired it. Louis's hand slid beneath the table as he rose, removing the gun that had been concealed beneath it earlier by the man who had accompanied the cleaning crew. In the same movement, his other hand buried the glass in Vassily's face. By then, Vassily had his own gun drawn, but it was too late for him. The first two bullets took him in the chest, but Louis caught him before he fell, shielding himself with the body as he fired upon the men at the bar. One managed to get off a shot, but it impacted harmlessly upon the woodwork above Louis's head. Barely seconds later, only four men remained alive in the room: the Priest, the bartender, and the two men who would soon kill them both.

The Priest had not moved. The second gun that had been concealed beneath the table was now in Angel's hand, and it was pointing directly at the Priest. Angel had remained motionless while the killing went on behind him. He trusted his partner. He trusted him as he loved him, which was completely.

"All of this for a private detective," said the Priest.

"He's a friend," said Angel. "And it's not just about him."

"Then what?" The Priest spoke calmly. "Whatever it is, we can reach an accommodation. You have made your point. Your friend is safe."

"You expect us to believe that? Frankly, you don't seem like the forgiving type."

"You know what type I am? The type that wants to live."

Angel considered this. "It's good to have an ambition," he said. "That one seems kind of narrow, though."

"It encompasses a great deal."

"I guess so."

"And as for what happened here, well, if you show me mercy, then mercy will be shown to you."

"I don't think so," said Angel. "I saw what was done to those children you farmed out. I *know* what was done to them. I don't think you're due mercy."

"It was business," said the Priest. "It was nothing personal."

"It's funny," said Angel, "I hear that a lot." He raised the gun, drawing a bead slowly upward from the Priest's belly, passing his heart, his throat, before stopping at his face. "Well, this isn't business. This *is* personal."

He shot the Priest once in the head, then stood. Louis was staring down the barrel of his gun at the bartender, who was flat on the floor, his hands spread wide.

"Get up," said Louis.

The bartender started to rise and Louis shot him, watching impassively as he folded in upon himself and lay still on the filthy carpet. Angel stared at his partner.

"Why?" he asked.

"No witnesses, not today."

Louis moved swiftly to the door. Angel followed. He opened the door, glanced quickly outside, then nodded at Louis. Together, they ran for the Oldsmobile parked across the street.

"And?" asked Angel, as he got into the passenger seat and Louis climbed behind the wheel.

"You think he knew what went on there, how his boss made his money?"

"I guess."

"Then he should have found a job someplace else."

The car pulled away from the curb. The doors above the club opened and two men emerged with guns in their hands. They were about to fire when the Oldsmobile made a hard left and disappeared from view.

"Will it come back on us?"

"He got above himself. He attracted attention. His days were numbered. We just accelerated the inevitable."

"You sure of that?"

"We walk on this one. We did some people a favor back there, and not just Parker. A problem was solved, and they got to keep their hands clean."

"And they'll go back to running kids into the country."

"That's a problem for another time."

"Tell me that we'll deal with it, that we won't walk away."

"I promise," said Louis. "We'll do what we can down the line."

They ditched the Olds four blocks away in favor of their own Lexus. The car boasted a Sirius satellite radio and, by mutual agreement, each was allowed to choose a station on alternate evenings and the other was not allowed to complain about the selection. Tonight was Angel's choice, so they listened to First Wave all the way back to Manhattan.

And thus the journey home passed in an almost companionable silence.

Farther south, the second link in the chain of killings was about to be forged.

There were only a handful of people in the bar when the predator entered, and he spotted his kill almost immediately: a sad, overweight little man with beaten-down shoulders, balding and sweaty, wearing a pair of brown trousers that had seen neither an iron nor a laundry in at least a week, and brown brogues that had probably cost him a lot some years before but that he could now no longer afford to replace. He was nursing a bourbon, the faintest trace of amber liquid coloring the melted ice at the bottom of the glass. At last, resignedly, he drained it. The bartender asked him if he wanted another. The fat man checked his wallet, then nodded. A generous shot was poured for him, but then the bartender could afford to be generous. It came from the cheapest bottle on the shelf.

The predator took in every detail of the fat man: his stubby fingers, the wedding band embedded in the flesh of one; the twin handles of fat at his sides; the belly that flopped over the cheap leather belt; the sweat marks beneath the arms of his shirt; the sheen of perspiration on his face, his forehead, his pate.

Because you're always sweating, aren't you? Even in winter, you sweat, the effort of hauling around your soft, gelatinous bulk almost too much for your heart to bear. You sweat when you wear a T-shirt and shorts in summer, and when the snow comes you sweat beneath layers of clothing. What is your wife like, I wonder? Is she fat and repugnant like you or has she tried to keep her figure in the hope that she might attract someone better while you're out on the road, even if that someone merely uses her for a night? (For she will surely be using him in return.) Do you think about those possibilities as you hustle from town to town, barely eking out a living, always laughing harder than you should, paying for drinks that you can't afford in order to curry favor, picking up the tab at restaurants that others choose in the hope that an order might follow? You have spent your life running, little man, always praying that the big break will come, but it never does. Well, your problems are about to come to an end. I am your salvation.

The predator ordered a beer, but it was just for show and he barely touched it. He didn't like his faculties to be dulled when he worked, not even fractionally. He caught a glimpse of himself in a mirror against the wall: tall, hair graying, body lean beneath his leather jacket and dark trousers. His complexion was sallow. He liked to follow the sun, but the demands of his chosen vocation meant that such a luxury was not always possible.

After all, people sometimes had to be killed in places where the sun was not shining, and his bills had to be paid.

Yet pickings had been thin these last few months. In truth, he was mildly concerned. It had not always been thus. Once, he had enjoyed a considerable reputation. He had been a Reaper, and that name had carried a certain weight. Now he still had a reputation, but it was not entirely a good one. He was known as a man with certain appetites who had simply learned to channel them into his work, but who was sometimes overcome by them. He understood that he had overstepped the mark at least once during the past twelve months. The kill was supposed to have been simple and fast, not protracted and painful. It had caused confusion, and had angered those who had hired him. Since then, work had become less plentiful, and without work his appetites needed to find another outlet.

He had been following the kill for two days. It was practice as much as pleasure. He always thought of them as "kills." They were never targets, and he never used the word "potential." As far as he was concerned, once he focused upon them they were already dead. He could have chosen a more challenging individual, a more interesting kill, but there was something about the fat man that repelled him, a lingering stench of sadness and failure that suggested the world would be no poorer without him. By his actions, the fat man had drawn the predator to him, like the slowest animal in the herd attracting the attention of a cheetah.

And so they stayed that way, predator and prey sharing the same space, listening to the same music, for almost an hour, until the fat man rose to go to the men's room, and the time came to end the dance that had begun forty-eight hours earlier, a dance in which the fat man did not even know he was a participant. The predator followed him, keeping ten paces back. He allowed the men's room door to settle in its frame before entering. Only the fat man was inside, standing at a urinal, his face creased with effort and pain.

Bladder trouble. Kidney stones, perhaps. I will end it all.

The doors to both stalls were open as the predator approached. There was nobody inside either. The knife was already in his hand, and he heard a satisfying click, the sound of a blade locking into position.

And then, a second later, the sound came again, and he realized that the first click had not come from his own blade, but the blade of another. The speed of his every motion increased, even as his throat suddenly grew dry and he heard the pounding of his heart. The fat man was also moving now, his right hand a blur of pink and silver, and then the predator felt a pressure at his chest, followed by a sharp pain that quickly spread through his body, paralyzing him as it grew, so that when he tried to walk his legs would not answer the signals from his brain and instead he collapsed on the cold, damp tiles, his knife falling from the fingers of his right hand as his left clasped the horned handle of the throwing blade now lodged in his heart. Blood pumped from the wound and began to spread upon the floor. A pair of brown brogues carefully stepped aside to avoid the growing stain.

With all of his failing strength, the predator raised his head and stared into the face of the fat man, but the fat man was not as he had once seemed. Fat was now muscle, slumped shoulders were straight, and even the perspiration had disappeared, evaporating into the cool evening air. There was only death and purpose, and for an instant the two had become one.

The predator saw scarring at the man's neck, and knew that he had been burned at some time in the past. Even as the predator lay dying, he began to make associations, to fill in the blanks.

"You should have been more careful, William," said the fat man. "One should never confuse business with pleasure."

The predator made a sound in his throat, and his mouth moved. He might have been trying to form words, but no words would come. Still, the fat man knew what he was trying to say.

"Who am I?" he said. "Oh, you knew me once. The years have changed me: age, the actions of others, the surgeon's knife. My name is Bliss."

The predator's eyes rolled in desperation as he began to understand, and his fingers clawed at the tiled floor in a vain effort to reach his knife. Bliss watched for a moment, then leaned down and twisted the blade in the predator's heart before pulling it free. He wiped the knife upon the dead man's shirt before taking a small glass bottle from the inside pocket of his jacket and holding it to the wound in the predator's chest, using a little pressure to increase the flow. When the bottle was full, he screwed a cap on it and left the men's room, his body changing as he walked, becoming once again the torpid, sweaty carrier of a failure's soul. Nobody, not even the bartender, looked at him as he left, and by the time the predator's body was found and the police summoned, Bliss was long gone.

The final killing took place on a patch of bare ground about twenty miles south of the St. Lawrence River in the northern Adirondacks. This was land shaped by fire and drought, by farming and railroads, by blowdowns and mining. For a time, iron brought in more revenue than lumber, and the railroads cut a swath through the forests, the sparks from their smokestacks sometimes starting fires that could take as many as five thousand men to bring under control.

One of those old railroads, now abandoned, curved through a forest of hemlock, maple, birch, and small beech before emerging into a patch of clear ground, a relic of the Big Blowdown of 1950 that had never been repaired. Only a single hemlock had survived the storm, and now a man knelt in its shadow upon the damp earth. Beside him was a gravestone. The kneeling man had read the name carved upon it when he was brought to this place. It had been displayed for him in a flashlight's beam, before the beating had begun. There was a house in the distance, lights burning in one of the upper windows. He thought that he had seen a figure seated at the glass, watching as they tore him apart methodically with their fists.

They had taken him in his cabin near Lake Placid. There was a girl with him. He had asked them not to hurt her. They had bound and gagged her and left her weeping in the bathroom. It was a small mercy that they had not killed her, but no such mercy would be shown to him.

He could no longer see properly. One eye had closed itself entirely, never to reopen, not in this world. His lips had split, and he had lost teeth. There were ribs broken: he had no idea how many. The punishment had been methodical, but not sadistic. They had wanted information and, after a time, he had provided it. Then the beating had stopped. Since then, he had remained kneeling on the soft earth, his knees slowly sinking into the ground, presaging the final burial that was to come.

A van appeared from the direction of the house. It followed a well-worn track to the grave, then stopped. The back doors opened, and he heard the sound of machinery as a ramp was lowered.

The kneeling man turned his head. An elderly, hunched figure was being pushed slowly down the ramp in a wheelchair. He was swaddled in blankets like a withered infant, and his head was protected from the evening chill by a red wool hat. His face was almost totally obscured by the oxygen mask over his mouth and nose, fed by a tank mounted on the back of the chair. Only the eyes, brown and milky, were visible. The chair was being pushed by a man in his early forties, who halted when the chair was feet from where the kneeling man waited.

The old man removed his mask with trembling fingers.

"Do you know who I am?" he asked.

The kneeling man nodded, but the other continued as though he had not given an answer. He pointed a finger at the gravestone.

"My firstborn, my son," he said. "You had him killed. Why?"

"What does it matter?" He struggled to enunciate.

"It matters to me."

"Go to hell." The effort made his lips begin to bleed again. "I've told them all that I know."

The old man held the mask to his face and drew a rasping breath before he spoke again.

"It took me a long time to find you," he said. "You hid yourself well, you and the others responsible. Cowards, all of you. You thought I'd lose myself in grief, but I did not. I never forgot, never stopped searching. I swore that their blood would be spilt upon his grave."

The kneeling man looked away and spat on the ground beneath the stone. "Finish it," he said. "I don't care about your grief."

The old man raised an emaciated hand. A shadow passed over the kneeling man and two shots were fired into his back. He fell forward onto the grave, and his blood began to seep into the ground. The old man nodded contentedly to himself.

"It has begun."

CHAPTER TWO

WILLIE BREW STOOD IN the men's room of Nate's Tap Joint and stared at himself in the battered mirror above the similarly battered sink. He decided that he didn't look sixty. In the right light, he could pass for fifty-five. Okay, fifty-six. Unfortunately, he had yet to find that particular light. It certainly wasn't in Nate's men's room, where the light was so bright that taking a leak felt like it was being performed under interrogation.

Willie was bald. He had lost most of his hair by the time he was thirty. After that, he'd experimented with various ways of disguising his baldness: combovers, hats, even a wig. He'd gone for an expensive one, the kind made from realistic-looking fibers. He figured he'd picked the wrong color or something, because even little kids used to laugh at him, and the guys who hung around the auto shop when they had nothing better to do, which was most of the time, had opened a book on the various shades of red his head assumed as he passed through the light and shade of the garage. Willie had enough troubles without becoming an object of amusement for the seldom gainfully employed, like some Coney Island freak: "Come see the Wig Guy: A Modern Marvel. All the Colors of the Rainbow . . ." He'd thrown away the wig after six months. Now he was just happy if his head didn't shine too brightly in public.

He tugged at the skin below his cheekbones. There were deep-set wrinkles around his mouth and eyes that might have passed for laughter lines if Willie Brew was the kind of guy who did a whole lot of laughing, which he wasn't. Willie did a brief count of the lines and wondered just how funny someone would have to find the world to build up that many wrinkles. Anyone who found the world that amusing was insane. There were broken veins on his nose, relics of his troubled middle years, and a few of his teeth felt loose. Somewhere along the path of life, he had also picked up a couple of extra chins.

Perhaps he did look sixty after all.

His eyesight remained good, although this merely enabled him to see more clearly the effects of the aging process upon him. He wondered if people with bad eyesight ever saw themselves as they truly were. Bad eyesight was the equivalent of those soft filters they used to take pictures of movie stars. You could have a third eye in the center of your forehead and, as long as it didn't see any better than the other two, you could fool yourself into believing that you looked like Cary Grant.

He stepped back and examined his paunch, supporting it with his hands like an expectant mother showing off her bump, an image that made him quickly release his grip and wipe his hands instinctively on his pants, as though he'd been caught doing something dirty. He'd always had a paunch. He was just one of those guys. From the time he came out of the womb, he'd looked like his diet consisted entirely of pizza and beer, which wasn't true. Willie actually ate pretty well for a single man. The problem was that he led what Arno, his assistant, described as a "classic indolent lifestyle," which Willie took to mean that he didn't run around in Spandex like a moron. Willie tried to picture himself in Spandex, and decided that he'd already had too much to drink if that was the kind of thing he was imagining alone in a men's room on his birthday night.

He had changed out of his bib overalls for the occasion, which had been traumatic in itself. Willie was a guy born for overalls. They were loose fitting, which was important for a man of his age and girth. They gave him useful pockets in which to keep things, and a place to store his hands when he wasn't using them without looking like a slob. Out of overalls, everything felt too tight, and he had too much stuff and too few holes in which to keep it. Tonight, he bulged in places where a man shouldn't bulge.

Willie was wearing black Sta-Prest trousers, a white shirt veering toward yellow due to age, and a gray jacket that he liked to think of as a classic of tailoring but was, in fact, just old. He was also sporting the new tie that Arno had handed to him that morning with the words, "Happy birthday, boss. You gonna retire now and leave me the place?" It was an expensive tie: black silk embroidered with thin strands of gold. This wasn't the kind you picked up in Chinatown or Little Italy from a guy selling do-rags and knockoff watches on the side of the street, everything wrapped in plastic and bearing a name like "Guci" or "Armoni" for rubes who couldn't tell the difference, or who figured that nobody else could. No, the tie was pretty tasteful, given that Arno had bought it. Willie figured that maybe he'd had a little help in choosing it since, as far as Willie could recall from a funeral that they had attended together earlier in the year, Arno only had one tie in his wardrobe, and that one was maroon polyester and stained with axle grease.

The thing about it was, Willie didn't *feel* sixty. He'd lived through a lot—Vietnam, a painful divorce, some heart trouble a couple of years back—and it had certainly aged him on the outside (those lines, and his few remaining gray hairs, were hard earned), but inside he felt like he always had, or at least the way he had since he was in his mid- to late twenties. That was when he had been at his peak. He'd survived two years in the Marines, and had returned home to a woman who'd loved him enough to become his wife. Okay, so maybe she hadn't exactly been Lassie in the faithful companion stakes, but that came later. For a time, they had seemed pretty happy. He'd borrowed some money from his father-in-law, started renting premises in Queens, over by Kissena Park, and applied the mechanical skills that he had honed in the military to maintaining and repairing automobiles. It turned out that he was even better at it than he had thought, and there was always enough business to keep him occupied, so that after a few years he had hired a small Scandinavian guy with bristly hair and the attitude of a junkyard dog to help him out. Thirty years later, Arno was still with him, and still had the attitude of a junkyard dog, albeit one whose gums hurt and who could no longer scamper after female dogs with the same vigor that he once had shown.

Vietnam: Willie hadn't come back scarred from his time in Nam, either physically or psychologically, or not so that he could tell. He'd landed in March 1965, part of the Third Marine Division assigned to create enclaves surrounding vital airstrips. Willie ended up in Chu Lai, sixty miles south of Da Nang, where the Seabees constructed a four-thousand-foot aluminum runway in twenty-three days amid cactus and shifting sands. It was still one of the finest feats of engineering under pressure that Willie had ever witnessed.

He had just turned nineteen when he signed up for service. He didn't even wait for the draft to find him. His old man, who had come here in the twenties and had served in the military himself during World War II, told him that he owed something to his country, and Willie didn't question his judgment. By the time he came home his father's friends were breaking heads down on Wall Street and over at Washington Square Park, teaching the long-hairs a little something about patriotism. Willie neither condoned it nor objected to it. He'd done his time, but he could understand why other kids might not want to follow in his footsteps. It was a matter for their conscience, not his. Some of his buddies had served, too, and they had all returned home more or less intact. One of them had lost an arm to a grenade hidden in a loaf of bread, but he could have lost a lot more. Another came back minus his left foot. He'd stepped on a bear trap, and the jaws had snapped shut above his ankle. The funny thing about those bear traps—funny if you didn't have your foot caught in one—was that they needed a key to open them, and bear trap keys weren't the kind of thing you just happened to have in your pack. The bear trap itself would be chained to a slab of concrete buried deep in the ground, so the only way to get the wounded soldier to safety was to dig up the whole arrangement, often while under fire, and then transport it back to camp, where a doctor would be waiting, along with a couple of men armed with hacksaws and cutting torches.

Both of those guys were gone now. They'd died young. Willie had attended their funerals. They were gone, but he was still here.

Sixty years, thirty-four of them in the same business, most in the same building. Only once had the security of his postservice existence been threatened. That was during the divorce, when his wife had sought half of all that he owned, and he was faced with the possibility of being forced to sell his beloved auto shop in order to meet her demands. While he might have been kept busy with a steady stream of repairs, there wasn't a whole lot of money in the bank and much of Queens hadn't been like it was now. Then there was no gentrification, no single men and women driving expensive automobiles that they didn't know how to service for themselves. People drove their cars until the wheels came off, and then came to Willie looking for a way to get another three, six, nine months out of them, just until things improved, until there was a little cash to spare. There were cops being shot on the streets, and turf wars, and protection money to be handed over, even if it was paid in kind by carrying out repairs for free, or by not asking questions when someone required a quick spray job on a car that was so hot it ticked. Elmhurst and Jackson Heights became Little Colombia, and Queens was the main entry point for cocaine shipments into the United States, the money laundered through check-cashing businesses and travel agencies. Colombians were dying every day in Willie's neighborhood. He had even known a couple of them, including Pedro Méndez, who campaigned for the antidrug president Cesar Trujillo and took three in the head, chest, and back for his troubles. Willie had serviced Pedro's car the week before his death. It was a different city then, almost unrecognizable from the one that existed today.

But then Queens had always been different. It wasn't like Brooklyn, or the Bronx. It was disparate. It sprawled. People didn't write affectionate books about it. It didn't have a Pete Hamill to mythologize it. "Someplace in Queens": if Willie had a buck for every time he'd heard someone use that phrase, he'd be a wealthy man. For those who lived outside the borough, everywhere within it was just "someplace in Queens." To them, Queens was like the ocean: big and unknowable, and if you dropped something into it, it got lost and it stayed lost.

And, despite it all, Willie had loved almost every minute of his life there. Then his wife had tried to take it away from him, and even with Arno adding to the fund the money that he had saved there still wasn't enough to pay her off. To cap it all, the landlord had put the building up for sale, so even if Willie managed to satisfy his old lady's demands he still wasn't sure that he would have a business once the premises were sold. He had been left with forty-eight hours to make a decision, forty-eight hours to write off nearly twenty years of effort and commitment (he was thinking of the garage, not the marriage), when a tall black man in an expensive suit and a long black overcoat arrived at the door of the little office in which Willie tried, and usually failed, to keep track of his paperwork, and offered him a way out.

The man knocked gently on the glass. Willie looked up and asked what he could do for him. The man closed the door behind him, and something in Willie's stomach tensed. He might have been a mechanic in the military, but he'd learned how to fire a gun, and he'd had to use it more than once, although as far as he knew he'd never managed to kill anybody with it, mainly because he hadn't really tried. Mostly, he had just done his best to avoid getting his own head shot off. He wanted to fix things, not break them, didn't matter if they were jeeps, helicopters, or human beings.

In turn, he'd been surrounded by other men who were like him, and some who were not, the kind who were willing and able to kill if push came to shove. There were the ones who did so reluctantly, or pragmatically, and there were a couple who were just plain psychotic, who liked what they did and got off on the carnage they wreaked. And then there were those—and he could have counted them on his thumbs—who were naturals, who killed cold-bloodedly and without remorse, who derived satisfaction from the exercise of a skill with which they had been born. They had something quiet and still inside them, something that could not be touched, but Willie often suspected that the thing inside them was hollow, and it contained a raging maelstrom that they had either learned to accommodate or declined to acknowledge, like the great protective frame that houses a nuclear reactor. Willie had tried to stay away from such men, but now he sensed that, once again, he was in the presence of one of them.

It was dark outside, and Arno had just gone home. He had wanted to stay with Willie, knowing that, if things didn't work out, tomorrow would be their final day in the shop, and he didn't want to lose a single minute that might otherwise have been spent in its environs, but Willie had sent him on his way so that he could be alone. He understood Arno's need to be there because he felt it himself, but this was still his business, his place. Tonight, he would sleep here, surrounded by the sights and smells that meant most to him in the world. He could not imagine a life without them. Perhaps, he thought, he could get some work in a body shop elsewhere, although he would find it difficult to toil for someone else after so many years as his own boss. In time, he might even be able to set himself up again in other premises, if he could save enough money. His bank had been sympathetic to his plight, but finally unhelpful. He was a man in the throes of a painful and potentially ruinous divorce, with a business (soon to be half a business, and that was no business at all) that was profitable but not profitable enough, and such a man was not worth the bank's time or money.

Now his solitude had been disturbed by the visitor, and to Willie's burdens had been added a strong helping of unease. Willie could have sworn that he had locked the door behind Arno when he left, but either he hadn't done it properly or this was an individual who wasn't about to let the small matter of a locked door stand in the way of whatever business he might wish to conduct.

"Sorry, we're closed," said Willie.

"So I see," said the man. "My name is Louis."

He extended a hand. Willie, who was never one to be ruder than necessary, shook it.

"Listen, I'm happy to meet you, but it doesn't change anything," said Willie. "We're closed. I'd tell you to come back another day, but I got my hands full just finishing what's out there already, and I'm not even sure if I'll still be here once the sun sets tomorrow."

"I understand," said Louis. "I heard that you were in trouble. I can help you out of it."

Willie bristled. He thought he knew what was coming. He'd seen enough jumped-up loan sharks in his time not to be dumb enough to put his head between their jaws. His wife was about to take half of all that he had. This guy was trying to take what was left.

"I don't know what you heard," Willie replied, "and I could give a damn. I can take care of my own problems. Now, if you don't mind, I got things to do."

He wanted to turn his back on the man in a gesture of dismissal, but despite his bravado he felt that the only thing worse than facing the visitor would be not facing him. You didn't turn your back on a man like this, and not only because you might end up with a knife in it. There was a dignity about him, a stillness. If he was a loan shark, then he wasn't a typical one. Willie might have differed on occasion with some of his customers (and, indeed, Arno) on the definition of how much rudeness was appropriate in the course of one's daily affairs, but he wasn't about to cross this man, not if he could help it. He'd talk his way out of it politely. It would be a strain, but Willie would manage it.

"You're going to lose this place," said Louis. "I don't want that to happen."

Willie sighed. The conversation, it seemed, was not at an end.

"What's it to you if I do?" he asked.

"Call me a Good Samaritan. I'm worried about the neighborhood."

"Then run for mayor. I'll vote for you."

The man smiled. "I prefer to keep a lower profile."

Willie held his gaze. "I'll bet you do."

"I'll invest in your business. I'll give you exactly 50 percent of what it's worth. In return you'll pay me a dollar a year as interest on the loan until it's paid off."

Willie's jaw went slack. This guy was either the worst loan shark in the business, or there was a catch in the deal big enough to snap Willie in two.

"A dollar a year," he said, once he'd managed to get his mouth under control again.

"I know. I drive a hard bargain. Tell you what, I'll leave you to think about it overnight. I hear your wife has given you forty-eight hours to reach a decision, and half of them are already gone. I guess I'm just not as reasonable as she is."

"Nobody ever called my old lady reasonable before," said Willie.

"She sounds like a special person," said Louis. His expression was studiedly neutral.

"She used to be," said Willie. "Not so much anymore."

Louis handed Willie a card. On it was a telephone number, and the image of a snake being crushed underfoot by a winged angel, but nothing else.

"There's no name on the card," said Willie.

"No, there isn't."

"Hardly worth having a business card that doesn't have a business on it. Must be hard to make a living."

"You'd think, wouldn't you?"

"What do you do, kill snakes?"

And the words were no sooner out of Willie's mouth than he regretted them, his mind uttering a silent "Goddamn" as it realized that it had lost the race to catch up with his tongue.

"Kind of. I'm in pest control."

"Pest control. Right."

The man extended his hand once again in farewell. Almost in a daze, Willie shook it.

"Louis," said Willie. "That's it, just Louis?"

"Just Louis," said the man. "Oh, and as of today, I'm your new landlord."

And that was how it had begun.

Willie splashed water on his face. From outside, he heard laughter, and a voice that sounded like Arno's giving his opinion on the Mets, an entirely negative view that seemed to involve only the word "Mets" and a seemingly infinite series of variations on a second word that Arno, who prided himself on his sophistication when he wasn't on his fourth double vodka, liked to refer to as "the copulative." Arno was funny like that. He might have looked like an aging rat, but he knew more words than *Webster's*. Willie had been to Arno's apartment only once, and nearly had his skull fractured when a pile of novels came toppling down on his head. Every available space seemed to be occupied by newspapers, books, and the occasional car part. On those rare occasions when Arno was late for work, Willie was tormented by images of him lying unconscious beneath an entire stack of encyclopedias from the 1950s, or smoking away like a piece of fish beneath layer upon layer of smoldering newsprint. Well, maybe "tormented" was putting it kind of strongly. "Mildly bothered" might have been closer to the mark.

Someone had written *Jake is a male slut* in lipstick at the bottom right-hand corner of the glass. Willie hoped that the culprit was a woman, although homosexuality didn't bother him so much now. Love and let love, that was his motto. Anyway, that black gentleman who had saved his business (and, let's face it, his life, because he'd always had a weakness for booze, and by the time the divorce was reaching its filthy nadir he was putting away a bottle of Four Roses a day, and say what you like about Four Roses but gentle it ain't) had a partner named Angel, and while it wasn't as if there were wedding bells in the offing, or an announcement in the Sunday edition of the *New York Times,* they were just about the closest-knit couple that Willie had ever encountered. "The couple that slays together stays together," as Arno had once put it, and Willie had instinctively looked over his shoulder in the quiet of the garage, half expecting to see a black figure looming unhappily over him, a smaller one beside him looking equally discontented. It wasn't that they scared him, or not much—that feeling had passed a long time ago, or so he liked to tell himself—but he hated to think that their feelings might be hurt. He had said as much to Arno, and Arno had apologized and had never issued a similar utterance since, but sometimes Willie wondered if Arno had been so far off the mark, all things considered.

The door of the men's room opened. Arno's head popped through the gap.

"The hell are you doing?" he asked.

"Washing my hands."

"Well, hurry up. There's a party waiting for you out here." Arno paused as he saw the writing on the mirror. "Who's Jake?" he asked. "Hey, did you write that?"

He ducked just in time to avoid being hit by a wadded paper towel, and then Willie Brew, sixty years old and sometime associate of two of the most lethal men in the city, went out to join his birthday party.

CHAPTER THREE

THE INTERIOR OF NATE'S was dimly lit. It was always that way. Even in summer, when streams of harsh sunlight struck the windows, the beams seemed to melt against the glass and then drizzle like honey through the panes, their energy dissipated as though they, like the patrons inside, had, in the transition from beyond to within, absorbed just a little too much alcohol to be truly useful for the rest of the day. Apart from an area two feet square beside the double doors, no part of Nate's had seen unfiltered natural illumination for more than half a century.

And yet Nate's was not a cheerless place. White fairy lights adorned the bar all year round, and each table was lit by a candle in a glass lamp seated on an iron bowl. The bowls were secured to the wood of the tables with inch-long screws (Nate was no fool) but the candles were scrupulously monitored, and as soon as they began to flicker they were replaced by a waitress or, on quiet evenings, by Nate himself, who was small, sixtyish, and jug-eared, and was said to have once bitten a man's nose off in a bar fight down in Baja when he was in the Navy. No one had ever asked Nate if that was true because Nate would happily talk to anyone about ball scores, the idiots who ran the city of New York and the country whose space the city occupied, and the general well-being of friends and family, but as soon as someone tried to get more personal with him, Nate would wander off to clean glasses, or check the taps, or replenish the candles, and the unwise party who had inadvertently offended him would be left to wait on a refill and rue his brashness. Nate's was not that kind of place, as Nate liked to point out, although nobody had ever managed to nail him down on just what kind of place Nate's was, exactly. Nate liked it that way, and so did the people who frequented his bar.

Nate's, like its owner, was a relic of another time, when this part of Queens was predominantly Irish, before the Indians and the Afghans and the Mexicans and the Colombians came along and began carving it up into their own little enclaves. Nate wasn't Irish, and neither was his bar: even on St. Patrick's Day, Nate wasn't about to change his white fairy lights for green ones, or begin drawing shamrocks on the heads of his patrons' beer. No, it was more to do with a certain state of mind, a particular attitude. Surrounded by foreign smells and strange accents, in a city that was constantly changing,

Nate's represented solidity. It was an old-world bar. You came here to drink, and to eat good, simple food that didn't pander to dietary fads or concerns about cholesterol. You behaved yourself. If you used foul language, you kept your voice down, particularly if there were ladies present. You paid your tab at the end of the night, and you tipped appropriately. The chairs were comfortable, the restrooms, occasional graffiti apart, were clean, and Nate's pouring hand was neither too heavy nor too light. He made good cocktails, but he didn't do shooters. "You want shooters, go to Hooters," as he once told some college kids who had made the mistake of asking for a tray of Dive Bombers. In fact, as Nate said later, once he had thrown their asses out, their first mistake was coming into his bar to begin with. Nate did not like college kids, which was not to say that he was not proud of the local boys who had made good by going on to further education. He knew their parents, and their grandparents. They were not "college kids." They were his kids, and they would always be welcome in his bar, although he still wouldn't serve them shooters, not even if a shooter was going to cure them of cancer. A man had to have standards.

The bar did not have a private room, but there were four tables at the back that were cut off from the rest of the premises by a wall of wood inset with three frosted-glass panes, and it was there that the party to celebrate the sixtieth birthday of Willie Brew was taking place. In truth, the party had spread out a little as the evening drew on. There was a noisy core of six or seven seated around Arno, then a second table of four or five that was quieter, mellowed by Jameson and the general good nature of those gathered there. A third was occupied by assorted wives and girlfriends, of which Willie had initially not entirely approved. Willie had been under the impression that this was to be a men-only night, but he supposed that, under the circumstances, he could afford to be tolerant, as long as nonmales kept themselves to themselves, within reason. Actually, he supposed that, deep down, he was a little flattered that they had come along. Willie was gruff, and he was by no means a looker. Since his wife left him, the only females with whom he had enjoyed actual physical contact were metal and had headlights where their boobs should have been, and he had almost forgotten how good it felt to be hugged by a woman, and smothered in perfume and kisses. He had blushed down to his ankles as a series of what might generally be termed "women of a certain age" had, either singly or in pairs, reminded him of the charms of the fairer sex by pressing said charms firmly against Willie's body. One of the reasons he had headed for the men's room was to remove the lipstick traces from his cheeks and mouth so that he no longer looked, as Arno had put it, like an overweight Cupid advertising a poor man's Valentine's Day.

Now, as he stood at the men's room door, he took in the assorted faces as though seeing them afresh. The first thing that struck him was that he knew a lot of people with criminal pasts. There was Groucho, the hot-wire expert, who might have made a good mechanic if he could have been trusted not to boost and then sell the cars on which he was supposed to be working. Beside him was Tommy Q, who was the most indiscreet man Willie had ever met, an individual apparently born without a filter between his mouth and his brain. Tommy Q, a purveyor of illegally copied movies, music, and computer software, was such a pirate that he should have sported an eye patch and carried a parrot on his shoulder. Willie had once, in a fit of madness, bought a bootleg copy of a movie from Tommy, the soundtrack to which had consisted almost entirely of the sounds of someone munching popcorn, and a couple having sex nearby, or as close to it as they could get in a crowded movie theater. In fact, thought Willie, it had been pretty similar to the *actual* experience of seeing a movie in New York on a Friday night, which was precisely why Willie didn't go to the movies in the first place. Tommy Q's inexpertly wrapped birthday tribute to Willie sat on top of the pile of gifts in one corner. It looked, thought Willie, suspiciously like a collection of pirated DVDs.

Then there were those who should have been there but, for vastly different reasons, were not. Coffin Ed was doing two-to-five in Snake River over in Oregon for desecrating a corpse. Willie wasn't sure what the precise wording of the charge had been and, to be honest, he didn't want to know. Willie wasn't the kind of man to judge another's sexual proclivities, and one naked person being found in a position of intimacy with another naked person didn't bother him in the slightest, but when one of the naked people was in something less than the fullest bloom of health, then that was slightly more problematic. Willie had always thought there was something kind of creepy about Coffin Ed. It was hard to feel entirely comfortable around a man who had attempted to make a living from stealing corpses and holding them for ransom. Willie had just assumed that Coffin Ed kept the corpses in a freezer somewhere until the ransom was paid, not in his bed.

Meanwhile, Jay, who used to do some part-time work for Willie, and who was the best transmission guy Willie had ever met, had died five years earlier. A heart attack had taken him in his sleep, and Willie supposed that it wasn't such a bad way to go. Still, he missed Jay. The old man had been a rock of decency and common sense, qualities that were sadly lacking in some of the other individuals gathered in Nate's bar that night. Old man? Willie shook his head sadly.

Funny how Jay had always seemed old to him, but now Willie was only five years younger than Jay was when he died.

His gaze moved on, lingering briefly on the women (some of whom, he had to say, were looking pretty attractive now that his beer intake had softened their lines); passing over Nate at the bar, who was reluctantly making up some complicated cocktail for a pair of suits; glancing at the faces of strangers, men and women cocooned in the comforting dusk, their features glowing in the candlelight. Standing where he was, half hidden by shadows, Willie felt momentarily cut off from all that was happening, a ghost at his own banquet, and he realized that he liked the sensation.

A small side table had been set up for the buffet, but now only the scattered remains of fried chicken and beef tips and firehouse chili lay upon it, along with a half-demolished birthday cake. In a corner to the right of the table, seated apart from the rest, were three men. One of them was Louis, grayer now than he had been on the first day that they had met and a little less intimidating, but that was simply a consequence of the years that Willie had known him. To those unfamiliar with him, Louis could still be very intimidating indeed.

To Louis's right sat Angel, nearly a foot shorter than his partner. He had dressed up for the night, which meant only that he looked marginally less untidy than usual. Hell, he had even shaved. It made him look younger. Willie Brew knew a little of Angel's past, and suspected more. He was a good judge of people, better than he was given credit for. Willie had met a guy once who had known Angel's old man, and a bigger sonofabitch had rarely walked this earth, the guy said. He had hinted darkly at abuse, at the farming out of the boy for money, for booze, and sometimes just for the fun of it. Willie had kept these things to himself, but it partly explained why there was such a fierce bond between Angel and Louis. Even though he knew nothing of Louis's upbringing, he sensed that they were both men who had endured too much in childhood, and each had found an echo of himself in the other.

But it was the third man who really troubled Willie. Angel and Louis, silent partners in his business, were, in their way, less of an enigma than their companion. They did not make Willie feel that, in their presence, the world was in danger of shifting out of kilter, that here was a thing unknowable, even alien. By contrast, that was the effect this other had upon him. He respected the third man, even liked him, but there was something about him . . . What was that word Arno had used? "Ethereal." Willie had been forced to look it up later. It wasn't quite right, but it was close. "Otherworldly," maybe. Whenever Willie spent time with him, he was reminded of churches and incense, of sermons filled with the threat of hellfire and damnation, memories from his childhood as an altar boy. It made no sense, but there it was. He carried with him a hint of night. In some ways, he reminded Willie of men whom he had known in Vietnam, the ones who had come through the experience fundamentally altered by what they had seen and done, so that even in ordinary conversation there was a sense that a part of themselves was detached from what was going on around them, that it resided in another place where it was always dark and half-glimpsed figures chittered in the shadows.

He was also dangerous, this man, as lethal as the two men beside him, although their lethality was part of their nature, and they had accommodated themselves to it, whereas he struggled against his. He had been a cop once, but then his wife and little girl got killed, and killed bad. He found the one who had done it, though, found him and put an end to him. He'd put an end to others since then, foul, vicious men and women, judging from what Willie had learned, and Angel and Louis had helped him. In doing so, they had all suffered. There had been pain, injuries, torments. Louis had a damaged left hand, the bones smashed by a bullet. Angel had spent months in a hospital enduring grafts on his back, and the experience had drained some of the life from him. He would die sooner because of it, of that Willie was certain. The third man had lost his PI's license not so long ago, and things still weren't right with his girlfriend, and probably never would be, so that he didn't see his new daughter as often as he might have liked. Last Willie heard, he was working behind a bar in Portland. That wouldn't continue for long, not with a man like that. He was a magnet for trouble, and the ones who came to him for help brought dragons in their wake.

In his company, Willie called him Charlie, and Arno called him Mr. Parker. Once upon a time people had called him Bird, but that was a nickname from his days on the force, and Angel had told Willie that he didn't care for it. But when he wasn't around, Willie and Arno always referred to him as "the Detective." They had never discussed it, never agreed between themselves that this was what he should be called. It had just emerged naturally over time. That was how Willie always thought of him: the Detective, with a capital D. It had the right ring of respect about it. Respect, and maybe just a little fear.

The Detective didn't look too threatening, not at first glance. There he differed from Louis, who would still have looked threatening to a casual observer even if he'd been surrounded by dancing fairies and dicky birds. The Detective was slightly taller than average, maybe five-ten or so. His hair was dark, almost black, with gray seeping in around the temples. There were scars on his chin and beside his right eye. He looked to be of medium build, but there was muscle under there. His eyes were blue, shading to green depending upon how the light caught them. The pupils were always small and dark. Even when he seemed to be relaxed, as he was now at Willie's party, there was a part of him that remained guarded and hidden, that was wound so tight his eyes wouldn't even let the light in. They were the sort of eyes, Willie thought, that made people look away. Some folk, you caught their eyes and maybe you smiled at them instinctively, because if that stuff about the eyes being the windows of the soul was true then what was at the heart of those people was essentially good, and that somehow communicated itself to whomever they met. The Detective was different. Not that he wasn't a good man: Willie had heard enough about him to understand that he was the kind who didn't like to turn away from another's pain, the kind who couldn't put a pillow over his ears to drown out the cries of strangers. Those scars he had were badges of courage, and Willie knew that there were others hidden beneath his clothes, and still more deep inside, right beneath the skin and down to the soul. No, it was just that whatever goodness was there coexisted with rage and grief and loss. The Detective struggled against the corruption of that goodness by those darker elements, but he did not always succeed, and you could see the evidence of that struggle in his eyes.

"Hey." It was Arno. "The hell is wrong with you tonight? You look like the IRS just called."

Willie shrugged. "Guess it's hitting an age with a zero at the end. Makes you thoughtful."

"Like you're gonna start making me coffee in the morning, and asking me how I slept?"

Willie punched him on the arm. "No, you knucklehead. Thoughtful, like when you start thinking about stuff, remembering."

"Well, stop it. It never helped you before, and you're too old to start getting good at it now."

"Yeah, I guess you're right." A beer was thrust into his hand, a Brooklyn Lager. He'd begun to drink it only recently. He liked the idea that there was an independent brewery over in Williamsburg once again, and he felt that he should support it. It helped that the stuff they brewed there tasted good, so it wasn't like he had to make any allowances.

He cast a final look at the three men in the corner. Angel returned it and raised his glass in salute. Beside him, Louis did the same, and Willie lifted his bottle in acknowledgment. A feeling of warmth and gratitude washed over him, so strong that it made his cheeks glow and his eyes water. He knew what these men had done in the past, and what they were capable of doing now. Something had shifted in their world, though. Maybe it was the influence of the third man, but they were the good guys, in their way. He tried to remember something someone had said about them once, something about angels.

Ah, that was it. They were on the side of the angels, even if the angels weren't entirely sure that this was a good thing.

And then he recalled who it was that had said it: it was the third man, Parker. The Detective. As if on cue, the Detective turned around, and Willie felt himself trapped in his regard. The Detective smiled, and Willie smiled back. Even as he did so, he could not shake off the sensation that the Detective knew exactly what Willie had been thinking.

Willie shivered. He'd been lying when he'd told Arno that it was his birthday that was making him act funny. That was part of it, but it wasn't the whole story. No, for the last couple of days Willie had been getting the feeling that something was wrong. It wasn't anything that he could put his finger on. The day before, there had been a blue Chevy Malibu parked across the street from the auto shop, two men sitting in the front seat, and it seemed to Willie like they were watching him, because when he started paying attention to them they moved off. Later, he dismissed it as paranoia, but he was certain that he had seen the car again today, this time parked farther down the street, the same two men once again occupying the front seats. He thought of mentioning the sightings to Louis, then dismissed it. It wasn't the time or the place. Maybe he was just feeling weird because of the day, because he was now entering his seventh decade. Still, he couldn't quite shake off the belief that something was bent out of shape slightly. It was like when his wife had filed for divorce, and the shop was about to be taken away from him, the knowledge that a crack had appeared in his existence, that his world was about to be transformed by something from outside, something hostile and dangerous.

And there was nothing that Willie could do to stop it.

CHAPTER FOUR

IT WAS AFTER 1:00 A.M. Most of the revelers had gone home, and only Arno and Willie and a man named Happy Saul remained of the main group. Happy Saul had suffered nerve damage to his face as a child, and it had contorted his mouth into a permanently fixed grin. Nobody ever sat next to Happy Saul at a funeral. It looked bad. Unusually—for it was often the case that men with nicknames like "Happy" or "Smiley" tended to be seriously angry and depressed individuals, the kind who never saw a bell tower without experiencing visions of themselves picking off bystanders with a rifle—Happy Saul was a contented guy, and good company. At that very moment, he was telling Willie and Arno a joke so inconceivably filthy that Willie was sure he was going straight to hell just for listening to it.

Angel and Louis were now alone in the corner. The Detective had gone. He didn't drink much anymore, and he had an early start back to

Maine the next morning. Before he left, Willie opened the gift that the Detective had brought: it was a bill of acceptance for a delivery of old packing crates, signed by Henry Ford himself, framed with a picture of the great man above it.

"I thought you could hang it in the shop," said the Detective, as Willie gazed at the photograph, his fingertips tracing the signature beneath.

"I'll do that," said Willie. "It'll have pride of place in the office. Nothing else around it. Nothing." He was touched, and a little guilty. His earlier thoughts about the Detective now seemed ungenerous. Even if they were true, there was more to him than his demons. He shook the Detective's hand. "Thank you," he said. "For this, and for coming along tonight."

"Wouldn't have missed it. Be seeing you, Willie."

"Yeah, next time."

Willie had returned to Arno and Happy Saul.

"Nice thing to get," said Arno, holding the frame in his hands.

"Yeah," said Willie. He was watching the Detective as he said goodnight to Nate and headed into the night. Even though Willie was at least two sheets to the wind, there was an expression on his face that Arno had never seen before, and it worried him.

"Yeah, it is . . ."

• • •

The two men sat close together, but not too close, Louis's arm draped casually across the seat behind his partner's head. Nate didn't have a problem with their relationship. Neither did Arno, or Willie, or even Happy Saul, although if Happy Saul did have a problem there would have been no way to tell without asking him. But not everyone in Nate's was so liberal minded, and while Angel and Louis would happily have confronted, and then quietly pummeled, anyone who had the temerity to question their sexuality or any displays of mutual affection that they might have felt inclined to show, they preferred to keep a low profile and avoid such encounters, in part so that they wouldn't cause trouble for Nate, and in part because other aspects of their lives demanded that they remain inconspicuous whenever possible, inasmuch as a tall, immaculately attired black man who could cause sweat to break out on an iceberg on a cold day and a small, shabby person who, when he walked down the street, made it look like the garbagemen had missed some of the trash could fail to attract attention to themselves.

They had moved on to brandy, and Nate had broken out his best snifter glasses for the occasion. The glasses were big enough to house goldfish. There was music playing in the background: *Sinatra-Basie* from '62, Frank singing about how love is the tender trap. Nate was polishing down the bar, humming along contentedly to the song. Usually, Nate would have started to close up by now, but he appeared in no hurry to make people leave. It was one of those nights, the kind where it felt like the clocks have been stopped and all those inside were safely insulated from the troubles and demands of the world. Nate was content to let them stay that way for a while. It was his gift to them.

"Looks like Willie had a good time," said Louis. Willie was swaying slightly on his chair, and his eyes had the dazed look of a man who has recently been hit on the head with a frying pan.

"Yeah," said Angel. "I think some of those women wanted to give him a special gift all of their own. He's lucky to be wearing his clothes."

"We're all lucky that he's wearing his clothes."

"There is that. He seems kind of, I don't know, not himself tonight?"

"It's the occasion. Makes a man philosophical. Makes him dwell on his mortality."

"That's a cheerful thought. Maybe we could start a line of greeting cards, put that on them. Happy Mortality Day."

"You been pretty quiet tonight as well."

"You complain when I talk too much."

"Only when you got nothing to say."

"I always have something to say."

"That's your problem right there. There's a balance. Maybe Willie could install a filter on you." His fingers gently brushed the back of his partner's neck. "You gonna tell me what's up?"

Although there was nobody within earshot, Angel still glanced casually around before he spoke. It never hurt to be careful.

"I heard something. You remember William Wilson, better known as Billy Boy?"

Louis nodded. "Yeah, I know who he is."

"Was."

Louis was silent for a moment. "What happened to him?"

"Died in a men's room down in Sweetwater, Texas."

"Natural causes?"

"Heart failure. Brought on by someone sticking a blade through it."

"That don't sound right. He was good. He was an animal, and a freak, but he was good. Hard to get close enough to take him with a knife."

"I hear there were rumors that he'd been overstepping the mark, adding flourishes to simple jobs."

"I heard that, too." There had always been something wrong with Billy Boy. Louis had seen it from the start, which was why he had decided not to work with him, once he was in a position to pick and choose. "He always did like inflicting pain."

"Seems like someone decided that he'd done it once too often."

"Could have been one of those things: a bar, booze, someone decides to pull a knife, gets his friends to help," said Louis, but he didn't sound like he believed what he was saying. He was just thinking aloud, ruling out possibilities by releasing them into the air, like canaries in the coal mine of his mind.

"Could have been, except the place was near empty when it happened, and we're talking about Billy Boy. I remember what you told me about him, from the old days. Whoever took him must have been a whole lot better than good."

"Billy was getting old."

"He was younger than you."

"Not much, and I *know* I'm getting old."

"I know it, too."

"That you're getting old?"

"No, that you're getting old."

Louis's eyes briefly turned to slits.

"I ever tell you how funny I find you?" he asked.

"No, come to mention it, you don't."

"It's cause you ain't. At least now you know why. The blade enter from the front, or the back?"

"Front."

"There a paper out on him?"

"Someone would have heard."

"Could be that someone did. Where'd you get this from?"

"Saw it on the internet. I made a call or two."

Louis rolled the glass in his hands, warming the brandy and smelling the aromas that arose. He was annoyed. He should have been told about Billy Boy, even as a courtesy. That was the way things were done. There were too many markers in his past to allow such matters to go unmentioned.

"You always keep tabs on the people I used to work with?" he said.

"It's not a full-time job. There aren't many of them left."

"There aren't *any* of them left now, not with Billy Boy gone."

"That's not true."

Louis thought for a moment. "No, I guess not."

"Which brings me to the next thing," said Angel.

"Go on."

"The cops interviewed everyone who was in the bar when they found him. Only one person had left: a little fat guy in a cheap suit, sat at the bar and drank no-name whiskey from the well, didn't look like he could afford to change his drawers more than once every second day."

Louis sipped his brandy, letting it rest in his mouth before releasing it to warm his throat.

"Anything else?"

"Bartender said he thought he saw some scarring just above the collar of the guy's shirt, like he'd been in a fire once. Thought he saw some at his right wrist as well."

"Lot of people get burned." Louis said the words with a strangeness to his tone. It might almost have been called dispassionate, had there not been the sense that behind it a great depth of feeling lay hidden.

"But not all of them go on to take someone like Billy Boy with a knife. You think it's him?"

"A blade," said Louis thoughtfully. "They find it in the body?"

"No. Took it with him when he left."

"Wouldn't want to leave a good knife behind. He was a shooter, but he always did prefer to finish them up close."

"If it's him."

"If it's him," echoed Louis.

"Been a long time, if it is."

Louis's right foot beat a slow, steady cadence upon the floor.

"He suffered. It would have taken time for him to recover, to heal. He'd have changed his appearance again, like he did before. And he wouldn't come out of hiding for a standard job. Someone must have been real pissed at Billy Boy."

"It's not only about the money, though, right?"

"No, not if it's him."

"If he's back, Billy Boy might just be the start. There's the small matter of you trying to burn him alive."

"There is that. He'll still be hurting, even now, and he won't be what he was."

"He was still good enough to take Billy Boy."

"If it's him." It sounded like a mantra. Perhaps it was. Louis had always known that Bliss would come back some day. If he had returned, it would be almost a relief. The waiting would be over. "It's because he was so good to begin with. Even with a little shaved off, he'd still be better than most. Better than Billy Boy, that's for sure."

"Billy Boy's no loss."

"No, he ain't."

"But having Bliss back in the world isn't so good either."

"No."

"I'd kinda hoped that he was dead." Much of this had been before Angel's time, before he and Louis had met, although he and Louis had encountered Billy Boy once, out in California. It was an accidental meeting at a service station, and Louis and Billy Boy had circled each other warily, like wolves before a fight. Angel hadn't thought much of Billy Boy as a human being then, although he accepted that he might have been prejudiced by what Louis had told him. Of Bliss, he knew only of what he had done to Louis, and what had been done to him in return. Louis had told him of it because he knew that it was not over.

"He won't be dead until someone makes him dead, and there's no money in that," said Louis. "No money, and no percentage."

"Unless you knew he had your name on his list."

"I don't believe he sends out notifications."

"No, I guess not."

Angel tossed back half of his brandy, and began to cough.

"You sip it, man," said Louis. "It ain't Alka-Seltzer."

"A beer would have been better."

"You have no class."

"Only by association."

Louis considered for a moment.

"Well," he said, "there is that . . ."

The apartment shared by the two men was not as those who knew the couple only casually might have imagined it to be, given their disparate dress codes, attitudes to life, and general demeanor. It occupied the top two floors of a three-story over-basement building on the farthest reaches of the Upper West Side, where the gap between rich and poor began to narrow significantly. The apartment was scrupulously tidy. Although they shared a bedroom, each had his own room in which to retire and in which to pursue his particular interests, and while Angel's room bore the unmistakable signs of one whose skill lay in the picking of locks and the undermining of security systems—shelves of manuals, assorted tools, a workbench covered with both electrical and mechanical components—there was an order to it that would have been apparent to any craftsman. Louis's room was starker. There was a laptop computer, a desk, and a chair. The shelves were lined with music and books, the music leaning, perhaps surprisingly, toward country, with an entire section for black artists: Dwight Quick, Vicki Vann, Carl Ray, and Cowboy Troy Coleman from the moderns, DeFord Bailey and Stoney Edwards from the earlier period, along with a little Charlie Pride, Ray Charles's *Modern Sounds in Country and Western*, some Bobby Womack, and *From Where I Stand*, a boxed set detailing the black experience in country music. Louis found it hard to understand why so many others of his race failed to connect with this music: it spoke of rural poverty, of love, of despair, of faithfulness and infidelity, and these were experiences known to all men, black as well as white. Just as poor black people had more in common with poor whites than with wealthy blacks, so too this music offered a means of expression to those who had endured all of the trauma and sadness with which it dealt, regardless of color. Nevertheless, he had resigned himself to being in a minority as far as this belief was concerned, and although he had almost managed to convince his partner of the merits of some things at which he might previously have scoffed, including regular haircuts and clothing stores that did not specialize in end-of-line sales, black country music—in fact, *any* country music—remained one of Angel's many enduring blind spots.

The apartment consisted of a modern kitchen, rarely used, that led into a large living room cum dining room, and Angel's workshop, all on the lower floor. On the upper floor, there was a luxurious bathroom that Louis had appropriated for himself, leaving the en-suite shower room to his partner; Louis's office; a smaller guest bedroom, with a tiny shower room, neither of which had ever been used; and the main bedroom, which was lined with closet space and, apart from the odd book, remained, by mutual effort and consent, in a state of interior design catalog neatness. There was a gun safe behind the mirror in the guest shower room. Whenever they were in the apartment, the safe remained open. At night, they each kept a weapon close at hand in the main bedroom. When the apartment was empty, the gun safe was kept locked and the mirror carefully put back in its original position using a hinge-and-lock mechanism operated by a small click switch a finger's length behind the glass. They took care of the cleaning and maintenance of the apartment themselves. No strangers were ever admitted, nor friends or acquaintances, of which there were few in any case.

They hid in plain sight, these men. They used prepaid cellphones, switching them regularly, but they never paid for the devices themselves: instead, homeless men and women were given money to make the purchases in stores scattered over four states, and a middleman was used to collect and pass on the phones. Even then, the cells were used only when absolutely necessary. Most of their calls were made from pay phones.

There was no internet connection in their apartment. A computer was kept in an office rented by one of Louis's many shell companies, which they used on occasion for more delicate searches, but often a cyber café was sufficient for their needs. They avoided email, although when required they employed Hushmail to send encrypted messages, or embedded codes in seemingly innocuous communications.

Wherever possible, they used cash, not credit cards. They were part of no loyalty programs, and they bought Metrocards for the subway as they needed them, disposing of them when they were exhausted and replacing them with new ones instead of recharging the originals. Utilities were paid for through a lawyer's office. They had learned the best routes to take on foot and by car to avoid security cameras, and the lights that illuminated the license plates on the vehicles they used all contained infrared bulbs designed to flood video cameras operating at near infrared frequency.

There were also other, more unusual, protections in place. The basement and first floor of their building were rented by an elderly lady named Mrs. Evelyn Bondarchuk, who kept Pomeranians and appeared to have cornered the market in chintz and bone china. There had once been a Mr. Bondarchuk, but he was taken from his young bride at a tragically early age, a consequence of a misunderstanding between Mr. Bondarchuk and a passing train, Mr. Bondarchuk being drunk at the time and having mistaken the track for a public urinal. Mrs. Bondarchuk had never married again, in part because no one could ever have taken the place of her much-loved, if dissolute, husband, but also because anyone who did would, by definition, have been equally or significantly more dissolute than his predecessor, and Mrs. Bondarchuk did not need such aggravation in her life. Thus a corner of her living room remained a slightly dusty shrine to the memory of her departed husband, and Mrs. Bondarchuk lavished her affection instead on generations of Pomeranians, who are not generally considered to be dissolute animals.

Mrs. Bondarchuk's apartment was rent controlled. She paid a laughably small monthly sum to a company called Leroy Frank Properties, Inc., that appeared to be little more than a box number in Lower Manhattan. Leroy Frank Properties, Inc., had bought the building in the early eighties, and Mrs. Bondarchuk had feared for a time that her tenancy might be affected by the sale, but instead she was assured, by letter, that all would remain as it had been and she was welcome to see out her days, surrounded by Pomeranians, in the apartment in which she had dwelt for the best part of thirty years. In fact, she was even permitted to expand her fiefdom into the basement below as well, which had been unoccupied since its previous tenant died some years earlier. Such things were unheard of in the city, Mrs. Bondarchuk knew, and she did her best to ensure that, as far as she was concerned, they remained so. She did not tell anyone of her good fortune, apart from her good friend Mrs. Naughtie, and then only after swearing her to silence. Mrs. Bondarchuk was a clever woman. She understood that something unusual was happening in her building, but as it did not appear to be hampering her existence and was instead improving it significantly, she behaved sensibly and allowed matters to take their course.

The only significant change occurred when the couple upstairs, who were both accountants, eventually retired and moved to a house in Vermont, and their place was taken by a quiet, beautifully dressed black man and a smaller, noticeably less well-dressed individual who looked like he might have come to steal her jewelry, which, had fate not introduced him to his current partner, might well have been the case. Still, they were very polite gentlemen. Mrs. Bondarchuk suspected that they were gay. It gave her quite a frisson for, by the standards of the city, she led a very sheltered life.

If any problems arose with her apartment, Mrs. Bondarchuk left a message with a delightful young woman named Amy, who answered the phone for Leroy Frank Properties, Inc. Actually, Amy answered the phone for a great many businesses, none of which needed or wanted an actual physical presence in the city. Leroy Frank Properties, Inc., owned a number of premises in New York, of which the one on the Upper West Side was the sole residential property. Amy was under explicit instructions to deal with Mrs. Bondarchuk's problems promptly, at the very latest by close of business on the day the call was received. A premium was to be paid to the relevant plumber, electrician, carpenter, or other professional to ensure that this was the case. A list of approved individuals was kept in a file in Amy's desk, all of whom were aware of the particular needs of Leroy Frank Properties, Inc., in relation to this building.

Mrs. Bondarchuk knew the first names of the two men who lived above her, and referred to them, respectively, as "Mr. Louis" and "Mr.

Angel," but she had never connected the black man, Louis, to Leroy Frank Properties, Inc., even though "Leroy Frank" was not a million miles removed from "Le Roi Français" and, while there had been a great many French kings, the name most commonly found among them was, of course, Louis. No, Mrs. Bondarchuk made no such connection, for it was none of Mrs. Bondarchuk's business to think about such matters, and her life was, for her, quite idyllic, so she had no desire to go poking her nose into dark corners. She had enough money on which to live quite comfortably; she had quiet neighbors; and the soundtrack to her life was the yapping of happy Pomeranians and the soothing strings of the Mantovani Orchestra, which, she had discovered, could provide an album for every occasion. And because she valued her situation so highly, Mrs. Bondarchuk guarded every facet of it very closely indeed. When the tradesmen came to fix a leak or change a light bulb, they did so under the unflinching stare of Mrs. Bondarchuk and assorted small dogs. The mailman never got beyond the doorstep. Likewise delivery men, salesmen, small children at Halloween, large children at any time, and any adult who was not her old friend and fellow widow, Mrs. Naughtie, with whom she played an often bad-tempered series of backgammon games, fueled by cheap sherry, every Thursday night.

Leroy Frank Properties, Inc., had installed an expensive and complicated alarm system when it had taken over the ownership of the building, and Mrs. Bondarchuk understood the workings of that system intimately. Mrs. Bondarchuk did not know it but, in her way, she was as essential to the security and peace of mind of the two men who lived above her as the guns that they occasionally carried in the course of their work. She was the Cerberus at the gates of their underworld.

Now, as she lay in her bed and listened to "Swedish Rhapsody" on the little CD player that Mr. Angel and Mr. Louis had given her for Christmas that year (Mrs. Bondarchuk preferred to go to bed late and wake up late: she had never been a morning person); she heard them enter, heard the soft weeping of the alarm before they silenced it with the code, and then a final single beep as the door closed and they reset the system.

"Night, night, Mrs. Bondarchuk," called Mr. Angel from the hallway.

She did not reply, but merely smiled as she stopped the music and turned off her light. They were home, and she always slept better when they were around.

For some reason that she could not quite fathom, they made her feel very safe indeed.

That night, Louis lay awake while Angel slept. He thought about his past, and the hidden nature of the world. He thought about lives taken and lives lost, about his momma and the women who had raised him. He thought about Bliss. He followed the threads in the patterns of his life, pausing where they overlapped, where one connected with another.

And then he closed his eyes, and waited for the Burning Man to come.

It was a small town, a sundown town. That term meant something for the boy and those like him. True, there was no longer a sign advertising that fact at the town limits, which counted as progress in some small way, although there might just as well have been, since most everyone beyond the age of seven could recall where it had stood, just below the gate to Virgil Jellicote's farm. Old Virgil had made sure that the sign wasn't obscured by dirt or, as had once occurred during the period of unrest that followed the killing of Errol Rich, by the judicious application of some black paint, so that the sign was transformed from "Nigger, Don't Let The Sun Set On You In This Town" to "White Folks, Don't Let The Sun Set On You In This Town." Old Virgil had been mightily troubled by that act of vandalism; other people, too, and not all of them white. What was done to Errol Rich was wrong, but riling the cops and the town council by screwing with their beloved sign was just plain dumb, although when the police came asking who might have been responsible for the damage, they were greeted only with silence. Being dumb wasn't a crime, not yet, and the law had plenty of other ways in which it could punish people of color without another being added to the list.

The town wasn't even unusual in its overt exclusion of the black population. It was one of thousands of such towns across the United States, and even whole counties had turned sundown when their county seat did. Half of all the towns in Ore-

gon, Ohio, Indiana, the Cumberlands, and the Ozarks were, at one point, sundown towns. God help the black man who found himself in, say, Jonesboro, Illinois, after dark, or nearby Anna (which was known, to both whites and blacks, as "Ain't No Niggers Allowed," and would continue to have signs to that effect on Highway 127 as late as the 1970s), or Appleton, Wisconsin, or suburbs like Levittown on Long Island; Livonia, Michigan; or Cedar Key, Florida. And, hey, that goes for your Jews, your Chinese, your Mexicans, and your Native Americans, too. Be on your way now, son. Time's a killin' . . .

The thing about the boy's hometown was that it was a pretty place. It was clean, and there wasn't much cussing, not in public. Main Street belonged on a postcard, and the flowers growing in its pots were always appropriate to the season. It was small, though. In fact, it was so small that it barely qualified as a town by any reasonable reckoning, but nobody in those parts referred to anywhere as a village. The place in which you lived was a town or it was nothing at all. There was something substantial about a town. A town meant neighbors, and laws, and order on the streets. A town meant sidewalks, and barbershops, and church on Sundays. To call somewhere a town was to recognize a certain standard of living, of behavior. Sure, folk might go off the rails now and again, but what was important was that everyone knew where those rails were. All derailments were purely temporary. That train kept on running, and all good people made sure they were on board for the whole of the journey, allowing for some unforeseen stops along the way.

But, for the boy, it had never really been a town, not for him. True, it had all the characteristics of a town, however small a space they might have occupied. There were stores, and a movie theater, and a couple of churches, although none for the Catholics, who had to drive eight miles east to Maylersville or twelve miles south to Ludlow if they wanted to worship their own misguided version of the Lord. There were houses, too, with well-kept front lawns and white picket fences and sprinklers that hissed unthreateningly on hot summer days. There were lawyers, and doctors, and florists, and undertakers. If you looked at it the right way, the town had everything necessary to ensure a perfectly adequate degree of service for those who chose to call it home.

The problem, as the boy saw it, was that all of those people were white. The town was built for white people and run by white people. The people behind the counters of the stores were white, and the people on the other side of the counters were mostly white, too. The lawyers were white and the cops were white and the florists were white. Black people could be seen in town, but they were always moving: carrying, delivering, lifting, hauling. Only white people were allowed to stand still. Black people did what they had to do, then left. After nightfall, there were only white folk on the streets.

It wasn't that anyone was cruel to the coloreds as a rule, or vicious, or intemperate in manner. It was simply understood by both sides that this was the way things worked. Blacks had their own stores, their own juke joints, their own places of worship, their own ways of doing things. They had their own town, in a sense, although it was one that did not trouble the planners or figure on any census. By and large, white folks didn't interfere with them, as long as nobody caused any trouble. The blacks lived out in the woods and the swamps, and some of them had pretty nice houses, too, all things considered. No one begrudged them what they had built for themselves. Hell, it wasn't unknown for white men to give some of these black businesses a little custom now and then, especially when those businesses facilitated the provision of exotic flesh for discerning gentlemen whose tastes ran in that direction, so it wasn't like the two races never mingled, or the twain never met. The twain met more often than many people liked to think, and there was good money to be made from those encounters.

But no one on either side ever forgot that the law was white. Justice might be blind, but the law wasn't. Justice was aspirational, but the law was actual. The law was real. It had uniforms, and weapons. It smelt of sweat and tobacco. It drove a big car with a star on the door. White people had justice. Black folks had the law.

The boy understood all of this instinctively. Nobody had been forced to explain it to him. His momma hadn't sat him down before she died and gone through the subtleties of law versus justice with him as it applied to the black community. As far as anyone was concerned, there wasn't a black community. There were just blacks. A community implied organization, and there were a great many people who associated organization with threat. Unions organized. Communists organized. Black people did not organize, not here. Maybe elsewhere, and there were those who said that the tide was changing, but not in this town. Here, everything worked fine just the way it was.

And that was why the boy was so troubling to the policeman who watched him through the two-way mirror on the wall. The mirror was one of the few concessions to modernity in the town's little police department. There was no a/c, even though the units had been installed. The problem with the units was that they kept blowing all of the fuses in the building on account of how the wiring was no good, or so the local electrician had explained. For the a/c to work properly, the whole building would have to be gutted and rewired, and that was going to be an expensive job in a structure this old. The town fathers were reluctant to sanction this expenditure, not if its sole purpose was to ensure that Chief Wooster didn't break a sweat during the hot summer months. Truth was, there were those who felt that it wouldn't do the chief the least bit of harm to break some sweat now and again, the chief being, according to the general consensus, a lard-ass with a heart that was seriously overworked, and not due to his general affection for humanity.

So the little room from which the chief was observing the boy was cooled only by a desk fan, and the desk fan wasn't worth a gnat's fart in the enclosed space. The chief's uniform was pasted to his body so that even the outline of his belly button was clearly visible through the tan cotton, and the sweat was running down his face in rivulets, near blinding him sometimes if he failed to judge properly the sweep of his handkerchief across his forehead.

And yet he did not move. Instead, he stared curiously at the boy, willing him to break. Chief Wooster might have been a lard-ass, and his view of his fellow men and women was certainly colored by a cynicism bordering on misanthropy, but he was no fool. The boy interested him. The boy had managed to kill his mother's lover, a man named Deber, without laying a finger on him, of that the chief was certain, and Deber had been nobody's idea of an easy mark. Deber had himself done time for a murder committed when he was barely thirteen, and there had been others since then, even if no one had been able to pin them on him. One of the killings of which Deber was suspected was the murder of a pretty young black woman down in the city. The son of that pretty young black woman was now sitting on the other side of the mirror being interrogated by two detectives from the state police. They weren't getting any further with the boy than the chief's own men had, and the chief's men had been far less gentle than the detectives. The bruises to the boy's face and the swelling beneath his right eye were testament to that.

Clark, one of the men in question, told the chief that the boy had pissed blood when they had taken him down to the bathroom to clean him up. The chief had told them to ease up on the boy after that. He wanted a confession, not a corpse.

It had taken the state cops a day to organize themselves sufficiently to make the journey north. During that twenty-four-hour period, the chief's men had worked the boy pretty hard. They'd started with beatings, then threats against the boy's family, who had provided him with an alibi. The cops had fed him soda spiked with Ex-Lax, then tied him to the chair and left him there. The chief had watched the boy fight against the urge to void himself, his mouth trembling with the effort, his nostrils flaring, his hands clasped into fists. When he was certain that the boy could take the pain no longer, he'd sent Clark in to make him an offer: confess to the Deber killing and they'd haul him straight to the bathroom. Otherwise, they'd let nature take its course and leave him to sit in what resulted. The boy simply shook his head. The chief almost admired his resilience, except it was making him look bad. He instructed Clark to accompany the boy to the men's room before he burst, as he didn't want him stinking up the building's only interrogation room. Clark had acquiesced, albeit reluctantly. Afterward, he had taken the boy out to the yard and hosed him off on the ground, his trousers around his ankles and the other cops jeering as the water jetted painfully against his privates.

Threats against his family hadn't worked either. He came from a house full of women. Wooster knew them. They were good people. Wooster wasn't a racist. There were good blacks and bad blacks, just like there were good whites and bad whites. It wouldn't be true to say that the chief treated them all equally. Had he tried, even if he'd had the inclination, he wouldn't have lasted a week in his current position, let alone six years. Instead, he treated blacks and poor whites pretty much the same. Wealthy whites required more careful handling. Wealthy blacks he didn't have to worry about, because he didn't know any.

Wooster believed in preventive policing. People ended up in his cells only when they'd done something seriously wrong, or when every other attempt to persuade them to follow the path of righteous and decent behavior had failed. He knew the people in his charge, and he made sure that his men knew them, too. The boy and his family had not once required his attention during the first five years that he had been chief, not until Deber appeared and wormed his way into the affections of the boy's mother, if that was truly what he had done. There had been nothing in Deber to suggest that he was capable of arousing the affections of anyone, and the chief suspected that threats and fear had been more responsible for the gestation of the relationship than any depth of feeling on the part of either party.

Then the mother had been killed, her battered body found lying in an alleyway behind a liquor store. There had been reports that Deber had been seen in that same liquor store less than an hour before the discovery of the body, and someone told of hearing a male voice and a female voice raised in argument at about that time. Deber, though, was like the boy now seated in the interrogation room: he hadn't broken, and the killing of the boy's mother remained unsolved. Deber had returned to the house full of women and taken up with the boy's aunt, or so local gossip had it. The women were frightened of him, and had good cause to be, but he should have been frightened of them, too. They were strong and clever, and nobody thought it likely that they would tolerate the presence of Deber in their house for much longer.

And then, not long after the commencement of that particular relationship, someone had taken the metal whistle that Deber used to summon his work crews, separated its two halves, and replaced the pea with a wad of homemade explosive. When Deber had blown the whistle, the charge had torn most of his face off. He'd lived for a couple of days afterward, blinded and in agony, despite the efforts of the doctors to keep him medicated, then had passed away. The chief was pretty sure that, wherever Deber now was, his agonies were continuing and were likely to do so for all eternity. Deber was no loss to the world, but that didn't change the fact that a man had been killed, and the person responsible had to be found. It wasn't good to have people wandering around freely creating booby traps out of household items, didn't matter if they were targeting blacks or whites. Guns and knives were one thing. They were commonplace, just like the people who used them. There was nothing particularly unnerving, beyond the occasional brutality of the act itself, about a man who'd carve up another man because he crossed him on a bad day, or one who'd put a bullet in the head of the guy next to him in an argument over a woman, or a debt, or a pair of shoes. As chief, Wooster knew where he stood with men, and women, of that stripe. They were neither strange nor startling. On the other hand, someone who could kill a man with his own whistle represented a whole new way of thinking with regard to ending lives, and one that Chief Wooster was in no hurry to encourage or embrace.

Wooster had obtained a warrant for the boy's arrest on the day Deber had died. The state cops had laughed down the phone at him when he'd informed them of what he'd done. Deber, they told him, had so many enemies that their suspect list resembled a phone book. He had been killed by a miniature explosive device, cunningly constructed and designed to ensure that only its intended target would be affected, and that the target would not survive. It had involved a degree of planning not usually associated with fifteen-year-old Negroes living in a shack by a swamp. Wooster had pointed out that the Negro in question was attending a high school that, thanks to a charitable donation from a southern trust fund, had a reasonably well-equipped science lab, and one that could easily have provided the iodine crystals and ammonium that an examination of the remains of the whistle had revealed as the constituent components of the explosive used to kill Deber. In fact, Wooster continued, they were precisely the components that a bright kid, not some expert assassin, might use to create an explosive, although, according to the report on the whistle, it was a miracle that it hadn't blown up long before it reached Deber's mouth, as nitrogen tri-iodide was a notoriously unstable compound that was supersensitive to friction. The technician who had examined the whistle suggested that the compound, even the reconstructed item itself, had probably been kept soaked in water for as long as possible by the killer, so that it had only just begun to dry out by the time the victim had raised it to his mouth for the final time. It was this information about the nature of the explosive used, and the absence of any other leads, that had convinced the state police to send, however reluctantly, two detectives to interview the boy.

Now one of those detectives stood and left the interrogation room. A moment later, the door to the chief's little observation cell opened and the same detective entered, a cold soda in his hand.

"We're not getting anywhere with this kid," he said.

"You need to keep trying," said Wooster.

"Looks like you did some trying of your own."

"He fell over on the way to the men's room."

"Yeah? How many times?"

"He bounced. I didn't keep count."

"You sure you read him his rights?"

"Someone did. Not me."

"He ask for a lawyer?"

"If he did, I didn't hear him."

The detective took a long draught of the soda. Some of it dribbled down his chin, like tobacco spit.

"He didn't do this. It was too slick."

Wooster wiped his brow with his sodden handkerchief.

"Too slick?" he said. "I knew Deber. I knew the people he ran with. They're not the slick kind. If someone in his own circle, or someone he'd crossed, wanted him dead, they'd have shot him or stabbed him, maybe cut his balls off first just to send a message. They wouldn't have wasted their time separating and then soldering a whistle so they could pack it with just enough explosive to tear his face off and turn his brain to sludge. They're not that smart. That kid, though—" He stood and pointed at the glass. "—that kid is smart: smart enough to break into his school and smart enough to put together a little homemade blasting powder. Plus he had motive: Deber killed his mother and was fucking his aunt, and Deber wasn't the gentle kind in the sack."

"There's no proof that Deber killed his mother."

"Proof." Wooster almost spat the word. "I don't need proof. Some things I just know."

"Yeah, well, the courts look at things differently. I'm friends with the men who interviewed Deber. They did everything short of hooking him up to a battery and frying him to make him talk. He didn't

break. No evidence. No witnesses. No confession. No case."

In the interrogation room beyond, the boy's head moved slightly, as though the men's voices had carried to him, even through the thick walls. Wooster thought he might even have seen the ghost of a smile.

"You know what else I think?" said Wooster. His voice was softer now.

"Go on, Sherlock. I'm listening."

Sherlock, thought Wooster. You patronizing piece of shit. I knew your daddy, and he wasn't much better than you are. He was a nobody, couldn't find his shoes in the morning if someone didn't hand them to him, and you're still less of a cop than he was.

"I think," said Wooster, "that if that kid hadn't killed Deber, then Deber would have killed him. I don't think either of them had a choice. If it wasn't the boy sitting in there, it would be Deber."

The detective gulped down the remains of his soda. Something in the evenness of Wooster's tone suggested to him that he had overstepped the mark seconds earlier. He tried to make amends.

"Look, Chief, you may be right. There's something about that kid, I'll give you that, but there's only so much longer we can keep going with this before we have to decide whether to shit or get off the pot."

"Just a few more hours. You talk to him about the women, about maybe using a threat against them to loosen him up some?"

"Not yet. Did you?"

"Tried. It was the only time he spoke."

"What did he say?"

"He told me that I wasn't the kind of man who'd hurt women."

"Yeah?"

"Yeah."

"Was he right?"

The chief sighed. "I guess so."

"Shit. There are other ways, though. Informal ways."

The two men looked at each other. Eventually, the chief shook his head.

"I don't think you're that kind of man either."

"No, I don't believe that I am." The detective crushed the soda can and aimed it, inexpertly, at a trash basket. It bounced off the edge and landed in the corner of the room.

"I hope you shoot better than that," said Wooster.

"Why, you figure I'm going to have to shoot somebody?"

"If only things were so easy."

The detective patted Wooster on the shouder, then instantly regretted it as his hand was soaked with the chief's sweat. He wiped it surreptitiously on his trouser leg.

"We'll try again," he said.

"Do that," said Wooster. "He killed him. I know he killed him."

He didn't look at the detective as he left the room. Instead, his eyes remained fixed on the young black man in the room, and the young black man stared back at him.

Two hours later, Wooster was at his desk, drinking water and swatting at flies. The two detectives had taken a break from the questioning and the stifling heat of the interrogation room. They were sitting outside the station house in their shirtsleeves, smoking, the remains of hamburgers and fries on the steps beside them. Wooster knew that the interrogation was almost at an end. They had nothing. After almost two full days of questioning, the boy had uttered only two sentences. The second was his judgment of Wooster. The first was to tell them his name.

"My name is Louis."

Louis, the way Wooster's brother-in-law, who lived down in Louisiana, might have pronounced it. The French way. Not Lewis, but Lou-ee.

He watched the two detectives speaking softly to each other. One of them came back inside.

"We're going to get a beer," he said.

Wooster nodded. They were done. If they came back at all, it would only be to get their car, assuming they could remember where they'd left it.

In the waiting area outside, across from the main desk, a black woman was sitting, clutching her handbag. She was the boy's grandmother, but she could have been his mother, her face was so youthful. Ever since the boy's arrest, one or another of the women in the boy's family had kept silent vigil on the same cold, hard chair. They all had a dignified air about them, a sense that they were almost doing the room a service by sitting in it. This one, though, the eldest of them, made Wooster uneasy. There were stories told about her. People went to her to have their fortunes read, to find out the sex of their unborn infant, or to have their minds put at rest about missing relatives or the souls of dead children. Wooster didn't believe in any of that stuff, but he still treated the woman with respect. She didn't demand it. She didn't have to. Only a fool would fail to recognize that it was her due.

Seeing her there now, waiting patiently, certain in the knowledge that the boy would soon be released into her charge, Wooster could spot the similarities between the woman and her grandson. It wasn't merely physical, although both carried themselves with the same slim grace. No, something of her own disconcerting calm had transferred itself to him. For some reason, Wooster thought of dark, still waters, of sinking into their depths, going deeper and deeper, down, down until suddenly pink jaws opened amid pale luminescence and the nature of the thing itself, the creature that hid in those unknown reaches, was finally and fatally revealed.

Wooster figured his day couldn't get a whole lot worse, although as far as he was concerned this business wasn't done with, no sir, not by a long shot. The boy could go home to his aunts and his grandmother and whoever else shared their little coven in the woods, but Wooster would be watching him. Wher-

ever that boy walked, Wooster would be stepping on his shadow. He'd break that boy yet.

And there was still the fag card left to play. Wooster had his suspicions about the boy. He'd heard stories. The only women with whom Louis spent time were those in his own household, and over at the Negro school he'd had to fight his corner a couple of times. Wooster knew that kids were often wrong about these things: any sign of sensitivity, of weakness, of femininity in a man and they would be on it like flies to a cut. Most of the time they were wrong, but sometimes they got it right. There were sodomy laws in this state, and Wooster had no difficulty in enforcing them. If he could get the kid on a sodomy beef, then that could be used as leverage on the Deber killing. Spending time in the pen on a queer charge was pretty much a guarantee of pain and misery right there. Better to go in with a reputation for having taken another man's life. At least that bought some respect. Wooster wasn't even interested in seeing the boy go to the chair. It would be enough for him to have proven others wrong: the state cops, his own people who had laughed at him behind his back for believing that a Negro boy could have committed a crime of such sophistication. Wooster wondered if he could bait a hook for the boy. There were one or two men in the town who wouldn't be above offering themselves up for the chance of a little dark meat. All it would take would be an agreed location, a specific time, and Wooster's fortuitous arrival on the scene. The older man would be allowed to walk, but the boy would not. It was a possibility.

As things happened, though, Wooster's day was about to worsen considerably, despite his own convictions to the contrary, and any plans for entrapment would soon turn to dust.

"Chief?" It was Seth Kavanagh, the youngest of his men. Irish Catholic. Mick through and through. There had been issues with some of the people in the town when Wooster hired him, and he'd even had a friendly visit from Little Tom Rudge and a couple of his fellow pillowcase-wearers, suggesting that he might want to reconsider hiring Kavanagh given that this was a Baptist town. Wooster listened to their pitch, then gave them the bum's rush. Little Tom and his kind made Wooster's skin crawl, but more than that, he felt incipient guilt whenever they came his way. He knew about the things that they had done. He knew about Negroes being beaten for still being within the town limits at sundown, even if those town limits seemed to change according to how much the local crackers had drunk at the time. He knew about unexplained fires in Negro cabins, and rapes that were brushed away as a little fun that had gotten out of hand.

And he knew about Errol Rich, and what had been done to him in front of a great many of the very people who praised God alongside Wooster in church every Sunday. Oh, yes, Wooster knew all about that, and he had enough self-knowledge to recognize his complicity in that act, even if he had been nowhere near the old tree from which Errol had been hanged and burned. Wooster hadn't cemented his grip on the town, not at that point, and by the time he heard about what was happening it was too late to do anything to stop it, or so he told himself. He'd made it clear, though, in the aftermath, that such an act was never to take place again, not in this town, not if he had any say in the matter. It was murder, and Wooster wouldn't condone it. It also got the Negroes all steamed up for no good cause. It overstepped the mark to the point where their anger threatened to overcome their fear. Furthermore—and it was this point, more than any other, that got shitbags like Little Tom thinking—it had the potential to bring the feds down on their heads, and they weren't understanding of the way things were done in small towns like this one. They didn't understand, and they didn't care. They were looking to make an example of people who didn't appreciate that the times they were a-changin', as that folk singer fella liked to put it.

And that was another reason for making sure that the boy Louis was punished for what he had done to Deber. If he got away with murder this time, then what would follow? Maybe he might take it into his head to move on to the men who had killed Errol Rich, the ones who had driven the car out from underneath his feet so that he kicked at dead summer air; the ones who had doused him in gasoline; the ones who had lit the torch and applied it to his clothes, turning him into a beacon in the night. Because there were whispers about Errol Rich and the boy's mother, too, and you could be certain that the boy had heard them. A man's father dies like that, and it could be that he would take it upon himself to avenge him. Damn, Wooster knew that he would, in the same situation.

Now here was Kavanagh, another of Wooster's little experiments in social change, bothering him with shit that he was certain he could do without. Wooster wiped his face with his handkerchief, then wrung it dry into his trash basket.

"What is it?"

He didn't look up. Once again, his gaze was fixed upon the wall before him, as though boring through it and the observation room beyond to reach the boy who had defied him for so long.

"Company."

Wooster turned in his chair. Through the window behind him, he watched the men emerge from their cars. One was a standard-issue Ford. He smelt government, a suspicion confirmed when Ray Vallance rolled down the passenger-side window and tossed a cigarette butt on the chief's yard. Vallance was the ASAC of the local FBI field office. He was an okay guy, as far as the feds went. He wasn't trying to move folks faster than they could walk on this civil rights thing, but he wouldn't let them dawdle either. Still, Wooster would have words with him about that butt. It showed disrespect.

The second car was too good to have come from any government pool. It was tan, with matching leather upholstery, and the man who got out on the driver's side looked more like a chauffeur than an agent, although Wooster thought that he also seemed like one mean sonofabitch, and he was pretty certain that the bulge underneath his left arm didn't come from a tumor. He opened the right rear passenger door, and a third man joined them. He looked old, but Wooster guessed that he wasn't much older than he himself was. He was just the kind of man who had always looked old. He reminded the chief of that old English actor, Wilfrid-Something-Something, guy was in the movie of My Fair Lady *that had come out a few years back. Wooster had seen it with his wife. It had been better than he was expecting, he seemed to recall. Well, that guy, the Wilfrid guy, he had always looked old, too, even when he was young. Now here was one of his near relatives, up close and in the flesh.*

Vallance seemed to sigh in his seat, then got out of the car and led two of his fellow agents to the door of the chief's office, bypassing the cop at the desk to enter the main area.

"Chief Wooster," he said, nodding with a pretence of amiability.

"Special Agent Vallance," said Wooster. He didn't stand. Vallance had never addressed him by anything but his first name before, and Wooster had returned the familiarity, even when there was business at hand. Vallance was giving him the nod, letting him know that this was serious, that both he and Wooster were being watched. Still, Wooster wasn't

about to stand down on his own turf without a fight, and there was the matter of that butt to consider.

Wooster looked past Vallance to where the other four men stood, the old-looking guy in the middle of the pack, smaller than the others but with his own quiet authority.

"What you got here, a wedding party?" asked Wooster.

"Can we talk inside?"

"Sure." Wooster rose and spread his hands expansively. "Everybody's welcome here."

Only Vallance and the older man entered, the latter closing the door behind them. Wooster could feel the eyes of his men and his secretary on him, boring through the glass. Knowing that he was on show before his own people made him step up to the plate. He straightened his shoulders and stood taller, his back to the window, not bothering to adjust the blinds, so that they had the sun in their eyes.

"What's the deal, Agent Vallance?"

"The deal is that boy you're sweating back there."

"Everybody sweats here."

"Not like him."

"Boy is a suspect in a murder investigation."

"So I hear. What have you got on him?"

"Got probable cause. Man he killed may have murdered his mother."

"May have?"

"He ain't around to ask no more."

"From what I hear, he was asked before he left this world. He didn't fess up to anything."

"He did it, though. Anyone believes he didn't is ready to meet Santa Claus."

"So, probable cause. That all you got?"

"So far."

"The boy bending?"

"The boy's not the kind to bend. But he'll break, in the end."

"You seem real sure of that."

"He's a boy, not a man, and I've broken better men than he'll ever be. You want to tell me what this is about? I don't think you have jurisdiction here, Ray." Wooster had given up being polite. "This isn't a federal beef."

"We think it is."

"How do you figure that?"

"Dead man was a crew chief on the new road by the Orismachee Swamp. That's a federal reserve."

"Will be a federal reserve," Wooster corrected him. "It's still just swamp now."

"Nope, that swamp, and the road that's being built, have just come under federal jurisdiction. Declaration was made yesterday. Rushed through. I got the paperwork here."

He reached into his inside jacket pocket, produced a sheaf of typed documents, and handed them to Wooster. The chief found his glasses, perched them on his nose, and read the small print.

"So", he said, when he was done, "that don't change a thing. Crime was committed before this declaration was made. It's still my jurisdiction."

"We can agree to differ on that one, Chief, but it doesn't matter anyhow. Read closer. It's a retrospective declaration, back to the first of the month, just before road construction began. It's a budgetary thing, they tell me. You know how the government works."

Wooster examined the paper again. He found the dates in question. His brow furrowed, and then blood soared to his cheeks and forehead as his anger grew.

"This is bullshit. The hell should this bother you anyway? It's colored on colored. It's not a rights issue."

"This is now a federal matter, Chief. We're not pressing charges. You've got to cut the boy loose."

Wooster knew that the case was slipping away from him, and with it some of his authority and his standing with his own staff. He would never be able to recover it. Vallance had made him his bitch, and the boy in that cell was going to skate, and laugh at Wooster while he was doing it.

And Wilfrid back there, with his prematurely graying hair and his neat, if slightly threadbare, clothes, had something to do with it, of that Wooster was sure.

"And where do you fit into all this?" he asked, now directing the full force of his ire at his second visitor.

"I apologize," said the little man. He stepped forward and stretched out a perfectly manicured hand. "My name is Gabriel."

Wooster didn't move to shake the hand that had been offered to him. He simply left it to hang in the air until Gabriel allowed it to fall. Screw you, he thought. Screw you, and Vallance, and good manners. Screw you all.

"You haven't answered my question," said Wooster.

"I'm here as a guest of Special Agent Vallance."

"You work for the government."

"I supply services to the government, yes."

That wasn't the same thing, and Wooster knew it. He was smart enough to grasp the underlying meaning of what had just been said. Suddenly, he got the sense that he was very much out of his depth, and that however angry he was, it would be unwise to ask any more questions of Gabriel. He had been trussed up like a hog ready for the spit. All that remained was for someone to shove a spike in his ass and all the way up through his mouth, and Wooster intended to avoid that fate at all costs, even if it meant giving up the boy.

He sat down in his office chair and opened a file. He didn't notice what it was, and he didn't read what was written on its pages.

"Take him," he said. "He's all yours."

"Thank you, Chief," said Gabriel. "Once again, my apologies for any inconvenience caused."

Wooster didn't look up. He heard them leave his office, and the door close softly behind them.

Chief Wooster. The big fish. Well, he'd just been shown the reality of his situation. He was a little fish in a small pond who'd somehow drifted into deep waters, and a shark had flashed its teeth at him.

He stared at the closed office door, visualizing again the wall beyond, the observation room behind it, and the boy in his cell, except now it was Gabriel watching him, not Wooster. Sharks. Deep waters. Unknown things coiling and uncoiling in their depths. Gabriel watching the boy, the boy watching Gabriel, until the two blended together to become a single organism that lost itself in a blood-dark sea.

CHAPTER FIVE

WILLIE BREW'S HEAD HURT.

Things hadn't started out too badly. He'd woken feeling dehydrated, and aware that, despite the fact he hadn't shifted position an inch in the night, he still hadn't slept properly. Maybe I'll get away with it, he thought. Maybe the gods are smiling on me, just this once. But by the time he reached the auto shop his head had started to pound. He was sweaty and nauseated by noon, and he knew things would go downhill from there. He just wanted the day to come to an end so that he could go home, go back to bed, and wake up the next morning with a clear head and a deep and abiding sense of regret.

It had been this way with him ever since he had given up hard liquor. In the good old, bad old days, he could have knocked back the guts of a bottle of even the worst rail booze and still been able to function properly the next morning. Now he rarely drank anything but beer, and then usually in moderation, because beer killed him in a way liquor never had. Except a man didn't reach the big six-oh every day, and some form of celebration was not only in order, but expected by his friends. Now he was paying the price for seven hours of pretty consistent drinking.

Even lunch hadn't helped. The auto shop was located in an alley just off 75th Street between 37th and Roosevelt, close by the offices of an Indian attorney who specialized in immigration and visas, an astute choice of business address on the attorney's part as this area had more Indians than some parts of India. Thirty-seventh Avenue itself had Italian, Afghan, and Argentinian restaurants, among others, but once you hit 74th Street it was Indian all the way. The street had even been renamed Kalpana Chawla Way, after the Indian astronaut who had been killed in the *Columbia* shuttle disaster in 2003, and men in Sikh turbans handed out menus throughout the day to all who passed by.

This was Willie's patch. He had grown up here, and he hoped that he would die here. He had biked out to LaGuardia and Shea Stadium as a kid, throwing stones at the rats along the way. It had mostly been the Irish and the Jews who lived here then. Ninety-fourth Street used to be known as the Mason-Dixon line, because beyond that it was all black. Willie didn't think he'd even seen a black face below 94th until the late sixties, although by the 1980s there were some white kids attending the mostly black school up on 98th. Funny thing was, the white kids seemed to get on pretty well with the black ones. They grew up close to them, played basketball with them, and stood alongside them when interlopers trespassed on their territory. Then, in the 1980s, things began to change, and most of the Irish left for Rockaway. The gangs came in, spreading outward from Roosevelt. Willie had stayed, and faced them down, although he'd been forced to put bars on the windows of the little apartment in which he lived not far from where the auto shop now stood. Arno, meanwhile, had always lived up on Forley Street, which was Little Mexico now, and he still didn't speak a word of Spanish. Below 83rd it was more Colombian than Mexican, and felt like another city: guys stood on the sidewalk hawking their wares, shouting and haggling in Spanish, and the stores sold music and movies that no white person was ever going to buy. Even the movies showing at the Jackson 123 had Spanish subtitles. Through it all, Willie had survived. He'd hadn't cut and run when times got tough, and when Louis had been forced to sell the building down by Kissena, Willie had taken the opportunity to relocate closer to home, and now he, and his business, were as much a part of the history of the place as Nate's was. It didn't help his hangover, though.

They'd eaten at one of the buffets, avoiding, as always, the goat curry that seemed to be a staple of the cuisine in this part of the city. "You ever even seen a goat?" Arno had once asked Willie, and he had to admit that he had not, or certainly not in Queens. He figured that any goat that found itself wandering around Seventy-fourth Street wasn't going to live for very long anyway, given the clear demand for dishes of which it was the main ingredient. Instead they stuck to the chicken, loading up on rice and naan bread. It was Arno who had converted Willie to the joys of Indian food, goat apart, and he had found that, once you stayed away from the hot stuff and concentrated on the bread and rice, it provided pretty good soakage after a night on the tiles.

Now they were back at the auto shop, and Willie was counting down the minutes until they could close up and go home. Softly, he cursed the Brooklyn Brewery and all of its works.

"A bad workman blames his tools," said Arno.

"What?" Willie hadn't been in the mood for Arno all day. The little Swede or Dane or whatever the hell he was had no right to be looking so spruce. After all, they'd finished the night propping up the bar together, talking about old times and departed friends. Some of those friends were even human, although most of them had four wheels and V8 engines. Arno had no qualms about drinking liquor. His only stipulation was that it had to be clear, so it was always gin or vodka for him, and Arno had matched Willie with a double vodka tonic for every beer. Yet here he was, bright and cheerful at the end of a grim day for Willie, listening in on his private conversations with the gods of brewing. Arno never seemed to get a hangover. It had to be something to do with his metabolism. He just burned it off.

Today, Willie hated Arno.

"It's not the brewery's fault," continued Arno. "Nobody made you drink all that beer."

"*You* made me drink all that beer," Willie pointed out. "I wanted to go home."

"No, you just thought you wanted to go home. You really wanted to keep celebrating. With me," he added, grinning like an idiot.

"I see you every day," said Willie. "I even see you Sundays at church. You haunt me. You're like the ghost, and I'm Mrs. Muir, except she ended up liking the ghost."

He considered his analogy and decided there was something suspect about it, but he was too weary to withdraw it. "Why the hell did I want to celebrate with you anyway?"

"Because I'm your best friend."

"Don't say that. I'll just despair."

"You got a better friend than me?"

"No. I don't know. Listen, you're just supposed to work for me, and even that's doubtful."

"I know you don't mean that."

"I do."

"Not listening."

"Dammit, I'm serious."

"Tra-la-la." Arno disappeared into the little storage room to the left of the main work area, trilling at the top of his voice, a finger lodged firmly in each ear. Willie considered throwing a wheel nut at him, and then decided against it. It would require too much effort, and anyway, he didn't trust his own aim today. He might miss Arno and hit something valuable.

He sat down on a crate, propped his elbows on his thighs, then rested his head in his hands and closed his eyes. It was almost eight, and dark outside. They always worked until eight on Thursdays, but in a few minutes they could safely lock up and call it a night. He would get Arno to take in the signs advertising that you could get your brakes fixed for $49.99 and your oil changed for $14.99. Then he would watch TV for a while at home before crawling into bed.

He wondered later if he had fallen asleep for a few moments right there and then, because when he opened his eyes there were two men standing in front of him. He made them for out-of-towners immediately. He could almost smell the cow turds. Both were of medium height, the older of the two probably in his early forties, with dark hair that hung untidily past his collar, and sideburns that extended out in sharp points at the end to join a goatee, as though all of his hair, head and facial both, was part of a single arrangement that could be taken off at night and draped over a mannequin's skull. He wore a brown, yellow, and green golf shirt under a brown corduroy jacket, and brown jeans over cheap imitation Timberlands.

Willie hated golf shirts almost as much as he hated golfers. Whenever anyone came into the shop dressed for the course, or with clubs in the back of the car, Willie would lie and tell them he was too busy to be of service. There might have been golfers who weren't assholes, but Willie hadn't met enough of them to be able to give the whole sorry species the benefit of the doubt. Also, in his experience, the more expensive the car a golfer drove, the bigger the asshole he was. His intense dislike of golfers extended to the entire golfing wardrobe, and that went double for phlegm-colored golf shirts and anyone sorry enough to wear one either in private or in public, and most particularly in Willie Brew's place of business when he was nursing a hangover.

The second man was broader than the first, and, despite the moderate chill in the air, was dressed only in a faded denim jacket over a T-shirt and distressed jeans. He was chewing gum, and wore the kind of shit-eating grin that suggested here, in the flesh, was not only a jerk, but the kind of jerk who considered it a poor day indeed that didn't involve inflicting a little pain and misery on another human being.

And this was the thing: they were both looking at Willie like he was already dead.

Willie knew who they were. He knew that, not far from the front entrance to his beloved auto shop, there would be a blue Chevy Malibu parked, ready to whisk these men back to wherever they had come from as soon as their work here was done. He should have said something the first time he saw the car. Now it was too late.

Willie stood. He still had a lug wrench in his right hand.

"We're closed, fellas," said Willie.

But these men were not here about a car, and anything that Willie said to the contrary was just delaying the inevitable, a pretense for which they would have no patience. They were here on business, and Willie tried to figure out if there was anyone he had bugged so much that they'd want to sic two guys like this on him. He decided that he couldn't find a name. There was nobody who hated him this much. This wasn't about him. A message was being sent, and it would be sent through Willie, through the breaking of his bones and the ending of his life.

Then the gum chewer produced a gun from beneath his jacket. He didn't even point it at Willie, just let it dangle by his side like it was the most natural thing in the world to walk into a man's premises and prepare to kill him. He kept his thumb and forefinger in position while he stretched the remaining fingers, an athlete giving his muscles a final loosening before stepping into the blocks.

"Drop the wrench," said his goateed buddy.

Willie did. It made a loud clang as it hit the concrete floor.

"You don't look so good," said Goatee. Willie tried to place the accent, but couldn't. There might have been some Canadian in there someplace. Not that it mattered, not now.

"I had a rough night."

"Well, I hate to say it, but your day ain't about to get much better."

Goatee punched Willie hard. Willie didn't have a chance to prepare for the blow. It hit him full in the center of the face and broke his nose. Willie went down on his knees, his hands already raised to catch the first flow of blood. He heard the second man snicker, then move off. The door to the storage area opened. Willie peered through his fingers, and saw the gum chewer enter the room, his gun raised now. For once in his life, Willie prayed, don't let Arno do anything dumb.

Goatee now had his own gun in his hand.

"You know," he continued, "you ought to be more particular about who you go into business with. I mean, I know men who keep company with faggots. I don't respect 'em, and I can't say that I much like what they do together, but it happens. Then, Lord knows, I've known men to keep company with killers. You might say that I am one of those men, and my buddy back there is as well. We're both like that, in a way: we kill people, and we keep each other company while we do it. But you, you're covering all the bases at once. Hanging out with fag killers: that's quite something. Guess you ought not to be surprised at what comes next."

He pointed the gun at Willie's head, and Willie closed his eyes. He heard a shot, and grimaced, but the sound hadn't come from up close. Instead, it echoed inside the storage room. The noise distracted Goatee for an instant. His head turned, and in that moment Willie was on him. He picked up the wrench as he came, raising it almost to his shoulder and then bringing it down sharply just above the man's gun hand. He thought that he felt a bone snap, and then the gun was on the floor and Willie's weight was forcing the other man back against the trunk of the red Olds on which Arno had been working. Even with one hand injured, Goatee was still fast. His left hand lashed out, catching Willie's busted nose and sending fresh daggers of pain through his face, blinding him for an instant. Willie kicked with his right foot, and the steel toe cap of his work boot connected with a thigh, deadening it so that his opponent stumbled as he stretched to reach his gun. The action caused Willie to lose his own balance, and he fell. He managed to knock the gun away with the side of his foot, sending it skidding into the shadows of the garage, just as he heard a second shot and glass breaking. He tried to make himself smaller, to find some cover, and when he looked up the back window of the Olds had shattered and Goatee was moving away quickly, still limping on his dead leg. There was a third shot, and Goatee's right shoulder was pushed forward, even as he slipped out of the garage door and disappeared into the night, his departure hastened by a final shot that struck the brickwork nearby.

Arno was standing at the entrance to the storage room, a gun in his hand. The gun wasn't very steady, and looked too big for Arno to hold. Arno didn't like guns and, as far as Willie knew, had never fired one before. It was a wonder that he'd managed to hit his target at all. Arno moved cautiously toward the garage door. There was the sound of a car starting up, then driving away.

Willie struggled to his feet. "What happened to the other fella?" he asked.

"I hit him with a hammer," said Arno. He was very pale. "His gun went off when he fell. You okay?"

Willie nodded. His nose hurt like damnation, but he was alive. His hands were shaking, and now he felt sure that he was going to vomit. He reached out and gently removed the gun from Arno's hand, putting the safety on as he did so.

"What was all that about?" asked Arno.

"I need to make a call," said Willie. "Find some wire and tie up the guy in the storage room."

Arno didn't move. "I don't think we're gonna have to do that, boss," he said.

Willie looked at him. "Jesus, how hard did you hit him?"

"It was a *hammer*. How hard do you think?"

Willie shook his head, although he wasn't sure whether in despair or admiration.

"I'm working with fucking Rambo now," he said. "I don't even know how you managed to wing that other guy."

"I was aiming for his feet," said Arno.

"What were you trying to do, make him dance? Aiming for his feet. Jesus. Lock the doors."

Arno did as he was told. Willie went into his office and picked up the phone. He knew by heart the number that he dialed.

The call transferred to a machine. Then he tried the service, and the woman named Amy took his number and said that she'd pass on the message. Finally, he tried the cell, using this week's number, to be utilized only in the gravest of emergencies, but a voice told him that the phone was off.

For Louis and Angel had troubles of their own.

Mrs. Bondarchuk was in the hallway when she heard the buzzer sound. She looked through one of the frosted-glass panes of the inner door and saw a man standing on the stoop outside the main door. He was dressed in a blue uniform and had a package in one hand and a clipboard in the other. Mrs. Bondarchuk pressed the intercom switch just as the buzzer sounded again. Her Pomeranians began yapping.

"Can I help you?" she asked, in a tone that suggested any help would be a long time coming. Mrs. Bondarchuk was wary of all strangers, and especially men. She knew what men were like. There wasn't a one that could be trusted, the two gentlemen who lived upstairs excepted.

"Delivery," the voice came back.

"Delivery for whom?"

There was a pause.

"Mrs. Evelyn Bondarchuk."

"Leave it inside," said Mrs. Bondarchuk, hitting the switch that opened the outer door only.

"Are you Mrs. Bondarchuk?" said the delivery man, as he stepped into the entrance.

"Who else would I be?"

"Need you to sign for it."

There was an inch-wide slot in the inner door for just such eventualities.

"Put it through the hole," said Mrs. Bondarchuk.

"Lady, I can't do that. It's important. I need to hold on to it."

"What am I going to do with a clipboard?" asked Mrs. Bondarchuk. "Sell it and fly to Russia? Put the clipboard through the hole."

The front door closed behind the man. She could see him properly now. He had dark hair and bad skin.

"Come on lady, be reasonable. Open up and sign."

Mrs. Bondarchuk didn't like the suggestion that she was being in any way unreasonable.

"I can't do that. You'll have to go, and you can take your parcel with you. Leave the number and I'll collect it myself."

"This is stupid, Mrs. Bondarchuk. If you don't accept it, I got to haul it all the way downtown again. You know, it could get lost," the man said, his implication clear. "Maybe it's perishable. What then?"

"Then it'll start to smell," said Mrs. Bondarchuk, "and you'll have to throw it away. Leave now, please."

But the man did not leave. Instead, he drew a pistol from beneath his uniform and aimed it at the glass. It had a cylinder attached to the end of it. Mrs. Bondarchuk had seen enough cop shows to know a silencer when she saw one.

"You dumb old bitch," he said as Mrs. Bondarchuk's finger left the intercom button, ending their conversation, while her left hand hit the silent alarm. The man glanced over his shoulder at the empty street behind him, then aimed the pistol at the glass and fired twice. The sound was like a pair of paper bags bursting, and almost simultaneously two impact marks appeared in front of Mrs. Bondarchuk's face, but the glass did not break. Like most things about the building, Mrs. Bondarchuk included, it was more formidable than it first appeared.

The man outside seemed to realize that his efforts were in vain. He slammed his gloved hand once against the glass, as though hoping to dislodge it from its frame, then opened the main door again and ran onto the street. For a time, all was quiet. Then Mrs. Bondarchuk heard noises from the basement at the back of the house. She checked her watch. Five minutes had passed since she had hit the silent alarm. If, after ten minutes, nobody came, her instructions were to call the police. Her two gentlemen had been very specific about this when the new security system was installed, and it had been repeated in an official letter to Mrs. Bondarchuk from Mr. Leroy Frank himself. It informed her that a private security firm, a very exclusive one, was employed to monitor Mr. Frank's properties in order to take some of the pressure from the city's finest. In the event of trouble, someone would be with her in less than ten minutes. If, after that time, no help had arrived, only then should she call the police.

The sounds from the back of the house persisted. She hushed her Pomeranians and quietly made her way downstairs to where the back door opened onto a small paved area where the trash cans were kept. The door was reinforced steel, and there was a spy hole in the center. She looked through it and saw two men, both of them wearing courier uniforms, attaching something to the exterior of the door. One of them, the man who had fired at the front door, looked up, and guessed that she was there from the change in the light. He waved a slab of white material, like a piece of builder's putty. Something that resembled the stub of a pencil stuck out of one end, with a wire attached.

"You ought to step back from the door," he said, his voice muffled by the steel yet audible. "Better still, lie against it, see what happens."

Mrs. Bondarchuk moved away, her hands pressed to her mouth.

"No," she said. "Oh, no."

She had to call the police. She retreated farther. She needed to get back to her apartment, needed to summon help. Mr. Leroy Frank's security people had not come. They had let her down, just when she most needed them. She began to run, and realized that she was crying. Her ears were filled with the sound of yapping Pomeranians.

Twin shots came from outside the door. They were much louder than the earlier shots, and they were followed by the sound of something heavy falling against the metal outside. Mrs. Bondarchuk froze, then turned in the direction of the door. She raised the tips of her fingers to her mouth. They trembled, tapping lightly on her fleshy lips.

"Mrs. Bondarchuk?" someone called, and she recognized Mr. Angel's voice. "You okay in there?"

"Yes," she said. "Yes. Who were those men?"

"We don't know, Mrs. Bondarchuk."

We.

"Have they gone?"

There was a pause.

"Uh, in a way," said Mr. Angel.

Mrs. Bondarchuk went back to her apartment, closed and locked the door, and sat with a pair of Pomeranians on her lap until Mr. Angel came to see her some time later with a chocolate cake from Zabar's. Together, they ate a slice of cake each and drank a glass of milk, and nice Mr. Angel did his best to put Mrs. Bondarchuk's mind at rest.

CHAPTER SIX

TO WILLIE'S SURPRISE, AND to Arno's relief, the man in the storeroom wasn't dead. His skull was fractured, and he was bleeding from his ears, which Willie didn't consider to be a good sign, but he was definitely still breathing. This took the decision on what to do next out of Willie's hands. He wasn't about to let a stranger die on his floor, so he called 911 and, while they waited for the ambulance and the inevitable cops to arrive, he and Arno got their stories straight. It was a bungled holdup, pure and simple. The men had been looking for money and a car. They were armed and, in fear of their lives, Willie and Arno had tackled them, leaving one unconscious on the floor and forcing the other to flee, wounded.

Willie took one further precaution. With Arno's help, and using a candle that he warmed and flattened on the radiator, he took the unconscious man's prints by pressing his fingers against the warm wax. He then placed the candle behind a pile of old documents in the office closet, and locked the door. The man wasn't carrying a wallet or any other form of ID, which Willie thought was odd. He knew that the cops would probably print him, but he also understood that Louis might want to make some inquiries of his own. To further assist Louis in any such endeavor, Willie told Arno to take some pictures of the guy, using his cellphone. Willie's cellphone didn't take photos. It was so low-tech that it made a tin can on the end of a piece of string look like a viable alternative, but that was just the way Willie liked it.

Both Willie and Arno played their parts to perfection when the cops arrived: they were honest men faced with the threat of harm and, possibly, death, who had fought back against their aggressors and now stood, shocked but most definitely alive, in the center of the small business they had so determinedly defended. It wasn't far off the mark either. The cops listened sympathetically, then advised them both to come down to the station the next morning in order to make formal statements. Arno asked if he was going to need a lawyer, but the detective in charge told him that he didn't think so. Off the record, he said that it was unlikely any charges would be pressed even if the mook died. No DA liked prosecuting an unpopular case, and Arno was in a position to offer an ironclad self-defense plea. The next step, he said, was to identify the gentleman in question, since the only items in his pockets were gum, a roll of tens, twenties, and fifties, and a spare clip for his gun. Willie and Arno did their best to look surprised at this news.

Willie reckoned they were 99 percent done when a pair of new arrivals, one male and one female, entered the garage. They both wore dark suits, and when they showed their IDs to the patrolman at the garage door he looked over his shoulder when they had passed and mouthed the word "feds" to his colleagues inside, as if they hadn't already guessed who the visitors were.

Willie's face had been taped up by one of the medics. The medic had reset Willie's nose in his office, thus saving him a trip to the hospital, and it was now throbbing balefully. Added to the nausea that he was still experiencing from his hangover and the comedown from the adrenaline rush of the fight, Willie was having trouble remembering the last time he'd felt so bad. Now, as he sat on a stool beside the busted Olds, Arno nearby, he watched the two agents approach and, with a dart of his eyes, signaled to Arno that there was trouble on its way. Willie was no expert on law enforcement, or the niceties of jurisdiction, but he had lived in Queens long enough to know that the FBI didn't show up every time someone waved a gun in an auto shop, otherwise they'd never have time to do anything else.

The man was black and introduced himself as Special Agent Wesley Bruce. His partner,

Special Agent Sidra Lewis, was a bottle blonde with piercing blue eyes and a set scowl on her face that suggested she believed everyone she met in the course of her work was guilty of something, even if it was only of thinking they were better than she was. They separated Arno and Willie, the woman taking Arno into the back office while Bruce leaned against the hood of the Olds, folded his arms, and gave Willie a big, unfriendly grin that reminded him of the way the gum chewer had smiled before Arno had knocked the smile from his face with a chunk of metal.

"So, how you doing?" asked Bruce.

"I been better," said Willie, which were just about the first completely honest words he'd uttered since the cops had arrived. He got the feeling that big old Special Agent Wesley Bruce here was well aware of that fact.

"Looks like our two friends picked the wrong guys to mess with."

"I guess so."

"You say they were looking for a car?"

"A car, and money."

"You got much money here?"

"Not a lot. Most people pay by check or credit card. We still get some that like to work with cash, though. Old habits die hard around here."

"I'll bet," said Bruce, as though Willie were not talking about cash payments but something else entirely. Willie tried to figure out what that might be, but there were so many possibilities from which to choose, legal and illegal, that he was spoiled for choice. Finally, Willie made the connection: like everything else that night, it was about Louis and Angel. The understanding did not affect his demeanor, but it made him dislike Special Agent Bruce even more than he already did.

In the meantime, Bruce gave Willie the hard eye. "I'll bet," he said again. He waited. Willie could hear Arno's voice coming from the office. He was talking a lot more than Willie was. In fact, Special Agent Lewis appeared to be having trouble just getting a word in.

Welcome to my world, thought Willie.

Eventually, Bruce seemed to realize that Willie wasn't about to break down and confess to every unsolved crime on the books, and resumed his questioning.

"So they wouldn't have raked in a whole lot of money for their trouble, even if they had managed to get away with it."

"Couple of hundred maybe, including petty cash."

"Lot of grief for a couple of hundred. There must have been easier pickings for them."

"We don't have a camera."

"Excuse me?"

"Security cameras. We don't use 'em. Most places do now, but we don't. Maybe they figured we didn't have them, and thought, what the hell, let's try it."

"Desperate times, desperate measures."

"Something like that."

"They strike you as desperate men?"

Willie considered the question. "Well, they weren't friendly. I don't know from desperate."

"I mean, they strike you as the kind of men who needed money?"

"Everybody needs money," replied Willie simply.

"Except our friend who got his head stoved in had four or five hundred in cash on him, not to mention a very nice gun. Doesn't strike me that he was hurting enough to take down an auto shop for a double century."

"I got no insights into the criminal mind. That's your department."

"No insights into the criminal mind, huh?" Bruce seemed to find this funny. He even laughed, although it didn't sound natural. It was as if someone had written the words "Ha. Ha. Ha." in front of him, then held a gun to his head and told him to read them aloud.

"What about the car?" said Bruce, when he was done laughing.

"What about it?"

"According to what you told the police, they drove here, and the other, uh, 'alleged' thief got away in the same vehicle. Why would they need a car if they already had one?"

"Could be they were planning a robbery and wanted something that couldn't be linked to them."

"Would have meant killing you and your buddy, then, just so you couldn't identify them or the car."

"Well, that's why one of them ended up wearing a hammer instead of a hat. Look, Mr. Bruce—"

"I prefer 'Special Agent Bruce.'"

Willie stared at Bruce impassively. There was a moment of strained silence between the two men, until Willie sighed theatrically and continued.

"*Special Agent* Bruce, I don't understand what your problem is here. We didn't get a chance to make these guys a cup of coffee so they could sit down and explain their motives to us. They came in, busted my nose, told me what they wanted, and you know the rest."

"Yeah, I know. You're heroes. There's already a guy from the *Post* outside, waiting to take your picture. You're going to be famous. Should be good for business."

"Sure," said Willie, a touch uneasily.

"You don't sound too happy about it," said Bruce.

"Who needs that kind of publicity?"

Bruce's grin widened. "Exactly!" he said. "That's just my point. Who needs it? Not you, and maybe not your partner in this operation."

"I don't know what you're talking about."

"Don't you? Who bailed you out when you were in trouble back in the day? Your ex-wife wanted you to sell the business as part of a divorce settlement, right? Things weren't looking good for you and then, suddenly, poof! You got the money to pay her off without having to sell. Where'd the money come from?"

Special Agent Bruce seemed to know a lot about Willie's business. Willie wasn't sure that he approved of his tax dollars being spent in this way.

"A Good Samaritan," he said.

"What was his name?"

"Came through an agency. I don't recall any names."

"Yeah, Last Hope Investments, which was in existence for about as long as a mayfly."

"Long enough to help me out. That's all that matters to me."

"You ever pay back the loan?"

"I tried but, like you say, Last Hope don't exist no more."

"Hardly surprising, if they go around making loans and then not seeking payment on them. Curious name, too, don't you think?"

"Not my problem. I declared the loan. I'm all straight."

"Who owns this building?"

"Property company."

"Leroy Frank Properties, Incorporated."

"That's it."

"You pay rent to Leroy Frank?"

"Fifteen hundred a month."

"Not much for a big place like this."

"It's enough."

"You ever meet Leroy Frank?"

"You think if I worked in a Trump building I'd meet Donald?"

"You might do, if he was a friend of yours."

"I don't think Donald Trump is friends with many of his tenants. He's the Donald, not—"

"—not Leroy Frank," Bruce finished for him.

Willie shook his head, a simple man faced with someone who seemed intent upon deliberately misinterpreting everything that was said.

"I told you: I never met no Leroy Frank. I cover my rent, I run my business, I pay my taxes, and I never even got so much as a parking ticket in my life, so I'm all square with the law."

"Well," said Bruce, "you must be just about the honestest man between here and Jersey."

"Maybe even farther than that," said Willie. "I met people from Jersey."

Bruce scowled.

"I'm from Jersey," he said.

"Maybe you're the exception," said Willie.

Bruce looked momentarily confused, then decided to let that particular conversation slide.

"He's hard to trace, this Leroy Frank," he resumed. "Quite the paper trail around his companies. Oh, it's all clean and aboveboard, don't get me wrong, but he's a mystery. Hard for a man to stay so *enigmatic* these days."

Willie said nothing.

"You know, what with this threat of terrorism and all, we've been spending a lot more time looking into finances that don't add up like they should," said Bruce. "It's easier than it used to be. We got more powers than before. Of course, if you're innocent then you've got nothing to fear—"

"I hear Joe McCarthy used to say that," said Willie, "but I think he was lying."

Bruce realized that he wasn't getting anywhere for the present. He took his considerable weight off the Olds, which seemed to groan with relief. His grin faded and his scowl returned. Willie figured it was only ever going to be a short vacation for that scowl at the best of times.

"Well, I guess I'll be going, but we'll be seeing each other again," said Bruce. "You happen to meet the mysterious Leroy Frank, you tell him I said hi. Unfortunate that all of this should happen in one of his properties. Be a shame if someone suggested to the press that it might be worth looking into the ownership of this place. It could threaten his anonymity, force him out into the light."

"I just pay my money into the bank," said Willie. "The only question I ask is, 'Can I get a receipt?'"

Special Agent Lewis emerged from the office. If anything, her expression looked more pinched than before, and she was practically shaking with frustration. Willie suppressed a smile. Arno did that to people. Trying to get answers from him when he didn't want to give them was like trying to straighten a snake. Bruce picked up immediately on his partner's unhappiness, but didn't comment upon it.

"Like I said, we'll be back," he told Willie.

"We'll be here," said Willie.

As the two agents departed, Arno appeared beside him.

"Gee, that lady was tense," he said. "I liked her, though. We had a nice talk."

"About what?"

"Ethics."

"Ethics?"

"Yeah, you know. Ethics. The rights and wrongs of things."

Willie shook his head. "Go home," he said. "You're making my head hurt even more."

He called Arno's name just as the little man was preparing to disappear into the night. "Be careful what you say on the telephone," he told him.

Arno looked puzzled. "All I ever say on the telephone is 'It's not ready yet,'" he said. "That, and, 'It's going to cost you extra.' You think the FBI might be interested in that?"

Willie scowled. Everybody, it seemed, was a comedian. "Who knows what they're interested in," he said. "Just watch what you say. Don't speak to any of those reporters outside. And show some respect, dammit. I pay your wages."

"Yeah, yeah," said Arno as the door closed slowly behind him. "Me, I'm gonna buy a yacht with my money this week . . ."

Louis made the call just as soon as the bodies had been disposed of. It was a matter of priorities. He left his name with the answering service, thinking, as he did so, that the voice on the end of the line sounded very similar to that of the woman who answered all calls for Leroy Frank. Maybe they incubated them somewhere, like chickens.

His call was returned ten minutes later. "Mister De Angelis says he will be available at twelve twenty-six tomorrow, around seven," the neutral female voice told him.

Louis thanked her, and said that he understood perfectly. As he hung up the phone, memories of previous meetings flooded back to him, and he almost smiled. De Angelis: of the angels. Now there was a misnomer.

Shortly after seven the next evening, Louis stood on the corner of Lexington and 84th. It was already dark. The sidewalks on this odd little stretch of the city's thoroughfares were relatively quiet, for most of its businesses, the odd bar and restaurant excepted, were already closed. A damp mist had descended over Manhattan, presaging rain and lending an air of unreality to the vista, as though a photographic image had been placed over the cityscape. To the left, the vintage sign over Lascoff's drugstore was still illuminated, and if one squinted, it was possible to imagine this stretch of Lexington as it might have looked more than half a century earlier.

The Lexington Candy Shop and Luncheonette was a throwback to that era. In fact, its roots were older still: it had been founded by old Soterios in 1925 as a chocolate manufactury and soda fountain, then passed on to his son, Peter Philis, who had, in turn, passed it on to his son, the current owner, John Philis, who still operated the register and greeted his customers by name. Its windows were filled with special edition Coca-Cola bottles, along with a plastic train set, some photos of celebrities, and a bat signed by the Mets' pure hitter Rusty Staub. It had been known as "Soda Candy" to generations of children, for that was what was written above its door, and its façade had remained unchanged for as long as anyone could remember. Louis could see two of its white-coated staff still moving around inside, although the front door was now locked, for the Lexington Candy Shop and Luncheonette only opened from seven until seven, Monday to Saturday. Nevertheless, the green plastic mat remained outside the door, waiting to be taken in for the night. On it was written Soda Candy's numerical address: 1226.

Louis crossed the street and knocked on the glass. One of the men cleaning up glanced sharply to his left, then emerged from behind the counter and admitted Louis, acknowledging him only with a nod. He closed and locked the door before he and his companion abandoned their tasks and disappeared behind another door at the back marked "No Admittance. Staff Only."

The place was just as Louis remembered it, although it had been many years since he had been inside. There was still the green counter, its surface marked by decades of hot plates and cups, and the green vinyl stools that rotated fully on their base, a source of endless amusement to children. Behind the counter stood twin gas-fired coffee urns, and a green 1942 Hamilton Beach malted machine and matching Borden's powdered malt dispenser, along with an automatic juicer from the same period.

Soda Candy was famous for its lemonade, made to order, the lemons squeezed while you watched, then stirred with sugar syrup and poured into a glass with crushed ice. Two glasses of that same lemonade now stood before the man who occupied the corner booth. The staff members had dimmed the fluorescents before they left, so it seemed to Louis that the old man who waited for him had somehow sucked the illumination from the room, like a black hole in human form, a fissure in time and space absorbing everything around him, the good and the bad, light and not-light, fueling his own existence at the cost of all who came into his sphere of influence.

It had been some years since Louis and the man named Gabriel had met, but two men whose lives had once been so closely linked could never truly sever the bond between them. In a sense, it was Gabriel who had brought Louis into being, who had taken a boy with undeniable talents and forged him into a man who could be wielded as a weapon. It was to Gabriel that those who needed to avail themselves of Louis's services had once come. He was the point of contact, the filter. His precise status was nebulous. He was a fixer, a facilitator. There was no blood on his hands, or none that one could see. Louis trusted him, to a degree, and distrusted him to a larger degree. There was too much about Gabriel that was unknown, and unknowable. Still, Louis was conscious of something that resembled affection for his old master.

He was smaller than Louis remembered, shrinking with age. His hair and beard were very white, and he seemed lost in his big black overcoat. His right hand trembled slightly as he gripped his glass and raised it to his lips, and some of the lemonade slopped onto the tabletop.

"Kind of cold for lemonade?" said Louis.

"Cold doesn't trouble me," Gabriel replied. "And one can get coffee anywhere, even if the coffee here is particularly good. I suspect it may be to do with the gas urns. But great lemonade, well, that is rarer, and one should grasp the opportunity to taste it when it arises."

"If you say so," said Louis as he slipped into a seat opposite, careful to keep both the staff exit and the main door in view, and placed the newspaper he had been holding in the center of the table. He didn't touch the glass.

"You know, they filmed parts of *Three Days of the Condor* here? I think Redford sat just where you are sitting now."

"You told me that before," said Louis. "A long time ago."

"Did I?" said Gabriel. He sounded regretful. "It seemed appropriate to mention it, given the circumstances." He coughed. "It's been a long time: a decade or more, ever since you discovered your conscience."

"It was always there. I just never paid too much attention to it before."

"I knew I was losing you long before our paths diverged."

"Because?"

"You started asking 'Why?'"

"It began to seem relevant."

"Relevance is relative. In our line of work, there are those who consider the question 'Why?'

to be a prelude to 'How deep would you like to be buried?' and 'Roses or lilies?'"

"But you weren't one of those people?"

Gabriel shrugged. "I wouldn't say that. I just wasn't ready to feed you to the dogs. I tried to ease your concerns, though, before I allowed you to go free."

" 'Allowed' me?"

"Permit an old man to indulge himself. After all, not everyone got to walk away."

"There weren't many left when I did."

"And none like you."

Louis did not acknowledge the compliment.

"And, if I may say so, my moral compass was surer than you gave me credit for," said Gabriel.

"I'm not certain I believe that, no offense meant."

"None taken. It is true, though. I was always careful about the work I farmed out to you. There were times when I walked a thin line, but I do not believe that I ever willingly overstepped it, at least, not where you were concerned."

"I appreciate that. I just think the line got thinner as time went on."

"Perhaps," Gabriel conceded, "perhaps. So, what happened last night? I understand you received visitors?"

Louis was not surprised that Gabriel was aware of what had occurred at the apartment building. At the very least, he would have made inquiries after Louis's call was received, although

Louis suspected that Gabriel knew of what had happened before the call was even made. Someone would have told him. That was how the old systems worked, and that was why the silence over Billy Boy's death had disturbed him so much.

"It was amateur hour," said Louis.

"Yes. The auto shop was a surprise, though. It appeared unnecessary and crude, unless someone was trying to send out a message. If so, then why target your residence at the same time?"

"I don't know," said Louis. "And it made the papers. Willie won't like the publicity. I don't like it either. It'll draw attention. Already has."

Gabriel dismissed Louis's concerns with a wave of his hand. "The papers have no interest in who owns buildings, merely who dies in them and who has sex in them, and not necessarily in that order."

"I wasn't talking about reporters."

Gabriel glanced out of the window, as if expecting agents of the state to suddenly materialize from the gloom. He seemed disappointed when they did not. Louis wondered how distant Gabriel now was from his former life. He no longer had his assassins, his Reapers, to call upon, but he would not have resigned himself to a quiet retirement. He knew too much already, but he always desired to know more. Perhaps he no longer dispatched killers to do dirty work for others, but he remained a part of that world.

Discreetly, Louis tapped the newspaper. Inside it was the flattened candle holding the wounded man's prints and copies of the photographs taken with Arno's cellphone, as well as additional prints from the two men who had died at the apartment building.

"I brought you some items that caught my eye. I'd like you to take a look at them."

"I'm sure the police will be looking at them, too."

"Maybe you can do it more quickly. A favor from your friends."

"They're not the kind who give favors without asking something in return."

"Then you're going to owe them two, because I have another one to ask."

"Name it."

"There were two federal agents nosing around Willie's place. They were asking questions about Leroy Frank."

"I've heard nothing about an investigation. It could be that they found a thread elsewhere and something has unraveled. Then again, they've become so much more dogged in recent years. There was a time when terrorism used to be good for business. Now it's all become very complicated: the slightest hint of a suspicious payment and there are all kinds of questions being asked, even of someone as blameless in such matters as Leroy Frank."

"Well, it could be embarrassing for a lot of people if they keep tugging on threads."

"I'm sure that something can be done," said Gabriel. "In the meantime, the matters in hand are more pressing: who did this, and how can we ensure that it does not happen again?"

" 'We'?"

"I feel a certain responsibility for your well-being, even after all this time. Also, in a sense, your problems are my problems, especially if they relate to something that occurred on my watch, as it were. It could, of course, be the case that it's related to your other activities. Your friend Parker has a way of making interesting enemies."

"Willie said the guy never mentioned Parker. It was about me."

"Good."

"Good?"

"It narrows the field. I haven't heard anything about a price on your head and, as you say, this was amateur hour. Anyone who put a paper out on you would be sure to hire more professional staff. If I were you, I'd be rather offended that someone might think you could be dealt with in such an uncouth fashion."

"Yeah, I'm all torn up. Speaking of which, I hope you sent flowers for Billy Boy."

Gabriel nodded sympathetically. "It wasn't entirely unexpected. His illness was quite advanced. Radical surgery was called for. It appears somebody took it upon himself to offer it."

"I'm sure he would have liked a second opinion."

"He got the best treatment available. The end, when it came, was quite swift."

"Blissful, even."

A spasm of unease animated Gabriel's face.

"I should have been told," said Louis.

"What have you heard?"

"Rumors, that's all."

"It's been a long time since anyone encountered him. It had been suggested that he was dead."

"Wishful thinking."

"Does he frighten you?" asked Gabriel slyly, calm now returning to his face.

"Do I have reason to be frightened?"

"None of which I'm aware. But in the case of the gentleman to whom you're referring, I wouldn't be privy to that kind of information. He's been off the radar for a long time, but you two do have a history. If he did return, he might be in the mood to renew old acquaintances."

"Not very reassuring for me. Maybe not very reassuring for you either."

"I'm an old man."

"He's killed old men before."

"I am different."

Louis conceded the point.

"Still, you and your partner handled yesterday's upsets rather well. I imagine that you'd present quite a challenge to him, even after all these years. What did you do with the trash?"

"I had it taken away. Landfill."

"And the old lady?"

"We bought her chocolate cake."

"Would that everyone were so easily mollified. How are your friends from the auto shop?"

"Shaken. I told them to close up for a few days. They're staying at a hotel."

Gabriel finished his lemonade and stood, picking up the newspaper as he did so and sliding it into his coat pocket.

"I should have something for you in a day or two," he said.

"I'd appreciate it."

"Well, it's not good to have this kind of thing going on. It makes everyone look bad."

"And we can't have that."

"Indeed not. Walk safely."

And with that, Gabriel was gone.

CHAPTER SEVEN

TWO MORNINGS LATER, GABRIEL held another meeting, this time in Central Park. The sky was clear and blue, unmarred by clouds after the gloom of the previous days, and there was a crispness to the air, a cleanliness, as though, however briefly, some of the fumes and filth of the city had been miraculously purged from it during the night. It was a day from childhood, but as he grew older Gabriel struggled to remember a time when he was young. The fragments of memory that remained to him seemed to involve another person, one unrelated to himself yet distantly familiar nonetheless. The sensation was similar to watching an old movie and recalling that, yes, one had seen this film before, and it had meant something, once upon a time.

He hated getting old. He hated *being* old. Seeing Louis had reminded him of all that he had once been, of the power and influence that he had wielded. There was still a little of it left, though. He no longer had Reapers at his beck and call, willing to do his bidding or the bidding of others for money, but favors were owed to him for favors done, for confidences kept, for problems buried and lives ended. Gabriel had stored his secrets away carefully, for he knew that his own life depended upon them. They were his security, and a currency to draw upon when necessary.

A younger man joined him, falling casually into step beside him. He was taller than Gabriel by a head, but Gabriel had almost three decades of often bitter experience on his companion. His code name was Mercury, after the god of spies and spooks, but Gabriel knew him as Milton. He suspected that it might be his real name, too, for, although an educated man, Milton's knowledge did not appear to extend into the field of literature, and an allusion to *Paradise Lost* by Gabriel early in their relationship had been met with a blank look. Then again, one never knew with agency men, and particularly ones of Milton's pedigree. One might have offered Milton intimate evidence of his own sexual preferences, complete with photographs, illustrations, and even former partners, to a similar end: a blank look. Blank. It was an appropriate word, in this case. Everything about Milton suggested a man who had been created in a laboratory in order to attract no attention whatsoever: average height, average looks, average hair, average clothing. There was nothing remarkable about him at all. In fact, so unremarkable was he that the eye tended to skate over him, barely registering his presence, and then instantly forgetting what it had seen. One had to be an exceptional individual to go through life so unnoticed.

Milton and Gabriel strolled by the lake, walking slowly enough to allow joggers to outpace them but fast enough that they could not be followed themselves without noticing. Milton wore a gray wool overcoat and a gray scarf, and his black shoes shone in the bright sunlight. Beside him, Gabriel, his white hair sprouting untidily from beneath a woolen cap, looked like a genial tramp. After some minutes had passed, Milton spoke.

"It's good to see you again," he said. His voice was as average as the rest of him, so that even Gabriel, who had known him for many years, could not tell if the words were meant or not. He decided that the sentiment might be genuine. It was not, as far as he could recall, something Milton said very often.

"And you," Gabriel lied, and Milton smiled, any offense caused by the untruth exceeded by his happiness at catching it. Milton, thought Gabriel, was the kind of man who was only at ease when the world was disappointing him, and therefore living down to his expectations. "I didn't expect you to come in person."

"It's rare that we have a chance to meet these days. Our paths no longer cross as once they did."

"I'm an old man," said Gabriel, and he was reminded of the context in which he had used those same words earlier in the week. He wondered if he had been correct then, if his age and his previous status might be enough to protect him from Bliss's predation. The thought had troubled him. He bore some responsibility for what had been done to Bliss, although Bliss could hardly have been surprised when retribution was visited upon him for his own actions, but the animosity between Bliss and Louis was of a deeper, more personal nature. No, if Bliss had returned, Gabriel would not be in his sights.

"Not so old," said Milton, and now it was his turn to lie.

"Old enough that I can see the tunnel at the end of the light," said Gabriel. "Anyway, it's a new world with new rules. I find it harder to recognize my place in it."

"The rules are still the same," said Milton. "There are just fewer of them."

"You sound almost nostalgic."

"Perhaps I am. I miss dealing with equals, with those who think as I do. I no longer understand our enemies. Their purpose is too vague. They don't even know what it is themselves. They have no ideology. They have only their faith."

"People enjoy fighting for their religion," said Gabriel. "It's inconsequential enough to matter deeply to them."

Milton didn't say anything in response. Gabriel suspected that Milton was a worshipper. Not a Jew. Catholic maybe, although he lacked the imagination to be a good one. No, Milton was probably a Protestant of indistinct color, a member of some particularly joyless congregation that thrived on hard benches and long sermons. The image of Milton in church led Gabriel to imagine what Mrs. Milton might look like, if there was such a person. Milton did not wear a wedding band, but that meant nothing. It was in the nature of such men to give as little as possible away. From something as simple as a wedding band, a whole existence might be imagined. Gabriel pictured Milton's wife as a pinched woman, as stern and unyielding as her religion, the kind who would spit the word "love."

"So, you've had contact with our lost sheep," said Milton, changing the subject.

"He seemed well."

"Apart from the fact that somebody appears to be trying to kill him."

"Apart from that."

"The police drew a blank on the first set of prints," said Milton. "So did we. A candle: that was quite ingenious. The gun found at the garage was clean, too, according to the police reports. No previous use."

"That's surprising."

"Why?"

"They were amateurs. Amateurs tend to make small mistakes before they make large ones."

"Sometimes. Perhaps these gentlemen dived in headfirst, and went straight from zero to minus one."

Gabriel shook his head. It didn't fit. He pushed it to the back of his mind, leaving it to simmer like a pot on a stove.

"We did, however, have more luck with one of the second sets. Curious that the owners of those prints have yet to surface."

"Landfill," said Gabriel. "It's difficult to surface when you're under thirty feet of earth."

"Indeed. The prints came from a man named Mark Van Der Saar. Unusual name. Dutch. There aren't many Van Der Saars in this part of the world. This particular Van Der Saar did three years upstate at the Gouverneur Correctional Facility for firearms offenses."

"Is that where he was from?"

"Massena. Close enough."

"Employers?"

"We're looking into it. One of his known accomplices is, or was, given Mr. Van Der Saar's recently acquired status as a decedent, a man named Kyle Benton. Benton did four years at the Ogdensburg Correctional Facility, also, incidentally, for firearms offenses. Ogdensburg, too, is located upstate, in case you didn't know."

"Thank you for the geography lesson. Please, go on."

"Benton works for Arthur Leehagen."

The rhythm of Gabriel's footsteps faltered for a moment, then recovered itself.

"A name from the past," he said. "That's all you have?"

"So far. I thought you'd be impressed: it's more than you had before you met me."

They walked on in silence while Gabriel considered what he had been told. He shifted pieces of the puzzle around in his mind. Louis. Arthur Leehagen. Billy Boy. It was all so long ago, and he felt a soft surge of satisfaction as he fitted the pieces together, establishing the connection.

"Do you know of two FBI agents named Bruce and Lewis?" he asked, once he was content with his conclusions. Milton had glanced at his watch, a clear sign that their meeting was about to come to an end.

"Should I?"

"They were looking into our mutual friend's affairs."

"I'm not sure that 'friend' is a word I'd use in this case."

"He has been friendly enough to keep his mouth shut for many years. I should think that is more amicable behavior than you're used to."

Milton didn't contradict him, and Gabriel knew that he had scored a point.

"What kind of interest are they showing?"

"They seem to be delving into his property investments."

Milton withdrew a gloved hand from his pocket and waved it disdainfully in the air.

"It's all of this post-9/11 bullshit," he said. Gabriel was shocked to hear him swear. Milton rarely showed such depth of feeling. "They're under instruction to follow paper trails: unusual business investments, financial dealings that seem suspicious, property and transport holdings that don't add up. They are the bane of our lives."

"He's not a terrorist."

"Most of them aren't, but along the way useful information is sometimes unearthed and followed up. It probably got passed on to these agents, and now they're curious."

"They're more than curious. They seem to know something of his background."

"It's hardly a state secret."

"Oh, but some of it is," said Gabriel.

The two men stopped, squinting against the sunlight, their breaths mingling in the dry air.

"He has a reputation," said Milton. "He's been keeping bad company, if such a thing were humanly possible given his own nature."

"I assume you're referring to the private investigator."

"Parker. And I believe he's a former investigator. His license has been revoked."

"Perhaps he's found some more peaceful ways of occupying his time."

"I doubt it. From what little I know of him, he feeds on trouble."

"Yet, if I did not know better, I might have said that Louis was almost fond of him."

"Fond enough to kill for him. If he has attracted attention, then he has brought it on himself. The only wonder is that it has taken the FBI so long to come knocking on his door."

"That's all very well," said Gabriel, "but there is as much that is unknown about him as known, and I'm certain you would prefer matters to remain this way."

"I hope that's not a threat."

Gabriel placed a hand on the younger man's arm, patting lightly the sleeve of his overcoat.

"You know me better than that," he said. "What I mean is that any investigation will eventually come up against a brick wall, a brick wall constructed by you and your colleagues. But such barriers are not impregnable, and the right questions asked in the right places could produce information that would be inconvenient to both parties."

"We could always get rid of him," said Milton. He said it with a smile on his face, but the remark still drew a wary look from Gabriel.

"If you were going to do that, you would have done it long ago," said Gabriel. "And would you have disposed of me, too?"

Milton began to walk again, Gabriel falling into step alongside him.

"With regret," said Milton.

"Somehow, I find that almost consoling," said Gabriel.

"What do you want me to do?" asked Milton.

"Call off the dogs."

"You think it's that easy? The FBI doesn't care much for other agencies interfering in its affairs."

"I thought you were all on the same side."

"We are: our own. Nevertheless, I'll talk to some people and see what I can do."

"I would be most grateful. After all, you'd be protecting a valuable asset."

"A once-valuable asset," Milton corrected, "unless, of course, he's in the market for some work."

"Unfortunately, he appears to have chosen another path."

"It's a shame. He was good. One of the best."

"Which reminds me," said Gabriel, as though it were a mere afterthought and not something that had been preying on his mind since he had learned of the death of Billy Boy. "What do you know of Bliss?"

"I know Laphroaig and a good cigar," said Milton. "Or isn't that what you meant?"

"Not quite."

"We lost contact with him many years ago. He was never on our Christmas card list to begin with. I found him distasteful. I shed no tears when he fell from grace."

"But you used him."

"Once or twice, and always through you. I learned to hold my breath, and I washed my hands afterward. As I understand it, you and your 'friend' contrived to put an end to his career."

"We were moderately successful," said Gabriel.

"Moderately. You should have used more explosive."

"We only wanted him dead, not half the people who might have been standing nearby when it happened."

"In some circles, such humanity might be taken as a sign of weakness."

"Which is why I have devoted such time and energy to reducing the size of those circles. As, I think, have you."

Milton inclined his head in modest agreement.

"Nevertheless, there are indications that Bliss may be back on the radar."

"Really?" For the first time, Milton looked directly at Gabriel. "I wonder why."

Gabriel had learned to read faces and tones of voice, to balance words spoken against gestures made, to pick up on the slightest of inflections that might give the lie to what was being said. As he listened to Milton speak, he felt certain that he had not been told all that the other man knew of what was taking place.

"Perhaps if you heard anything more, you might be inclined to give me a call."

"Perhaps," said Milton.

Gabriel reached out his hand. Milton took it and, as they shook, Gabriel neatly slid a piece of paper beneath the cuff of Milton's shirt.

"A small token of gratitude," said Gabriel. "A container that you might be ill-advised to allow to leave the yard in question."

Milton nodded his thanks. "When you see the lost sheep, pass on my regards."

"I'll be sure to do that. I know he thinks fondly of you."

Milton grimaced. "You know," he said, "I don't find that very comforting at all."

Gabriel contacted Louis later that evening, again through their respective answering services. They spoke for only a few minutes in a cab taking Gabriel to the Performance Space on Broadway. The driver was absorbed in a lengthy and animated telephone conversation being conducted entirely in Urdu. Gabriel had amused himself earlier in the journey by attempting to follow what was being said.

"I had a call," said Gabriel. "It came from a gentleman who works for Nicholas Hoyle."

"Hoyle? The millionaire?"

"Millionaire, recluse, whatever."

"And what did he say?"

"It appears that Mr. Hoyle would like to meet you. He says he has information that could be useful to you, information concerning the events of recent days."

"Neutral territory?"

Gabriel shifted in his seat. "No. Hoyle never leaves his penthouse. He is, by all accounts, a most peculiar man. You'll have to go to him."

"That's not the way things are done," said Louis.

"He approached you through me. *That* is the way things are done. He would be aware of any consequences that might arise should he fail to observe the usual niceties."

"He could have sent those men to draw me out."

"If he was intent upon that, he could simply have hired better help and finished the job there and then. Anyway, he has no reason to move against you, or none of which I am aware, unless you have angered him in the course of some of your recent activities."

He arched a questioning eyebrow at Louis.

"Doesn't ring any bells," said Louis.

"Then again," said Gabriel, "I can't imagine that you and your friend from Maine leave many loose ends. Cancer offers a better survival rate than crossing you. Given that, I imagine Hoyle has some mutually beneficial arrangement in mind. The choice is yours, though. I am merely passing on the message."

"In my position, what would you do?"

"I would speak to him. So far, we're no closer to finding out anything about the men involved or who was behind them."

Gabriel darted a look at Louis. The lie had passed him by. That was good. Gabriel would wait to hear from Louis what Hoyle had to say. In the meantime, he had begun to make inquiries about Arthur Leehagen. He was not yet ready to share with Louis what Milton had told him. In everything that he did, Gabriel protected himself first and foremost. Despite any affection he might have retained for Louis, he would feed him to wild dogs before he put himself at risk.

"So they were amateurs, but their boss isn't? Still makes no sense, unless we're back to the possibility that someone wants to draw me into the open."

"You're not as hard to find as you might like to believe, as recent events have proved. We're missing something here, and Hoyle may be the one to enlighten us. He doesn't issue invitations to his abode every day. Under other circumstances, it might be considered quite an honor."

Louis watched the city flash by the window. Everything—the cab, the people, the lights—seemed to be moving too fast. Louis was a man who liked to be in control, but that control was being ceded to others: Gabriel, his unseen contacts, and now Nicholas Hoyle.

"All right, make the arrangements."

"I will. You'll have to go unarmed. Hoyle doesn't allow weapons inside the penthouse."

"Gets better and better."

"I'm sure that you can handle anything that may arise. Incidentally, I raised the federal matter with some potentially interested parties. I believe it will be dealt with to your satisfaction."

"And who might those interested parties be?"

"Oh, you know better than to ask that. Now, if you'd just let me out here, I'll be on my way. And please pay the cab driver. It's the least that you can do for me after all that I've done for you."

Bliss drove north, an anonymous figure on an anonymous highway, just another pair of headlights burning whitely in the dark. Soon he would leave the road and find a place to rest for the night. Rest, not sleep. He had not slept properly in many years, and he lived in constant pain. He desired peaceful oblivion more than almost anything else on earth, but he had learned to survive on a few hours of slumber brought on by the exhaustion that eventually overcame his residual agonies. The treatment of his injuries, and his efforts to stay ahead of his pursuers, had depleted him not only physically, but financially, too. He had been forced to resurface, but he had chosen his paymaster carefully. In Leehagen, he had found someone who could satisfy both his financial and his personal needs.

The bottle containing Billy Boy's blood lay in a padded box at the bottom of Bliss's small suitcase. Leehagen had wanted him killed on his land, but Bliss had refused. It was too dangerous. But as the knife left his hand, and he saw the look of understanding on Billy Boy's face before he died, Bliss knew that his gifts were still intact. It gave him confidence for what was to come.

That night, as he lay on his bed in a modest, clean motel room, humming softly to himself, he thought of Louis with the ardor of a lover journeying to meet his betrothed.

CHAPTER EIGHT

THE HEADQUARTERS OF HOYLE Enterprises stood a few blocks from the UN, so the surrounding streets were a Babel of diplomatic plates, creating uneasy relationships between bitter international enemies now forced to share valuable parking space. Hoyle's building was unremarkable: it was older and smaller than most of the adjacent towers and stood at the eastern extreme of a public area that extended partially into the vicinity of the neighboring blocks to the north, south, and west, creating a natural boundary between Hoyle and the edifices around him.

In the twenty-four hours since the meeting with Gabriel, Louis and Angel had sourced the blueprints for Hoyle's building, and Angel, aided by a bored Willie Brew and a slightly less bored Arno, had watched it for an entire day. It was a precaution, an effort to establish some sense of the rhythms of the building, of how deliveries were dealt with, of shift changes and lunch breaks among the security guards. It wasn't long enough to form any accurate determination of the risks involved in entering, but it was better than nothing.

Actually, to Willie it was worse than doing nothing. He could have been doing nothing in the relative comfort of his own apartment, instead of doing something that he wasn't enjoying far from any comfort at all. Arno had spent most of their watch reading, which seemed to Willie to defeat the purpose of keeping an eye on the building to begin with, but then Willie supposed that Arno was just killing time, too. Louis was reluctant to have them return to the auto shop just yet, which meant that Willie could either sit in his apartment and watch TV that didn't interest him, or sit in a car and watch a building that didn't interest him either. One good thing had resulted from their efforts: Willie had decided that, Louis or no Louis, he and Arno were going back to work soon. Even after only a couple of days of lounging around, Willie felt as though something was dying inside him.

Hoyle's penthouse occupied the top three floors of the building. The remainder was given over to his offices. While Hoyle-owned companies were involved in mining, property, insurance, and pharmaceutical research, among other interests, the beating heart of his operation lay behind the modest façade of the Manhattan office. This was the parent company, and it was in this building that all power ultimately resided. A small but steady stream of people moved in and out of the lobby throughout the day, the flow increasing between twelve and two, and becoming almost entirely one-way traffic after five. Angel had spotted nothing untoward during his period of surveillance, and neither had Willie or Arno. There were no men carrying RPGs stationed behind the pillars, and he could see no heavy artillery hidden among the potted plants.

Then again, as Gabriel had noted, Hoyle had approached Louis through the proper channels, a peculiarly old-world notion in this modern age, and one that depended for its force upon Gabriel's reputation and the favors owed to him by others. If there were any breach of protocol, Hoyle would be aware of the possible repercussions. As far as Gabriel was concerned, therefore, Louis had no cause to be any warier than usual, which meant that Louis and Angel were very wary indeed as they entered the building shortly after eight that evening.

There was one security guard behind the desk, and he merely nodded them through. Only one elevator was open in the lobby, and it had no buttons inside or out. The interior was mirrored. There was no visible camera. Angel figured that meant there were probably at least three: one behind each mirrored wall, and maybe a pinhole fourth behind the small video screen displaying the numbers of the passing floors. The elevator was also likely to be miked, so neither man spoke. They merely watched their reflections in the gleaming brass of the doors, one apparently contentedly, the other critically. Angel didn't like mirrors. As Louis had once pointed out, mirrors didn't like him either, remarking that "even your reflection probably leaves a stain."

When the display read "PH," the elevator stopped and the doors opened silently. There were two men waiting for them in an otherwise empty foyer, with more mirrors on the walls and a vase of freshly cut flowers standing on a small marble plinth. Both men wore black suits and matching funeral ties, and both carried metal detector wands. They swept them over Angel and Louis, pausing to check belts, coins, and watches, then indicated that they should proceed. A pair of carved wood doors, Oriental in origin, and clearly old, opened to reveal a third man. He was dressed more casually than the others: black trousers and a black wool jacket over an open-collared white shirt. His hair was neither too long nor too short and was pushed casually over his ears at the sides, as though he cared just enough to keep it tidy, and nothing more. His eyes were brown, and Angel detected in his features a mixture of amusement, frustration, and professional jealousy. He had the build of a swimmer: broad across the shoulders, but slender and muscular overall. The jacket hung loose enough to hide a gun, and was unbuttoned.

Angel felt Louis relax slightly, but the response was the opposite of what it appeared to be. When Louis relaxed, it was an indication that a threat was at hand and he was preparing to act, as when an archer releases a breath simultaneously with the flight of the arrow, channeling all of the tension into the flighted missile itself. The two men regarded each other silently for a few moments, then the waiting man spoke.

"My name is Simeon," he said. "I'm Mr. Hoyle's personal assistant. Thank you for joining us. Mr. Hoyle will be with you presently."

Angel wasn't sure what Simeon's duties as an assistant entailed, but he was pretty certain that they didn't involve typing or answering the phone. Neither was he simply a bodyguard, unlike the men who had searched them. No, Angel had met Simeon's type before, and so had Louis. Here was a specialist, and Angel wondered why a businessman, albeit a wealthy, reclusive one like Nicholas Hoyle, might require someone with the abilities that Simeon undoubtedly possessed.

Simeon's gaze moved briefly to Angel, decided that there was nothing there worth lingering upon, then returned to Louis. He retreated into the room behind him, extending his right hand in a gesture of welcome. He did not turn his back on Louis. It came across as a sign of respect as well as of caution.

They entered a large, open-plan living area, dimly lit, with bookshelves from floor to ceiling, occupied by a combination of books, sculptures, and ancient weaponry: blades and axes and daggers, all mounted on transparent glass supports. The room was so cold that Angel felt goose bumps rise. The floorboards were made of reclaimed wood, and the couches and chairs were dark and comfortable, giving the impression that here was the habitation of a man of arms and letters, a throwback to another era. The room itself might even have been from another century, were it not for a glass wall that looked down upon an enclosed swimming pool, the water rippling slightly and casting its patterns on the interior walls. Although the contrast was initially disconcerting, Angel decided that it complemented, rather than undermined, the decor. Unless one was close to the glass, the sunken pool was invisible, so all that remained were the ghosts of the ripples upon the walls. It was like being in the cabin of a great ship at sea.

"Boy, it's blue," said Angel, as he stared down at the water, and it was: unnaturally so, as though a dye had been added to it. Angel decided that, even if he was the swimming kind, he wouldn't have taken a dip in that pool. It looked like a chemical vat.

"The pool is professionally treated every week," said Simeon. "Mr. Hoyle likes his cleanliness."

There was an edge to his voice when he spoke, a mild undertone of sarcasm. It made Louis wonder just how committed Simeon was to his boss. Louis had previously met men who were more than bodyguards to their employers, but less than friends. They were like guard dogs who grow to love the men who feed them scraps, doting on moments of affection and viewing any anger directed toward them as evidence of a failure on their part. Simeon didn't seem like that kind of guy. This was a financial arrangement, pure and simple, and as long as Hoyle continued to put money into Simeon's account, Simeon would continue to guard Hoyle's life. Both parties knew exactly where they stood, and Louis guessed that both Hoyle and Simeon liked it that way.

"Hey, is Simeon your first name or your last name?" asked Angel.

"Does it matter?"

"Just trying to make conversation."

"You're not very good at it," said Simeon.

Angel looked downcast. "I get that a lot."

Louis was examining a lance point on one of the shelves. He didn't touch it, merely moved its glass base carefully in order to view it point-on, as though it were aimed at his face.

"It's from a Hyksos lance," said Simeon. "They invaded Egypt seventeen hundred years before Christ and formed the Fifteenth Dynasty."

"You read that somewhere?" asked Louis.

"No, Mr. Hoyle read it somewhere. He was kind enough to share the knowledge with me, and now I'm passing it on to you."

"Interesting. You should run tours." Louis turned to Simeon. "You work for him long?"

"Long enough."

"That could be taken two ways."

"Guess so."

"Where did you serve?"

"What makes you think I'm ex-military?"

"I have good eyes."

Simeon considered his reply. "Marines."

"Let me guess: Recon."

"No. Antiterrorist, out of Norfolk."

Antiterrorist: that meant FAST, the Marines' Fleet Antiterrorist Security Team, formed at the end of the 1980s to provide additional short-term protection when the threat was beyond the capabilities of the usual security forces. Simeon would have been trained in threat assessment, the preparation of security plans, guarding VIPs protection. Despite himself, Louis was impressed.

"This must make a pleasant change for you," said Angel, joining them. "Now you don't have to lift anything heavier than a wand." He smiled guilelessly. "It's like being a fairy godfather."

Louis had moved on to what appeared to be a knife and ax combined, with a vicious triangular blade.

"That's a ko dagger-ax." Another man had entered the room from a door to the right. He had a full head of silver hair, neatly trimmed, and wore a long-sleeved red polo shirt and tan chinos. His shoes were brown penny loafers, scuffed and comfortable. He was lightly tanned. When he smiled, he revealed teeth that were slightly uneven, and not excessively white. His blue eyes were magnified behind the lenses of his glasses. Whatever else he was, he did not appear to be vain, or had ceased to make the more obvious concessions to vanity. The only peculiar aspect of his appearance was the pair of white gloves that covered his hands. "I'm Nicholas Hoyle. Welcome, gentlemen, welcome."

He joined Louis at the shelf, clearly enjoying the opportunity to show off his collection. "Eleventh or tenth century B.C.," he continued, lifting the weapon so Louis could examine it more closely. "They were all the rage in Pa-Shu during the Eastern Chou, but that one originated in Shansi."

He replaced the ax and moved on. "This item is interesting." He carefully moved a curved dagger from its plinth. "It's late Shang, thirteenth to twelfth century B.C. See, there's a rattle at the end of its hilt." He shook the blade gently. "Not for silent killing, I imagine."

Finally, he moved on to a crude-looking ax that stood on a shelf of its own. "This is one of the oldest weapons I own," he said. "Hungshan, from the Liao river region of northeast China. Neolithic. Three thousand years old, at least, perhaps even four thousand or more. Here, take it."

He handed the ax to Louis. Behind him, Angel saw Simeon stiffen slightly. Even after all these years, the ax was clearly capable of inflicting damage. It looked much more recent than it was, a testament to the skill that had gone into its construction. Louis saw that the top of the ax head had been carved to resemble an eagle. He ran the tip of his index finger along the carving.

"It's religious in nature," said Hoyle. "The first messenger from the Celestial Ruler was believed to have been a bird. Eagles were thought to transmit human wishes to the gods; in this case, one presumes, the death of an enemy."

"It's an impressive collection," said Louis, returning the ax to him.

"I began collecting when I was a boy," said Hoyle. "I started with minié balls gathered from the Kennesaw Mountain Battlefield. My father was a Civil War aficionado and liked to take us on battlefield vacations. My mother, I seem to recall, was generally unimpressed. I even created my own mix of tallow and beeswax to lubricate them, just like the soldiers did to prevent bore fouling from black powder residue. Otherwise—"

"They'd stick in the barrel," Louis finished. "I know. I used to collect them myself."

"And where was that?" asked Hoyle.

"Doesn't matter," said Louis. "It was a long time ago."

"Well," said Hoyle. He seemed embarrassed that he had overstepped some mark with Louis by asking about his past. It wasn't a situation with which he appeared to be familiar. To hide his discomfort, he indicated a pair of armchairs and twin couches surrounding a low redwood table. Louis took one of the chairs, Hoyle another, while Angel sat on a couch. Alcohol was offered, but Angel and Louis declined. Instead, green tea was served, and some Japanese candies that stuck to Angel's teeth and filled his mouth with a taste of lemon and horseradish that was not unpleasant, merely peculiar.

"You'll forgive me for not shaking hands," said Hoyle. He managed the neat trick of making it sound like a request, a favor granted by another even if the decision had been entirely his own. "Even with my gloves on, I tend to be cautious about such matters. The human hand is home to both resident and transient bacteria, a veritable cesspool of germs, but it is the transients of whom we must be most acutely aware. My immune system is not what it once was—a congenital weakness—and now I no longer venture beyond these walls. Nevertheless, I remain in good health, but precautions must be taken, particularly where visitors are concerned. I hope you're not offended."

Neither Angel nor Louis looked offended. Louis remained impassive. Angel appeared bewildered. He glanced discreetly at his hands. They looked clean, but he knew what a cesspool was. He sipped some green tea. It didn't taste of very much at all. He considered using it to wash his hands.

"I hear you've been having difficulties," said Hoyle. He addressed his comments to Louis alone. Angel was used to such behavior. It didn't trouble him. It meant that, in the event of a problem, he usually had an advantage over those, like Simeon and his master, who had underestimated him.

"You seem to be well informed," said Louis.

"I make it my business to be," replied Hoyle. "In this case, your interests and mine appear to have coincided. I know who sent those men to your home and the business premises in Queens. I know why they were sent. I also know that the situation is likely to deteriorate further unless you act promptly."

Louis waited.

"In 1983," Hoyle continued, "you killed a man named Luther Berger. He was shot in the back of the head at close range as he left a business meeting in San Antonio. You were paid fifty thousand dollars for the hit. It was good money, in those days, even split with the driver of your getaway vehicle. In keeping with protocol, you didn't ask why Berger had been targeted.

"Unfortunately, though, his name wasn't really Luther Berger. He was Jon Leehagen, or 'Jonny Lee' as he was sometimes called. His father is a man named Arthur Leehagen. Arthur Leehagen did not take kindly to the killing of his older son. He has spent a very long time trying to find out who was behind his murder. In the last twelve months, he has made considerable progress. The man who hired you through Gabriel—his name was Ballantine, incidentally, although you never met him—died a week ago. He was taken to Leehagen's property, killed, and his remains fed to hogs. Leehagen has also been able to establish your identity, and the identity of the driver of the vehicle that removed you from the scene. I believe he was known to you as Billy Boy. He, like Ballantine, has since been killed: stabbed in a restroom, as I understand it, although you may know more about the circumstances than I do.

"The men who attacked your home and the auto shop in Queens were sent by Leehagen. More will follow. I don't doubt that you're capable of handling most of them, but, rather like terrorists, they only have to get lucky once, while you will have to be both lucky, and proficient, all of the time. I also imagine that you would prefer not to have any more attention drawn to yourself or your business operations than is absolutely necessary. Therefore, it is incumbent upon you to act sooner rather than later."

"And how would you know all of this?"

"Because I am at war with Arthur Leehagen," said Hoyle. "I make it a point to know as much as possible about his actions."

"And assuming any of this is true, why are you so eager to share it with us?" asked Louis.

"There is bad blood between Leehagen and me. It goes back a very long way. We grew up not far from each other, but our lives have taken somewhat divergent paths. Despite that, fate has seen fit to bring us into conflict on occasion. I would like to outlive him, and I would like that process to begin as soon as possible."

"Must be real bad blood," said Louis.

Hoyle nodded at Simeon. A portable DVD player was placed upon the table. Simeon hit the "Play" button. After a second or two, a grainy film commenced.

"This arrived two months ago," said Hoyle. He did not look at the screen. Instead, he watched the reflection of the ripples upon the wall behind them.

The film showed a pretty blond woman, perhaps in her late twenties or early thirties. The woman appeared to be dead, and her face and hair were smeared with mud. She was naked, but most of her body was obscured by the massive heads of the hogs that were feeding on her. Angel looked away. Simeon hit "Pause," freezing the image.

"Who is she?"

"My daughter, Loretta," said Hoyle. "She was seeing Leehagen's surviving son, Michael. She was doing so out of spite. She blamed me for all that was wrong with her life. Sleeping with the son of a man whom I despised seemed, to her, fitting revenge, but she underestimated the Leehagen family's capacity for violence, and vengeance."

"Why would he do that?" asked Louis quietly.

Hoyle looked away, unable to meet Louis's eye. "It doesn't matter," he said, the clear implication being that whatever had provoked such a response had been similarly vile.

"Why didn't you go to the police?"

"Because there was no proof that Leehagen did this. I know the recording came from him—I can feel it—but even if I managed to convince the police that Leehagen was responsible, I guarantee that there would be nothing of my daughter left for them to find, assuming they could even locate the hog farm in question. There is also the matter of my own dealings with Leehagen. Neither of us is entirely innocent, but it has gone too far for us to stop now."

He gestured at Simeon, who picked up the DVD player and removed it to a darkened alcove, then disappeared into one of the back rooms.

"I should add that you were not my first port of call in this matter," said Hoyle. "I first hired a man named Kandic, a Serb, to kill Leehagen's remaining son, and, if possible, Leehagen himself. I was informed that Kandic was the best in the business."

"And how did that work out?" asked Louis.

Simeon returned. In his hands was a glass jar, and in the jar lay a human head. The corneas had been drained of color by the embalming fluid, and the skin had been bleached to the color of bone. The flesh at the base of the neck was ragged and torn.

"Not very well," said Hoyle drily. "This arrived one week ago. Either I was misled when I was told that Kandic was the best, or it's bad news for anyone who might consider following in his footsteps."

"And now you want Leehagen to pay for what happened to your daughter."

"I want this to end. It will do so only when one of us is dead. Naturally, as I said, I would prefer it if Leehagen predeceased me."

Louis stood. The movement caused the two men by the door to reach for their weapons, but Simeon stilled them with a wave of his hand.

"Well," said Louis, "this has all been very interesting. I don't know where you get your information from, but you should talk to your source, because he's feeding you some poor product. I don't know about any Luther Berger, and I've never handled a gun in my life. I'm a businessman, that's all. I'd also be careful about saying some of those things out loud again. It could get you into trouble with the law."

Louis walked to the door, Angel behind him. Nobody tried to stop them, and no one said anything until they had passed into the lobby and were waiting on the elevator.

"Thank you for your time, gentlemen," said Hoyle. "I'm sure I'll be hearing from you soon."

The elevator doors opened, Louis and Angel stepped inside, and rode in silence to the ground before disappearing into the streets.

Louis was silent as they drove from Hoyle's building. Around them, the city moved to its own hidden heartbeat, a rhythm that varied from hour to hour, tied to the movements of the individuals that inhabited it so that sometimes he found it hard to tell if the city dictated the lifestyles of its people, or the people influenced the life of the city.

"I thought the gloves were a nice touch," said Angel. "If his tan had been a little darker, he could have done Al Jolson."

There was no reply. A signal changed ahead of them, but Louis floored the gas and sped through the lights. Louis knew better than to risk attracting the attention of the cops, but now he seemed reluctant to stop for any reason. Angel could also see that he was driving with his mirrors, keeping a close watch on cars behind them, or passing on the left and right.

Angel looked out of his window, watching storefronts flash by.

"What are we going to do?" he asked. His tone, though soft and neutral, indicated to his partner that a response of some kind would be wise.

"I make some calls. I find out how much of what Hoyle told us is true."

"You don't trust him?"

"I don't trust anyone with that much money."

"The head in the jar was pretty convincing. You really never hear of the guy he hired?"

"No, I never did."

"Can't have been too good at his job, if you never heard of him."

"The fact that his head currently resides in a jar would tend to support that," said Louis.

"So?"

"If Hoyle is telling even some of the truth, then we're going to have to move against this Leehagen," said Louis. "We'll need to do it fast. He'll know that we're looking for whoever is trying to light us up. He needs to get to us before we figure it out. So, like I told you, I'll make some calls, and we'll take it from there."

Angel sighed. "And I was starting to enjoy the quiet life."

"Yeah, but you need the noise to appreciate the silence."

Angel looked at him. "What are you: Buddha?"

"I must have read it someplace."

"Yeah, in a fortune cookie."

"You got a soul like a raisin, you know that?"

"Just drive. My raisin-like soul needs peace."

Angel went back to staring out of the window, but his eyes took in nothing of what they saw.

CHAPTER NINE

ANGEL SAT ALONE AT his workbench. Before him were scattered the components of an assortment of keyless entry systems: push-button handsets, hard-wired keypads, wireless remote deadbolts, and even a proximity card reader and a fingerprint reader, the latter alone representing about two thousand dollars worth of butchered electronics. Angel liked to keep up with developments in his area of expertise. Most of the equipment he was examining was capable of being used for both commercial and domestic purposes, but homeowners and contractors had, in his experience, yet to embrace the new technology. Equally, most locksmiths were not adept at dealing with keyless locks. Many were suspicious of the new systems, regarding them as being more open to corruption or breakdown. The reality was that electronic systems had fewer moving parts and, once they were installed, were potentially much harder to access than traditional mechanical systems. Angel could pick a five-pin tumbler lock with a screwdriver and a pin. A biometric reader was another matter entirely.

Usually, he would be fascinated by the equipment he had disassembled, like an anatomist given an opportunity to examine the internal organs of a particularly fine specimen, but on this occasion his mind was elsewhere. The attack on the apartment building had unnerved him, and the evening's developments at Hoyle's apartment had done nothing to set his mind at ease. In the aftermath of the attacks, he and Louis had discussed the possibility of lying low for a time, but had quickly discounted it. To begin with, there was Mrs. Bondarchuk, who refused to move, arguing that it would disturb her Pomeranians. She also pointed out that her grandfather had refused to flee from the Communists in Russia, fighting on with the Whites, and that her father had fought the Nazis at Stalingrad. They had not run, and neither would she. The fact that both her grandfather and father had died in the course of their respective stands against their foes did not affect her argument in any way.

Louis, in turn, did not believe that their enemies would attack them again at the apartment. Between that incident, and the encounter at the auto shop, three men had been lost. At the very least, they would be licking their wounds. A little time had been bought, and it could best be used at their home, not at some makeshift safe house, or in a vulnerable hotel. Angel had acquiesced, but there was something in the way Louis spoke that had disturbed him.

He wants them to come, he thought. *He wants this to continue. He* likes *it.*

Angel had never told a soul that Louis sometimes frightened him. He had not even told Louis, although he wondered if Louis might not have guessed that fact for himself. It was not that he feared Louis might turn on him. While his partner could charitably be described as "acid-tongued" on occasion, none of the violence of which he was capable had ever been directed at Angel. No, what frightened Angel was Louis's *need* for that violence. There was a hunger inside him that could only be fed by it, and Angel did not fully understand the source of that hunger. Oh, he knew a great deal about Louis's past. Not everything, though: there were parts of it that remained hidden, even from him, but then it was also true that Angel had not told Louis everything about himself either. After all, no relationship could function or survive under the burden of total honesty.

But the details of Louis's past were not enough to explain the man that he had become, not for Angel. When faced with a threat to his own safety and that of the women with whom he lived, the young Louis had acted immediately to remove that threat. He had set out, quite cold-bloodedly, to kill the man named Deber whom he suspected of murdering his mother, and who had now returned to the house that she had occupied with her own mother, her sisters, and her young son, to replace her with another. Louis had smelt his mother's blood upon him, and Deber in turn, his senses attuned to potential threats, had seen the desire for vengeance bubbling beneath the placid surface of the boy. Their small world could not contain both of them, and Deber had felt certain that, when the time came for the boy to act, he would do so in the way of a hotheaded young man. It would be direct: a blade, or a cheap gun acquired for the purpose. Deber would see him coming. The boy would want to look into Deber's eyes as he died, for that was the kind of revenge that a child sought. There could be no gratification at a distance, Deber believed.

But the boy was not like that. From his earliest years, there was something inside him that could not be touched, an old soul living in a young body. Deber was cunning and cruel, but the boy was clever and dispassionate. Deber did not die from a bullet wound, or a knife to the chest or belly. He did not see death coming for him, for death arrived camouflaged. It came in the guise of a cheap metal whistle, an item of which Deber was inordinately fond. He used it to summon the boy for meals, to get the attention of his woman, to organize the gangs of men whose work he oversaw. When he raised it to his mouth on that fateful morning, he might just have had enough time to wonder why it did not emit its usual shrill call before the small ball of homemade explosive blew his face and part of his skull away. The boy's last memory of Deber was of a small, dapper man leaving the house to drive to work, the whistle hanging on a chain around his neck. He did not need to see the whistle being raised, to witness the burst of red and black that came with the explosion, to stare down upon the ruined human being dying in a pauper's bed, in order to achieve satisfaction.

Deber's murder had come naturally to Louis, so it would not be true to say that his first fatal act of violence had set him on the path to becoming what he now was. He had always had that capacity within him, and the catalyst for its eruption into the world had been largely unimportant. But once it was unleashed, it flowed through his veins as naturally as blood.

Angel, too, had killed, but the reasons behind the killings had been less complicated than those that motivated Louis. Angel had killed, variously, because he had to; because had he not done so he himself would have died; and because, most of all, it had seemed like the thing to do at the time. He was not haunted or tormented by those whom he had killed. He wondered, on occasion, if that meant there was something wrong with him. He suspected that it did. But Angel had no *urge* to kill. He did not seek out violent men in order to confront them, or to test himself against them. Had someone informed him that, from this day forth, he would never have to hold a gun again and would live out his days doing nothing more challenging than breaking locks and eating fried food, he would have been content to do so, as long as Louis was by his side. But therein lay the problem: a life like that was beyond Louis, and to embrace such an existence would have meant sacrificing his partner. Angel's violence was born out of circumstance; Louis's was elemental.

That was, in part, why they had remained close to Charlie Parker over the years. Angel owed a debt to the private detective, who had done his best, as a cop, to protect Angel from those who would have harmed him while he was in prison. Angel had never fully understood why Parker had chosen to do that. Angel had helped him with information from time to time, as long as it didn't involve naming too many names, and he was sure, although they had never spoken of it, that Parker knew something of Angel's past, of the abuse that he had endured as a child. But there were a lot of criminals out there who could point to troubled childhoods, some of them even worse than Angel's; pity or empathy were not enough to explain why Parker had chosen to help and, ultimately, befriend him. It was almost, thought Angel, as though Parker had known what was to come. No, not *known.* That wasn't it. There were things about Parker that were unusual, even downright spooky, but he wasn't a seer. Perhaps it was just something as simple as meeting another human being and understanding, immediately and deeply, that this was an individual who belonged in one's life, for reasons readily apparent or yet to be revealed.

Louis had found difficulty in understanding that, at least at the start. Louis did not want cops or ex-cops in his life. Yet he knew what Parker had done for Angel, knew that Angel would not be alive were it not for the strange, troubled private detective who seemed about to break under the weight of his grief and loss, yet somehow refused to do so. In time, Louis had seen something of himself in the other man. They began by respecting each other, and that had developed into a kind of friendship, albeit one that had been tested on more than one occasion.

But what Louis and Parker had in common more than anything else, Angel believed, was a kind of darkness. A version of Louis's fire burned in Parker; a stranger yet more refined form of Louis's hunger gnawed at him. In a way, they used each other, but each did so with the knowledge, and consent, of his peer.

Things had changed, though, in recent months. Parker was no longer a licensed PI. He felt that he was being watched by those who had taken his license away, that a wrong move could put him in jail, or draw attention to his friends, to Louis and Angel. Angel wasn't certain how they had managed to avoid that attention until now. They had been careful and professional, and luck had played a part at times, but those factors in themselves should not have been enough, could not have been enough. It was an enigma.

But with Parker out of commission, Louis had been denied one of the outlets for his urges. He had begun to speak of taking on jobs again. The move against the Russians had been inspired less by the immediate threat to Parker than by Louis's desire to flex his muscles. Now it seemed that he and Angel were under attack from forces they had not yet fully identified. And what most disturbed Angel was the suspicion that Louis was secretly pleased at this development.

Then there was Gabriel, who bore some responsibility for their current situation, since, if what Hoyle had told them was true, it was he who had dispatched Louis to kill Leehagen's son to begin with. Angel had never met the old man, but he knew all about him. The relationship that existed between Gabriel and Louis was ineffably complex. Louis seemed to feel that he owed some debt to Gabriel, even though Angel believed that Gabriel had manipulated and, possibly, corrupted Louis for his own ends. Now Gabriel was, however peripherally, back in Louis's life, like a hibernating spider spurred into motion by the warmth of the sun and the vibrations of insects close to its dusty web. It suggested to Angel that aspects of Louis's past, his old life, were now leaching into the present, and poisoning it as they came.

If Louis sometimes frightened Angel, then Angel remained frustratingly unknowable to his partner. Despite all that had happened to him, there was a gentleness at the heart of Angel that might almost have been construed as a weakness. Angel felt things: compassion, empathy, sorrow. He felt them for those who were most like him, troubled children in particular, for Louis knew that every adult who was abused as a child holds that child forever in his heart. That did not make his emotions any less admirable, and Louis recognized that he himself had been colored and changed by the years he had spent in the company of this odd, disheveled man. He had been humanized by him, yet what was a virtue in Angel had become a chink in Louis's armor. But then the moment he began to have feelings for Angel he had sacrificed a crucial element of his defenses. His forces, in a sense, had been divided. Where once he had only to worry about himself—and that concern was tied up with the nature of his profession—he now had to contend with his fears for another. When Angel had almost been taken from him, held to ransom and mutilated by a family that had no intention of ever releasing him alive, Louis had seen, for an instant, what he would become without his partner: a creature of pure rage who would be consumed by his own fire.

What he did not tell Angel was that part of him devoutly wished for such a consummation.

Parker, too, had altered him, for in the detective Louis saw elements of both Angel and himself combined: he had Angel's compassion, his desire not to let the weak be ground down by the strong and the ruthless, but also something of Louis's willingness, even need, to strike out, to judge and to inflict punishment. There was a delicate balance between Parker and Louis, the latter knew: Parker held the worst of Louis back, but Louis allowed the worst of Parker to find an outlet. And Angel? Well, Angel was the pivot around whom the other two moved, a confidant of both, containing within himself echoes of Louis and Parker. Yet wasn't that true of all of them? It was what bound them together, that and an emerging sense that Parker was moving toward a confrontation of which they, too, were destined to be a part.

He had never imagined that he would end up tied to such a man as Angel. In fact, for many years he had chosen not to acknowledge his sexuality to himself. It was a shameful thing when he was young, and he had suppressed it so well that any expression of it had proved difficult for him as he grew older.

And then this strange person had tried to burgle his apartment. He hadn't even done it particularly well, the proof being that he had ended up under Louis's gun while attempting to get his television out of a window. Who, Louis often wondered, enters an apartment that is clearly tastefully decorated, with some small, easily transportable *objets d'art*, and then tries to steal a heavy TV set? It was no wonder that Angel had ended up in jail. As a thief, he was a spectacular failure, but as a lockpicker, well, that was where his true genius lay. In that, he was gifted. It was, Louis suspected, God's little joke on Angel: he would give him the skills required to gain access to any locked room, but would then deprive him of the guile required to make practical use of those skills, short, of course, of actually becoming a locksmith and earning an honest day's work for an honest day's pay, a concept that Angel found repugnant.

Almost as repugnant to Louis was his partner's distinctive fashion sense. At first, Louis thought it was an affectation; that, or pure cheapness. Angel would scour the bargain racks at Filene's, TJ Maxx, Marshalls, anywhere that primary colors were gathered together in unlikely combinations. He didn't care much for outlet malls, unless their stores, too, had a rail that had been discounted so much that the stores were pretty much paying customers to take stuff away. No, outlet malls were too easy. Angel liked the hunt, the thrill of the chase, that moment of pleasure that came from unexpectedly finding a lime-green Armani shirt reduced to one tenth of its original price, and a pair of designer jeans to match, assuming by "matching" one meant "clashing unbearably." The thing about it was, Angel would be immensely, genuinely proud of his purchases, and it had taken years for Louis to realize that, every time he commented unfavorably on his partner's choice of attire, something inside Angel cringed, like a child that has tried to please a parent by cooking a meal, only to get all of the ingredients wrong and find himself chastised instead of praised for his efforts. It didn't matter that, when it came to clothing, Angel seemed to be colorblind. This was *designer* clothing. It had cost him next to nothing, but it was good quality and had a label that people would know. As a child, Angel had probably dreamed of wearing nice clothes, of owning expensive things, but as an adult he could not justify to himself the expense of such items. They were meant for others, not for him. He did not consider himself worthy of them. But he could cheat by buying them for next to nothing, since no justification would be required if they were cheap.

Louis had once bought Angel a beautiful Brioni jacket as a gift, and the garment had languished in a closet for years. When Louis had eventually confronted Angel about it, Angel had explained that it was too expensive to wear, and he wasn't the kind of guy who wore expensive clothes. Louis hadn't understood the response then, and he wasn't sure that he understood it a whole lot better now, but he had since learned to bite his tongue when Angel presented his latest purchases for approval, unless faced with provocation beyond the tolerance of mortal man to endure. For his part, Angel had started to learn that a bargain wasn't a bargain if no one could look at it without shades or antinausea medication. An accommodation of sorts had therefore been reached.

Now, while Angel sat in his workroom and stared vacantly at the electronic components arrayed before him, Louis was in an anonymous office ten blocks away, a computer screen glowing before him, wondering if it might not be better to deal with Leehagen himself, to leave Angel behind. The thought lasted about as long as a bug in an oven. Angel would not stay. It was not in him to do so. Yet, unlike Angel, this was Louis's purpose: to hunt, to provide the ultimate solution to any problem. He enjoyed it. Ever since the emergence of the Leehagen threat, he had felt more alive than he had at any other point in the last year. Old muscles were returning to life, old instincts coming to the fore. He, and the things and people that mattered to him, were in danger, but he felt himself capable of meeting and neutralizing the threat. Angel would stand alongside him, but he would not share Louis's pleasure in what was to come, and Louis would try to hide his own as best he could. It was not a pleasure in killing, he told himself, but the pleasure that a craftsman takes in exercising his skills. Without that opportunity, well, he was just a man, and Louis did not care for being "just" anything.

His fingers danced on the keyboard as he began tracking Arthur Leehagen.

Gabriel sat in Wooster's observation room. The boy was tall, although a little too slim, but that would change. He was handsome now, and would be handsome yet. There was a stillness to him that boded well. Despite his hours of interrogation, he held his head high. His eyes were bright and watchful. He did not blink often.

After a couple of minutes had passed, the boy's posture changed slightly. He tensed, and his head tilted, like an animal that has sensed the approach of another but has not yet decided if it represents a threat. He knew that he was being watched and that it was no longer Wooster who was observing him.

Gabriel leaned forward in his seat and touched the glass, running his fingers over the boy's head, his cheekbones, his chin, like a breeder checking the quality of a thoroughbred horse. Yes, he thought, you have the potential to become what I need.

There is a Reaper in you.

Gabriel knew that the vast majority of men were not born killers. True, there were many who believed themselves to be capable of killing, and it was possible to condition men to become killers, but few were born with that innate ability to take the life of another. In fact, throughout history it had been known that men in combat demonstrated a marked reluctance to kill, and would not do so even to save their own lives, or the lives of their comrades. During World War II, it was estimated that as few as 15 percent of all American riflemen in combat ac-

tually fired their weapons at the enemy. Some would fire wide or high, if they fired at all. Others would take on ancillary tasks such as carrying messages, transporting ammunition, even rescuing under fire fellow soldiers who had been injured, sometimes at far greater risk to themselves than might have been the case had they stayed in position and used their weapons. In other words, this was not a matter of cowardice, but a consequence of an innate resistance among humans to the killing of their own species.

All of that would change, of course, with improvements in the conditioning of soldiers to kill. Yet conditioning was one thing, while finding a man for whom that conditioning was not required was quite another. At times of fear or anger, human beings stop thinking with their forebrain, which is, in effect, the first, intellectual filter against killing, and start thinking with their midbrain, their animal side, which acts as a second filter. While there were those who suggested that, at this stage, the "fight or flight" mechanism came into play, the range of responses was actually more complex than that. In fact, to fight or to flee was the final choice, once posturing or submission had been eliminated.

Overcoming that second filter was one of the aims of conditioning, but there were those in whom that midbrain filter was absent. They were sociopaths, and in a sense, the purpose of conditioning was to create a pseudosociopath, one who could be controlled, one who would obey orders to fight and kill. A sociopath obeyed no orders, and therefore could not be controlled. A properly trained and conditioned soldier was a weapon in himself. In that process, of course, something good was lost, perhaps even the best part of the human being involved: it was the understanding that we do not exist merely as independent entities, but are part of a collective whole and that each death lessens that whole and, by extension, ourselves. Military training required that understanding to be nullified, that realization to be cauterized. The problem was that, like the early surgical procedures of ancients, this process of cauterization was based upon an inadequate understanding of the workings of human beings.

Fears of death or injury were not the main causes of mental breakdowns in combat; in fact, they were found to be among the least important factors. Nor was exhaustion, although it could be a contributor. Rather, it was the burden of killing, and of killing up close and knowing that it was your bullet or your bayonet that had brought a life to an end. Sailors did not suffer psychiatric casualties to any similar degree. Neither did bomber pilots dropping their loads high above cities that might have been, from their distant vantage point, entirely empty of citizens. The difference was one of proximity, of, for want of a better term, intimacy. This was death heard and smelled and tasted and felt. This was to face the aggression and hostility of another directed entirely at oneself, and to be forced to acknowledge one's own aggression and hatred in turn. It was to recognize that one had become, potentially, both victim and executioner. This was a denial of one's own humanity, and the humanity of others.

The boy named Louis was unusual. Here was an individual who had responded to a hostile stimulus in a forebrained way, approaching the threat as a problem to be solved. It wasn't simply that the second, midbrain filter had been overcome; instead, Gabriel wondered if the issue had ever even reached that stage. This was a cold-blooded, premeditated killing. It indicated significant potential. The difficulty, from Gabriel's point of view, lay in the physical distance from the killing itself that the boy had maintained. Gabriel understood the relationship between physical proximity and the trauma of killing. It was harder to kill someone up close with a knife than it was to shoot him at long range with a sniper's rifle. Similarly, the sense of elation that frequently came with a kill was increasingly short-lived the closer the killer was to the victim, because in that situation guilt was as close as the body. Gabriel had even known soldiers to comfort the man whose life they had taken as he lay dying, whispering apologies for what had been done.

In real terms, the apparent ease with which the boy had killed suggested a possible dissociation, a reluctance or inability to recognize the consequences of his actions; that, or an intellectual understanding that he had murdered someone combined with an emotional denial of the act, and with that any real responsibility for it. He would have to be tested fur-

ther so that his true nature might be revealed. The boy did not appear to be showing signs of undue stress. He had, it seemed, handled himself calmly when faced with sometimes violent interrogation. He had not broken. He was not seeking an opportunity to confess, to expiate his guilt. True, stress might reveal itself later, but for the moment he appeared relatively untroubled by what he had done. It was only a small percentage of men, that elusive 2 percent, who, under the right circumstances, could kill without remorse. Those circumstances did not necessarily involve personal risk, or even a risk to the lives of others. It was, at one level, a matter of conditioning and situation. At some point, the boy would have to be placed in the right environment in order to see how he might respond. If he did not react correctly, that would be the end of the matter. It might also, Gabriel knew, mean the boy's death.

There was also the matter of how he would respond to authority. It was one thing to kill for oneself, and quite another to kill because someone told you to do so. Soldiers were more likely to fire their weapons when their leaders were present, and were more effective when they were bound to that leader by their respect for him. Gabriel was in a different position: his charges had to be willing to do what he told them even while he himself was far away. He was like a general, but without subordinates in the field who could ensure that his orders were carried out to the letter. In turn, leaders in combat had a degree of legitimacy that came from their status in the hierarchy of their nations, but Gabriel's position was far more ambiguous.

For all of these reasons, Gabriel picked those whom he used with great care. True sociopaths were of no use to him, because they did not respect authority. The younger his charges were, the better, because the young were more open to manipulation. He tried to look for weaknesses to exploit, ways to fill the gaps in their lives. The boy Louis lacked a father figure, but he had not been so desperate to find one that he was prepared to acquiesce to Deber's authority, or to flee from him in order to seek another when it became apparent that Deber considered him a threat. Gabriel would have to tread lightly. Louis's trust would be hard-earned.

But from what Gabriel had learned, Louis was also a natural loner. He had no close friends, and he lived as the only male in a household of women. He was not the kind who would form relationships within larger groups, which meant that, if his natural instincts were channeled, he would not seek absolution for his actions from others. Absolution was one thing Gabriel could not offer, and that, in turn, was why he preferred those who were not unduly troubled by guilt. Neither did he want those who might identify excessively with their victims. To do what he required of them necessitated emotional distance, and on occasion Gabriel was prepared to alter his approach in order to exploit social, moral, or cultural differences between his Reapers and their victims. Nevertheless, he did not seek to eradicate empathy entirely, for the absence of empathy was another indicator of sociopathy. Some empathy was a necessary restraint upon hostile or sadistic behavior. A delicate balance had to be maintained. It was the difference between being prepared to hurt someone when required, and hurting someone when one desired.

According to what Gabriel had learned before his arrival at the little police department, the boy was a fighter, one who would stand his ground when provoked. That was good. It indicated an important predisposition to aggression, even a longing for an opportunity to display it. Louis's experiences with Deber had been the trigger for what followed but, to complete the analogy, the weapon had already been loaded long before then. There were also rumors that the boy was a homosexual; if not a practicing one, for he was still very young, then he had at least exhibited sufficient tendencies to allow rumors about his sexuality to circulate locally. Gabriel, as in so many other areas, was enlightened about matters of individual sexuality. He distinguished between those aspects that were aberrant—a predilection toward violence, for example, or the impulse to abuse children—and those that were not. Aberrant sexual behavior indicated a degree of unreliability that tended to exhibit itself in other areas as well, and rendered its practitioners unsuitable for Gabriel's purposes. Gabriel was not a homosexual, but he understood the nature of sexual desire, just as he understood the nature of aggression and hostility, for the two were not as distant as some liked to believe. While there were some aspects of human behavior that could be controlled and altered, there were some that could not, and one's sexual orientation was among them. Louis's sexuality interested Gabriel only in the sense that it might make him vulnerable or conflicted. Such weaknesses could be exploited.

And so Gabriel watched Louis through the glass, and the boy stared back. Five minutes passed in this way, and at the end Gabriel nodded once to himself in apparent satisfaction, then stood and left the room to face the fifteen-year-old killer.

Like any good leader, Gabriel loved his people, in his fashion, even though he was prepared, at all times, to sacrifice them if the need arose. Over the years that followed, Louis fulfilled, and even exceeded, Gabriel's expectations, except in one regard: he refused to kill women on Gabriel's orders. It was, Gabriel supposed, a legacy of his upbringing, and Gabriel made allowances for it, for he did indeed love Louis. He became like a son to him and Gabriel, in turn, became the father of the man.

Gabriel stepped into the interrogation room and took a seat across the table from Louis. The room smelled of perspiration and other less pleasant things, but Gabriel did not give any indication that he noticed. The boy's face was shiny with sweat.

Gabriel unplugged the tape recorder from the wall, then sat across from Louis and placed his hands upon the table. "My name is Gabriel," he said. "And you, I believe, are Louis."

The boy did not answer, but simply regarded the older man silently, waiting to see what might be revealed.

"You're free to go, by the way," said Gabriel. "You will not be charged with the commission of any crime."

This time, the boy reacted. His mouth opened slightly, and his eyebrows lifted an inch. He looked at the door.

"Yes, you can walk out of here right now, if you choose," Gabriel continued. "Nobody will try to stop you. Your grandmother is waiting outside for you. She will take you back to your little cabin. You can sleep in your own bed, be among familiar things. All will be as it once was."

He smiled. The boy had not moved.

"Or don't you believe that?"

"What do you want?" said Louis.

"Want? I want to help you. I think you are a very unusual young man. I might even go so far as to say that you're gifted, although your gift is one that might not be appreciated in circles such as these."

He waved his right hand gently, taking in the interrogation room, the station house, Wooster, the law . . .

"I can help you to find your place in the world. In return, your skills can be put to better use than they would be here. You see, if you stay in this town you'll overstep the mark. You'll be challenged, threatened.

That threat may come from the police, or from others. You'll respond to it, but you're known now. You won't get away a second time with what you did, and you'll die for it."

"I don't know what you're talking about."

Gabriel wagged a finger, but it was not a disapproving gesture.

"Very good, very good," he said. He chuckled, then allowed sound to drift into silence before he spoke again.

"Let me tell you what will happen next. Deber had friends, or perhaps 'acquaintances' would be a better word for them. They are men like him, and worse. They cannot allow his death to go unremarked.. It would damage their own reputations, and suggest a degree of weakness that might leave them open to attack by others. Already, they will know that you have been questioned about what happened to him, and they will not be as skeptical as the state police. If you return to your home, they will find you and they will kill you. Perhaps, along the way, they will hurt the women who share that home with you. Even if you run, they will come after you."

"Why should you care?"

"Care? I don't care. I can walk away from here, and leave you and your family to your fate, and it will cause me not a moment's regret. Or you can hear my offer, and perhaps something mutually beneficial may result. Your problem is that you do not know me, and therefore cannot trust me. I fully under-

stand your predicament. I realize that you will need time to consider what I am suggesting—"

"I don't know what you're suggesting," said Louis. "You haven't said."

He is almost droll, thought Gabriel. He is old beyond his years.

"I offer discipline, training. I offer a way for you to channel your anger, to use your talents."

"Protection?"

"I can help you to protect yourself."

"And my family?"

"They're at risk only as long as you remain here, and only if they know where you are."

"So I can go with you, or I can walk out of here?"

"That's right."

Louis pursed his lips in thought.

"Thank you for your time, sir," he said, after some moments had passed. "I'm going to leave now."

Gabriel nodded. He reached into his jacket pocket and produced an envelope. He handed it to the boy. After a moment's hesitation, Louis took it and opened it. He tried to hide his reaction to what was inside, but the widening of his eyes betrayed him.

"There's a thousand dollars in that envelope," said Gabriel. "There's also a card with a telephone number on it. Through that number I can be reached at any time, day or night. You think about my offer, but remember what I said: you can't go home again. You need to get far away from here—far, far away—

and then you need to figure out what you're going to do when those men come calling on you. Because they will."

Louis closed the envelope and left the room. Gabriel did not follow him. He did not have to. He knew the boy would leave this town. If he did not, then Gabriel had misjudged him and he was of no use to him anyway. The money did not matter. Gabriel had faith in his own judgment. The money would come back to him many times over.

After he was released, Louis walked back with his grandmother to the cabin in the woods. They did not speak, even though it was a two-mile walk. When they reached home, Louis packed a bag with his clothes and some mementos of his mother—photos, one or two items of jewelry that had been passed on to him—then took two hundred dollars from the envelope and secreted the cash in various pockets, in a slash in the waistband of his trousers, and in one of his shoes. The remainder he divided into two piles, slipping the smaller into the right front pocket of his jeans and the rest back into the envelope. Then he kissed good-bye to the women who had raised him, handed the envelope and the five hundred dollars it contained to his grandmother, and got a ride on Mr. Otis's truck to the bus station. He asked to make only one stop along the way. Mr. Otis was reluctant to oblige him, but he saw what Wooster had seen in the boy, and what Gabriel had seen, too, and he understood that he was not to be crossed, not in this thing or in any other. So Mr. Otis pulled up just past Little Tom's bar, his truck hidden by the bushes that lined the road and watched the boy walk into the dirt lot, then disappear from view.

Mr. Otis began to sweat.

Little Tom looked up from the newspaper that lay open on the bar. There were no customers to distract him, not yet, and the radio was tuned to a football game. He liked these quiet moments. For the rest of the night he would serve drinks and make small talk with his customers. He would discuss sports, the weather, men's relationships with their womenfolk (for women did not trouble Little Tom's bar, any more than the coloreds did, and thus the bar was a refuge for a certain type of man). Little Tom understood the role his bar performed: no decisions of great import were made here, and no conversations of any consequence took place. There was no trouble, for Little Tom would not tolerate it, and no drunkenness, for Little Tom did not approve of that either. When a man had consumed what Little Tom adjudged to be "enough," he would be sent on his way with some words of advice about driving carefully and not getting into any arguments once he was home. The police were rarely called to Little Tom's premises. He was in good standing with the town fathers.

None of this distracted from the fact that, like many men who practiced a public and superficial version of what they considered to be a reasonable way of life, Little Tom was an animal, a creature of violent and abusive appetites, sexually incontinent and filled with loathing for all those who were different from himself: women, especially those who would not touch him unless money was involved; Jews, although he did not know any; churchgoers of any liberal stripe or persuasion; Polish, Irish, Germans, and any others who spoke American with an accent or who had names that Little Tom could not pronounce with ease; and all coloreds, without exception.

Now, a young black man was standing on the threshold of Little Tom's bar, watching him as he read his newspaper. Little Tom didn't know how long the colored had been standing there, but however long it had been, it was too long.

"Be on your way, boy," said Little Tom. "This ain't a place for you."

The boy did not move. Little Tom shifted position and began to walk toward the raised hatch in the bar. Along the way, he picked up the bat that lay beneath the bar. There was a shotgun there, too, but Little Tom figured that the sight of the bat would be enough.

"You hear what I said? Be about your business."

The boy spoke. "I know what you did," he said.

Little Tom stopped. The boy's composure unnerved him. His tone was even, and he had not blinked since Little Tom had first noticed him, not once. His gaze seemed to penetrate Little Tom's skull and crawl like a spider over the surface of his brain.

"The hell are you talking about?"

"I know what you did to Errol Rich."

Little Tom grinned. The grin grew slowly, spreading like oil. So that was what this was about: a colored, a nigger, letting his anger get the better of his senses. Well, Little Tom knew all about dealing with coloreds who couldn't keep a civil tongue in their mouths in front of a white man.

"He got what was coming to him," said Little Tom. "You're about to get what's coming to you, too."

He moved swiftly, swinging the bat as he came, striking up instead of down, aiming for the boy's ribs, but the boy stepped nimbly forward, into the stroke instead of away from it, so that the bat struck the wood of the door frame at the same time as fingers gripped Little Tom's throat and spun him against the wall. The impact of the bat on the wood sent a painful vibration up Little Tom's arm, so that it was still weak when the edge of the boy's left hand hit it, causing the bat to fall to the floor.

Little Tom was too surprised to react. No colored had ever touched him before, not even a black woman, for Little Tom did not consort with other races, either forcibly or with their consent. He smelled the boy's breath as he leaned closer. The fingers tightened on his throat, and then he heard the back door of the bar open and a man shouted something. The grip upon him eased a little, and then he was flung to one side, tripping over a stool and landing heavily.

"Hey," said the voice, and Little Tom recognized Willard Hoag's gravelly tones. "The fuck do you think you're doing, boy?"

The boy picked up the bat and turned to face the new threat. Hoag, unarmed, stopped. The boy looked at Little Tom.

"Another time," he said.

He backed out of the bar, taking the bat with him. Seconds after he left, the bat came crashing through Little Tom's window, showering the floor with glass. Little Tom heard a truck pull away, but when he got to the road it was no longer in sight, and he never did find out who had driven the colored to his place. It troubled him for a long time, even after he discovered the boy's identity and found a way to pass it on to those who had their own reasons for dealing with him. As he grew older, the memory of the offense grew dim. Lots of memories faded, for by the time that he died, Little Tom was succumbing to dementia, even if he managed to hide its effects from those who frequented his increasingly ailing little bar, as the business went into decline along with its owner. Thus it was that when the boy eventually returned as a man, and made Little Tom pay the price for what he had done to Errol Rich, Little Tom was unable to connect him to the only colored who had ever laid a hand upon him.

And as for why Louis took so long to avenge Errol Rich's death, well, as he liked to tell Angel, Little Tom was worth killing, but he wasn't worth traveling very far to kill, so Louis just waited until he happened to be in the neighborhood. It was, he said, a matter of convenience.

That came later, though. For now, he headed west, and he did not stop until he could see and smell the ocean. He found a place in which to live and work, and there he waited for the men to come.

CHAPTER TEN

LOUIS WAS EARLY FOR the meeting with Gabriel at Nate's. He didn't like being early for encounters of this kind. He preferred to keep people waiting for him, aware always of the potential psychological advantages to be gained in even the most apparently innocuous of encounters. It might have seemed that such precautions would be unnecessary in any meeting between Gabriel and himself, as they had known each other for many years, but both men were acutely aware of how difficult their relationship was. They were not equals, and although Gabriel had been more of a father figure to Louis than any other man in his life, taking the boy under his wing when he was still a teenager, teaching him how to survive in the world by honing his own natural skills, both men understood why he had done so. If one were to regard Louis's instincts as a form of corruption, his willingness to use violence, even to the point of murder, as moral weakness rather than strength of character, then Gabriel had exploited that corruption, deepening and enhancing it in order to turn Louis into a weapon that could be used effectively against others. Louis was not so naive as to believe that, had he not met Gabriel, he might otherwise have been saved from himself. He knew that, had Gabriel not entered his life, he would probably be dead by now, but he had paid a price for the salvation of sorts offered by the older man. When Louis, the last of the Reapers, had walked away from Gabriel, he had done so with no regrets and without turning his back, and for many years after he had been wary, conscious that there were those who might prefer it if he were silenced forever, and that Gabriel might well be among them.

The old man had been part of Louis's life for longer than almost anyone else he had known, the few surviving female members of his own family apart, and he kept even them at a distance, salving his conscience by ensuring that they never wanted for money, even as he acknowledged to himself that they had little need of what he sent them and that his gifts were more for his own peace of mind than theirs. But Gabriel had been there from the crucial later years of his adolescence, then all through his adulthood until Louis had severed their ties. Now they were together again, one in his middle age, the other in his declining years. They had seen each other grow older, and it was strange to think that, when they had first met, Gabriel had been younger than Louis himself was now.

Louis glanced at his watch. He was particularly unhappy about being early on this occasion, for he was in no mood to wait. He felt the tension building within himself, but he did not try to dissipate it. He recognized it as anticipation. Louis knew that there was conflict and violence on its way, and his body and mind were preparing for it. The tension was part of that, and it was good. The months of normality, of indolence, of ordinary life, had come to an end. Even when he and Angel had traveled to Maine earlier that year to help Parker deal with the revenger, Merrick, there had been little call for his specialized services, and he had returned to New York frustrated and disappointed. They had been glorified bodyguards, nothing more. Now he and Angel were under threat, and he was preparing to respond. What troubled him was that he did not yet have a clear picture of what form that threat had taken. That was why he was here, waiting in the old bar not far from Willie Brew's auto shop. Gabriel had promised him clarification and confirmation of the information offered by Hoyle, and Gabriel, whatever his faults, was not one to renege on his promises.

The delivery door at the back of the bar opened with a soft creak, and Gabriel entered. The door had been kept unlocked for him at

Louis's request, Nate leaving them to their own devices in the otherwise empty bar. Nate knew better than to bother them. The bar was another of Louis's silent investments, a place in which to meet and in which to store some essentials should he ever need to go to ground: cash, a small quantity of diamonds and Krugerrands, a gun and ammunition. They were kept in a locked box in a safe behind shelves in Nate's office, and only Louis held the combination. He had nests like this in five different locations throughout New York and New England, two of which, this one included, were unknown even to Angel.

Gabriel took a seat and signaled to Nate for a coffee. Nothing was said until the cup arrived and they were alone again. Gabriel sipped at his coffee, his little finger held carefully away from the handle. The old man, thought Louis, had always observed the niceties of civilized behavior, even when he was arranging for men and women to be wiped from the face of the earth.

"Tell me," said Louis.

Gabriel shifted uneasily.

"Ballantine disappeared on the twelfth. He was under investigation by the SEC. His assets were about to be frozen. Someone, it seems, sent the authorities details of insider trading by companies of which Ballantine was a director. He was facing a series of indictments. It was assumed that he was in hiding, or had fled the jurisdiction."

"Is there any evidence to suggest otherwise?"

"He has a wife and three children. They have been interviewed, and they seemed genuinely at a loss to explain his absence. He hasn't been in contact with them. His passport was found in his desk at home. There was a floor safe in one of his closets. His wife didn't have the combination, or said she didn't. A court order was obtained to open it. There was nearly one hundred thousand dollars in cash inside, along with almost twice that amount in negotiable bonds."

"Not the kind of baubles a man on the run would leave behind."

"Hardly. Especially not so conscientious a family man as Mr. Ballantine."

Sarcasm dripped like snake venom from Gabriel's words.

"Too clean to be clean?"

"He owned a house in the Adirondacks through one of his companies. A place in which to entertain clients, one assumes. And to be entertained in turn."

"Did you find the entertainer?"

"A prostitute. Quite upmarket. She had been advised to keep quiet, even though she knew little enough. Men came. They took Ballantine. They left her."

"Did you know that he had disappeared before I asked you to look into this?"

Gabriel met Louis's gaze, but it was a calculated effort.

"I don't keep up with the activities of all my former clients."

"That's a lie."

Gabriel shrugged. "Not entirely. Some remain on the radar for good reasons, but others I let slide. Ballantine I did not concern myself with. He was an intermediary, nothing more. He used me. On occasion I used him, too, but so did many others. You, of all people, should know how these things work."

"That's right. It's why I'm trying to figure out how much you've been hiding from me."

For the first time since he had arrived, Gabriel smiled. "We all need secrets. Even you."

"Was Kandic one of yours?"

"No. After you left me, my interest in such matters ceased. There is a new breed of independent contractor out there now, some of them veterans of the conflicts in Chechnya and Bosnia. They're war criminals. Half of them are on the run from the UN, the other half from their own people. Kandic was running from both. He was a former member of the Scorpions, a Serbian police unit linked to atrocities in the Balkans, but it seems that he had a history to hide long before he began killing old men in Kosovo. When the tide began to turn, he sold out his own comrades to the Muslims and made his way over here. I haven't yet managed to trace the means by which he was hired by Hoyle."

"Was he any good?"

"I'm sure that he came highly recommended."

"Yeah, I'd like to see the reference. It probably didn't mention that he was prone to decapitation. Is that all you have for me?"

"Nearly." Hoyle had confirmed what Milton had told Gabriel: there was a link to Leehagen. Now Gabriel explained what he knew of the man named Kyle Benton, and his connection to both Leehagen and one of the men who had died outside Louis's building, although he did not tell Louis how long he had known about Benton.

"I'm looking into the rest," he concluded. "These things take time."

"How long?"

"A few days. No more than that. Did you believe all that Hoyle told you?"

"I saw a head in a jar, and a girl being eaten by hogs. They both looked real enough. Did you know that Luther Berger was really Jon Leehagen?"

"Yes."

"And you didn't tell me."

"Would it have made any difference?"

"Not then," Louis conceded. "Did you know who his father was?"

"I was aware of him. He was a creature of contradictions. A hoodlum from the sticks, and an astute businessman. An ignorant man, but with low cunning. A cattle breeder and a pimp, but with mines to his name. An abuser and trafficker of women, who loved his sons. Not a threat, not in the circles in which you and I moved. Now he has cancer of the lungs, liver, and pancreas. He cannot breathe unaided. He is virtually housebound, apart from occasional excursions around his property in his wheelchair to feel fresh air upon his face. Therein lies the problem. I suspect that Hoyle may be right: if Leehagen is behind this, then he will keep coming at you, because he has nothing to lose. He will want you to die before he does."

"And the enmity with Hoyle?"

"True, from what I can find out. They have long been rivals in business affairs, and were once rivals in love. She chose Leehagen, and gave him his two sons. She died of cancer, perhaps the same form of the disease that is now killing Leehagen himself. Their mutual antagonism is well known, although its precise roots appear to be lost in the past."

"Did his son deserve to die?"

"You know," said Gabriel, "I think I preferred you when you weren't so scrupulous."

"That's not answering the question."

Gabriel raised his hands in a gesture of resignation. "What does 'deserving' mean? The son was not so different from the father. His sins were fewer, but that was a consequence of age, not effort. A believer in God would say that one sin was enough to damn him. If that is true, then he was damned a hundred times over."

For a moment, Louis's features, usually so impassive, altered. He looked weary. Gabriel saw the change, but did not comment upon it. Nevertheless, in that instant Gabriel's opinion of his protégé altered. He had, he supposed, entertained hopes that Louis might yet prove useful once again. He had been good at what he did, good at killing, but to maintain that edge required sacrifice. Call it what you would—conscience, compassion, humanity—but it had to be left bloody and lifeless upon the altar of one's craft. Somehow, a little of the decency had been left in Louis's soul, and over the last decade it had prospered and grown. Yet perhaps Gabriel, too, had failed to smother all of his natural feelings toward the younger man beneath a blanket of pragmatism. He would assist him in this one last matter, and then their relationship would have to come to an unconditional end. There was too much weakness in Louis now for Gabriel to be able to risk keeping the lines of communication open. Weakness was like a virus: it transferred itself from host to host, from system to system. Gabriel had survived in his various incarnations through a combination of luck, ruthlessness, and an ability to spot the flaws in human beings. He planned to live for a great many more years. His work had kept him young inside.

Without such amusements, he would have withered and died, or so it sometimes seemed to him. Gabriel, despite all of his many talents and his instinct for survival, lacked the self-knowledge to understand that he had withered inside a long time before.

"And Bliss?" asked Louis.

"I have heard nothing."

"Billy Boy was driving the car on the day that we took out Leehagen's son."

"I am aware of that."

"Now he's dead, and Ballantine's gone—dead, according to Hoyle. If those killings are also linked to Leehagen, then only you and I are left."

"Well, then, the sooner we clear this whole affair up, the happier we will both be." Gabriel stood. "I'll be in touch when I have more to offer," he said. "You can make your final decision then."

He left the same way that he had entered. Louis remained seated, considering all that he had been told. It was more than he had before he arrived, yet it was still not enough.

From his perch on a garage roof, Angel followed Gabriel's progress, watching as the sinister old man walked slowly up the alley, watching as he reached the street and looked left and right, as though undecided about which path beckoned him, watching as an old Bronco with out-of-state plates passed slowly, watching as flames leapt in the darkness of its interior, watching as the old man bucked and clouds of blood shot from his back as the bullets exited, watching as he folded to the ground, the redness pooling around him, the life seeping from him with every failing beat of his heart . . .

Watching, feeling shock, but no regret.

"He'll live. For now."

Louis and Angel were back in their apartment. It was late afternoon. The call had come through to Louis. Angel did not know from whom, and he did not ask. He only listened as his lover repeated what he had been told.

"He's a tough old bastard," said Angel.

There was no warmth to his tone. Louis recognized its absence.

"He would have let you die, if it suited him. It wouldn't have cost him a moment's thought."

"No, that's not true," said Louis. "He would have spared a moment for me." He stood at the window, his face reflected in the glass. Angel, damaged himself, wondered how much more damaged in turn this man whom he loved could be to retain such affection for a creature like Gabriel. Perhaps it was true that all men love their fathers, no matter how terrible the things they do to their sons: there is a part of us that remains forever in debt to those responsible for our existence. After all, Angel had wept when the news of his own father's death had reached him, and

Angel's father had sold him to pedophiles and sexual predators for drinking money. Angel sometimes thought that he had wept all the harder because of it, wept for all that his father had not been as much as for what he was.

"If Hoyle is right, then Leehagen found Ballantine," said Louis. "Maybe Ballantine gave him Gabriel."

"I thought he always insulated himself," said Angel.

"He did, but they knew each other, and there was probably only one layer, one buffer, between Ballantine and Gabriel, if that. It looks like Leehagen found it, and from there made the final connection."

"What now?" asked Angel.

"We go back to Hoyle, then I kill Leehagen. This won't stop otherwise."

"Are you doing it for your sake, or for Gabriel's?"

"Does it matter?" Louis replied.

And in that moment, had he been there to witness it, Gabriel might have seen something of the old Louis, the one he had nurtured and coaxed into being, shining darkly.

Benton called from a phone box on Roosevelt Avenue.

"It's done," he said. Benton's wrist and shoulder ached, and he was sure that the latter had begun to bleed again. He could feel dampness and warmth there. He should not have taken it upon himself to fire the shots at the old man, not with the wounds that he had received at the auto shop, but he was angry, and anxious to make up for his failure on that occasion.

"Good," said Michael Leehagen. "You can come home now." He hung up the phone and walked down the hall to the bedroom in which his father lay sleeping. Michael watched over him for a couple of minutes, but did not wake him. He would tell him of what had transpired when he awoke.

Michael had no idea who the old man really was. Ballantine had spoken of him only in the most general of terms. It was enough that he had been involved in his brother's slaying, and was meeting Louis, the man directly responsible for his brother's death. The attack would be one more incentive for Louis to strike back, one more reason for him to travel north. At last Michael had begun to understand his father's reasoning: blood called for blood, and it should be spilled where his brother lay at uneasy rest. He still believed that his father was overestimating the potential threat posed by Louis and his partner once they were lured north, and there had been no need to involve the third party, the hunter, the one named Bliss, but his father was not to be dissuaded, and Michael had given up the argument almost as soon as it had begun. It didn't matter. It was his father's money and, ultimately, his father's revenge. Michael would acquiesce to the old man's wishes, for he loved his father very much, and when he was dead, all that was once his would become his son's.

Michael Leehagen might have been a king in waiting, but he was loyal to the old ruler.

CHAPTER ELEVEN

THEY DIDN'T GIVE HOYLE notice of their arrival. They simply turned up in the lobby after hours and told one of the security staff to inform Simeon that Mr. Hoyle had visitors. The guard didn't seem unusually troubled by the request. Angel guessed that, given the fact of Hoyle's residency in the building, and his reluctance to face the world on its own terms, the guards had grown used to human traffic at odd hours.

"What name should I give?" asked the guard.

Louis did not answer. He merely stood beneath the lens of the nearest camera, his face clearly visible.

"I think he'll know who it is," said Angel.

The call was made. Three minutes went by, during which an attractive woman in a tight-fitting black skirt and white blouse passed through the lobby and eyed Louis appreciatively. Almost imperceptibly, except to Angel, Louis's posture changed.

"You just preened," said Angel.

"I don't think so."

"Yeah, you did. You stood straighter. You *became* straight. You de-gayed."

The doors of the private elevator opened in the lobby, and the guard gestured at them to enter. They walked toward it.

Louis shrugged. "A man likes to be appreciated."

"I think you're confused about your sexuality."

"I got an eye for beauty," said Louis. He paused. "So does she."

"Yeah," said Angel, "but she'll never love you as much as you do."

"It is a burden," said Louis, as the doors closed.

"You're telling me."

Only Simeon was waiting for them in the lobby when they arrived at Hoyle's penthouse. He was dressed in black pants and a long-sleeved black shirt. This time, the gun that he wore was clearly visible: a Smith & Wesson 5906, housed in a Horseshoe holster.

"Customized?" asked Louis.

"Maryland," said Simeon. "Had it dehorned." He drew the gun smoothly and rapidly and held it so that they could see where the sharp edges had been removed from the front and rear sights, the magazine release, the trigger guard extension, and the hammer. The display functioned both as a surprising act of vanity on Simeon's part that Angel would not have associated with a man like him, and also as a warning: they had arrived unscheduled, and at a late hour. Simeon was wary of them.

He put the gun back in its holster and wanded them almost casually, then showed them once again into the room overlooking the pool. This time, the pattern created by the ripples on the wall was distorted and irregular, and Angel could hear the sound of someone swimming. He wandered over to the glass and watched Hoyle performing butterfly strokes through the water.

"He swim a lot?" he asked Simeon.

"Morning and evening," said Simeon.

"He ever let anyone else use that pool?"

"No."

"I guess he's not the sharing kind."

"He shares information," said Simeon. "He's sharing it with you."

"Yeah, he's a regular fountain of knowledge."

Angel turned away and joined Louis at the same table at which they had sat with Hoyle earlier in the week. Simeon stood nearby, allowing them to see him, and him to see them.

"How come you work for this guy?" asked Louis at last. The sounds of swimming had ceased. "Can't be too much call for your talents, stuck all the way up here with someone who don't get out much."

"He pays well."

"That all?"

"You serve?"

"No."

"Then you wouldn't know. Paying well covers a lot of sins."

"He got a lot of sins to cover?"

"Maybe. It comes to that, we're all sinners."

"Guess so. Still, those Marine skills of yours, they'll get rusty, sins or no sins."

"I practice."

"Not the same."

Angel saw Simeon twitch slightly.

"You implying that I might need to use them soon?"

"No. Just saying that it's easy to take these things for granted. You don't stay sharp and they may not be there for you when you need them."

"We won't know until that day comes."

"No, we won't."

Angel closed his eyes and sighed. There was enough testosterone in the room to make a wig bald. They were one step away from arm wrestling. At that moment, Hoyle entered. He was wearing a white robe and slippers, and was drying his hair with a towel, although he did so while wearing the ubiquitous white gloves.

"I'm glad that you came back," he said. "I just wish it could have been under better circumstances. How is your—" He searched for the right word to describe Gabriel, then fixed on " 'friend'?"

"Shot," said Louis simply.

"So I gathered," said Hoyle. "I appreciate the confirmation, though."

He took a seat across from them and handed the damp towel to Simeon, who did his best not to bristle at being reduced to the status of pool boy in front of Louis. "I presume that the attack on Gabriel is the reason you've returned. Leehagen is taunting you, as well as attempting to punish another of those whom he blames for his son's death."

"You seem sure that it was Leehagen who targeted him," said Louis.

"Who else could it be? No one else would be foolish enough to attack a man of Gabriel's standing. I'm aware of his connections. To move against him would be unwise, unless one had nothing to lose by doing so."

Louis was forced to agree. In the circles in which Gabriel moved, there was a tacit understanding that the provider of the manpower was not responsible for what occurred once that manpower was put to use. Louis was reminded of Gabriel's description of Leehagen: a dying man, desperate for revenge before the life left him entirely.

"So," said Hoyle. "Let us be clear. Perhaps you're wondering if this apartment is wired, or if anything that you say here might find its way to some branch of the law enforcement community. I can assure you that the apartment is clean, and that I have no interest in involving the law in this matter. I want you to kill Arthur Leehagen. I will provide you with whatever information I can to facilitate his demise, and I will pay you handsomely for the job."

Hoyle nodded to Simeon. A file was produced from a drawer and passed to Hoyle. He placed it on the table before them.

"This is everything that I have on Leehagen," said Hoyle, "or everything that I believe might prove useful to you."

Louis opened the file. As he flipped through its contents, he saw that some of the material replicated what he had uncovered himself, but much was new. There were sheafs of closely typed pages detailing the Leehagen family history, business interests, and other enterprises, some of them, judging by photocopies of police reports and letters from the attorney general's office, criminal in nature. They were followed by photographs of an impressive house, satellite images of forests and roads, local maps, and, last of all, a picture of a balding, corpulent man with a series of flabby chins folding into a barrel chest. He was wearing a black suit and a collarless shirt. What was left of his hair was long and unkempt. Dark pig eyes were lost in the flesh of his face.

"That's Leehagen," said Hoyle. "The photograph was taken five years ago. I understand that his cancer has taken its toll upon him since then."

Hoyle reached for one of the satellite images, and pointed to a white block at its center. "This is the main house. Leehagen lives there with his son. He has a nurse who lives in her own small apartment adjoining it. About a quarter of a mile to the west, perhaps a little farther"—he grabbed another photograph, and placed it beside the first—"are cattle pens. Leehagen used to keep a herd of Ayrshire cattle."

"That's not cattle land," said Louis.

"It didn't matter to Leehagen. He liked them. Fancied himself as a breeder. He felled forest so they could graze, and utilized areas that had been cleared by storm damage. I think they made him feel like a gentleman farmer."

"What happened to them?" asked Angel.

"He sent them for slaughter a month ago. They were his cattle. They weren't going to outlive him."

"What's this?" asked Louis. He pointed to a series of photographs of a small industrial structure with what appeared to be a town nearby. A thin straight line ran along the bottom of a number of the photographs: a railway line.

"That's Winslow," said Hoyle. He placed two standard maps side by side in front of Louis and Angel. "Look at them. See any difference between them?"

Angel looked. In one, the town of Winslow was clearly marked. In another, there was no sign of the town at all.

"The first map is from the 1970s. The second is only a year or two old. Winslow doesn't exist anymore. Nobody lives there. There used to be a talc mine near the town—that's what you can see to the east in some of the pictures—owned by the Leehagen family, but it gave out in the 1980s. People started to leave, and Leehagen began buying up the vacant properties. Those who didn't want to go were forced out. Oh, he paid them, so it was all aboveboard, but it was made clear what would happen if they didn't leave. It's all private land now, lying to the northeast of Leehagen's house. You know anything about talc mining, sir?"

"No," said Louis.

"It's a nasty business. The miners were exposed to tremolite asbestos dust in the mines. A lot of the companies involved knew that the talc contained asbestos, the Leehagens included, but chose not to inform their workers about either its presence or the prevalence of asbestos-related diseases in their mines. We're talking mainly about scarring of the lungs, silicosis, and incidents of mesothelioma, which is a rare asbestos-related cancer. Even those who weren't directly involved in mining began developing lung problems. The Leehagens defended themselves by denying that industrial talc contains asbestos or poses a cancer risk, which I believe is a lie. This stuff ended up in kids' crayons, and you know what kids do with crayons, right? They put them in their mouths."

"With due respect, what does this have to do with the matter in hand?" asked Louis.

"Well, it was how Leehagen managed to empty Winslow. He offered financial settlements to the families, most of whom had relatives who had worked in the mines. The settlements indemnified Leehagen and his descendants against any future action. He screwed those people to the wall. The amounts they received were far less than they might have been awarded had they been prepared to take their cases to court, but then this was the 1980s. I don't think they even knew what was making them sick, and most of them were already dead when the first cases from elsewhere began coming before the courts a decade or more later. That's the kind of man Leehagen is. It is ironic, though, that his own cancers may well have been caused by the mines that made him wealthy. They killed his wife"—when Hoyle said the word "wife," he winced slightly—"and now they're killing him."

Hoyle found another map, this one depicting the course of a river. "After he'd emptied the town, he got permission to redirect a local stream, the Roubaud, on some spurious environmental grounds. Effectively, the redirection allowed him to cut himself off. It functions as a moat. There are only two roads that cross it into his land. Behind Leehagen's house is Fallen Elk Lake, so he has water at his back as well. He's sown the lake bed with rocks and wire to prevent anyone from gaining access to the house from that direction, so the only way onto his land is over one of the two bridges spanning the stream."

Hoyle pointed them out on the map, then traced the roads that led from them with his finger. They formed the shape of an inverted funnel, cut at four points by two inner roads that ran through the property parallel to the eastern shore of the lake.

"Are they watched?" asked Angel.

"Not consistently, but there are still homes nearby. Some of them are rented by Leehagen to the families of the men who used to tend his cattle, or who work his property. There are a couple of others that belong to people who've reached an arrangement with him. They stay out of his affairs, and he lets them live where they've always lived. They're mainly on the northern road. The southern road is quieter. It would be possible for a vehicle going down either of those roads to get pretty close to Leehagen's house, although the southern road would be the safer bet, but if the alarm was raised then both those bridges could be closed before any trespassers had a chance to escape."

"How many men does he have?"

"A dozen or so close to him, I'd guess. They stay in touch on the land through a dedicated, secure high-frequency network. Some have served time, but the rest are little more than local thugs."

"You guess?" said Angel.

"Leehagen is a recluse, just as I am. His disease has made him one. The little that I do know about his current circumstances was dearly bought." He moved on. "Then there's his son and heir, Michael." Hoyle found another photograph, this time of a man in his forties with something of Leehagen Senior in his eyes, but who weighed considerably less. He was wearing jeans and a checked shirt and cradled a hunting rifle in his arms. An eight-point buck lay at his feet, the animal's head resting on a log so that it faced the camera. Louis recalled the man whom he had killed in San Antonio, Jonny Lee. He had looked more like his father, from what Louis could remember of him.

"This one is quite recent," said Hoyle. "Michael looks after most of his father's business affairs, legal and otherwise. He's the family's link to the outside world. Compared to his father, he's quite the bon viveur, but by any normal standards he is almost as reclusive. He ventures out a couple of times a year, but usually people come to him."

"Including your daughter," said Louis.

"Yes," said Hoyle. "I want Michael killed as well. I'll pay extra for him."

Louis sat back. Beside him, Angel was silent.

"I never pretended that this was going to be easy," said Hoyle. "If I could have dealt with this matter without the involvement of those outside my own circle, then I would have. But it seemed to me that we had a shared interest in putting an end to Leehagen, and that you might succeed where others had failed."

"And this is all you have?" asked Louis.

"All that might prove useful, yes."

"You still haven't told us how your beef with Leehagen began," said Angel.

"He stole my wife," said Hoyle. "Or the woman who might have been my wife. He stole her, and she died because of it. She worked at the mine, helping with paperwork. Leehagen believed that it would be good for her to earn her keep."

"This is over a *woman*?" said Angel.

"We're rivals in many matters, Leehagen and I. I bested him repeatedly. In the process, I alienated the woman I loved. She went to Leehagen as a means of getting back at me. He was, I should add, not always so repellent in appearance. He has been ill for many years, even before the cancer took hold. His medication affected his weight."

"So your woman went to Leehagen—"

"And she died," finished Hoyle. "In retaliation, I stepped up my efforts to ruin him. I fed information about him to business rivals, to criminals. He came back at me. I retaliated again. Now we are where we are, each of us sealed away in our respective fortresses, each nursing a deep hatred of the other. I want this thing ended. Even weak and ill, I begrudge him his existence. So here is my offer: if you kill him, I will pay you $500,000, with a $250,000 bonus if his son dies alongside him. As a gesture of good faith, I will pay you $250,000 of the bounty on the father in advance, and $100,000 on that of the son. The balance will be placed in escrow, to be paid over on completion of the job."

He replaced the photographs and maps in the file, closed it, and eased it gently toward Louis. After only a moment's hesitation, Louis took it.

The call woke Michael Leehagen from a stupor. He staggered to the phone in his dressing gown, his eyes bleary and his voice hoarse.

"Yes?"

"What have you done?"

Michael recognized the voice instantly. It dispelled the last vestiges of sleep from him as surely as if he had stood in the face of a raging, icy gale.

"What do you mean?"

"The old man. Who gave you the authority to target him?" There was a calmness to Bliss's voice that made Michael's bladder tighten.

"Authority? I gave myself the authority. We got his name from Ballantine. He set my brother up, and he was meeting with Louis. He'll make the connection. It will bring him here for sure."

"Yes," said Bliss. "Yes, it will. But it's not how these things are done." He sounded distracted, as though this was not a development that he had anticipated or desired. It made no sense to Michael. "You should have spoken to me first."

"With respect, you're not the most contactable of men."

"Then you should have waited until I called you!" This time, the anger in Bliss's voice was clear.

"I'm sorry," said Michael. "I didn't think there would be a problem."

"No." Michael heard him breathe in deeply, calming himself. "You couldn't have known. You may have to prepare for reprisals if the attack is connected to you. Some people won't like it."

Michael had no idea what Bliss was talking about. His father wanted everyone involved in Jonny Lee's death wiped from the face of the earth. How things were done elsewhere was of no consequence to him. He was interested only in the end result. He waited for Bliss to continue.

"Call your men back from the city," said Bliss, and now he sounded weary. "All of them. Do you understand?"

"They're already on their way."

"Good. Who fired the shots?"

"I don't think that—"

"I asked you a question."

"Benton. Benton fired the shots."

"Benton," said Bliss, seemingly committing the name to memory, and Michael wondered if he had somehow condemned Benton by naming him.

"When are you coming up here?"

"Soon," said Bliss, "soon . . ."

CHAPTER TWELVE

LOUIS STARED DOWN AT the man on the bed. Gabriel looked even smaller and more ancient than before, so old that he was nearly unrecognizable to Louis. Even in the space of a day, he seemed to have lost too much weight. His skin was gray, marked with a deep yellow in places where a salve had been applied to it. His eyes were sunken in blue-black pools, so that they seemed bruised, like those of a fighter who has spent too long trapped against the ropes, pummeled into unconsciousness by his opponent. His breathing was shallow, hardly there at all. The gunshot wounds, covered by a layer of dressings, had allowed some of his critical, and already dwindling, life force to dissipate, as though, had he been a witness to the shooting, Louis might have perceived it emerging from the exit holes, a pale cloud amid the blood. It would never return. It was lost, and an elemental part of Gabriel had been lost with it. If he survived, he would not be the same. Like all men, he had always been fighting death, the pace of the struggle increasing as the years drew on, but now death had the upper hand and would not relinquish it.

He had expected a police presence near the old man, but there was none. It troubled him, until he realized that others would be keeping vigil over Gabriel now. There was a small camera fixed to the upper-right-hand corner of the room, but he could not tell if it was a recent addition to the decor. He assumed that they were watching him. He waited for them to show themselves, but they did not come. Still, the fact that he had been allowed to get so close to Gabriel meant they knew who he was. It did not concern him. They had always known where to find him, if they chose.

He touched Gabriel's hand, black on white. There was a tenderness to the gesture, and a sense of regret, but something else played across Louis's face: a kind of hatred.

You created me, thought Louis. *Without you, what would I have become?*

The door behind him opened. He had seen the nurse approaching, her shape reflected in the polished wall behind Gabriel's bed.

"Sir, you'll have to leave now," she said.

He acknowledged her with a slight inclination of his head, then leaned down and kissed Gabriel gently on the cheek, like Judas consigning his Savior to death. He was both a man without a father, and a man with many fathers. Gabriel was one of them, and Louis had yet to find a way to forgive him for all that he had done.

Milton stood in a small office steps away from Gabriel's room. The door was marked "Private," and behind it sat a desk, two chairs, and an array of monitoring equipment, including both video and audio recording facilities. It was known in the law enforcement community as the Auxiliary Nurses' Station, or ANSTAT, and was a shared resource, which meant that, in theory, all agencies had an equal call on its use. In reality, there was a pecking order that had to be observed, and Milton was king rooster. He hovered over the two armed agents, watching as Louis left Gabriel's room and the nurse closed the door softly behind him.

"Action, sir?"

"None," said Milton, after only a moment's hesitation. "Let him go."

They stood in Louis's office, Hoyle's papers and maps spread across Louis's desk. Louis had added his own notes and observations with a red pen. This would be the last time that all of the information they had would be presented in this way. Once this discussion was over, it would be destroyed: shredded, and then burned. On a chair nearby lay fresh maps, and copies of the photographs and satellite images that they would show to the others.

"How many?" asked Angel.

"To do the job, or to do the job right?"

"To do it right."

"Sixteen, at least. Two to hold each of the bridges, maybe more. Four in the town for backup. Two teams of four approaching the property cross-country. And, if we lived in an ideal world, a big-ass chopper to take them all out once they were done. Even then, there would be problems with communication. There's no cellphone coverage that deep into the mountains. The trees and the gradient of the land mean that there's no line of sight, so walkie-talkies are out of the question for us."

"Satellite phones?"

"Yeah, and maybe we could send the cops a letter of confession as well."

Angel shrugged. At least he'd asked.

"So how many do we have?"

"Ten, ourselves included."

"We could bring in Parker. That would give us eleven."

Louis shook his head. "This is our game. Let's play it, see what numbers we roll."

He picked up four images, photographs of Leehagen's house taken with increasing degrees of magnification, and set them alongside one another, comparing angles, revealed points of access, weaknesses, strengths.

And Angel walked away, leaving him to his plans.

• • •

They both understood that this was not the way such things were done. There should have been background checks carried out, weeks—even months—of preparation, alternative entry and exit strategies examined, yet they did none of these things. In part, they recognized the urgency of the situation. Their friends, their home, had been targeted. Gabriel had been grievously wounded. Even without the information provided by Hoyle, they knew that it was in the nature of a man who would act in such a reckless way not to retreat after initial reverses. He would come at them again and again until he succeeded, and everyone close to them was at risk as a consequence.

As in most matters that concerned them both, it was Angel who was the more perceptive, the one who recognized underlying motives, the one who instinctively homed in on the feelings of others. Despite all that remained hidden about his partner, he was attuned to the other man's rhythms, his modes of thought and methods of reasoning, in a way that he believed was alien to Louis in their relationship. For a man who had lived so long in a gray world, drained of morality and conscience, Louis was always most comfortable with what was black and white. He was not prone to self-examination, and when he did analyze himself he did so entirely at one remove, as though he were a detached observer of his own follies and failings. Angel sometimes wondered if that was a consequence of the lifestyle he had chosen, but he suspected that it was probably an integral aspect of Louis's makeup, as much a part of him as his color and his sexuality, a thing stamped upon his consciousness before he even left his mother's womb, waiting to be called into being as the boy grew older. Gabriel had recognized that single-mindedness, and had harnessed it.

Now circumstances had intervened and, in a way, Louis was once again serving Gabriel, although this time as his avenger. The problem was that his desire to act, to strike, to release some of that pent-up energy had made him incautious. They were moving too quickly against Leehagen. There were too many gaps in their knowledge, too many sides upon which they were exposed.

So Angel broke a cardinal rule. He confided in another. Not everything, but enough that, if things began to fall apart, someone would know where to look for them, and whom to punish.

That evening, they ate together at River on Amsterdam. It was a quiet meal, even by their standards. Afterward, they had a beer in Pete's, once the office crowd had departed along with the free munchies, and half watched the Celtics make dull work of the Knicks. To amuse himself, Angel counted the number of people who were using hand sanitizer, and stopped once it threatened to move into double figures. Hand sanitizer: what was the city coming to, he wondered. I mean, he could understand the logic of it. Not everyone who used the subway was exactly spotlessly clean, and he'd taken cab rides that had required him to send his clothes to the laundry the following day just to get the stink out, but seriously, he wasn't sure that a little bottle of mild hand sanitizer was the answer. There was stuff breeding in the city that could survive a nuclear attack, and not just cockroaches. Angel had read somewhere that they'd found the gonorrhea virus in the Gowanus Canal. On one level, it was hardly surprising: the only thing that you couldn't find in the Gowanus Canal was fish, or at least any fish that you could eat and live for longer than a day or two once you'd consumed it, but how dirty did a stretch of water have to be to contract a social disease?

Usually, he would have shared these thoughts with his partner, but Louis was elsewhere, his eyes on the flow of the game but his mind intent upon very different strategies. Angel finished his beer. Louis still had half a glass left, but there was more life in the Gowanus.

"We done?" said Angel.

"Sure," said Louis.

"We can watch the end of the game, if you want."

Louis's eyes drifted lazily toward him. "There's a game?" he said.

"I guess there is, somewhere."

"Yeah, somewhere."

They walked through the brightly lit streets, side by side, together but apart. Outside a bar at the corner of 75th, Navy boys were shouting come-ons to the young women strolling by, drawing smiles and daggered glances in equal measure. One of the sailors had an unlit cigarette in his mouth as he stood at the door of the bar. He patted his pockets for a lighter or a book of matches, then looked up to see Angel and Louis approaching.

"Buddy, you got a light?" he asked.

Louis reached into his pocket and withdrew a brass Zippo. A man, he believed, should never be without a lighter or a gun. He flipped and flicked, and the sailor shielded the flame instinctively with his left hand.

"Thanks," he said.

"No problem," said Louis.

"Where you from?" asked Angel.

"Iowa."

"The hell is someone from Iowa doing in the Navy?"

The sailor shrugged. "Thought it might be good to see some ocean."

"Yeah, not a lot of ocean in Iowa," said Angel. "So, you seen enough yet?"

The sailor looked downcast. "Buddy, I seen enough ocean to last me a lifetime." He took a long drag on his cigarette and tapped the heel of a shiny black shoe upon the ground.

"Terror firmer," said Angel.

"Amen to that. Thanks for the light."

"Our pleasure," said Louis.

He and Angel walked on.

"Why would anyone join the Navy?" asked Angel.

"Damned if I know. Iowa. There's a guy only ever saw pictures of the sea, and decided it was for him. Dreamers, man. They forget they have to wake up sometime."

And in that moment their silence became more companionable than it had previously been, and Angel resigned himself to what was being done, because he was a dreamer, too.

II

The harvest is plentiful, but the laborers are few.

—MATTHEW 9:37

CHAPTER THIRTEEN

THE MEETING WAS HELD in one of the private dining rooms of a members' club between Park and Madison, almost within complaining distance of the latest Guggenheim exhibition. There was no sign on the wall beside the door to indicate the nature of the establishment, perhaps because it was not necessary. Those who needed to know its location were already aware of it, and even a casual observer would have realized that here was a place defined by its exclusivity: if one had to ask what it was, then one had no business doing so, since the answer, if given, would be entirely irrelevant to one's circumstances.

The precise nature of the club's exclusivity was difficult to explain. It was more recently established than similar institutions in the vicinity, although it was by no means without history. Because of its relative youth, it had never turned away a prospective member on the grounds of race, sex, or creed. Neither was great wealth a prerequisite of membership, since there were those on its books who might have struggled to pay for a round of drinks in an institution less tolerant of its members' occasional struggles with solvency. Instead, the club operated a policy that might most accurately have been described as reasonably benevolent protectionism, based upon the understanding that it was a club that existed for those who disliked clubs, either because of an inherently antisocial bent or because they preferred others to know as little about their business as possible. Phones of any kind were forbidden in the public areas. Conversation was tolerated if it was conducted in the kind of whispers usually considered audible only to bats and dogs. Its formal dining room was one of the quietest places to eat in the city, in part because of the virtual ban on any form of vocal communication, but mostly because its members generally preferred to dine in the private rooms, where all business was guaranteed to remain undisclosed, for the club prided itself on its discretion, even unto death. The waiters were one step removed from being deaf, dumb, and blind; there were no security cameras; and nobody was ever referred to by name, unless they indicated a preference for such familiarity. Membership cards carried only a number. The top two floors contained twelve tastefully, although not opulently, furnished bedrooms for those who chose to spend the night in the city and preferred not to trouble themselves with hotels. The only questions ever asked of guests tended to involve variations upon certain themes, like whether they might like more wine, and if they might, perhaps, require some assistance making their way up the stairs to bed.

There were eight men, including Angel and Louis, gathered on this particular evening in what was unofficially known as "The Presidential Room," a reference to a famous night when a holder of the highest office in the land had used the room to satisfy a number of his needs, of which eating was only one.

The men ate at a circular table, dining on red meat—venison and fillet steak—and drinking Dark Horse shiraz from South Africa. When the table was cleared, and coffee and digestifs had been served to those who required them, Louis locked the door and spread his maps and graphs before them. He went over the plan once, without interruption. The six guests listened intently, while Angel watched their faces carefully for any flickers, any reactions that might indicate that others shared his own doubts. He saw nothing. Even when they began asking questions, they were purely on matters of detail. The reasons for what was about to take place did not concern them. Neither did the risks, not unduly. They were being well paid for their time and expertise, and they trusted Louis. They were men used to fighting and they understood that their compensation was generous precisely because of the dangers involved.

At least three—the Englishman, Blake; Marsh, from Alabama; and the mongrel Lynott, a man who had more accents than the average continent—were veterans of any number of foreign conflicts, their allegiances determined by mood, money, and morality, and generally in that order. The two Harrys—Hara and Harada—were Japanese, or said they were, although they possessed passports from four or five Asian countries. They looked like the kind of tourists one saw at the Grand Canyon, mugging cheerfully for the camera and making peace signs for the folks back home. They were both small and dark, and Harada wore black-framed glasses that he always pushed up on the bridge of his nose with his middle finger before speaking, a tic that had led Angel to wonder if it wasn't simply a subtle way of giving the world the bird whenever he opened his mouth. He and Hara looked so innocuous that Angel found them deeply unsettling. He had heard of some of the things they had done. He hadn't been sure whether to believe the stories or not until the two Harrys passed on a movie to him that they claimed had made them laugh harder than anything they had seen before, tears already rolling down their cheeks as they exchanged favorite plot points in their native tongue. Angel had blocked out the name of the movie for the sake of his own sanity, although he had a memory of acupuncture needles being inserted between a guy's eyelid and eyeball and then being "pinged" gently with a fingertip. What was particularly disturbing was that the movie had been the Harrys' Christmas present to him. Angel wasn't a guy to go around branding people as abnormal without good reason, but he figured the Harrys should have been strangled at birth. They were their mothers' little joke at the world's expense.

The sixth member of the team was Weis, a tall Swiss who had once served in the pope's guard. He and Lynott seemed to have some minor beef going, if the look that passed between them when they had realized they were to dine together was anything to go by. It was just one more reason for Angel to feel uneasy. Those kinds of tensions, especially in a small team, tended to spread out and make everyone edgy. Still, they all knew one another, even if only by reputation, and Weis and Blake were soon deep in conversation about mutual acquaintances, both living and dead, while Lynott appeared to have found a point of shared interest with the Harrys, which confirmed Angel's suspicions about all three of them.

By the end of the evening, the teams had been decided: Weis and Blake would secure the northern bridge, Lynott and Marsh the southern. The Harrys would work the road between the two bridges, traveling back and forth at regular intervals. If required, they could move to support either of the bridge teams, or take it upon themselves to hold a bridge if one of those teams had to cross the river to support Angel and Louis in their escape.

It was decided that they would leave the next day, staggering their departures, staying in pre-assigned motels within easy reach of their target. Shortly before dawn, when each team was in position, Angel and Louis would cross the Roubaud to kill Arthur Leehagen, his son Michael, and anyone else who got in the way of this stated aim.

When their six guests had departed, and the check had been settled, Angel and Louis separated. Angel returned to their apartment, while Louis went downtown to a loft in TriBeCa. There he shared a final glass of wine with a couple named Abigail and Philip Endall. The Endalls looked like any normal, well-to-do couple in their late thirties, although normal was not a word that applied to their chosen line of work. As they sat around the dining table, Louis went through a variation of his original plan with them. The Endalls were the jokers in Louis's pack. He had no intention of tackling Leehagen with only Angel by his side. Before any of the other teams were even in place, the Endalls would be on Leehagen's land, waiting.

• • •

That night, Angel lay awake in the darkness. Louis sensed his sleeplessness.

"What is it?" asked Louis.

"You didn't tell them about the fifth team."

"They didn't need to know. Nobody needs to know every detail except us."

Angel didn't reply. Louis moved beside him, and the bedside light went on.

"What is it with you?" said Louis. "You been like a lost dog these last two days."

Angel turned to look at him. "This isn't right," he said. "I'll go along with it, but it isn't right."

"Taking Leehagen?"

"No, the way you're going about it. Pieces aren't fitting the way that they should."

"You talking about Weis and Lynott? They'll be fine. We keep them away from each other, that's all."

"Not just them. It's this small team, and the holes in Hoyle's story."

"What holes?"

"I can't put my finger on them. It just doesn't ring true, not all of it."

"Gabriel confirmed what Hoyle told us."

"What, that there was a beef between him and Leehagen? Big deal. You think that's enough of a reason to kill someone's daughter and feed her to hogs, to pay the best part of a million dollars in bounty on the heads of two men? No, I don't like it. It seemed like even Gabriel was holding something back. You said so yourself after you spoke to him. Then there's Bliss . . ."

"We don't know that he's out there."

"I smell him all over Billy Boy."

"You're turning into an old woman. Next you'll be talking about getting a cat, and clipping coupons."

"I'm telling you: something is off."

"You that worried, then stay here."

"You know I can't do that."

"Then get some sleep. I don't need you any edgier than you already are for this."

Louis turned out the light, leaving Angel in darkness. He did not sleep, but Louis did. It was a gift that he had: nothing ever got in the way of his rest. He did not dream that night, or he could not remember if he did, but he woke up just before dawn, Angel at last sleeping beside him, and his nostrils were filled with the smell of burning.

Their names were Alderman Rector and Atlas Griggs. Alderman was out of Oneida, Tennessee, a town where, as a child, he had witnessed police and civilians hunt down a Negro hobo who had stepped off a freight train at the wrong station. The man was pursued through the woods as he fled for his life until, after an hour had gone by, his bullet-riddled body was dragged through the dirt and left by the station house for all to see. His mother had named him Alderman out of spite for the white people who were determined that such a title would never be available to him in reality, and she stressed to the boy the importance of always being neatly dressed and of never giving a man, white or black, an excuse to disrespect him. That was why, when Griggs tracked him down at the cockfight, Alderman was dressed in a canary-yellow suit, a cream shirt, and a blood-orange tie, with two-tone cream and brown shoes on his feet and, screwed down so hard upon his head that it left a permanent ring in his hair, a yellow hat with a red feather in the band. Only when you got up close could you see the stains on the suit, the fraying on the collar of the shirt, the ripples in the tie where the elastic in the fabric had begun to give, and the bubbles of hardened glue holding his shoe leather together. Alderman owned only two suits, a yellow and a brown, and they were both items of dead men's clothing, bought from the widows before the coffin lid had been screwed down on their previous owners, but, as he often pointed out to Griggs, that was two suits more than a whole lot of other men owned, whatever the color of their skin.

Alderman—nobody ever called him Rector, as though his Christian name had become the title that would always be denied him—was five-ten and so thin that he looked almost mummified, his high-yellow skin tight against his bones, with little flesh to suggest that Alderman was anything more than an animated corpse. His eyes were sunk deep in their sockets, and his cheekbones were so pronounced that they threatened to shred his skin when he ate. His hair grew out in soft, dark curls that were turning to gray, and he had lost most of the teeth on the lower left side of his mouth to a bunch of crackers in Boone County, Arkansas, so that his jaws didn't sit right, giving him the ruminative expression of one who had just been burdened with a piece of unsettling information. He was always softly spoken, forcing others to lean in closer to hear him, sometimes to their cost. Alderman might not have been strong, but he was fast, intelligent, and unflinching when it came to doing injury to others. He kept his fingernails deliberately long and sharp in order to do maximum damage to the eyes, and thus he had blinded two men with his bare hands. He kept a switchblade beneath the band of his watch, the band just tight enough to keep the knife in place but loose enough to allow it to be released into Alderman's hand with a flick of his wrist. He preferred small guns, .22s mostly, because they were easier to con-

ceal and lethally effective up close, and Alderman liked to do his killing where he could feel the breath of the dying upon him.

Alderman was respectful to women. He had been married once, but the woman had died and he had not taken another wife. He did not use prostitutes or dally with women of low character, and he disapproved of others who did so. For that reason, he had only barely tolerated Deber, who had been a sexual sadist and a serial exploiter of women. But Deber had a way of insinuating himself into situations that provided opportunities for enrichment, like a snake or a rat squeezing itself through cracks and holes in order to reach the juiciest prey. The money that came Alderman's way as a result enabled him to indulge his sole true vice, which was gambling. Alderman had no control over it. It consumed him, and that was how a clever man who occasionally pulled off some low- to medium-sized jobs came to own only two stained suits that were once the property of other men.

Griggs, by contrast, was not intelligent, or not unusually so, but he was loyal and dependable and possessed of an unusual degree of strength and personal courage. He wasn't much taller than Alderman, but he had fifty pounds on him. His head was almost perfectly round, the ears tiny and set fast against his skull, and his skin was black with a hint of red to it in the right light. Deber had been his second cousin, and the two men would trawl for women in the towns and cities through which they passed.

Deber had charm, even if it didn't run deep enough to drown a bug, and Griggs was handsome in a meaty way, so they did okay together, and Griggs's adoration of his cousin had blinded him to the more unsavory aspects of Deber's dealings with women: the blood, the bruising, and, on the night that he had killed the woman with whom he was living, the sight of a body lying broken in the alleyway behind a liquor store, her skirt hoisted up around her waist, her lower body naked, violated by Deber even as she was dying.

The final fight was just about to start when Griggs arrived at the old potato shed that housed the pit. It was August, almost at the end of the season, and the birds that had survived bore traces of their earlier fights. There were no white faces to be seen. The interior of the shed was so warm that most of the men present had dispensed with their shirts entirely, and were drinking cheap beers from buckets filled to overflowing with ice in an effort to cool themselves down. It smelled of sweat and urine, of excrement and the cock blood spattered around the inside of the pit and soaking into its dirt base. Only Alderman appeared untroubled by the heat. He was seated on a barrel, a thin roll of bills in his left hand, his attention fixed on the pit below.

Two men finished sharpening the gaffs on their birds' legs and entered the pit. Instantly, the pitch and volume of the spectators' voices altered as they sought some final betting action before the fight began, exchanging hand signals and shouts, seeking confirmation that their wagers had been recorded. Alderman did not join them. He had already placed his bet. Alderman left nothing until the last minute.

The breeders crouched at either side of the pit, their roosters pecking at the air, sensing that combat was imminent. The birds were introduced to each other, their hackles rising in instinctive hatred, and then they were released. Griggs worked his way through the crowd as the birds fought, catching occasional glimpses of flashing spikes, of blood spatter landing on arms, chests, faces. He saw a man instinctively lick the warm blood from his lips with the tip of his tongue, his eyes never moving from the combat below. One of the birds, a yellow-hackled rooster, got spiked in the neck and began to flag. The breeder withdrew it temporarily, blowing on its head to revive it, then sucking the blood from its beak before returning it to the fray, but it was clear that the rooster had had enough. It went cold, refusing to respond to the attacks of its opponent. It was counted out, and the fight declared over. The losing breeder picked up the distressed bird in his arms, looked at it sadly, then wrung its neck.

Alderman had not moved from his barrel, and Griggs could tell that the night had not gone well for him.

"Bullshit, man," said Alderman, his voice like that of a mourner whispering prayers for the dead, or a soft brush sweeping ashes from a stone floor. "That was all bullshit."

Griggs leaned against the wall and lit a cigarette, in part to get some of the smell of the pit out of his nostrils. Griggs had never been much for cockfighting. He wasn't a gambler, and he had grown up in the city. This wasn't his place.

"Got some news for you," he said, "something might ought to cheer you up."

"Uh-huh," said Alderman. He did not look at Griggs, but began counting and recounting his money, as though hoping that the act of moving it through his fingers might multiply it, or reveal a previously unseen twenty among the fives and ones.

"The boy that done Deber. Could be I know where he's at."

Alderman finished counting and slipped the bills into a scuffed brown leather wallet, then placed the wallet carefully in the inside pocket of his jacket and closed the button. They had been searching for the boy for ten weeks now. They had tried intimidating the women at the cabin, pulling up outside it in their big old, beaten-up Ford, all false smiles and implied threats, but the boy's grandmother had fronted them right there on her porch, and then three men had appeared from the trees, locals looking out for their own, and he and Griggs had moved on. Alderman figured that even if they did know where he was, the women wouldn't tell them, not even if they took a knife to one of them. He could see it in the matriarch's eyes as she stood there before her open door, her hands on her hips as she cussed them softly for what they were trying to do. Like Chief Wooster, Alder-

man knew something of the woman's reputation. They weren't ordinary cuss words she was using against them. It made no nevermind to Alderman, who didn't believe in God or the devil, but he admired the woman's demeanor, and was respectful of her even as he tried to communicate to her the level of damage he and Atlas were prepared to inflict in order to find the boy.

"So where he at?" he asked Griggs.

"San Diego."

"Boy's a long way from home. How'd you come by it?"

"Friend told a friend. Met a man in a bar, they got talking, you know how it is. Man heard we was looking for a young nigger, heard there might be money in it. Said a boy like ours showed up in San Diego looking for work about two months back. Got him a job as a kitchen boy in a diner."

"This man have a name?"

"White guy, didn't give no name. Heard about the boy from some redneck owns a bar in the boy's hometown. But I made some calls, got someone out there to take a look at the boy at his place of work. It's him, sounds like."

"Long way to go to be wrong."

"Got Del Mar out there. Not far to Tijuana neither. It's him, though. I know it."

Alderman got up from the barrel and stretched. There wasn't much to keep them here, and he did owe that boy: Deber had been close to setting up a score, and his death had fucked that up royally.

Without Deber, he and Atlas had been struggling. They needed to hook up with someone new, someone with juice, but the rumors about what the boy maybe had done to Deber had spread, and now he and Atlas weren't getting the respect that they ought to have. They needed to fix things with the boy before they could start making money again.

That night, they hit a mom and pop store and netted seventy-five dollars from the register and the safe. When Griggs put a knife to the woman's throat, her husband had come up with $120 more from a box in the storeroom. They left them tied up in the back of the store and turned the lights out, tearing the telephone from the wall before they departed. Alderman had been wearing an old gray overcoat over his suit and both he and Griggs had cloth sacks over their heads to hide their faces. He had made sure that they parked out of sight of the store before they went in, so their car couldn't be identified. It had been an easy takedown, not like some of the ones they'd done with Deber back in the day. Deber would have raped the woman at the store out of spite, right in front of her husband.

They stopped near Abilene at a bar owned by an old acquaintance of Griggs's, and where a man named Poorbridge Danticat, who knew of Alderman and Griggs and Deber, made a joke about Deber losing his head. Alderman and Griggs had waited for him in the parking lot afterward, and Griggs had beaten Poorbridge so badly that his jaw was removed almost entirely from his skull and one ear hung crookedly from a flap of skin. It would serve as a message. People needed to learn some respect.

All this because of Deber, thought Alderman, as they drove west. I never even liked him, and now we have to travel for days to kill a boy just cause Deber couldn't control himself with his woman. Well, they'd make the boy pay, make an example of him so that folk would know that he and Atlas took these things seriously. There was no other way. Business, after all, was business.

The diner stood on National Boulevard, not far from the X-rated Pussycat house. The Pussycat had started life as the Bush Theater in 1928, then became, at various stages in its history, the National, the Aboline, and the Paris, before finally joining the porn mainstream in the 1960s. When Louis arrived for work each morning shortly after five, the Pussycat was silent and sleeping, like an old harlot after a hard night's whoring, but by the time he left, twelve hours later, a steady stream of men had already begun to make use of the Pussycat's facilities, although, as Mr. Vasich, the Yugoslav owner of the diner, would often remark, "Ain't none of them staying longer than a cartoon."

Louis's job at Vasich's Number One Eatery, as a pink and yellow neon sign announced it, was to do whatever was required to keep the place functioning, short of actually cooking the food himself or taking money from its patrons. He washed, shucked, peeled, and polished. He helped carry in deliveries *and carry out garbage. He made sure that the restrooms were clean and there was paper in the stalls. For this he was paid the minimum wage of $1.40 an hour, from which Mr. Vasich deducted twenty cents an hour for room and board. He worked sixty hours each week, with Sundays off, although he could, if he chose, come in and work off the books for a couple of hours on Sunday morning, for which Mr. Vasich paid him a flat five dollars, no questions asked. Louis took the extra hours. He spent little of the money that he earned, apart from treating himself to an occasional movie on a Sunday afternoon, since Mr. Vasich fed him well at the eatery and gave him a room on the second floor with a bathroom across the hall. There was no access to the diner itself from where Louis stayed, and the rest of the rooms were given over to file storage and a collection of mismatched and broken furniture, only some of it connected to the business below.*

After two weeks had gone by, he took the bus down to Tijuana and, having walked the streets for two hours, eventually bought a Smith & Wesson Airweight alloy .38 and two boxes of ammunition from a store close to Sanchez Taboda. The man who sold it to him showed him, using a combination of broken English and simple, hands-on demonstration, how to release the cylinder and push back on the ejector rod to access the central ejector plate. The gun smelled clean, and the man gave Louis a brush and some oil to keep the weapon that way. When he was done, Louis tried to get a sandwich but all the bak-

eries and bread stores had been closed, apparently because a pesticide had been stored alongside the ingredients for making bread in a government warehouse in Mexicali, resulting in the deaths of a number of children, so he settled for half a chicken on a bed of wilted lettuce before returning to the United States.

He found an old bicycle in one of Mr. Vasich's storerooms and paid to have the tires repaired and the chain replaced. The following Sunday, he filled a bag with a bottle of water, a sandwich from the diner, a doughnut, some empty soda bottles, and the .38, and biked west until he had left the city behind. He stowed his bike in some bushes and walked away from the road until he came to a hollow filled with rock and scree. There he spent an hour firing at bottles, replacing them with rocks when only broken shards were left. It was the first time that he had held and fired a revolver, but he quickly got used to its weight and the sound that it made. Mostly, he fired from a range of not more than fifteen feet from his targets, figuring that, when it came down to it, he would probably be using the gun up close. Once he was satisfied with himself and his knowledge of the weapon, he buried the pieces of broken glass, carefully collected the spent cartridges, and biked back to the city.

The waiting came to an end on a warm, still August night. He woke to the sound of boards creaking outside his room. It was still dark outside, and he did not feel as though he had slept for long. He did not know how they had managed to get so close without being heard. The second-floor rooms were reached by way of rickety wooden stairs to the right of the building, and Louis always kept the main door locked at Mr. Vasich's insistence. Yet he was not surprised that they had found him at last. Gabriel had told him it would happen, and he had known it himself to be true. He slipped from beneath the sheets, wearing only his boxers, and reached for the .38 just as his bedroom door was kicked in and a fat man with a round head appeared in the doorway. Behind him, Louis could see another, smaller man hovering.

The big man had a long-barreled pistol in his hand, but it was not pointed at the boy, not yet. Louis raised his own weapon. His hands shook, not from fear but from the sudden rush of adrenaline into his system. Still, the man at the door misunderstood.

"That's right, boy," said Griggs. "You got a gun, but it's hard to kill a man up close. It's real—"

Louis's gun spoke, and a hole blew dark blood from Griggs's chest. Louis walked forward, his finger pulling the trigger again, and the second shot hit Griggs in the side of the neck as he fell backward, almost taking Alderman Rector with him. Alderman fired the little .22, but the shot went wild and took out the windowpane to the right of Louis. The gun in Louis's hand was no longer shaking, and the next three shots impacted in a tight circle no bigger than a man's closed fist in the center of Alderman's torso. Alderman dropped his gun and turned, his right hand clutching at the wounds in his body as he tried to support himself against the wall. He managed a couple of steps before his legs crumpled and he fell flat on his stomach. He moaned at the pressure on the wounds, then started to crawl along the floor, pulling himself with his hands, pushing with his feet against Griggs's corpse. He heard footsteps behind him. Louis fired the last bullet into Alderman's back, and he stopped moving.

Louis stared at the gun in his hand. He was breathing fast, and his heart was beating so hard that it hurt. He went back to his room, dressed, and packed his bag. It didn't take him long, for he had never really unpacked it, understanding that the time would come when, if he survived, he would have to move again. He reloaded the .38, just in case these men had not come alone, then stepped over the two bodies and walked to the end of the hall. He opened the door and listened, then cast an eye over the yard below. There was no movement. A beat-up Ford was parked below, both of its front doors open, but there was nobody inside.

Louis ran down the stairs and turned the corner, just in time to catch a man's fist across his left temple. He collapsed to the ground, blinded by the pain. Even as he fell he tried to raise the .38, but a boot connected with his hand and forced it to the ground, stamping on his fingers until he was forced to release his grip. Hands grabbed hold of his shirtfront and hauled him to his feet, then pushed him around the corner until he felt the first step against the back of his calves. He sat down and saw clearly, for the first time, the man who had attacked him. He was six feet tall and white, his hair cut short like that of a cop, or a soldier. He wore a dark suit, a black tie, and a white shirt. Some of Louis's blood had landed on the material, staining it.

Behind him stood Gabriel.

Louis's eyes were watering, but he did not want the men to think that he was crying.

"They're dead," he said.

"Yes," said Gabriel. "Of course they are."

"You followed them here."

"I learned that they were on their way."

"And you didn't stop them."

"I had faith in you. I was right. You didn't need anyone else. You could take care of them yourself."

Louis heard sirens calling in the distance, drawing closer.

"How long do you think you will be able to evade the police?" asked Gabriel. "One day? Two?"

Louis did not reply.

"My offer still stands," said Gabriel. "In fact, more so than before, after tonight's little demonstration of your abilities. What do you say? The gas chamber at San Quentin, or me? Quickly, now. Time is wasting."

Louis watched Gabriel carefully, wondering how he had come to be here at just the right time, understanding that tonight had been a test but not certain how much of it Gabriel had orchestrated. Someone must have told those men where he was. Someone had betrayed him to them. Then again, it could have been a coincidence.

But Gabriel was here. He had known those men were coming, and he had waited to see what would transpire. Now he was offering help, and Louis did not know if he could trust him.

And Gabriel stared back at him, and knew his thoughts.

Louis stood. He nodded at Gabriel, picked up his bag, and followed him to the car. The driver picked up the .38, and Louis never saw it again. By the time the police arrived they were already heading north, and the boy who had worked at the eatery, the one who had left two men dead on Mr Vasich's floor, ceased to be, except in some small, hidden corner of his own soul.

CHAPTER FOURTEEN

THEY DROVE NORTH JUST after breakfast. Nobody followed them. As they left the city, Louis employed all the skills of evasion that he had learned—sudden stops, doubling back on himself, the use of dead ends and meandering roads through residential areas—yet he discerned no pattern among the vehicles in his wake, and neither did Angel. In the end, both were content that they had left the city unencumbered by unwanted attention

Their conversation of the previous night was not mentioned. It would serve no purpose to disinter it now. Instead, they behaved as they always did, interspersing periods of silence with comments on music, on business, or on whatever happened to strike them at the time.

"Philadelphia," said Angel. "City of Brotherly Love, my ass. You remember Jack Wade?"

"Cactus Jack."

"Hey, that's unkind. He had a skin condition. Nothing he could do about it. Anyway, he once tried to help an old lady across the street in Philly and she kneed him in the balls. Took his wallet, too, he said."

"It is one unfriendly city," Louis agreed.

Angel watched the scenery go by. "What's over there?" he asked.

"Where?"

"East. Is that Massachusetts?"

"Vermont."

"Least it's not New Hampshire. I always worry that someone's going to take a pot shot at us from the trees when we drive through New Hampshire."

"They do breed 'em tough there."

"Tough, and kind of dumb. You know, they refused to pass a law requiring people to wear seat belts?"

"I read that somewhere."

"You rent a car in New Hampshire, you start it up, and it doesn't make that 'beep-beep-beep' noise if you forget to put on your seat belt."

"No shit?"

"Yeah, instead, if you try to put it on, a voice calls you a pussy and tells you to grow a pair."

"Live free or die, man."

"I think that was referring to the forces of tyranny and oppression, not some guy who misjudges the brake time on his Prius."

"Cheap gas, though."

"Cheap gas. Cheap liquor. Easy availability of weapons."

"Yeah," said Louis. "Hard to see how that could go wrong."

They left the interstate close to Champlain. At Mooers, they took a right and headed through the Forks, then crossed the Great Chazy River, which was little more than a stream at that point. The towns all blended into one: there were volunteer fire departments, cemeteries, old abandoned filling stations at intersections, now replaced by glowing edifices at the town limits, the vintage pumps still standing like ancient soldiers guarding long-forgotten memorials. Some places looked more prosperous than others, but it was a relative term; everywhere, it seemed, they saw things for sale: cars, houses, businesses, stores with paper on the windows, no hint now left of their former purpose. Too many homes had wounded paintwork, too many lawns were littered with the entrails of vehicles, cannibalized for parts, and the discarded limbs of broken furniture. They passed through places that were hardly there at all: some towns seemed to exist only as a figment of some planner's imagination, like a joke on the map, a punchline to a gag that had never been told. Halloween jack-o'-lanterns glowed on porches and in yards. Ghosts danced around an old elm tree, the wind picking at their sheeted forms.

They stopped for a coffee at Dick's Country Store and Music Oasis at Churubusco, mainly because they liked its advertising: "500 Guitars, 1000 Guns." Angel figured that somebody had to be kidding, but Dick's was for real: to the right of the door was a little convenience store with a fridge full of bait worms, and to the left were two separate entrances. The first led into a guitar and musical instrument shop that seemed to be staffed by the usual benevolent guitar heads and amp aficionados. A young man with long dark hair sat on the floor, trying out a black Gibson guitar, his fingers picking a loose melody in the fading afternoon light. The second door, meanwhile, led into a pair of linked rooms filled with shotguns, pistols, knives, and ammunition, and was staffed by a pair of serious-looking men, one young, one old. A sign warned that a New York state pistol permit was required to even handle a gun. Beside it, a heavyset woman was filling out the paperwork for a four-hundred-dollar pistol.

"I'm buying it as a gift for someone," she explained.

"That's acceptable," said the older of the two men, although it wasn't clear if he was referring to the legality of the transfer or the nature of the gift. Angel and Louis looked on in bemusement, then returned to their car to drink the coffee, and continued north. A wind farm occupied the hills to the west, the blades unmoving, like playthings abandoned by the offspring of giants.

"It's a strange part of the country," said Angel.

"That it is."

"Lot of people out there who didn't vote for Hillary."

"Lot of people in here who didn't vote for Hillary either."

"Yeah, fifty percent of them. I don't care. I always liked her."

When they came to Burke, they spotted the first of the brown U.S. Border Patrol vehicles, and although they were only doing five above the limit, Louis slowed down. They almost missed the right onto Route 122 as it grew dark, and only a closed campground, its power outlets covered by upturned plastic trash cans, alerted them to the presence of the turning onto 37. A chimney stack for a house never built appeared on the left, concrete slowly succumbing to the onslaught of green, and then, about twelve miles from Massena, motels appeared, and a Mohawk casino, and Indian smoke shops. A sign advised that they were only a mile from the Canadian border. Another, draped across a warehouse, announced that "This is Mohawk Land, not NYS Land."

They were close now.

They stopped in Massena, checking in separately at an anonymous motel and booking different rooms. Louis slept. Angel watched TV, the volume at its lowest audible level, alert to the sound of cars entering the parking lot, of voices, to the presence of anonymous figures in the gathering dark. It was too early for him to fall easily into sleep. He was a night owl by nature. It was mornings that were hard for him. At last, he forced himself to turn off the television and lie back on the bed. Maybe he napped for a time, but he was awake when the clock by his bed indicated that it was after 4:00 A.M., and he stilled the alarm before it barely had a chance to sound.

Louis was already waiting in the car when Angel emerged from the room. No words were exchanged, no greetings. Instead, they drove from Massena in silence, their attention fixed on the road, on the darkness, and on the work that lay ahead.

CHAPTER FIFTEEN

LOUIS TURNED SOUTH SOME five miles west of Massena. After a further six miles, they passed a series of U-shaped pools filled with still water, and old mining works falling into decay, the only remnants of the Leehagen talc mine. Farther back, now slowly being reclaimed by nature, were the ruins of Winslow. They could not see them in the gloom, but Louis knew that they were there. He had seen them on Hoyle's photographs, and had memorized their position down to the nearest fraction of a mile, just as he knew the position of the two unmarked roads that curved southwest across the Roubaud Stream and into Leehagen's land.

They came to the first intersection after sixteen miles had appeared on the clock. It was marked "Private Property," and led to the first bridge over the Roubaud. Louis slowed. To their right, a flashlight blinked once from the trees: Lynott and Marsh, making their presence known. Louis and Angel followed the road for another three miles until they came to the second bridge. Again, they were signaled from somewhere deep among the trees: Blake and Weis.

The Endalls, meanwhile, had entered Leehagen's property under cover of darkness shortly after midnight and had traveled, on foot, to the ruins of the old cattle pens, there to keep watch on Leehagen's house and await the arrival of Angel and Louis. As with the three main pairs, there was no way to communicate with them now that the operation was under way. It did not matter. Everybody knew what had to be done. Phones would have helped, but they were not an option, not here.

The only ones who were not yet in place were Hara and Harada. They were still in Massena, and would leave only at a prearranged time once Angel and Louis had entered Leehagen's property, in order to avoid the possibility that a mini-convoy of cars might draw attention to what was about to occur.

Once Louis was satisfied that the bridge teams were in place, he crossed the southern bridge onto Leehagen's land. They saw no lights, passed no other cars, nor detected any signs of life on the road. Mostly, the land around them was forest, so they were hemmed in on both sides by trees, but on two occasions they came to man-made breaks in the tree line, hundreds of feet wide: Leehagen's grazing acres. After two miles, they took a dirt road north again, the forest beginning to thin here, until they came to an old barn, pinpointed on one of their maps, that stood beside an abandoned farm, and there they left the car. They were less than half a mile from Leehagen's house, and to drive any farther would be to risk alerting its residents, for it was quiet here.

They armed themselves with Glocks and a pair of Steyr TMP 9mm submachine guns fitted with suppressors and carried on slings, leaving the rest of their mobile armory in the trunk. This was to be a killing raid, fast and brutal, and they did not anticipate the need for longer-range weapons. The Steyrs were simple and effective: easily controllable despite an effective range of up to twenty-five meters; light, with an empty weight of just under three pounds; limited recoil; and a cyclic rate of nine hundred rounds per minute. They each added a spare thirty-round magazine for the Steyrs, and a spare clip for the Glocks.

Ahead of them lay the cattle pens, twin wooden single-story structures painted white. Nearby, a modern blue grain elevator towered over the lower buildings. Angel could smell the lingering odor of excrement and cow urine, and when he looked inside the first of the pens he could see that they had not been cleaned since the animals had been slaughtered. Louis checked the pens to the right, and once they were sure that both were empty, they moved on, using the buildings for cover until they came to the bottom of a small hill that overlooked the Leehagen house about a quarter of a mile to the west.

Louis had never had any intention of taking Leehagen with a long-range shot, even if the old man had been more mobile than he was. It was not one of his particular skills, even less so since the damage suffered to his left hand while they were in Louisiana with Parker some years before. Had such a shot been available to him, there was no way of knowing if Leehagen might actually have been fit enough to take the air that particular morning, and then there was always the weather to consider. After all, a sick man was hardly going to be wheeled around his property in the cold, and the forecast was for heavy rain. But there was also the son to be dealt with. Louis wanted him as well. If he killed the father and left the son alive, then the vendetta would continue. Both had to be taken out at the same time. That meant killing them in the house, with Louis and Angel entering while the Endalls provided cover. It would be done as quietly as possible with silenced weapons to limit the possibility of gunfire drawing unwanted attention to what was being done, but Louis knew that such hopes might well prove optimistic. He didn't believe that they could get in and out entirely unnoticed, and he recognized that they might well end up fighting their way off Leehagen's land. At least they would not have to do so alone, and Leehagen's men would be no match for their ten guns.

"Where are they?" whispered Angel.

Louis stared back at the empty pens. This was where they were supposed to rendezvous, but there was still no sign of the Endalls.

"Shit," hissed Louis. He considered their options. "Let's take a look at the house, see if there's any sign of movement."

"What?" asked Angel. "You're not going ahead without them?"

"I'm not doing anything yet. I just want to see the house."

Now it was Angel's turn to swear, but he followed Louis to the brow of the hill. The house lay before them, surrounded by a white picket fence. A lamp burned dimly in one of the upstairs windows, but otherwise all was quiet. Behind the house, the lake was a deeper patch of darkness extending toward unseen hills. Louis put a pair of binoculars to his eyes and scanned the property. Beside him, Angel did the same, although his attention was less on the house than on the deserted buildings behind him, so even as he looked to the north he was listening for the sounds of approach from the south.

They kept watch on the house for five minutes, and still the Endalls had not appeared. Angel was growing nervous.

"We need to—" began Angel, when Louis hushed him with a raised hand.

"That lit window," he said.

Angel put the binoculars to his eyes once more, and barely caught sight of what had alerted Louis before the white drapes fell back into place again: a woman at the window, and then a man pulling her away. The woman had blond hair, and Angel had clearly seen her face, if only for a second.

It was Loretta Hoyle, Nicholas Hoyle's deceased daughter, now apparently back from the dead.

"The last time we saw her, she was being eaten by hogs, right?" said Angel.

"That's right."

"She's looking good on it."

But already Louis was on his feet.

"We've been set up," he said. "We're out of here."

Lynott and Marsh were sitting in their Tahoe. It turned out that they had certain shared tastes in music, among other things. Marsh had brought his iPod, and the stereo had an MP3 socket, so they were now listening to Stan Getz's *Voices*. It was a little too close to the middle of the road for Lynott and did not, he felt, represent Getz at his best, but it was restful and suited his mood. From where they sat, just off a woodcutter's trail, they could see any cars that might pass before them, and part of the bridge on the other side of the road, but they remained invisible among the trees. Only someone approaching from the west on foot would have a chance of seeing them, and then only if he got up close. In the event of that happening, the person in question would have reason to regret his proximity.

On the backseat of the Tahoe were eleven pint bottles of water, a large flask of coffee, four prepacked sandwiches, and some muffins and candy bars. Again, this was Marsh's doing. Lynott had to give him credit for thinking ahead, even if he was starting to regret having some of the coffee and one of the bottles of water from the twelve-pack.

"I need to take a leak," he said. "You want me to do it in the empty bottle?"

Marsh looked at Lynott as if he had just asked if Marsh would like it if he took a leak on him.

"Now why would I want you to do that? You think I get off on seeing men urinate in bottles? I don't even get off on women doing that."

"Just thought I'd ask," said Lynott. "Some guys are sticklers for staying with the vehicle."

"Not when it comes to anything below the waist I'm not. Go find yourself a little privacy."

Lynott did as he was told. It was good to stretch his legs, and the air was cool and smelled of green leaves and clear water. He walked slowly into the woods, moving perpendicular to the gradient, taking care not to slip on the wet ground and fallen leaves. He found a suitable tree, then took a look over his shoulder to make sure that he still had the Tahoe in sight before turning his back and unzipping his fly. The only sound in the forest was the none-too-gentle trickle of liquid upon wood, and Lynott's accompanying sigh of relief and contentment.

Suddenly, a third sound was added to the mix: the shattering of glass, and a noise that was somewhere between a sigh and a cough. Lynott identified it immediately, and his gun was in his right hand even as he used his left to tuck his member back into his pants, ignoring the unwelcome trickle that accompanied the move. He took two steps before something impacted on the back of his skull, and then he was dead before he even realized that he was dying.

Angel resisted telling Louis that he'd told him so.

They moved along opposite sides of the cattle pens, their guns always moving, sighting down the barrels on the empty doorways, the dark windows, alert for even the slightest sign of movement.

They reached the barn unchallenged. It seemed unchanged from when they had left it, its doors closed to hide the car within. They paused and listened intently, but heard nothing. Louis signaled to Angel to open the left door, counting down from three. Angel's mouth was dry, and there was an ache in his belly. He licked some perspiration from his upper lip as Louis's fingers silently made the count then, as the final finger fell, he yanked the door open.

"It's clear," said Louis, then added, "but it's not good."

The car was resting too low to the ground on one side, like a lopsided smile. The tires on the right had both been slashed. The driver's-side window had been broken, and the hood had been raised and then allowed to fall back down without locking. Louis remained at the door, keeping watch, while Angel moved inside. He could detect no movement. An empty field stretched from the back of the barn toward the forest, but he could make out little in the distance apart from the shapes of the trees.

Angel squatted in front of the car and carefully raised the hood a fraction. He took a tiny Maglite from his pocket, switched it on, and held it between his teeth before picking up a piece of wood from the ground and slowly running it along the gap between the body of the car and the hood. There were no wires that he could find. He raised the hood a little farther with his left hand and, with the flashlight in his right, examined the engine. He could see no springs, no pads, no devices that might be activated by the raising of the hood. Nevertheless, he drew a deep breath before he lifted the hood fully. It took him only a moment to figure out what had been done. He could smell it before he saw it.

"They blew the fuse panel," he said. "This baby isn't going anywhere."

"Guess we walk."

"Kids?"

"You see the local gangbangers while we was passing through?"

"No, but this is, like, rural. Maybe they were hiding."

"Yeah, 'cause they was so scared of the big city boys."

Louis took one last look around, then stepped into the garage and headed straight for the trunk of the car. He put his finger upon the release button, then paused before pushing it and glanced at Angel.

"There was nothing up front," said Angel.

"That's reassuring. Maybe you want to take a couple of steps away, just in case."

"Hey, if you go, I go, too."

"Maybe I don't want you to go, too."

"You want someone to mourn for you later?"

"No, I just don't want you with me for eternity. Now step the fuck back."

Angel moved away. Louis hit the button, flinching only slightly as he did so. The trunk popped open, and Louis swore. Angel joined him.

Together, they stared into the trunk.

Weis and Blake had no music in their car, and they had long ago exhausted their store of mutual acquaintances. It did not trouble either of them. They were men who valued silence. Although, true to form, neither had said it aloud, each admired the other's essential stillness. The inability to remain quiet and unmoving for long was one of the reasons Weis detested Lynott. Their paths had last crossed in Chad, where they had nominally been fighting on the same side, but Weis considered Lynott to be unprofessional: a thief, and a man of low morals. But then, Weis was a man who hated easily, and already he had begun to notice Blake's breathing, which, stillness or no stillness, he felt was uncomfortably loud. There was nothing to be done about it, he supposed, short of suffocating him, and that seemed like an overreaction, even to Weis.

Curiously, Blake was thinking exactly the same thing about Weis but, unlike him, he was not a man who felt compelled to simmer quietly. He turned to Weis.

"Hey—" he said, and then the passenger-side window exploded beside Weis's head, the roar of the shotgun almost deafening Blake in his left ear, and suddenly Weis had a head no longer. A warm redness descended on Blake as Weis's torso toppled toward him, but by then Blake was already below window level, yanking the door handle and tumbling to the ground, his gun in his hand as he fired blindly, his vision clouded by Weis's blood, knowing that the noise and the fear of a stray round hitting its target might be enough to buy him crucial seconds. He must have been lucky, he realized, for as he blinked the blood away he saw a man in a green and brown camouflage poncho fall to the dirt, but Blake didn't stop to take in what he had done. All that mattered was to keep moving. If he stopped, he would die. He felt pain in his head and shoulder, and knew that some of the pellets must have hit him, but a combination of Weis and his good fortune in being seated a little farther forward than his late companion had saved him from the worst of the blast.

Shots impacted around him as he ran, and one passed so close to his left cheek that he felt the heat of its passage and thought that he could almost see the bullet as it flew, a spinning mass of gray tearing the air apart. Then the trees were growing thicker around him, and another shotgun blast shredded a branch not far from his head, but he kept moving, veering from left to right and back again as he went, using the trees for cover, giving them no clear shot at him. He heard the sounds of their pursuit, but he did not look back. To do that, he would have to stop, and if he stopped they would have him.

He took a deep breath into his lungs, preparing for a burst of speed that might buy him more vital time, and then his face collided with a hard object, and his nose broke and his teeth shattered, and for a moment he was blinded once again, this time by white light, not blood. He fell backward, but even as he did so his instinct for survival remained sharp, for he held on to the gun as he hit the ground and fired in the direction of the collision. He heard someone grunt, and then a body fell upon him, pinning him to the ground. The white light was fading now, and there was fresh pain in its place. The man was spasming against him, blood pouring from his mouth. Blake pushed him off, twisting his lower body to use both his own weight and the dying man's to free himself of the burden. He staggered to his feet, still dizzy from the force of the blow that he had received, and the first shot took him in the upper back, spinning him and sending him to the ground again. He tried to raise the gun but his arm wouldn't support the weight, and he could only lift it a couple of inches. Somehow he found the strength to fire, but the force of the recoil caused him to scream in agony and, involuntarily, he released his grip on the gun. He tried to lean over and reach for it with his left, but another bullet struck him, passing through his left arm and into his chest. He fell back upon the leaves and stared at the trees and the dark skies above.

A man's head appeared before him, his face obscured by a black ski mask. Two blue eyes blinked curiously at him. Then a third eye appeared, black and without emotion, and this one did not blink, not even as its pupil became a bullet and brought Blake's pain to an end.

Two bodies had been crammed into the trunk of Louis's car. The last of the season's flies had already found them. Abigail Endall had been blasted in the chest. There was a lot of damage, the peppering at the edges of the wound and the shredding of her shirt suggesting the shot had been fired from a short distance away, enough to allow the pellets to spread but not enough to dissipate the force of the blast. Her husband had been killed at close range with a single pistol shot to the head, the gun held so close to his forehead that Louis saw blistering and powder burns around the wound. Abigail's eyes were half closed, as though she were trapped between waking and sleeping.

"Help me get them out," said Louis.

He leaned into the trunk, but Angel stopped him with the palm of his hand.

"Shit," said Louis.

Once again, Angel took the Maglite and the stick and used it to check beneath the bodies as best he could. When he was satisfied that the corpses were not booby-trapped in any way, they first removed Abigail, who was lying on top of her husband, then Philip. The matting beneath the bodies had been pulled back, and a series of hidden clips had been activated in the base of the trunk, releasing the panels in the base and sides. The weapons stored there, and all of their ammunition, were gone. The spare tire had also been slashed, as a further precaution.

Angel looked at Louis, and said: "What now?"

• • •

Hara and Harada didn't make it much farther than Massena, and in that they were both unlucky and lucky: unlucky in the sense that they were now unable to participate any further in Louis's operation, and unluckier still when a routine search of their vehicle revealed their cache of weapons. The cops declined to give them the benefit of the doubt, and they ended up in a cell in the Massena police department on Main Street while the chief figured out what to do with them, and thus their lives were saved.

Slowly, Angel and Louis approached the barn doors.

"One hundred feet," said Louis.

"What is?"

"Distance between here and the forest to the east."

"If they're waiting for us, they'll take us as soon as we leave."

"You want them to take us here instead?"

Angel shook his head.

"You go left, I go right," said Louis. "You run, and you don't stop, no matter what. We clear?"

"Yeah, we're clear."

Louis nodded. "See you on the other side," he said.

And they ran.

III

Night's candles are burnt out, and
 jocund day
Stands tiptoe on the misty mountain
 tops.
I must be gone and live, or stay and die.

—WILLIAM SHAKESPEARE, *ROMEO AND JULIET*, III, V

CHAPTER SIXTEEN

GABRIEL OPENED HIS EYES. For a few moments, he had no awareness of where he was. There were unfamiliar sounds, and he was surrounded by too much white. This was not home: home was reds and purples and blacks, like the interior of a body, a cocoon of blood and muscle and tendon. Now, that protection had been stripped away, leaving his consciousness vulnerable and isolated in this strange sterile environment.

His responses were so sluggish that it took him time to recognize that he was in pain. It was dull, and it seemed to have no single locus, but it was there. His mouth was very dry. He tried to move his tongue, but it was stuck to his palate. Slowly, he formed spittle to release it, then licked his lips. He could not move his head more than an inch to the right or the left, not at first, and, anyway, it hurt him to do so. Instead, he worked on his arms, his hands, his fingers, his toes. As he did so, he tried to remember how he had come to be here. He had almost no recollection of anything that had happened after he had left Louis in the bar.

No, wait, there was something: a stumble, an old man's fear of falling, then a burning, like hot coals inserted deep into the core of his being. And sounds, faint but still audible, like the popping of distant balloons. Gunshots.

There were stinging sensations in the back of his left hand and in the crook of his right arm. He saw the drip needle in the soft skin on the right, then took in the green plastic connector at the top of the second needle that had been inserted into a vein in the back of his hand. He thought that he might have vague memories of waking before now, of lights shining in his eyes, of nurses and doctors bustling around him. In the interim, he had dreamed, or perhaps it had all been a dream.

Like most men, Gabriel had heard the myth that one's life flashed before one's eyes in the moments before death. In reality, as he had felt the cold rasp of death's scythe cutting through the air close by his face, its chill in stark contrast to the burning that had followed the impact of the bullets, he had experienced no such visions. Now, as he pieced together what had occurred, he recalled only a vague sense of surprise, as though he had bumped into a stranger on a street and, looking into his face to apologize, had recognized an old acquaintance, his arrival long anticipated.

No, the events of his life had come to him only later as he lay in a drug-induced stupor on the hospital bed, the narcotics causing the real and the imagined to mingle and interweave, so that he saw his now-departed wife surrounded by the children they had never had, an imaginary existence the absence of which brought no sense of regret. He saw young men and women dispatched to end the lives of others, but in his dreams only the dead returned, and they spoke no words of blame, for he felt no guilt at what he had done. For the most part, he had rescued them from lives that might otherwise have finished in prisons or poor men's bars. Some of them had come to violent ends through Gabriel's intervention, but that ending had been written for them long before they met him. He had merely altered the place of their termination, and the duration and fulfillment of the life that preceded it. They were his Reapers, his laborers in the field, and he had equipped them to the best of his abilities for the tasks that lay before them.

Only one walked in Gabriel's dreams as he did in life, and that was Louis. Gabriel had never quite understood the depth of his affection for this troubled man. His dream gave him an answer of sorts.

It was, he thought, because Louis had once been so like himself.

Gabriel heard a chair shift in the corner of the room. He opened his eyes a little wider. Carefully, he turned his head in the direction of the sound, and was pleased to find that he had more movement than before, even if the discomfort that it caused was still great. There was a shape against the window, a disturbance in the symmetry of the horizontal bars of the half-closed blinds. The shape grew larger as the man rose from his chair and approached the bed, and Gabriel recognized him as he drew closer.

"You're a difficult man to kill," said Milton.

Gabriel tried to speak, but his mouth and throat were still too dry. He gestured at the jug of water by his bedside, and winced at the pain the movement brought. It was that damned needle in the back of his hand. He could feel it in the vein. Gabriel had been hospitalized twice in the previous ten years: once for the removal of a benign tumor, the second time for a hairline fracture of his right femur, and on both occasions he had been strangely resentful of the connector in his hand. Odd, he thought: the injuries that have brought me to this place are more serious and painful than a thin strip of metal inserted into a blood vessel, and yet it is this upon which I choose to focus. It is because it is small, a nuisance rather than a trauma. It is understandable. Its purpose is known to me. And today, at this moment, it represents the first step in coming to terms with what has happened.

Milton poured a glass of water for him, then held it to Gabriel's mouth so that he could sip from it, supporting the old man's head gently with his right hand as he did so. It was a curiously intimate, tender gesture, yet Gabriel was resentful of it. Before, they had been equals, but they would never be so again, not after Milton had seen him reduced to this, not after he had touched his head in that way. Even though there was kindness in the action, Milton could not have been unaware of what it meant to Gabriel and his dignity, his sense of his own place in the complex universe that he inhabited. A little of the liquid dribbled down Gabriel's chin, and Milton wiped it for him with a tissue, compounding Gabriel's anger and embarrassment, but he did not show his true feelings, for that would be to surrender entirely to them and humiliate himself still further. Instead, he croaked a thank you and let his head sink back onto the pillows.

"What happened to me?" he asked, the words little more than a whisper.

"You were shot. Three bullets. One missed your heart by about an inch, another nicked your right lung. The third shattered your collarbone. I believe the appropriate thing to say in these situations is that you're lucky to be alive. Not for the first time, I might add."

He lowered his head slightly, as though to hide the expression upon his face, but Gabriel's eyes had briefly closed and he missed the gesture.

"How long?" asked Gabriel.

"Two days, or a little more. They seem to think you're some kind of medical marvel; that, or God was watching over you."

The ghost of a smile formed on Gabriel's lips. "Except God does not believe in men like us," he said, and was pleased to see a frown appear on Milton's face. "Why"—he paused to draw a breath—"are you here?"

"Can't one old friend visit another?"

"We're not friends."

"We are as close to friends as either of us have," said Milton, and Gabriel inclined his head slightly in reluctant agreement. "I've been watching over you," continued Milton. He gestured toward the camera in the corner.

"You're a little late."

"We were concerned that someone might try to finish the job."

"I don't believe you."

"It doesn't matter what you believe."

"And are you my only visitor?"

"No. There was another."

"Who?"

"Your favorite."

Gabriel smiled again.

"He believes this was linked to the earlier attacks," said Milton. "He's going after Leehagen."

The smile faded as Gabriel regarded Milton carefully.

"Why should Leehagen interest you?"

"I never claimed that he did," said Milton, as he waited to be questioned further. He thought that he saw something flit across Gabriel's features, a vague awareness of hidden knowledge. Milton leaned in closer to him. "But I have some information for you. You asked me to find out what I could about Leehagen and Hoyle; most of it I suspect you already know. There was an *anomaly*, though, for want of a better word."

Gabriel waited.

"The one who called himself Kandic wasn't hired to kill Leehagen."

Gabriel considered what he had been told. His mental functions were still impaired by the drugs, and his mind was clouded. He tried desperately to clear it, but the narcotic fug was too strong. Under other circumstances, he would have made the deductions required alone, but now he needed Milton to lead him. He swallowed, then spoke.

"Who was he sent to kill?"

"My source says Nicholas Hoyle."

"By Leehagen?"

Milton shook his head. "Someone further afield. Hoyle is involved in an oil deal in the Caspian. It appears that there are some who would prefer it if he was involved no longer. My source also says that whatever occurred between Hoyle and Leehagen in the past, it has now been forgotten, if the feud ever truly existed in the form that was claimed. It seems they have used the rumor of their mutual antagonism to their shared advantage. 'My enemy's enemy is my friend': at times, Hoyle's rivals have approached Leehagen, and Leehagen's enemies have approached Hoyle. Each man used the approaches to learn what he could to the other's advantage. It's an old game, and one that they've played well. They also share an interest in young women—*very* young women—or they did until Leehagen's illness began to take its toll. Leehagen still supplies Hoyle's needs. The girls have to be untouched. Virgins. Hoyle has a phobia about disease."

"But his daughter," said Gabriel. "His daughter was killed."

"If she was, it was not at Leehagen's instigation. It had nothing to do with him, or any feud, real or imagined, with Hoyle."

"Real or imagined," repeated Gabriel softly. He was feeling nauseous, and the pain seemed to have intensified. It was a trap, a ruse. He closed his eyes. What was that saying? There is no fool like an old fool.

"Help them," said Gabriel. He gripped the sleeve of Milton's jacket, ignoring the stinging in the back of his hand.

"And whom should I help?"

"Louis. The other. Angel."

Milton sat back in his chair, gently releasing the cloth of his jacket from Gabriel's fingers. It was a gesture of disengagement, of distancing.

"I can't do that," he said. "Even after what was done to you, I can't intervene. I won't."

The tension in Gabriel's body could not be sustained. He was weakening. He sagged back into the pillows, his breath now coming in short bursts, like that of a runner at the end of a long race. He knew that the end was coming.

Milton rose. "I'm sorry," he said.

"Tell Willie," said Gabriel. There was a blackness descending upon him. "Tell Willie Brew. Just that. All I ask."

And as he lost consciousness, he thought that he saw Milton nod.

The house stood on an acre of land, the building itself spreading over three floors and four thousand square feet. It was secure behind high walls, with motion-activated lights in the yard and an alarm linked to a private security firm that employed men known to have no qualms about drawing, and using, their weapons.

The house was occupied by a man named Emmanuel Lowein, his wife, Celice, and their two children, David and Julie, aged eleven and twelve, respectively. Also with them for the past two days were two men who spoke little and slept less. They kept the Loweins and their children away from the windows, ensured that the drapes remained closed, and monitored the grounds using a system of remote cameras.

Louis had never been in the safe house before, and he knew Bliss only by reputation. Lowein had information about a number of South American politicians that friends of Gabriel were very anxious to acquire. Lowein, in turn, wanted security for his family and a new life far from jungles and juntas. Gabriel was acting as the go-between, and Louis and Bliss had been assigned as added security while the negotiations were continuing. Lowein was a target, and there were those who were anxious that he should be silenced before he had a chance to share what he knew. Gabriel had long held the view that, in the event of an individual or individuals being targeted by professionals, one could do a lot worse than have men of a similar mind-set as part of the guard detail.

Bliss was almost a decade older than Louis. Unlike Louis, he had high-profile kills to his name, but there were rumors that he now wished to fade into the shadows for a time. Men in their line of work eventually began to accumulate a long list of enemies, principally among those who refused to acknowledge the separation between the killer and those who had ordered the kill. To the professionals, the Reapers, it made no sense: one might as well blame the rifle itself, or the bullet, or the bomb. Like them, the Reapers were simply tools to be applied toward the ultimate end. There was nothing personal about it. Nevertheless, such reasoning could not always be understood by those who had suffered loss, whether that loss was personal, professional, political, or financial in nature.

But Gabriel did not want Bliss to leave him, and did not seem to trust Bliss entirely now that he seemed intent upon ending their relationship and refusing to do Gabriel's bidding for much longer. Thus it was that Bliss had been assigned, with Louis, the temporary custody of the Lowein family. There would be no more kills for him for the time being, and perhaps not ever again.

It was a dull job, and they had passed the time as best they could. While the Loweins slept, Bliss spoke in the most general terms of his life as a Reaper, imparting to Louis occasional words of advice. He talked of sharpshooting, for one of Bliss's skills lay in the use of the rifle. He told Louis of the origins of the term "sniper" in the hunting of game fowl in India in the nineteenth century; of Hiram Berdan, the Civil War general who was an exponent of the art and helped to perfect the techniques still used by snipers to this day; of the Englishman, Major Hesketh-Pritchard, who organized the first Army School of Sniping, Observing, and Scouting during World War I in response to the German sniper attacks on British soldiers; of the Russian teams in World War II, and the less-efficient use of snipers by the Americans, who had yet to realize that arming a unit marksman with an M1, M1C, or M1903 was not the same as creating a sniper.

Louis listened. It seemed to him that the skills valued in a sniper were not without relevance to his own situation: intelligence, reliability, initiative, loyalty, stability, and discipline. It made sense to train repeatedly, to keep one's abilities honed; to maintain prime physical condition, because with that came confidence, stamina, and control; not to be a smoker, for an unsuppressed cough could betray a position, and the desire for a cigarette would bring with it nervousness, and irritation, and a commensurate lowering of efficiency; and to be emotionally balanced, without anxiety or remorse when it came to a kill.

Finally, Bliss told Louis of the importance of the "walkaway." Snipers, and Reapers, were weapons of opportunity. It was important to prepare, so that one was ready when the opportunity presented itself. Good preparation could create opportunities, but sometimes the opportunity would not present itself, and it was not wise to force the situation. Another chance would come, if one were patient and prepared.

But there would be times when all was not right, when one's instincts told one to leave, to drop everything and walk away. Bliss spoke of a job down in Chile. He had been tracking the target through his sight and was moments away from taking the shot, when one of the bodyguards had glanced up at the window where Bliss lay in wait. Bliss knew that he was invisible to the guard. It was almost dusk, and he was swathed in black, nonreflective material against a darkened window in an anonymous block of apartments. Even the muzzle of the rifle had been blackened. There was no way that the bodyguard's gaze should have fallen upon him, yet it had.

Bliss did not even consider taking the shot, although his finger was already tightening on the trigger. Instead, he had walked away. It was a setup. Someone had informed. He had escaped from the building with only seconds to spare, leaving his rifle behind. Gabriel had understood, and the leak was found and plugged.

"Remember," Bliss had said. "You only have one life. Your duty is to make it last. The trick is knowing when to stand, and when to walk away."

Now it was after two in the morning. The Loweins were asleep upstairs, the adults together in one room on the second floor, the children next door. The third floor was unoccupied. Twice every hour,

Louis or Bliss would check up on them. Downstairs, a radio played Connie Francis: a recording of some old show. It was Bliss's choice, not Louis's. He tolerated it out of deference to the older man.

Bliss had left him sitting in an armchair while he went upstairs to make sure all was okay with the Loweins. Only after five minutes had passed, and Bliss had not returned, did Louis stir from his chair. He walked to the hallway.

"Bliss?" he called.

There was no reply. He tried the walkie-talkie, but got only static in return.

He removed his gun from his holster and began to climb the stairs. The children's bedroom door was open, and the two kids were curled up in their beds. The nightlight by the wall had been turned off. When Louis had last checked, the light had been on. He knelt and flipped the switch.

There was blood on the sheets, and one of the spare pillows lay on the floor, feathers pouring from twin bullet holes. He moved closer to the first bed and pulled the sheet from David Lowein. The boy was dead, the blood soaking into the pillow under his head. He checked the other bed. David's sister had been shot once in the back.

Louis was about to call in help, then stopped. There was movement in the parents' bedroom. He could hear footsteps. He killed the nightlight and moved toward the connecting door. It stood slightly ajar. Slowly, he pushed it open, and waited.

Nothing.

He moved into the room, and a pale figure stumbled toward him. Celice Lowein's cream nightdress was soaked with blood from the wound to her chest. He thought that she was trying to reach for him, her left hand outstretched, red with her blood and the blood of her husband who lay dead on the bed behind her, but then realized that she was staring past him, using the last of her strength to find her children.

He put his hand out to stop her, and she came to rest against it, teetering on the balls of her feet. She looked at him, and her mouth opened. There was desolation in her eyes, and then even that was gone as the life left her and she collapsed on the floor.

Just too late he heard the footsteps behind him. He prepared to turn, but the gun touched the back of his head and he froze.

"Don't," said Bliss's voice.

"Why?" asked Louis.

"Money. Why else?"

"They'll find you."

"No, they won't. Kneel."

Louis knew that he was going to die, but he would not die on his knees. He twisted, his own weapon a dark blur in his hand, and then Bliss's gun spoke and all went black.

CHAPTER SEVENTEEN

WILLIE BREW AND ARNO had decided, after consultation with Louis, that the auto shop should reopen. Louis had been against it, fearing for their safety, but Willie and Arno had been entirely for it, fearing for their sanity if they were not allowed to return to their little haven of automobiles, engine parts, and overalls. They had cars to repair, they argued, and promises to keep. (Actually, Arno had preceded the latter with something about having miles to go before he slept, which Willie suspected might have been part of a poem or a song or something, and he had given Arno a scowl that left him in no doubt that such contributions were not only unwelcome, but might result in engine oil being poured down his throat.)

Absent from the surroundings of his beloved auto shop, and cut off from the routines that had sustained him for so many years, Willie had found himself thinking too much. With thoughts came regrets, and with regrets came the urge, always present, never forgotten, to drink more than was wise in order to lift his mood. It was almost a contradiction in terms, but Willie was by nature a solitary man who was happiest surrounded by others, and in the role to which he was best suited: dressed in blue bib overalls with grease on his hands, in intimate congress with a motorized vehicle. The private part of himself could retreat, comfortable in the knowledge that it was not required to be fully engaged for the commission of such routine acts, while something automatic kicked in and allowed another part of himself to play the role of the cranky yet ultimately genial proprietor. Without the latter character in which to lose himself temporarily, Willie was in danger of losing the best part of himself permanently.

For this reason, even on Sundays he and Arno could often be found in the shop, tinkering away while the radio played in the background, both men oil-smeared and at peace. There was always work to be done, for they had earned their reputation and there was no shortage of willing customers for their services. Willie had also been spurred on to greater efforts by his desire to pay back the loan that he had received from Louis all those years before. Although he was grateful for what had been done, he disliked being beholden to any man financially. Money cast a shadow over any relationship, and Willie's relationship with Louis was more unusual than most. It was predicated on the fact that Willie knew what Louis did, yet had to act as if he did not; that he was aware of the blood on this man's hands, and it did not concern him. The attack on his place of business, and the knowledge that he had come very close to dying in it, had added another problematical dimension to his involvement with Louis. Yet Willie knew that it could never end, not entirely, for the bonds that tied them together were not merely financial. Even so, by severing the monetary connection he would be making a statement about his own independence. Perhaps also on some deeper, half-acknowledged level, he was investing the paying off of the loan with a greater significance, as though it represented the more final separation for which he secretly wished.

But for now, here in these grubby premises, surrounded by familiar sights and smells, such matters could be forgotten. This was his place. Here, he had purpose. Here he could be both himself, and something more than himself. It was important to him to reclaim it after the attack. It had been violated by the incursion of the two armed men, but by returning to it and using it for the purpose for which it had been created, he and Arno could cleanse it of that stain.

In the end they had forced Louis to concede, helped by the fact that Angel was on their side. This was largely because, in certain matters,

Angel felt duty bound to take the opposite side to that of his partner in order to keep him on his toes, no matter how sensible a position said partner might be occupying at the time. In that way, at least, they resembled settled couples the world over. But Angel also understood Willie better than Louis did. He knew how important the auto shop was to him, and how much the attack had angered and shaken him. Willie, Angel knew, would rather have died under the gun in his shop than peacefully at home in his bed. In fact, Angel suspected that Willie's ultimate desire was to be crushed under some suitably extravagant piece of American engineering upon which he happened to be working at the time—a '62 Plymouth Fury, maybe, or a '57 Dodge Royal two-door sedan—just as Catherine the Great of Russia was often said to have died under the stallion with which she was about to copulate. The relationship between mechanics and cars, particularly classic cars, had always struck Angel as slightly odd, and the affection displayed for them by Willie and Arno as particularly unsettling. Sometimes, when he entered the garage, he half expected one or both of them to be found smoking a postcoital cigarette in the backseat of a forty-year-old automobile. Actually, he expected to find worse than that, but he preferred not to torture himself with images of Willie and Arno engaged in sexual acts of an automotive nature.

So now Willie and Arno were back in the place that they loved, the radio tuned, as it always was, to WCBS at 101.1. The station was on a fifties jag that night: Bobby Darin, Tennessee Ernie Ford, even Alvin and the Chipmunks—and here Willie, usually a man of some tolerance, was tempted to take a hammer to the speakers, especially when Arno, who could be an irritatingly uncanny mimic when he chose, began to sing along from under the hood of a '98 Dodge Durango with a busted radiator hose and twin white stripes down the body that appeared to have been painted by someone cross-eyed.

It was after ten, and yet they were still working, neither man troubled by the lateness of the hour. Familiar smells, familiar sounds. This was home to them. They were fixing things, and content to be doing so.

Well, reasonably content.

"For the love of sweet Jesus and His holy divine mother," said Willie, "cut that out!"

"Cut what out?"

"The singing."

"Was I singing?"

"Dammit, you know you were singing, if you can call it that. If you're gonna sing along to something, sing along to the Elegants or the Champs. You don't even do a bad Kitty Kalen, but not, not Alvin and the goddamned Chipmunks."

"David Seville," said Arno.

"Who?"

"That was the Alvin and the Chipmunks guy. David Seville. It was 1958 when he started, except he wasn't really David Seville, he was Ross Bagdasarian. Armenian, from Fresno."

"There's a Fresno in Armenia?"

"What? No, there's no Fresno in Armenia." Arno paused. "Not that I know of. No, he was of Armenian *descent.* His people just ended up in Fresno. Jeez, why is it so hard to talk to you? It's like dealing with a geriatric."

"Yeah, well, maybe it's because you don't know anything useful. How *come* you don't know anything useful anyway? You got all this stuff in your head—poetry, monster movies, even damned chipmunks—and you still can't find your way around a Dodge transmission without a map and a bag of supplies."

"If I'm so bad, how come you ain't fired me yet?"

"I have fired you. Three times."

"Yeah, well, how come you took me back again?"

"You work cheap. You're lousy at what you do, but at least you don't cost much to keep."

"Bad food," said Arno.

"And such small portions," said Willie, and the two men laughed. The sound was still echoing in the farthest corners of the auto shop when

Willie tapped lightly but audibly three times on the side of his work bench, a signal that they had agreed upon as a warning of potential trouble. From the corner of his eye, Willie saw Arno reach for a baseball bat that he had begun to keep close to hand as of that day, but otherwise the little man did not move. Willie shifted his right hand to the front pocket of his capacious overalls, where it gripped a compact Browning .380 that had come from Louis.

Then Arno heard it: two knocks on the door. The auto shop was locked down. Now there was someone outside in the dark, demanding to be let in.

"Shit," said Arno.

Willie stood. He held the Browning down by his side as he walked to the door and risked a glance through the interior grill and the Plexiglas of the window, trying not to make his head a target, then hit the exterior light.

The man standing outside was alone, and his hands were buried deep in the pockets of his overcoat. Willie couldn't tell for sure if he was armed. If he was, he wasn't waving it around.

"Are you Willie Brew?" the man asked.

"That's me," said Willie. He had never been much for the "who's asking" school of greeting and debate.

"I have a message for Louis."

"I don't know a Louis."

The man drew closer to the glass so that he could be certain that Willie would hear what he had to say, then continued as though Willie had never spoken.

"It comes from his guardian angel. Tell him to drop the job and come home, him and his friend. Tell them both to walk away. He asks, you're to say that Hoyle and Leehagen are intimately acquainted. Are you clear on that?"

And something told Willie that this man was, however confusingly, trying to do Louis a good turn, and to deny any further knowledge of him would not only be fruitless, but might also result in harm to the two men who were, after Arno, closest to Willie.

"If this message is so important, you ought to tell him yourself," said Willie.

"He's out of contact," he said. "Where he is, cells don't work. If he calls you, pass the message on to him."

"He won't call here," said Willie. "That's not how he operates."

"Then he's not coming back," said the man.

He turned to walk away. After a second's hesitation, Willie opened the door and followed him into the night, slipping the gun into the pocket of his overalls. The visitor was approaching the rear passenger-side door of a black Lincoln town car that had been parked out of Willie's line of sight. As Willie appeared, the driver's door opened and a man emerged. He didn't look like any chauffeur that Willie had ever seen. He was young, and neatly dressed in a gray suit, but he had eyes so dead they properly belonged in a jar somewhere. His right hand was hidden behind the door, but Willie knew instinctively that there was a gun in it. He gave silent thanks that he had not walked out of the garage with the little Browning visible. Instead, he held his hands away from his body, as though preparing to hug the man that he was following.

"Hey," said Willie.

The man stopped, his hand on the handle of the car door.

"Who are you?" asked Willie.

"My name is Milton. Louis will know who I am."

"That's no good to me. He's gone. They're both gone. Can't you do something? Can't you help them?"

"No."

"I'm not even sure where they are," said Willie, and he heard the hint of pleading in his voice, of desperation, and felt no shame. Angel had told him a little, but it had meant nothing to him. He was surprised that Angel had chosen to share any details at all with him, but he had been more concerned about returning to his beloved auto shop at the time. All he had was the name of a town upstate. What the hell use was that if they were in trouble? He wasn't a one-man army. He was just an overweight guy in overalls, with a gun that he didn't want to use.

But Louis and Angel were important to him. Whatever his fears and reservations, they had saved him, in their way. Willie was under no illusions: when Louis had first approached him, it was not out of altruism. It had suited him to have Willie in the building that he had acquired, for reasons that Willie himself still did not quite understand. Yet, self-interested or not, Louis had permitted Willie to keep doing what he loved. That was a long time ago, and things were different now. They had paid for his birthday party. They had even given him a gift: a Rolex Submariner Oyster, discreetly handed to him after everyone was gone from Nate's that night. It was one of the most beautiful things he had ever seen that did not have four wheels. Never had he even imagined that he would own something so lovely. He was wearing it now. Only for an instant had he considered putting it in a drawer and saving it for special wear. He didn't do "special." If he put it in a drawer, then it would stay there until he died. Better to wear it, and enjoy the fact of it upon his wrist.

He owed these men. He would do whatever he had to in order to help them, even if it meant getting down on his knees in the middle of the street before a stranger and his armed acolyte.

And the visitor relented, if only slightly.

"They're hunting a man named Arthur Leehagen. He lives upstate in the northern Adirondacks, not far from Massena. Now that you know where they are, what are you going to do about it?"

He opened the door and got into the car, pulling the door closed after him without another word to Willie. All the time, the man with the dead, unblinking eyes kept watch. Only when the rear door was closed, and his charge was safe, did he get into the front seat and drive away.

CHAPTER EIGHTEEN

ONCE AGAIN, THE AUTO shop was locked down. The radio had been silenced, and the lights around the two vehicles upon which Willie and Arno had been working were now extinguished, the cars standing raised in the gloom on their hydraulic lifts like forgotten patients on a pair of operating tables, abandoned by the surgeon for more deserving cases.

Willie and Arno were in the small office at the rear of the premises, surrounded by invoices and scribbled notes and oil-stained boxes. There was only one chair, which Willie was occupying. Arno squatted on the floor, small and thin, his head slightly too large for his body, a gargoyle evicted from its pedestal. Each had a cup in his hand, and a bottle of Maker's Mark stood on the desk between them. If ever there was a time for hard liquor, Willie supposed that this was it.

"Maybe it's not as bad as it sounds," said Arno. "They've been in trouble before, and they came out of it okay."

He didn't sound as though he entirely believed his own words, even if he desperately wanted to.

Willie took a sip of booze. It tasted terrible. He wasn't sure why he even kept it in his filing cabinet. It had been a gift from a grateful customer, although not one grateful enough to give a better bottle as a token of appreciation. Willie had been meaning to give it away for, oh, at least two years now, but he kept holding off just in case it came in useful for something. Tonight, it just had.

"After all, it's not like we can call the cops," said Arno.

"No."

"I mean, what would we tell them?" Arno's brow briefly furrowed in concentration, as though he were already trying to construct in his mind a plausible yet entirely fictitious explanation for some imaginary law enforcement officer.

"And it's not as if we can go up there and help them either. You can use a gun, but I never held one in my life until last week, and that didn't go so good. I nearly killed you with it."

Willie nodded glumly.

"Don't get me wrong," Arno continued. "I'll do whatever it takes to help them, up to a point, but I fix cars for a living. For what we're talking about here, that's not going to be too much use to anyone."

Willie put his mug aside. "I hate this stuff," he said wearily, and Arno wasn't sure if he was talking about the booze or something else. Willie rested his elbows on his desk, cupped his hands before him, and buried his face in them, his eyes closed, his fingertips almost touching across the bridge of his nose.

Arno watched his boss with an expression of tenderness on his face. It would be true to say that Arno loved Willie Brew. He loved him completely and devotedly, although had he ever chosen to say so out loud Willie would have had him committed. Willie had given him a place in which to work that was as much a sanctuary as Arno's cluttered, paper-filled apartment. He respected Arno's skills, even if he was scrupulously careful never to demonstrate that respect through either word or deed. He was Arno's closest friend, the one to whom Arno had turned when his beloved mother died, the man who had helped him carry her casket, walking alongside him with two anonymous undertakers behind. He was the finest mechanic Arno had ever met, and the most decent of men. Arno would have done anything for Willie Brew. He would even have died for him.

But he would not die for Louis and Angel. He liked Angel, who was at least friendly at times in a vaguely human, nonthreatening way. Louis, though, he did not like. Louis scared him to hell and back. He knew that this was a man whom he should respect, someone of power and lethality, but Arno respected Willie more. Willie had earned his respect through his actions, through his humanity. Louis required respect in the way a panther did, because only an idiot wouldn't respect something so potentially dangerous, but that didn't mean you wanted to spend any more time in the panther's cage than was absolutely necessary.

He recalled how Willie had spoken to him the morning after that first meeting with Louis. Willie had bought coffee and doughnuts, and the smell of them had been wafting from the office when Arno arrived for what he fully expected to be his last day in the auto shop. Willie had told him of Louis and his offer, and of how he felt that he had no choice but to accept it. That was how he put it, Arno remembered: he would take the loan, but only reluctantly. Willie was too wise to the ways of the world to imagine that such gifts came without conditions both acknowledged and unacknowledged. At the time, Arno had just been grateful that they would be able to continue in business, and he didn't care if the guy offering the loan had cloven hooves and horns coming out of his head. That changed once he met Louis, and saw the physical form that was about to cast a shadow over what had previously been a regular business. Angel had lightened that shadow a little, but for many years Arno and his beloved boss had still been forced to work under it, and Arno was human enough to resent that fact.

Now Angel and Louis were in trouble, and while Arno knew that they had acted in response to what had occurred earlier, that they had no choice in the matter and their own survival, and perhaps even the related survival of Arno and Willie, was dependent upon their actions, Arno wasn't so naive as to believe that, in the normal course of events, men with guns just arrived out of the blue to kill people because the mood struck. This was payback for something that had been done by Louis. Arno didn't want to see Angel and Louis dead, but he could understand why someone else might want to.

Willie stood and began rummaging through the papers on the desk. Eventually, after a box of nuts and assorted unpaid bills had tumbled to the floor, he found what he was looking for: his battered black address book. He thumbed through the pages, stopping at N–P.

"Who you gonna call?" asked Arno, and then added, in a misplaced attempt at humor: "Ghostbusters?"

A strange smile appeared on Willie Brew's lips. It made Arno even more nervous than he was already.

"In a way," said Willie.

Arno saw him pick up a pen and begin writing down a number: first a 1, followed by 2-0-7, and Arno then knew to whom they were turning for help. He poured himself another shot of Maker's Mark and added a little more to Willie's cup.

"For luck," he said.

After all, he figured, if the Detective was involved then someone was going to need it. He just hoped it wouldn't be Willie and him.

Willie went down the block to Nate's to make the call. He was concerned that the feds might be tapping the line in the auto shop. He had even been worried for a time that they might have planted a bug in his office, but despite the filth and the general clutter of his workplace Willie knew every inch of it intimately, and the slightest change in his environment would have been immediately apparent to him. The phone was another matter. He knew from watching HBO that they no longer needed to stick little devices in the receiver. This wasn't the Cold War. They could probably tell what you had for lunch just by pointing a gizmo at your belly. Willie was particularly cautious about cellphones, ever since Louis had informed him of just how easily they could be tracked and their communications intercepted. Louis had explained to him how a cellphone acts like a little electronic beacon, even when powered off, so that its owner's position could be pinpointed at any time. The only way to render yourself invisible was to take out the battery. That bothered Willie more than anything else, the idea that his every move might be tracked by unseen watchers in a bunker somewhere. Willie wasn't about to head off to Montana and live in a compound with guys who watched *Triumph of the Will* to get off, but equally he didn't see any point in making things easier for the government than they already were. It wasn't like Willie was a spy, it was just that he didn't much care for the idea of people eavesdropping on anything he might have to say, however inconsequential it might be, or monitoring his movements, and his involvement with Louis had made him realize that he could become, however tangentially, a target for any investigation that might focus on his business partner, so it paid to be careful.

Nate raised a hand in greeting to Willie when he entered the bar, but Willie merely grimaced in response.

"What can I get you?" asked Nate.

"I need to use your phone," said Willie. There was a crowd of loud young women at the back of the bar, where the public phone stood close to the men's room, and there was something in Willie's voice and expression that told Nate this wasn't the kind of call you wanted someone to overhear.

"Go in back," said Nate. "Use my office. Close the door."

Willie thanked him and slipped under the bar. He took a seat at Nate's desk, a desk that, in its general neatness and sense of order, bore no resemblance to his own. Nate's phone was an old rotary dial model, adapted for the modern age but still requiring the judicious application of a forefinger to make a call. The one time Willie was in a hurry, and trust Nate to have a phone that Edison could have built.

First of all, Willie called the answering service and left a message for Angel and Louis, repeating verbatim what the man named Milton had told him to say in the faint hope that one of them might pick it up before all of this went any further. Next he called Maine. The Detective wasn't home, so Willie decided to try the bar in Portland where he was now working. It took him a while to remember the name. Something Lost. The Lost Something. The Great Lost Bear, that was it. He got the number from 411, and the phone was answered by a woman. He could hear music playing in the background, but he couldn't identify it. After a couple of minutes, the Detective came on the line.

"It's Willie Brew," said Willie.

"How you doin', Willie?"

"Uh, up and down, up and down. You didn't see the papers?"

"No, I was out of town for a while, up in the County. I just got back this morning. Why?"

Willie gave him a summary of all that had happened. The Detective didn't ask any questions until Willie was done. He just listened. Willie liked that about him. The man might have made him nervous for reasons that he both could and could not put his finger on, but there was a calmness about him at times that reminded Willie of Louis.

"Do you know where they went?"

"Upstate. The guy who warned us mentioned somewhere near Massena, someone named Arthur Leehagen."

"Are there procedures in place for when something goes wrong?"

"There's an answering service. I leave a message, and then they can pick it up. They're supposed to check it every twelve hours when they're away. I've done that, but I don't know when last they called to check in and, y'know, it doesn't seem right just to wait around in the hope that it'll all work out."

The Detective didn't even bother to ask about cellphones.

"What was that name you were given again?"

"Leehagen. Arthur Leehagen."

"All right. You at the shop?"

"No, I'm down at Nate's. I'm worried that my phone might be tapped."

"Why would someone tap your phone?"

Willie explained about the visit by the feds.

"Hell. Shout me the number of where you are."

Willie gave it to him, then hung up the phone. There was a soft knock at the door.

"Yeah?"

Nate appeared. He had a snifter with two fingers of brandy in his hand.

"Thought you might need this," he said. "On the house."

Willie thanked him, but waved the glass away. "Not for me," he said. "I think it's going to be a long night."

"Somebody die?" asked Nate.

"Not yet," said Willie. "I'm just trying to keep it that way."

When he returned to the auto shop nearly an hour later, Arno was still sitting in the office, but the bottle of Maker's Mark had been put away, and instead there was the smell of brewing from the Mr. Coffee machine.

"You want some?" asked Arno.

"Sure."

Willie went to a shelf and removed a Triple A road atlas. He opened it to the New York page and began tracing a route with his finger. Arno filled a mug with coffee, added some creamer, then put it by his boss's right hand.

"So?" Arno asked.

"Road trip."

"You're going up there?"

"That's right."

"You think that's a good idea?"

Willie thought for a second. "No," he said. "Probably not."

"The Detective going too?"

"Yeah."

"Driving?"

"Yeah."

"Couldn't he fly? Wouldn't it be quicker?"

"With guns? He's not Air America."

Willie considered removing his bib overalls, then decided against it. He was happier wearing them, and anything that lightened his current mood wasn't to be dismissed easily. Instead, he shrugged on an old jacket over them.

"You stay here," he said to Arno. "In case they call."

"I wasn't going anyway," said Arno. "I told you. I'm not that kind of guy."

"I just thought you were going to offer, like in the westerns."

"You kidding? You ever see a Scandinavian western?"

Willie tried to remember if Charles Bronson had been Scandinavian. Actually, he thought that Bronson might have been Lithuanian. He was an -anian anyway, that much he knew.

"I guess not," he said at last.

Arno followed him to the rear of the auto shop, where Willie's old Shelby stood in the yard. It looked like it wouldn't go two miles without shedding parts and oil, but Arno knew that there wasn't a better-maintained automobile this side of New Jersey.

"Okay." Willie nodded at Arno. Arno nodded back. He suddenly felt like the little woman in the relationship. He was tempted to hug Willie, or straighten the collar on his shirt. Instead, he contented himself with simply shaking his boss's hand and advising him to be careful.

"Look after my place, now," said Willie. "And, listen, if all this goes to hell, you close up and walk away. Contact my lawyer. Old Friedman knows what to do. I put you in my will. You got no worries if I die."

Arno smiled. "I knew that, I'd have killed you myself long before now."

"Yeah, well that's why I didn't tell you. That, or you'd just be bitchin' at me for your cut all the time."

"Drive safe, boss."

"I will. Don't pay any bills while I'm away."

Willie climbed in the car, backed out of the yard. He raised a hand in farewell, then was gone. Arno went back inside, and saw that Willie hadn't even touched his coffee. It made him sad.

It was a long ride north, as long a drive as Willie had ever tackled without a proper break. He was tempted once or twice to stop for coffee or a soda, something with caffeine and sugar in it to keep him alert, but he had a bladder that was ten years older than he was and he didn't want to waste even more time by having to pull off the highway to relieve himself twenty minutes after he'd finished whatever he'd had to drink. He listened to WCBS until it began to fade, then found a Tony Bennett cassette in the glove compartment and let that play instead. There was a tightness in his gut. At first, he wondered if it was fear, but then he realized that it was anticipation. He had been coasting for a long time, living from day to day, doing what he loved but never stretching himself much, never testing himself. Willie had thought those days were behind him, that they were part of his youth, but he had been proved wrong. He patted the Browning in his jacket pocket. It seemed too small and light to be of use, but it also felt as if it was radiating heat, so that he could sense its warmth against the side of his leg. He tried to imagine using it, and found that he could not. This was a weapon for killing up close, and Willie had never had to look a man in the face when he fired off a shot at him. As for dying, he didn't believe that he was frightened of it: the manner of it, perhaps, but not the fact of it. After all, he had reached an age where dying had started to become an objective reality instead of an abstract concept.

No, the thing that worried him most was the possibility of letting Angel and Louis down, or the Detective. He didn't want that to happen. He wanted to do the right thing. He prayed for the courage to step up to the plate if the call came.

Willie reckoned it was six, maybe six and a half hours from Queens to where he was due to meet the Detective. At least it was highway most of the way, so he maintained a steady eighty for most of the journey, and it wasn't until he turned off 87 that the landscape and the road began to change in earnest and he was forced to slow down. Not that he could see any of it, but he didn't need to be a psychic to sense the change in atmosphere from the interstate to the county roads. The highway kept nature at bay: it was six lanes of fast-moving traffic, and Willie had only a limited degree of sympathy for any of the road-kill that he passed along the way. But when he left the interstate for the smaller roads, his mood and perspective changed. Here, nature was much closer. The trees crowded in upon him, and the only light that he had to guide him came from his own headlights and the warning reflectors occasionally embedded in the tarmac. It rained for a time, and the drops looked like starbursts exploding in his high beams. Something flew across his line of sight, so big and close that he was certain for an instant that it was going to crash through his windshield. At first, he thought it was a bat, until he realized that bats didn't grow that large, not outside of B movies, and that it was in fact an owl on the hunt for prey. He felt strangely elated by the sight: the only owls he had ever seen before were on TV, or in the zoo. Even then, he could not have guessed how big and heavy they appeared to be when in flight. He was relieved that he hadn't hit it at speed: the bird would have taken his head off.

Willie was a creature of the city, and of New York in particular. It wasn't that he considered green fields merely to be suburbs waiting to happen. He wasn't entirely without sensitive feelings. No, it was just that New York wasn't like other states: it was a place defined by its largest city in a way that nowhere else in the country was. When you mentioned New York to most people, either American or foreign, they didn't think of the Adirondacks, or the Saint Lawrence, or of forests and trees and waterfalls. They thought of a city, of skyscrapers and yellow cabs and concrete and glass. That, too, was Willie's New York. He could not equate it with its rural obverse.

He realized that Angel and Louis had probably come this way. He was shadowing them, driving in their tracks. The thought seemed to renew his sense of purpose. He checked his mileage and calculated that he had only an hour or so to go before he reached the place where he was supposed to meet the Detective. He felt his stomach tighten again. The gun was heavy in his pocket.

He drove on.

CHAPTER NINETEEN

JUST AS ANGEL AND Louis had hours before, Willie emerged from small towns and forests into a cluster of motels and casinos close to the Canadian border.

He'd only been this far upstate once before, and that was farther west, over at Niagara. He and his ex-wife had gone there for their honeymoon. In January. He must have been crazy but, then again, he had been in love, and neither of them was exactly a summer person. He'd had enough of heat and sweat in Vietnam, and she had simply wanted to see the falls. She told him they would be even more spectacular in winter, surrounded by ice and snow. He supposed they had been pretty impressive, although the chill that had entered his bones should have served as a warning for what was to come later in their married life. All things considered, he ought to have stuck her in a barrel right there and then and pushed her over the edge.

He spotted the Detective's Mustang parked outside the Bear's Den, a big truck stop and diner about ten miles from Massena, and experienced a sense of pride at the sight of the vehicle. He had sourced that car for the Detective, beating the dealer down on price until he thought the guy was going to start weeping on the lot. Willie had then brought the Mustang back to the shop and taken it to pieces, checking every moving part, substituting those that were worn or threatened to give up the ghost in a year or two. Seeing it here, far to the north, he felt the way a school principal might feel upon encountering a former student who had done particularly well for himself. He half expected the car to beep softly in recognition as he approached. After he had parked, he walked around the Mustang twice, giving both the interior and exterior a brief examination. When he was done, he sighed contentedly. There were one or two little nicks to the paintwork, and the treads on the right front tire were wearing thin, but otherwise she seemed to be in good condition. Still, he wanted to take a lengthy look under the hood soon. He was sure there were halfway-decent mechanics up in Maine, but they couldn't love his babies the way that he did. He patted the hood affectionately and entered the diner, passing some tattered stuffed bears in a glass case beside the main door, their fur rubbed bare in places. They made him depressed, and he quickened his step to put them from his sight.

It was shortly after 6:00 A.M., and the day was only just beginning to brighten. The rain had stopped falling for a while, but the sky was gray and brooding, and Willie knew that there would be more to come. The Bear's Den was a big place, and it was already half filled with people eating breakfast in the booths. They were smoking, too. It reminded Willie, once again, that NYC rules didn't apply up here. You tried lighting up over breakfast in the city and there would be a cop kneeling on your back before you could get to the funny pages, assuming your fellow diners didn't beat you to death first.

The Detective was seated in a red vinyl booth at the back of the room, a little fake hay bale made from wood shavings on the windowsill beside him, topped with a miniature scarecrow and plastic pumpkins. He was wearing dark-blue jeans, a black T-shirt, and a black military jacket. He hadn't removed the jacket, despite the warmth of the diner. Willie could guess why. There was a gun under there somewhere. The Detective was supposed to have surrendered all of his weapons after his permit and license were revoked, but Willie figured that only counted for the ones the cops knew about. Like Louis, the Detective wasn't the kind to go around advertising all of his possessions.

There was a cup of coffee before him, and the remains of bacon and poached eggs. Willie took the seat across from him and a waitress appeared. He ordered coffee and toast. He wasn't very hungry. He wasn't tired either, or not as tired as he had expected to be. That surprised him. Then again, he wasn't a big sleeper at the best of times. Four, maybe five hours a night was usually enough for him.

"I see you couldn't resist giving the Mustang a once-over," said the Detective. He was smiling.

"You send them out into the world, and all you can hope is that the world treats them the way it should," said Willie. "Like children."

He saw the Detective's smile flicker slightly, and wished that he hadn't mentioned children. You lose a child, especially the way this man had lost his, and it will always be a red, raw wound to you.

"She running okay?" asked Willie, moving on to safer ground.

"She's running fine."

"Helps not having her shot up by folk."

Willie had never quite forgiven the Detective for allowing his previous Mustang, also sourced by him, to be shot to pieces in some godforsaken Maine town. The car had been beyond salvation, although Willie had been forced to rely on Angel's testimony in that regard. Willie had offered to transport the car back down to Queens at his own expense to see what could be done, but Angel had put a consoling hand on Willie's shoulder and quietly suggested to him that this might not be a good idea. He reckoned the sight of what was left of the car would be too upsetting for Willie. It was the equivalent of a closed casket at a beloved relative's funeral.

"I do try to avoid getting shot up whenever I can," said the Detective.

How's that working out for you, Willie was tempted to ask. The Detective exerted a seemingly irresistible force of attraction over bullets, knives, fists, and just about anything else that could potentially do a body harm. Even sitting this close to him made Willie nervous.

The coffee and toast arrived, distracting him for a time from his concerns for his personal safety. The coffee tasted good, and he could feel his brain responding to the rush of sugar and caffeine.

"Is it okay to talk here?" asked Willie.

"I wouldn't. We can talk in the car. I take it they haven't called, though?"

"No." Suddenly, Willie's cell beeped. He found it in his overalls and felt his hopes rise, until he saw the message welcoming him to Canada.

"We're not in Canada, right?" he said.

"Not unless they've invaded quietly."

"Fucking Canadians," said Willie, turning his disappointment to anger and aiming it north. "Be just like them."

He went back to nibbling at his toast. He had a lot of questions he wanted to ask, not least of which was if they were up here alone. The Detective was good at what he did. Angel and Louis had said so often enough, and Willie had no reason to doubt their word, but he wasn't sure if two men would be able to handle whatever they were about to face. Much as he loved Angel and Louis, Willie had no pressing desire to throw himself on their pyre for no good reason. Suddenly, the gravity of the situation impacted upon him fully. He put down his piece of half-finished toast. What little appetite he had disappeared. He excused himself and went to the men's room, and there he doused his face and neck with cold water and dried himself with a wad of paper towels, then went back outside.

The check had been paid, and the Detective was waiting for him at the door. If he knew what Willie was feeling, he gave no indication of it.

"You need anything from your car?" the Detective asked.

"No. I got all I need here."

Instinctively Willie patted the Browning once again, and instantly felt ridiculous. He sounded like a gunfighter: a smug gunfighter, the kind that got shot at the end of the third reel. The Detective looked at him quizzically.

"You okay, Willie?"

"I didn't mean that to sound the way it did," said Willie apologetically. "You know, like I was

Dirty Harry or someone. I'm just not used to this kind of thing."

"If it's any consolation, I do this a lot, more than I'd like, and I'm not used to it either."

They both got into the Mustang, and the Detective pulled away from the curb. He drove for about a mile until he came to a deserted lot, then pulled in and killed the engine. The Detective produced a series of pages. They were satellite images, printed in high resolution from a computer. One showed a large residence. The second showed a town. On others there were roads, streams, fields.

"Where'd you get these, the CIA?" asked Willie.

"Google," said Parker. "I could plan an assault on China from a home computer. Arthur Leehagen has a compound south of here; that's the main house by the lake. It looks like there are two roads in and out, both heading roughly west. They cross a stream, which means Leehagen's land is almost entirely surrounded by water, except for two narrow tracts to the north and south where the stream comes close to the lake before veering away. The southern road veers northwest, and the northern road southwest, so they come close to meeting near Leehagen's house. Two other roads intersect them, running north to south, the first near the stream, the second about a mile or so in."

As he spoke, the Detective pointed out the details on one of the images. Willie didn't own a computer. He figured it was too late in life to worry about these things, and he had little enough spare time as it was. He had a vague notion of what a Google might be, but he couldn't have explained it to anyone in a way that made sense, not even to himself. Still, he was impressed by what the Detective was showing him. Wars had been fought with less detailed information in hand than this. Hell, he'd fought in one of them.

"You okay with the gun you've got?" asked the Detective.

"Louis gave it to me."

"It should be good, then. You fired a weapon recently?"

"Not since Vietnam."

"Well, they haven't changed much. Show me the gun."

Willie handed the Browning to the Detective. It weighed less than two pounds fully loaded, and had a blued finish. It was a pre-1995 model, as the magazine had a thirteen-round capacity, not a ten. The chamber was unloaded, according to the indicator on the extractor.

"Nice and light," said Parker. "Not new, but clean. You got a spare clip?"

Willie shook his head.

"With luck, you won't have to use it. If we have to empty clips, then we're probably outnumbered, so it won't matter too much either way."

Willie didn't find this entirely reassuring.

"Can I ask you something?" he said.

"Sure."

"Is it just us? I mean, no offense meant, but we ain't exactly Delta Force."

"No, it's not just us. There are others."

"Where are they?"

"They went on ahead. In fact—" Parker checked his watch. "—we ought to be joining them about now."

"I had another question," said Willie, as the Detective started the engine.

"Go ahead."

"Is there a plan?"

The Detective looked at him.

"Not getting shot," he replied.

"That's a good plan," said Willie, with feeling.

The Detective kept the headlights on as they drove. Willie thought they might be a little high, but he said nothing. He could worry about headlights another day. Getting shot was on his mind. He'd been shot at in Nam, but no bullets had even come close to him. He was kind of hoping to keep things that way. Still, it paid to know what to expect. He'd been around men who'd been shot, and the range of reactions had startled him. Some screamed and cried, others just stayed silent, holding all the pain inside, and then there were those who acted like it was a minor thing, as though the wind had just been taken out of them a little by a shard of hot metal buried deep in their flesh. Finally, he felt compelled to ask the question.

"You've been shot, right?" he asked the Detective.

"Yeah, I've been shot."

"What was it like?"

"I don't recommend it."

"You know, I'd figured that out for myself."

"I don't think mine was your typical experience. I was in freezing water, and I was probably already in shock when I got hit. It was a jacketed bullet, so it didn't spread out on impact, just passed straight through. It got me here." He pointed to his left side. "It was mainly fatty tissue. I don't even remember too much pain at first. I got out of the water and started walking. Then it began to hurt like hell. Bad, really bad. A woman—" Here, the Detective paused. Willie didn't interrupt, merely waited for him to continue. "—a woman I knew, she had some nursing experience. She sewed it up. I kept going for a couple of hours after that. I don't know how. I think I was still in shock, even then, and we were in trouble, Louis, Angel, and I. It happens that way, sometimes. People who've been injured find a way to keep going because they have to. I was running on adrenaline, and there was a girl missing. She was Walter Cole's daughter."

Willie knew about this. He had heard some of the story from Angel.

"A couple of days after it was over, I collapsed. The doctors said it was a delayed reaction to all that had happened. I'd lost some teeth, and I think what they did to repair that damage hurt almost as much as the gunshot. Anyway, it seemed to precipitate everything that followed, like my body had decided enough was enough. They tried to put me in the hospital, but I rested up at home instead. Took a while for the gunshot wound to stop hurting. When I turn a certain way, I think I can still feel a twinge. Like I said, I don't recommend it."

"Right," said Willie. "I'll remember that."

They turned off the main road, heading south. Eventually, the Detective slowed, searching for something to his right. A road appeared, marked "Private Property." The Detective turned onto it and followed it for a short distance until they came to a bridge, where he stopped the car. They sat there, neither of them moving. There was a light in the trees, and Willie thought that he could hear a repetitive beeping sound. He looked to his left and saw that the Detective had a gun in his right hand. Willie took the Browning from his jacket pocket and removed the safety. The Detective looked at him and nodded.

They got out of the car simultaneously and moved in the direction of the light. As they drew closer, Willie could see the vehicle more clearly. It was a Chevy Tahoe. Its side window had disintegrated, and the body of a man lay slumped over one of the seats, a ragged wound torn in his chest. The Detective skirted the Chevy, his gun raised, until he came to a second body farther into the woods. Willie joined him and looked down at the remains. The man was lying facedown with a hole in the back of his head.

"Who are they?" he asked.

"I don't know." He knelt and touched the man's skin with the back of his hand. "They've been dead for a while." He looked at their boots. They were clean, shining with what Willie thought was almost a military polish. There was only a little mud on them.

"Not from around here," said the Detective.

"No," said Willie. He looked away. "You think these guys came with Louis and Angel?"

The Detective thought about it. "They wouldn't have tried to take Leehagen alone, not with so much territory to cover. It would make sense to try to hold the bridges. So my guess is, yes, they were part of whatever Louis was planning, which means Leehagen's people found them and killed them."

He approached the bridge and stared across it toward the dark woods beyond.

"So where's the rest of the cavalry?" asked Willie.

The Detective sighed and gestured across the bridge. "In there. Somewhere."

"I'm guessing that's not where they're supposed to be, right?"

The Detective shook his head. "These guys are *never* where they're supposed to be."

CHAPTER TWENTY

THE TWO MEN WERE named Willis and Harding. Coincidentally, they shared a first name: Leonard. It was what had set them at each other's throats when they were small boys in a small town in a large state, the kind of town where it mattered who was Leonard Number One and who was Leonard Number Two.

As things turned out, the two boys were pretty evenly matched, and in time a bond of friendship had developed between them, a bond that was finally cemented when they stomped a man named Jessie Birchall to death outside a bar in Homosassa Springs, Florida, for having the temerity to suggest that Willis ought not to have touched Jessie's fiancée on the ass as she was making her way to the ladies' room. The fiancée in question claimed to have no memory of what the two young men had looked like when the police came to question her, even though one of the men had hit her hard enough to break her left cheekbone when she attempted to intervene on her fiancé's behalf, a forgetfulness not unconnected to the fact that Willis, his hands still warm with the dying man's blood, had whispered in her ear for thirty seconds while Jessie Birchall suffocated in redness on the garbage-strewn concrete of the parking lot, time enough to let his little lady know exactly what would happen to her if she saw fit to share with the law everything that she had witnessed. Actually, Jessie Birchall's fiancée hadn't liked him that much anyway, not enough to endure what Willis was proposing. She was only eighteen, and there would be other fiancés.

Eventually, Willis and Harding ended up in the pay of Arthur Leehagen, a man whose illegal means of making money sat easily, if discreetly, alongside his more legitimate business concerns. Willis and Harding, like a number of Leehagen's more specialized employees, were involved principally with the former activities, although they had proved useful whenever problems had arisen with the latter as well. When the cancers had begun to bloom like dark red flowers, it was Willis and Harding who had been sent out to talk to the more indignant sufferers, the ones who were threatening loudly to sue, or to go to the newspapers. Sometimes it took just one visit, although occasionally the two men had been forced to wait outside school gates to smile at mothers picking up their children, or to sit high in the bleachers during cheerleading practice, watching those short skirts ride up, their eyes lingering hungrily on thighs and breasts. And if the coach decided to ask them what they thought they were doing, well, the coach had kids, too. As Willis liked to say, there was plenty for everybody, boys and girls alike, and he was not a picky man. And if the cops were called, then Willis and Harding were Mr. Leehagen's men, and that was as good as diplomatic immunity right there.

And if someone was stubborn enough, or foolish enough, to ignore those warnings, well . . .

Willis and Harding might almost have been related, because they looked a little alike. Both were tall and rangy, with straw-blond hair darkening to red, and pale skin dotted with the kinds of freckles that joined together in places to form dark patches on their faces like the shadows cast by clouds. Nobody had ever asked them if they were related, though. Nobody ever asked them much of anything. They had been employed precisely because they were the type of men whom it seemed unwise to question. They spoke rarely, and when they did it was in tones so quiet and unobtrusive that they seemed to belie the substance of what was being said, yet left the listener in no doubt about their sincerity. It was whispered that they were gay, but in fact they were omnisexual. Their intimacy with each other had never extended to the physical, yet each was otherwise happy to sate his appetites wherever the opportunity lay. They had shared men and women, sometimes together, sometimes apart, the objects of their attentions sometimes submitting willingly, and sometimes not.

As the sky grew lighter that morning, and the rain briefly ceased, they were both identically dressed in jeans, black work boots, and billowing blue denim shirts as they sat in the cab of the truck, Willis driving, Harding staring out of the window, idly blowing cigarette smoke into the air. Their primary role in the operation was to keep watch on the northern bridge and its surrounds, as well as patroling the outer ring road of Leehagen's property in case, through some miracle, the two trapped men managed to break through the initial cordon.

Beside them were the guns they had used to kill Lynott and Marsh. Others had taken care of the second pair of men. Willis had felt a grim satisfaction that Benton, despite his protests, had been excluded. Willis didn't like Benton: he was a local bully boy who would never graduate to the majors. Willis was of the opinion that he and Harding should have been sent to New York, not Benton and his retard buddies, but Benton was a friend of Michael Leehagen's, and the old man's son had decided to give him a chance to prove himself. Well, Benton had proved something, that was for sure, but only that he was an asshole.

Now that the men at the bridges were dead, Willis and Harding were no longer concerned about further incursions, although they planned to stick to the outer road, just in case. Their thoughts had moved on to other matters. Like a number of Leehagen's employees, Harding didn't understand why they weren't simply being allowed to deal with the two intruders themselves. He didn't see the point in paying someone good money to do it for them. It never struck him that the man who would be arriving to kill them might have personal reasons for doing so.

He was distracted from his meditations by a single word from Willis.

"Look."

Harding looked. An enormous 4x4 was parked on the right-hand side of the road, facing in their direction. On either side of the road, pine trees stretched away into the distance. There was a man sitting on a log close to the truck. He was chewing on a candy bar, his legs stretched out in front of him. Beside him was a carton of milk. He did not appear to have a care in the world. Willis and Harding both simultaneously decided that this would have to change.

"The hell is he doing?" said Willis.

"Let's ask him."

They pulled up about ten feet from the monster truck and climbed out of the cab, shotguns now cradled loosely in their arms. The man nodded amiably at them.

"How you boys doin'?" he said. "It's a fine morning in God's country."

Willis and Harding considered this.

"This isn't God's country," said Willis. "It's Mr. Leehagen's. Even God doesn't come here without asking."

"Is that so? I didn't see no signs."

"You ought to have looked closer. They're out there, 'Private Property' printed clear as day on every one. Maybe you just don't read so good."

The man took another bite of his candy bar. "Aw," he said, his mouth full of peanuts and caramel, "maybe they were there and I just missed them. Too busy watching the sky, I guess. It is beautiful."

And it was, a series of oranges and yellows fighting against the dark clouds. It was the kind of morning sky that inspired poetry in the hearts of even the most tongue-tied of men, Willis and Harding excepted.

"You'd better move your truck," said Harding, in his quietest, most menacing voice.

"Can't do that, boys," said the man.

Harding's head turned slightly to one side, the way a bird's might at the sight of a worm struggling beneath its claws.

"I don't think I heard you right," he said.

"Oh, that's okay, I didn't think I heard you right either," said the man. "You talk kind of soft. You ought to speak up. Hard for a man to get another man's attention if he goes around whispering all the time." He took a deep breath, and when he spoke again his voice rumbled up from deep in his chest. "You need to get some breath in your lungs, give the words something to float on."

He finished his candy bar, then carefully tucked the wrapper into the pocket of his jacket. He reached for the carton of milk, but Harding kicked it over.

"Aw, I was looking forward to finishing that," said the man. "I'd been saving it."

"I said," repeated Harding, "that you better move your truck."

"And I told you that I can't do it."

Willis and Harding advanced. The man didn't move. Willis swung the butt of his shotgun around and used it to break the right headlamp of the 4x4.

"Hey, now—" said the man.

Willis ignored him, proceeding to the left headlamp and shattering that, too.

"Move the truck," said Harding.

"I'd love to, honest I would, but I really can't oblige."

Harding pumped a round into the chamber, placed the shotgun to his shoulder and fired. The windshield shattered, and the leather upholstery was pockmarked by shot and broken glass.

The man put his hands in the air. It wasn't a gesture of surrender, merely one of disappointment and disbelief.

"Aw, fellas, fellas," he said. "You know there was no need to do that, no need at all. That's a nice truck. You don't want to do things like that to a nice truck. It's—" He struggled for the right words. "—a matter of aesthetics."

"You're not listening to us."

"I am, but you're not listening to *me.* I told you: I'd like to move it, but I can't."

Harding turned the shotgun on him. If anything, his voice grew softer as he spoke again.

"I'm telling you for the last time. Move. Your. Truck."

"And I'm telling you for the last time that I can't."

"Why not?"

"Because it's not my truck," said the man, pointing behind Harding. "It's *their* truck."

Harding turned around. It was the second-last thing he ever did.

Dying was the last.

The Fulci brothers, Tony and Paulie, were not bad men. In fact, they had a very clearly developed, if simple, sense of right and wrong. Things that were definitely wrong included: hurting women and children; hurting any member of the Fulcis' distinctly small circle of friends; hurting anyone who hadn't done something to deserve it (which, admittedly, was open to differing interpretations, particularly on the part of those who had been on the receiving end of a pummeling from the Fulcis for what seemed, to the victims, like relatively minor infractions); and offending Louisa Fulci, their beloved mother, in any way whatsoever, which was a mortal sin and not open to discussion.

Things that were right included hurting anyone who broke the rules listed above and—well, that was about it. There were creatures swimming in ponds that had a more complicated moral outlook than the Fulcis.

They had come to Maine when they were in their early teens, after their father had been shot in a dispute over garbage collection routes in Irvington, New Jersey. Louisa Fulci wanted a better life for her sons than for them to be drawn inevitably into the criminality with which her late husband had been associated. Even at the ages of thirteen and fourteen respectively, Tony and Paulie looked like prime candidates for use as instruments of blunt force. They were then barely five feet four inches tall but each weighed as much as any two of his peers, and their body fat ratio was so low that a waif model would have wept for it.

Unfortunately, there are individuals whose physical appearance condemns them to a certain path in life. The Fulcis looked like criminals, and it seemed inevitable that criminals they would become. The possibility of their cheating fate was further hampered by their emotional and psychological makeup, which might charitably have been described as combustible. The Fulcis had fuses so short that they barely existed. As time went on, a great many medical professionals, including a number attached to prison welfare and probation services, attempted, unsuccessfully, to balance the Fulcis' moods by pharmaceutical intervention. What they discovered in the process was quite fascinating, and interesting papers for professional and academic study might well have resulted had the Fulcis been willing to stay still long enough to cooperate in their formulation.

In most cases of psychological disorder, aberrant behavior could be moderated and controlled through the judicious application of a cocktail of assorted medications. It was simply a matter of finding the right combination of drugs and encouraging the subject to take them regularly and continually. Where the Fulcis were concerned, though, it was discovered that the drugs would only operate effectively for a short period of time once they had lodged in their system, frequently one month or less. After that, their effectiveness dwindled, and upping the dosages did not result in any corresponding decrease in psychotic behavior. The medical professionals would then return to the drawing board, come up with another potential winning combination of blue, red, and green pills, only to discover that, once again, the Fulcis' natural inclinations appeared to reassert themselves. They were like organ recipients rejecting a donor kidney, or captive lab rats that, faced with an obstacle preventing them from reaching their food, gradually worked out a way to get around it.

One of the psychiatrists even went so far as to title a possible paper on the Fulcis. It was called *Viral Psychosis: A New Approach to Psychotic Behavior in Adults.* His theory was that the Fulcis' psychosis bore some resemblance to the manner in which certain viruses mutated in response to medical attempts to counter them. The Fulcis were psychotic in a way that went far beyond any normal conception of the term. The paper was never published because the psychiatrist was afraid of both the mockery of his peers and the potential damage that might be inflicted upon his person if the Fulcis discovered that he had referred to them as psychotic, even under the guise of protective pseudonyms. The Fulcis were not stupid. A senior law enforcement figure had once suggested that the Fulcis "couldn't even spell rehabilitation." This was untrue. The Fulcis could spell it. They just had no concept of how it might be applied to their own situation, for they had no insight into their own psychosis. They were happy. They loved their mother. They valued their friends. It was all very straightforward. As far as the Fulcis were concerned, rehabilitation was for criminals, and they were not criminals. They just looked like criminals, which wasn't the same thing at all.

Some branches of the law had been given cause to differ with the Fulcis' interpretation of their condition over the years. The brothers had been jailed in Seattle for the theft of $150,000 worth of Russian vodka from the port, even though they had only been hired to drive the trucks. Nevertheless, they were the ones who were found in possession of the booze, and they took the fall. They had also done time in Maine, Vermont, New Hampshire, and the Canadian maritime province of New Brunswick, mostly for offenses involving what their good friend Jackie Garner liked to call "transfers of ownership," occasionally involving a degree of violence if someone deliberately or inadvertently broke one of their rules. As with the law, ignorance was no defense.

But the most significant moment in their lives occurred when they were arrested for murder in Connecticut. The death in question was that of a bookie named Benny the Breather, who had engaged in a little creative accounting that did not meet with the approval of his bosses. These bosses were distantly related to some of the individuals who had been involved in the garbage disposal dispute that had ended the life of the Fulcis' father. Benny the Breather was so named in honor of a conviction for making lewd and lascivious telephone calls to various women who had been less than flattered by his attentions. Since Benny had made all of the calls from the comfort of his own bed, it hadn't taken the police long to track him down. In the course of his arrest, Benny had taken a nasty tumble down the stairs of his apartment block due to the fact that one of the women he had called was the wife of a sergeant at the local precinct. This fall had left Benny with a slight limp, so he was also sometimes known as Benny the Gimp. Benny hadn't cared much for either of his nicknames, and had been known to protest vociferously at the use of either of them, but the judicious introduction of a bullet to his head had solved the problem for all concerned.

Unfortunately, a good citizen had witnessed the crime and came forward with a description of the men responsible, which happened to match that of the Fulci brothers. They were hauled in, identified in a lineup, and tried for murder. Circumstantial evidence was enough to confirm their presence at the scene, which was nearly as surprising to the Fulcis as their initial identification in the lineup, given that they hadn't killed anyone, and certainly not Benny the Breather, aka Benny the Gimp.

The judge, taking into account psychiatric reports, sentenced them to life imprisonment, and they were sent to separate institutions: Paulie to the Level Four Corrigan Correctional Institution in Uncasville, and Tony to the Level Five Northern Correctional Institution in Somers. The latter was designed primarily to manage those inmates who had demonstrated an inability to adjust to confinement and posed a threat to the community, staff, and other inmates. Tony's immediate incarceration there—do not pass Go, do not collect two hundred dollars—was ordered because his mind began to shake off the shackles of his medication while his trial was still ongoing, resulting in an altercation that left one jailhouse cop with a broken jaw.

And there they might have remained—puzzled, hurt, and innocent—had one of the men who ordered the killing of Benny the Breather/Gimp not felt a pang of guilt at seeing two Italian-Americans wrongfully convicted of murder, particularly two Italian-Americans whose father had died in the service of a greater criminal good, leaving a widow who was regarded by one and all as a model of ethnic motherhood. Some calls were made, and it was suggested to a crusading attorney that the convictions in question were unsafe. The case against the Fulcis was further weakened when two similarly large gentlemen were arrested in New Haven following the attempted murder of a nightclub owner and were found to be in possession of the weapon that had killed Benny. Apparently, it had some kind of sentimental value to one of them, and he had been reluctant to part with it.

The result was that the Fulcis were pardoned and released after thirty-seven months in jail, and obtained a very nice settlement from the state of Connecticut for their troubles. This they used to ensure that their mother would be kept in comfort and style for the rest of her days. Louisa, in turn, gave the brothers a weekly allowance to do with as they chose. They chose mainly to buy beer and ribs, and a monster Dodge 4x4 that they customized to within an inch of its life. Next to their mother, and each other, it was their most cherished possession on earth.

It was this truck that Willis and Harding had just busted up with their shotguns.

"Wow," said Jackie Garner, because it was he who had been sitting by the side of the road, waiting for the Fulcis to finish their business in the woods, "you guys are so screwed."

Thus it was that when Harding turned around he saw two very large and very irate men emerging from the woods. One was hurriedly zipping up his fly. The other was staring unhappily at the truck. Their faces, which tended toward redness even at times of relative calm, had assumed the complexion of a pair of mutant plums. To Harding, they looked like trolls dressed in polyester, twin refrigerators in big-man pants and jackets. They couldn't even walk properly, they were so wide. Instead, they shambled from side to side, like wind-up robots. The sight of the two men lumbering in their direction was so confusing to Harding and Willis that it took them a moment or two to react, so that Harding was still raising his shotgun when Tony Fulci's fist connected with his face, breaking a number of bones simultaneously and sending him flying backward into Willis, who at that moment had lifted his own weapon and was about to fire. The shot tore through Harding and killed him instantly, even as Jackie Garner rose up and clubbed Willis across the back of the head with the butt of a pistol. Paulie then finished the job by pounding on Willis some more, until he was on the verge of departing this life and following his partner to his final reward, at which point Paulie desisted because his hand hurt.

Tony rounded on Jackie Garner.

"You was supposed to watch the fucking truck, Jackie," he said.

"I *was* watching the truck. They asked me to move it, but you had the keys. I didn't know they were going to start shooting it up."

"You still ought to have said something to them."

"I tried to say something."

"Yeah? Well it wasn't the right thing." Tony reached out and yanked the candy bar wrapper from Jackie's pocket. "How come you got time to finish a Three Musketeers bar but you ain't got time to watch the truck? You can't do both at once? I mean, the fuck, Jackie? You know, it's just—the fuck."

Jackie assumed a conciliatory pose and tone. "I'm sorry, Tony," he said. "I don't think they were reasonable men. You can't talk to unreasonable men."

"Well then, you ought not to have talked to them. You ought to have killed them."

"I can't just go killing people over a truck."

"It wasn't *a* truck. It was *our* truck."

His brother was tenderly stroking the hood of the truck and shaking his head. With a last despairing look at Jackie, Tony went over to join him.

"How bad does it look?"

"Upholstery's ripped to pieces, Tony. There's some holes to the paintwork, too. Lights are shot. It's a mess." He was on the verge of tears.

Tony patted his brother on the shoulder.

"We'll fix her up. Don't worry. We'll make her as good as new."

"Yeah?" Paulie looked up hopefully.

"Better than new. That right, Jackie?"

Jackie, sensing that the storm was already blowing over, offered his support for this view.

"If anyone can do it, you guys can."

Paulie got into the cab, having first carefully wiped it clear of glass, and started the truck. He let it run for a minute until he was satisfied that no damage had been done to the engine. Tony stood beside Jackie. Willis was still breathing, but only barely. Tony stared down at him. Jackie thought that he looked like he wanted to finish the job.

"You think Parker will be pissed at us?" he said.

The Fulcis admired Parker. They didn't want him to be angry.

"No," said Jackie. "I don't think he'll even be surprised."

Tony brightened. He and Paulie dumped Harding's body in the back of the dead men's pickup, then tied Willis's hands and legs with baling wire that they found in the cab and left him, unconscious, beside his dead colleague. Jackie then drove the truck into the woods and left it there, out of sight of the road.

"You think those guys were related?" Paulie asked his brother, as they waited for Jackie to return. "They looked like they was related."

"Maybe," said Tony.

"Pity they was such assholes," said Paulie.

"Yeah," said Tony. "Pity."

There was a radio on the dashboard of the truck. It crackled into life just as Jackie Garner finished hiding the truck in the woods.

"Willis," said a voice. "Willis, you there. Over."

Jackie nearly didn't answer it, then decided, aw, why not? He'd seen movies in which people found out the bad guy's plans by pretending to be someone else on a phone or a radio. He didn't see why it couldn't work on this occasion.

"This is Willis. Over."

There was a pause before the reply came.

"Willis?"

"Yeah, it's me. Over."

"Who is this?"

Dammit, thought Jackie, *this is harder than it looks in the movies. I ought to learn to leave well enough alone.*

"Sorry," he said. "Wrong number."

After all, there didn't seem to be anything else to say. He put the radio down, then hurried back to join the Fulcis. They looked up in surprise at the sight of Jackie running.

"Time to go," said Jackie. "Company's coming."

CHAPTER TWENTY-ONE

THEY DIDN'T DIE.

That was the first thing that struck Angel once they had made it to the trees: they were still alive. Running across the stretch of ground between the garage and the forest had been one of the most terrifying experiences of his life. All the time, he had been waiting for the moment of impact, the second when his body would buck as the first shot struck him, the sensation like a hard punch from a seasoned fighter, to be followed by searing pain and then . . . What? Death, either instant or slow. Another wound, Louis dragging him across the damp grass as he bled slickly, leaving a dark line as the life flowed from him, knowing that this time there would be no second chances, that he would die here, and Louis might die alongside him?

And so he had run hard, fighting the instinct to make himself as small as he could, knowing that to do so would slow him down. Be smaller, or be faster, that was the choice. In the end, he had opted for speed, every muscle in his body tense, his face contorted in expectation of the bullets that must inevitably begin to fly. He knew that he would be hit before he heard the shot that had taken him, so the silence, broken only by the sounds of breathing and footfalls, was of no consolation.

Both men zigzagged as they crossed the open ground, altering their pace and direction unexpectedly to throw off any shooters. The tree line began to loom closer, so close that, even in the murk, Angel could pick out details of bark and leaves. Farther back, the forest faded into shadows and gloom. There could be any number of men in there waiting for them, drawing a bead on the moving targets or holding their aim on a single spot, waiting for the target to come to them. Perhaps Angel would see the muzzle flash in the shadows before he died, the last flicker of light before the final darkness to come.

Fifteen feet. Ten. Five. Suddenly, they were among the trees. They dropped to the ground among the bushes, then crawled slowly away from where they had landed, careful to make as little noise as possible, avoiding undergrowth that might move and give away their positions. Angel glanced at Louis, who was about ten feet to his right. Louis raised a palm, indicating that he should stop. Something flew high above their heads in the trees, but neither man lifted his eyes to follow its progress. Instead, they waited, their attention fixed on the forest before them, their sight now adjusted to the darkness.

"They didn't shoot," said Angel. "How come they didn't shoot?"

"I don't know."

Louis searched the woods for movement, for any sign that they were being watched. He found nothing, but he knew that there were men out there somewhere. They were being toyed with.

He indicated that they should move forward. Using the trees as cover, they made slow, careful progress, each taking his turn to move, then pausing to cover the advance of the other, conscious that they needed to watch not just what lay ahead of them, but what might appear from behind. They saw nothing. The forest appeared to be clear, but neither man fooled himself into thinking that this meant their presence was unremarked. The bodies had been left in the trunk of their car for them to find, and the car itself had been put beyond use. A message had been sent. They were alive, but only at the whim of others.

Louis thought again of the woman at the window. Was it too much of a coincidence that she should have appeared at just the moment that he and Angel had fixed their sights upon the house? Perhaps they had been permitted to see her, and then they had responded exactly as anticipated: they had aborted their plan and returned to their vehicle, but by then the trap had been sprung. Now they had no choice but to keep moving and wait to see how events played out, so they continued through the forest, never allowing their guard to relax even slightly, constantly turning, watching, listening. They were exhausted by the time they had gone only three-quarters of a mile, but by then the trees had begun to thin, and there was open ground visible in front of them. It sloped upward to the inner ring road. Beyond it was more forest.

They stopped while they were still hidden, the road a raised spine before them. They could see no sign of movement upon it. Louis sniffed the air, trying to pick up any hint of cigarette smoke or food that might have carried on the breeze, indicating the presence of men nearby. There was none.

He and Angel were almost within touching distance.

"I go on three, you go on four," he whispered. The slight delay would make them harder targets if the road was being watched, the second man distracting from the first, sowing just enough confusion to give them an edge. He raised his right index and middle fingers, spreading them apart to form a V. "I go left, you go right. Don't stop until you get to the trees."

Angel nodded. They stayed low until they reached the edge of the forest, then Angel watched Louis's lips make the count. One. Two.

Three.

Louis sprinted for the road. A second later Angel was moving, veering away from his partner, zigzagging once again but not as violently as before, intent only on getting across the open road, where he would be most vulnerable, as quickly as possible.

They did not even make it to where the ground began to rise. The first shot sent a spume of dirt into the air a couple of inches from Angel's feet. The second and third struck the road itself, and then the scattered shots became a fusillade, forcing the two men back into the forest. They flattened themselves on the ground, and returned fire with the Steyrs, aiming at the muzzle flashes, keeping to short bursts in order to conserve their ammunition. Louis saw a figure running low, wearing a green combat jacket. He fired, but the man kept moving. He was beyond the limited range of the guns.

"Stop firing," he told Angel after each of them had exhausted a magazine, and instantly Angel did as he was told, reloading with his face pressed hard against the ground.

The shooting from the other side of the road did not cease, but neither did the shots draw any closer. Instead, the shooters seemed happy to knock bark from the trees behind them, too far over their heads to do any damage as long as they stayed down, or to send clouds of dust and gravel spurting from the surface of the road. Slowly,

Angel and Louis moved back into the cover of the trees.

Only then did the gunfire stop, although their ears still rang from the noise. They could see them now: a line of three men in hooded ponchos, barely visible in the woods on the other side of the road. One held his rifle at port arms while the others leaned against the trees to his left and right, rifles at their shoulders, sighting down the barrel at their targets. They did not seem troubled that Angel and Louis could see them. Then more men appeared from the north and south, following the road, and took up positions among the trees. Some of them even seemed to be smiling. It was a game, and they were winning. Angel dropped the Steyr and raised his Glock, but Louis reached out and indicated that he should hold his fire.

"No," he said.

They've strung themselves out along the road, thought Louis. *They took note of where we came in, then made an educated guess at where we'd come out. The line might have been thinner a little farther to the east or west, but they knew that they could reinforce it quickly.*

From somewhere on the other side of the road, he heard the crackle of a radio before it was lost in the sound of an approaching vehicle. A flatbed truck appeared from the south and stopped thirty or forty feet away from where

Angel and Louis knelt. They could see the shapes of two men in the cab. The truck idled. Nobody moved.

"What the hell is this?" asked Angel.

But Louis did not reply. He was performing calculations in his mind: times, distances, weapons. He tried to work out their chances of killing the two men in the truck if they used the cover of the forest to work their way south. They were good, but the chances of getting away from the pursuers who would inevitably follow were less favorable: close to zero, he reckoned.

And yet this couldn't go on indefinitely. They were being contained for a purpose. He wondered if there were men already moving in from behind, cutting them off. They were like foxes fleeing the hunters only to find that the entrance to their den had been sealed, forcing them to turn and face the dogs.

"We go back," he said.

"What?"

"They've closed off the road, for now. They also know where we're at, and that's not good. We use the forest while we can. There's a house to the northeast. It was on the satellite photographs. Could be we can lay our hands on a car or a truck there, or at least a phone."

"We could call the cops to come get us," said Angel. "Tell them we came here to kill someone by mistake."

Rain began to fall, large drops that made a slapping noise upon the leaves above them. Even though the sun had now almost risen, the sky above them remained cloudy and dark. The rain fell harder and faster, quickly soaking them to the skin, but the men watching from the woods did not move. The rain slid from their slickers and ponchos. They had been prepared for rain. They had been prepared for everything. Slowly, Louis and Angel retreated into the trees.

There was massive internal bleeding. His brain swelled inside his skull, causing more hemorrhaging. They fought for him, trying to prevent herniation, for that would be the end of him. They removed bone fragments, and a clot, and the bullet. Finally, all of their work would leave only the faintest of scars, hidden by his hair.

And while they battled to save him, Louis sat by a lake, surrounded by trees. Across the water, he could see the house in which he had grown up. It was empty now, fallen into ruin. It was no longer home. He could not go back there, so there was no life within its walls. There was no life anywhere. The woods were quiet, and no fish swam in the lake. He sat in the dead place, and he waited.

After a time, a man emerged from the darkness of the forest to the east. His face was gone, and his teeth were bared in his ruined skull. He had no eyes with which to see, but he turned his head toward Louis. The terrible wounds made him look as though he were grinning. Perhaps he was. Deber had always been grinning, even when he killed Louis's mother.

To the west, a light appeared, and the Burning Man took his place by the water, his mouth forming words, speaking soundlessly to his son of rage and wrath.

North: the house. South: Louis. East: Deber. West: the Burning Man. Compass points.

But Louis was not the southern point. He heard footsteps behind him, and a hand gently brushed the back of his neck. He tried to turn, but he could not.

And his grandmother's voice whispered: "These are not the only choices."

It was the beginning of the end, the seed that would lead to the slow flowering of a conscience.

The wound took a long time to heal. The bullet had penetrated his skull, but had not passed into his brain. His mother had always told him he had a hard head. Even after his survival was assured, he had trouble forming certain words and distinguishing colors, and his vision was blurred for months. He was tormented by phantom sounds, and by pains in his limbs. Gabriel was tempted to cut him loose, but Louis was special. He had been the youngest of Gabriel's recruits, and he still had the potential to exceed all of Gabriel's expectations. He responded quickly to therapy, in part because of his own natural strength, but also, Gabriel knew, out of a desire for revenge. Bliss had disappeared, but they would find him. They could not let what he had done go unpunished.

It took ten years to track him down. When he was found, Louis was sent to execute him.

He was living in Amsterdam as a Dutch national, under the name van Mierlo. Some surgery had been performed on him; not much, but just enough on the nose, eyes, and chin to ensure that if any of his old acquaintances crossed his path they would fail to recognize him immediately. It was all about buying time: hours, minutes, even seconds. Louis knew that Bliss would have spent the years since the Lowein incident preparing for the day when he might be found. He would be ready to run at any time. He would know his environment intimately, so that the slightest change in routine would alert him. He would always be armed. He would own a car, kept in a secure private parking garage not far from where he lived, but would rarely use it. It would be kept for emergencies, in case the airport or the trains were closed to him for any reason, or when alternative travel arrangements were denied him.

He stuck to taxis, catching them on the street instead of calling for them in advance, and never taking the first that came along, always waiting for the second, third, or even fourth. Once each month, he visited his lawyer in Rotterdam, taking the train from Centraal. He was renting a four-story building on Van Woustraat, but appeared to have done nothing to the first floor, living on the second and third. Louis guessed that both the first and fourth floors would be booby-trapped, and that a bolt hole of some kind existed in Bliss's living quarters, providing access to one of the adjoining buildings.

Louis wondered if Bliss knew that he was still alive. Probably, he thought. In the event that he was found, Bliss would expect Louis himself to come. He would be anticipating a knife, a gun to the head, just as Deber had so many years before. Perhaps he even feared an attempt to capture him and return him to the United States for Gabriel to deal with as he saw fit. But Louis would be present; of that Bliss was certain, because Bliss did not know Louis, not as Gabriel did and not, in his final, agonized days, as Deber had.

Louis left the Netherlands without Bliss ever catching sight of him, and another man took his place for the final days, but during Louis's time there he tracked Bliss, using Gabriel's assistance as well as his own initiative. They found bank accounts. The office of his lawyer was searched. Business interests, and properties owned, were identified. Even his car was found.

Then, during Louis's final days in Amsterdam, relations between the Dutch government and the transport unions deteriorated. A series of strikes was anticipated. One week later, Bliss went to his garage to pick up his car in order to drive to Rotterdam. There was a cassette player in the dashboard. He turned on the stereo as he maneuvered out of his space, the nose of the car angling upward with the slope, but instead of the anticipated Rolling Stones he heard a woman's voice. Connie Francis, he thought. It's Connie Francis singing "Who's Sorry Now?"

But I don't own any Connie Francis.

Oh, you clever boy.

He already had one foot on the ground when the mercury tilt switch activated, and the car, and Bliss, were engulfed in flame.

• • •

"He survived," Gabriel told Louis. "You should have found another way."

"That way seemed appropriate. Are you sure he's not dead?"

"There were no remains found in the car, but fragments of skin and clothing had adhered to the garage floor."

"How much skin?"

"A great deal, apparently. He must have been in considerable pain. We traced him to a doctor's surgery on Rokin. The doctor was dead when we found him, of course."

"If Bliss lives, he'll come back at us someday."

"Perhaps. Then again, it may be that all that is left is a charred husk with the man we knew trapped inside."

"I could find him again."

"No, I don't think so. He has money, and connections. This time, he'll bury himself deep. I think we shall have to wait for him to come to us, if he comes at all. Patience, Louis, patience . . ."

CHAPTER TWENTY-TWO

BLISS SAT IN THE dining room of Arthur Leehagen's house, the table at his back and an empty Hardigg Storm case at his feet. He wore a raincoat, and he held a soft waterproof hat in his hands. In front of him was a window, but until a short time before he had been able to see nothing through the glass and had, instead, focused entirely on his own reflection. He was not weary. He had come so far, and the moment for which he had long wished was almost upon him.

He recalled those first hours, when he was convinced that all of the skin had been seared from his body, the agony as he had stumbled into the night, his mind clouded entirely by pain. It had taken a great effort of will to compartmentalize his suffering, to clear a tiny corner of his consciousness so that reason could take over from instinct. He had made it to a phone, and that had been enough. He had money, and with money you could buy anything, if you had enough of it: a hiding place, transport, treatment for one's wounds, a new face, a new identity.

A chance to live.

But such pain. It had never gone away, not truly. It was said that one forgot the intensity of one's former agonies as time went on, but that was not true for Bliss. The memory of the pain that he endured had been seared both in and on him, in his spirit and on his body, and even though the physical reality of it had faded, the memory of it remained sharp and clear. Its ghost was enough to evoke all that had once been, and he had used that capacity to relive it in order to bring him to this place.

He heard footsteps behind him. Michael Leehagen spoke, but Bliss did not turn around to acknowledge his presence.

"There's been contact," Leehagen said.

"Where?"

"The inner ring, close by the southern intersection."

"Did your father's men do as they were told?"

There was a pause before Michael answered. Bliss knew that the reminder of his father's authority would rankle. It served no purpose other than to satisfy Bliss. It was a reminder that Michael had overstepped his limits in ordering the attack on Gabriel. Bliss had not forgotten it. There would be a reckoning once the job was done. Benton, the man who had pulled the trigger, would be the sacrificial lamb on the altar of Bliss's atonement for the shooting. It was for Bliss, and no other, to decide if Gabriel lived or died. Bliss understood that Gabriel could not have let his treachery go unpunished, and he bore him no animosity for the long hunt that had ensued. It was Louis that Bliss wanted. Louis had burned him. Louis had made it personal.

"They forced them back. They didn't aim to kill."

Bliss blew air through his nose, like an amused bull. "Even if they didn't, they probably wouldn't have hit anything, unless it was in error."

"They're good men."

"No, they're not. They're rural thugs. They're farmboys and squirrel eaters."

Michael didn't dispute the accuracy of the description.

"There's something else. We lost contact with two of our people, Willis and Harding, on the outer ring. A stranger came on their radio."

"Then I suggest you deal with the problem."

"We're doing that now. I just thought you should know."

Bliss stood, turning now for the first time but still ignoring the man who stood at the door. On the table behind him, resting on its Harris bipod, was a Chandler XM-3 sniper rifle with a titanium picatinny rail and recoil lug, and a

Nightforce NXS day optic sight. The Hardigg case also contained a universal night sight, which Bliss had not fitted in the hope that there would be enough light for him to track his prey. He stared through the window at the spreading dawn, masked somewhat by the rain that had begun to fall. Day was coming in earnest.

Beside the Chandler was a second rifle, a Surgeon XL. Bliss had been torn between the two, although "torn" was an exaggeration of the relative equanimity with which he now made his choice. Unusually for a man in his particular line of work, Bliss had no excessive fondness for guns. He had encountered those for whom the tools of their trade exerted an almost sexual attraction, but he felt no kinship with them. On the contrary: he considered their sensual regard for their weapons as a form of weakness, a symptom of a deeper malaise. In Bliss's experience, they were the kind of men who gave amusing names to their sexual organs, and who sought a release from killing similar to that which they found in the act of congress. Such beliefs were, for Bliss, the height of foolishness.

The XL was a .338 Lapua Magnum, with a Schmidt & Bender 5-25 x 56 scope mounted on its rail and a multiport jet muzzle brake to tame the recoil. The stock was Fiberglas, and altogether the gun weighed just slightly more than twenty pounds. He lifted the rifle, put his left arm through the sling, and let his left shoulder take the weight. He had always preferred his right, but since that day in Amsterdam he had learned to adapt in this matter as in so much else.

"You're going now?"

"Yes."

"How will you find them?"

"I'll smell them."

Leehagen's son wondered if the strange, scarred man was joking, and decided he was not. He said nothing more as he watched Bliss leave the house and walk across the lawn in search of his prey.

IV

For some of these,
It could not be the place
It is without blood.
These hunt, as they have done
But with claws and teeth grown perfect,

More deadly than they can believe.

—JAMES DICKEY (1923–97), "THE HEAVEN OF ANIMALS"

CHAPTER TWENTY-THREE

THEIR RETREAT FROM THE road was conducted in the same way as their approach to it had been: steady progress using the trees for cover, one moving while the other kept vigil, both constantly watching, listening. They waited for the hooded figures to advance upon them from the road, judging the distance so that any pursuers would be within range of the Steyrs, but they did not come.

The rain didn't look like it would ease up anytime soon. Angel was shivering, and his back hurt. The pain of his old wounds tended to come and go, but exposure to cold or damp, or long periods spent walking or running, always exacerbated it. Now he could feel a tightness where the grafts had taken, as though his skin were being stretched too tightly across his back.

As for Louis, he kept returning to the standoff at the road. It was clear that Leehagen's men wanted to keep them contained, and to kill them only as a last resort. Yet he couldn't see a way that he and Angel would be allowed to leave here alive. They had been drawn north for a purpose, and that purpose was to wipe them from the face of the earth. The Endalls had been killed, and Louis could only assume that the other teams had also been targeted. They were all good at what they did, but they had not expected that their every move would be known in advance. Leehagen had second-guessed them at every turn. He had anticipated their coming, and the presence of Loretta Hoyle at the house suggested that her father had been involved in the betrayal.

But the task of finishing them off had not been assigned to the men on the road, or to others of their kind. It seemed to have been gifted to another; it remained to be seen who that might be, but Louis had his suspicions.

To the southwest lay the cattle pens, the barn containing their car, and Leehagen's house. Was that where they were supposed to have died, taken unawares as they entered the property, believing their presence to be unknown to those sleeping within? If so, then their intended executioner had been waiting there for them, and would ultimately have to come after them if they did not go to him. Louis had almost abandoned any intention of trying to get to Leehagen. He would be protected, and the element of surprise had been lost, especially as it seemed that it had never been there to begin with. But now he had begun to reconsider. To move on Leehagen would be unexpected at least. They were being contained primarily to the east, where the main road lay, their captors anticipating that they would try to make a break for it and find a way out of the area. Louis didn't know how realistic their chances were on that score. It was a lot of ground to cover on foot, and even if they found a car and tried to bust out of the cordon, they were looking at a well-armed and mobile pursuit, and a series of raised roads that could easily be blocked. Their best chance in terms of transport lay in taking out one of the truck teams and hoping communications weren't so tight that any break in protocol or routine would be instantly noticed.

But if they went west, to Leehagen, they would be effectively trapping themselves between two lines: the men to the east, and whatever protection Leehagen had near the house, with the lake behind it cutting off any further retreat, unless they could steal a boat, assuming they could find their way through the rocks Leehagen had sown on the lake bed, and also assuming they could hold off Leehagen's men, because they sure as hell weren't going to be able to kill them all.

The farmhouse in the woods, recalled from Louis's examination of the satellite images, presented another option. They could call for help, barricading themselves inside in the hope of holding off their pursuers until rescue came. There were favors owed: a chopper could be on the ground in less than an hour. It would be a hot landing, but the men upon whom Louis might call would be used to that.

They came to the house. It was an old two-story structure painted in red, although the color had faded over time to a washed-out brown, so that it looked as though the dwelling was made of iron that had begun to rust, like a fragment of a ship that had come apart from the main structure and been left to rot almost within sight of water. The property was accessed by a dirt trail that hadn't been visible on the satellite photographs due to tree cover, although Louis had guessed that there had to be a road somewhere. There was no grass in the yard. Instead, it had been turned into a vegetable garden. To their right, chickens clucked invisibly in their hutches, surrounded by a wire pen to keep out predators. To their left stood an old woodshed, its door open and blocks already stacked and covered within in preparation for winter. Behind it, white smoke gusted from a green, wood-burning furnace.

There were lights inside the house, and more smoke rose from the chimney. An old truck was parked at the back door, its bed a wooden cage. It reeked of animals' excrement.

"How do you want to do this?" asked Angel, but the question was answered for him. The back door opened and a woman appeared on the sheltered porch. She looked as if she might have been in her forties, but her clothes were those of someone much older and there was too much gray in her hair for her years. Her face spoke of hard living, of disappointments, of hopes and dreams that had crumbled to dust in her hands.

She looked at the two men, taking in their weapons, and spoke.

"What do you want here?" she asked.

"Shelter, ma'am," said Louis. "The use of a telephone. Some help."

"You always come asking for help with guns in your hands?"

"No, ma'am."

"You could say we're victims of circumstance," said Angel.

"Well, I can't aid you. Go on now, you'd best be on your way."

Louis had to admire her courage. There weren't many women who'd tell two armed men to be about their business.

"I'm sorry, ma'am," he said. "I just don't think you understand what's happening here."

"We understand fine," said a voice from behind him. Louis didn't move. He knew what was coming. Seconds later, he felt the twin barrels nudge him from behind.

"You know what that was, son?"

"Yes, I do."

"Good. Let your gun fall down now. Your friend can do the same."

Louis did as he was told, allowing the Steyr to drop but letting his right hand drift toward the Glock at his waist. Small fingers appeared and snatched the Steyr away, then did the same with Angel's weapon.

"Your hand moves another inch, son, and I guarantee that you won't live to feel the next raindrop on your face."

Louis's hand froze. He was patted down hard, and the Glock was taken from him. The same voice asked Angel where his pistol was at, and Angel answered quickly and honestly. Glancing to his left, Louis saw a tall young man frisk Angel and take the gun from his waist. They were now completely unarmed.

He heard footsteps backing off behind him. Slowly, he turned. Angel was already looking at the two men who had emerged from behind the woodshed. One was probably in his sixties, wearing a wide-brimmed leather hat to protect him from the rain. The younger man, the one who had frisked them, was in his late twenties, and was bareheaded. His hair was close shaven, and the rainwater ran like tears down the cheeks of his intensely pale, blue-veined face. His left eye appeared to have no retina. It was entirely white, like his skin, as though something poisonous had seeped from the latter into the former, draining it of color. Both were armed, the older man with a shotgun, the younger with a varmint gun. Between them stood a little girl of no more than seven or eight who was dressed, incongruously, in a Minnie Mouse raincoat and bright red boots. The guns recently taken from Angel and Louis lay between her feet. She didn't seem troubled by the guns, or by the fact that the two men with her were pointing weapons at the visitors.

"You ought to have stayed back in New York," said the older man.

"How do you know we're from New York?" said Angel.

"Rumors. They were waiting for you to come. It was just a matter of when."

" 'They'?"

"Mr. Leehagen and his men."

"You work for Leehagen?"

"Everyone around here works for Mr. Leehagen, one way or another. If he don't pay you directly, then you live by what he pays others." He looked down at the little girl. "Go to your grandma, honey."

The little girl ran behind the legs of the younger man and danced her way to the shelter of the house, splashing through the puddles that were forming on the uneven ground. She climbed the steps to the porch and stood beside her grandmother, who put a protective hand around her granddaughter's shoulders. The girl smiled up at the older woman, then clapped her hands once with pleasure and excitement. Angel wondered who her father was. It didn't seem to be the younger of the two men, the pale creature with the washed-out eye. She was too pretty to be his, too vibrant. He looked like a corpse that hadn't yet realized it was dead.

"Thomas," said the woman at the door to the older man. There was a note of what might almost have been pleading in her voice. It struck Angel that she wasn't intervening out of any great concern for the two men who had trespassed onto the property. She just didn't want her husband to get into trouble by spilling blood.

"Just take her inside," said Thomas. "We'll deal with this."

The woman grabbed the girl by the hand and pulled her into the house. The girl didn't seem happy to miss the show, and it took an extra yank on her arm before she crossed the threshold and the door closed behind them. Even then, Angel could see her staring yearningly back at him, disappointment creasing her features.

"We don't want any trouble," said Angel.

"Really?" said the man named Thomas. He sounded skeptical, and tired. "It's a little late for that, don't you think?"

"We just want to get out of here alive," said Angel.

"I don't doubt that, son. My guess is you're going to have some problems on that score."

"You could help us."

"I could, that's true. I could, but I won't."

"Why not?"

"Because then I'd die in your place, assuming you managed to get out of this mess you're in, which I don't think is going to happen. Mr. Leehagen places a high premium on loyalty."

"Those men out there are going to kill us."

"You reap what you sow. I'm sure that's in the Bible, somewhere. My wife could tell you. She reads on it some, when the mood strikes her. Never spoke much to me."

He shifted his grip on the shotgun, and Louis tensed. Angel could sense him getting ready to spring, and Thomas seemed to sense it, too. The twin mouths of the shotgun steadied themselves on Louis. The wind changed direction, bringing the stink of whatever animals Thomas had transported to their doom in his truck to Angel, the smell of their dying as they voided themselves in fear.

"No," said Thomas, simply. "You do, and I'll be feeding your body to the hogs before day's end."

Hogs. Now Angel could hear them snuffling and grunting somewhere behind the house.

"You helped them make their movie," he said.

Thomas shifted uneasily. "I don't know nothing about that."

"How did they do it? A model? They get someone to lie in the mud and pretend to be eaten, fix it all up later in an editing suite. You tell us: how did they do it?"

"I don't know, and I don't care," said Thomas. "I got nothing against you personally, and I don't want to have to kill you here. Mr. Leehagen wouldn't like it. He's got other plans for you, I guess. Go on, now. You get away from here, and you don't come back. Your guns can stay with me. I don't trust you to keep your word when I let you go."

Louis spoke: "Without weapons, we don't stand a chance."

"You didn't stand a chance anyway."

"You seem to know a lot about it."

The old man smiled. It wasn't a malicious smile. Instead, there was a measure of pity in it.

"You came up here all primed to cause some hurt, and now the tables have been turned on you. What did you think would happen? That there'd be some old man in a big house and you'd kill him without anyone even raising a finger to stop you? You listen to me: I got no love for that sonofabitch, and I think the world would have been a better place if he'd never been born into it, but you made a mistake coming up here, and you'll live or die by that mistake. Like I said, you'll reap what you've sown." He gestured with the shotgun, indicating the woods through which they had come. "That way lies the road, and maybe your way out of here. Don't come back here. You do, and we'll kill you. I have my family to consider, Leehagen or no Leehagen."

"I believe you," said Louis.

"Good."

The two men stepped back as Angel and Louis moved away, the barrels of the guns never wavering. When they were almost out of sight, the old man called out.

"Hey," he said.

They stopped.

"You said that I knew a lot about this. I don't. I heard someone shoot his mouth off in a bar two nights ago, and then we was warned to keep an eye out for strangers. I figured what was coming. Those men out there, they don't want to kill you. They're saving you for someone else."

"Who?" asked Angel.

The old man shrugged. "Something about happiness," he said. "That's what they said."

"Happiness?"

"No, not happiness," said Thomas. His brow furrowed as he tried to remember the right word. "Bliss. That was it. They said bliss was coming your way."

Louis did not speak as they walked away. His arrogance, his anger, had brought them to this. Bliss. He looked at Angel trudging alongside him, lost in his own pain. The shorter man glanced up, and their eyes met. There seemed to be no blame in them, no wrath. This was what Louis had needed to do, and Angel had stood alongside him, despite his own reservations. If that was not love, what was? Suddenly Louis's feelings of warmth toward his partner were dispelled.

"You're an asshole," said Angel. "You know that?"

"Yeah, I know it."

"Good. I'm cold and I'm wet and I'm going to be killed by a man who collects other killers like scalps, and it's all your fault."

"I was just thinking that you hadn't blamed me for this. I was thinking how much I admired you for it."

"Are you out of your mind? Of course I blame you. And you can keep your admiration. I'd write that on your tombstone, but I'll be too dead to do it." Angel sneezed loudly. "Great. This is just great."

Louis looked at the sky. "Maybe it will stop raining."

"It's something to look forward to, I guess."

"We need guns."

"We'll have to kill someone to get them."

"We could go back and take them from the old man."

For a second or two, they considered it. They knew how it would play out. For all of the old man's bluster and the guns in their hands, he and his family would be no match for them. But there was a child in the house, and there had been something in Thomas's eyes that told Louis he would fight if they returned. There would be injuries, maybe even deaths. No, they would not go back there.

"They expect us to run, to try and break out of the cordon," said Louis. "They won't expect us to do what we came here to do."

"We try for Leehagen's house?"

"Yeah."

"In the absence of anything better, it sounds like a plan." Angel wrung rainwater from his jacket. "What are we going to do, drown him?"

"In the absence of anything better . . ."

They walked on.

"You really blame me for all this?" asked Louis, after a few minutes of silence had gone by.

Angel thought. "I blame myself."

Louis paused. "Is that true?"

"No," said Angel as he sneezed again. "I do blame you."

CHAPTER TWENTY-FOUR

WILLIE BREW AND THE Detective crossed the bridge and followed the road for a hundred yards or so until they came to an intersection. Well, you could call it an intersection, but as far as Willie was concerned it was two roads going exactly nowhere, one heading east to west, the other continuing south. Neither of them looked too inviting, but then any strip that didn't have a convenience store, a couple of fast-food outlets, and maybe a bar or two barely qualified as a road in Willie's book.

"Who are these guys, exactly?" asked Willie. The question had been troubling him since they had reached the bridge. He'd only been up in this godforsaken part of the world for an hour, and already he'd seen two dead bodies and, according to the Detective, the dead men had probably been on their side, which suggested to Willie that the odds in their favor had started to shrink. Now the rest of what passed for a rescue mission had disappeared, and the

Detective had appeared more disappointed than surprised at their absence. None of this was making Willie feel any more at ease, and he began to wonder if Arno hadn't been wise to stay where he was, and if he shouldn't have stayed right there with him.

At that moment, the biggest truck Willie had ever seen in his life appeared from the west. It was jet black, and its tires were so huge that even to stand on them and use them as a means of jumping to the ground was to risk breaking an ankle on impact. As it drew closer, Willie could see that the truck also seemed to be without its windshield, and both of its headlights were busted. The bench seats in the cab were big enough to seat four adults comfortably, but currently they seemed to be seating three men uncomfortably, especially since two of those men were wide enough to qualify as illegal structures if they stayed in the same place for too long. The man squashed between them, who was no Slim Jim himself, wore a look of beatific calm, as if this situation were not only familiar to him, but entirely welcome, despite the rain.

"Shit," said Willie, involuntarily. Suddenly, the Browning looked very small in his hand. The gun didn't look like it would have enough stopping power to make any of these men pause in their tracks. It would be like firing marshmallows at a trio of charging elephants.

"Relax," said the Detective. "They're with us."

He didn't sound particularly happy about it.

The truck came to a halt barely five feet from where they were. Until that point, it had been traveling so fast that Willie wasn't sure it was going to stop at all. Seen from up close, the two big guys looked mad as hell, and it seemed for a few crucial seconds that they were just going to drive right over the Mustang, crushing it beneath the wheels of their truck as they proceeded in the direction of whomever had incurred their wrath. Willie rated that particular individual's chances of survival at somewhere between minimal and extinct.

The Detective got out of the Mustang. Willie did likewise. The two big men climbed out of either side of the cab, using a footplate behind the wheels to jump down. Willie couldn't be certain, but he thought he felt the ground shake when they landed.

"Meet Tony and Paulie Fulci," said the Detective softly. "The guy in the middle is Jackie Garner. He's the sane one, although it's a relative term."

Willie hadn't heard of Jackie Garner, but he'd heard of the Fulcis. Angel had spoken of them in the tones usually reserved for forces of nature like hurricanes or earthquakes, the message being that, in common with such meteorological and seismic events, it was a pretty good idea to stay as far away from them as possible. As things stood, Willie was not far away from the Fulcis at all, and therefore had somehow entered a mobile disaster zone.

"What happened to your truck?" asked the Detective.

"Some guys happened," said Paulie. He jerked a thumb in Jackie's direction. "He didn't help, though."

"We've been through all this," said Jackie. "It was a misunderstanding."

"Yeah, well . . ." said Paulie. Clearly, the whole affair still rankled.

"Where are the guys in question?" asked the Detective.

There was some awkward shuffling of feet.

"One of them ain't doing so good," said Tony.

"How not good?"

"He's out cold. I ain't so sure he's going to wake up again either. I hit him kind of hard."

"And the others?"

"Other," corrected Jackie. "There were two of them."

"He ain't doing so good either," said Tony. His embarrassment deepened. "Actually, he ain't never going to do good again. It was kind of an accident," he concluded lamely.

To his credit, Willie thought, the Detective maintained an impassive façade.

"Did you find out anything useful from them before they started not doing so good?" he asked.

Tony shook his head and stared at the ground.

"We know how they're staying in contact, though," said Jackie Garner. "They got radios in their trucks." He thought for a moment. "There's some bad news there, too, though," he continued.

"Yeah?" said the Detective wearily.

"I answered one of their calls."

"You've got to be kidding."

"I thought I could find stuff out."

"And did you?"

"I found out that I'm not a mimic."

"Funny, Jackie."

"Sorry, man. I wasn't thinking."

"So they know we're here."

"I guess so."

The Detective turned away from the three men. Willie said nothing. It was like being back in Nam. This was another fuck-up, playing out right before his eyes. He was starting to feel weary now, and he was drenched. He also assumed that things were going to get worse before they got better.

Then they heard it, the noise breaking the awkward silence. There was a vehicle approaching. Instantly, the Detective began to move.

"Willie, get the Mustang out of sight," he said. "Take it toward the bridge. Paulie, get in the cab of the truck. Head east, but slowly. Let them see you. Jackie, Tony, into the trees with me. If it looks like they're on their way to church, don't shoot."

Nobody argued with him or questioned him. They did exactly as they were told. Willie got into the Mustang, turned it in a tight circle, and headed back the way he had come, pausing only when the intersection was out of sight. Then he killed the engine and waited. He was struggling to breathe, even though he hadn't exerted himself physically. He wondered if he was having a heart attack. He flexed his left arm to make sure that it wasn't going numb. He was sure that was one of the signs. The arm seemed to be moving okay. He adjusted the rearview mirror and kept his eyes on the road behind him. The Browning now lay on the passenger seat. He had one hand on the ignition key, the other hand on the stick. Anyone came around that corner that he didn't recognize and he was out of there. He would make a run for it. There would be nothing else for it.

Then the shooting started.

The Detective had taken up a position to the west of the road, Tony Fulci and Jackie to the east. A Bronco came into view, and the three men aimed their weapons. At the sight of Paulie pulling away in the big truck, the driver of the Bronco increased his speed. There was a man beside him in the passenger seat, a shotgun held across his body. A third man stood in the bed of the truck, leaning on the roof of the cab with a rifle in his hands as he tried to draw a bead on Paulie's rear window.

There was no warning. Two holes appeared almost simultaneously in the Bronco's windshield and the driver slumped over the wheel, his head striking the glass and smearing the blood that had splashed upon it. Instantly the truck began to swerve to the right. The passenger leaned over to try to arrest the turn, while the shooter in the bed held on to the crash bar for dear life. More shots came, pockmarking the windshield, and the truck veered off the road and crashed down the eastern slope. It struck a pine tree, the bull bars on the front minimizing the damage even as the rifleman was flung from the bed and landed heavily on the grass. He lay there, unmoving.

The Detective emerged from the cover of the trees first. Already, Tony and Jackie were running across the road to join him. He kept his gun fixed on the two men in the cab, but it was clear that both were already dead. The driver had been hit in the neck and chest. The passenger might have survived the initial gunfire, but he hadn't been wearing a belt when the truck hit the tree. He had been a big man, and the force of his head and body hitting the damaged windshield at speed had broken the glass, so that his upper body now lay on the hood of the truck while his right leg was tangled in the same belt that might have saved him.

The Detective walked to where Tony and Jackie were standing over the man on the ground. Jackie picked up the rifle and tossed it into the trees. The injured man was now moaning softly, and holding on to the top of his right leg. It was twisted at the knee, and his foot stood at an unnatural angle to the joint. The Detective winced at the sight. He knelt on the grass and leaned close to the man's ear.

"Hey," he said. "Can you hear me?"

The man nodded. His teeth were bared in agony.

"My leg—" he said.

"Your leg's broken. There's nothing we can do about it, not here."

"Hurts."

"I'll bet."

By now, Paulie had turned the truck around and was pulling up on the road above. The Detective indicated that he should stay where he was to watch the approaches, and Paulie acknowledged with a wave.

"You got anything in your truck you can give him for the pain?" the Detective asked Tony.

"There's some Jacks," said Tony. He thought for a moment. "And some pills and stuff. Doctors keep giving us so much, it's hard to keep track of it all. I'll go take a look in the glove compartment."

He lumbered off. The Detective returned his attention to the injured man.

"What's your name?"

"Fry." The man managed to gasp the word out. "Eddie Fry."

"Okay, Eddie, I want you to listen to me carefully. You're going to tell me exactly what's going on here, and then I'm going to give you something for the pain. If you don't tell me what I want to know, then one of these big men is going to stand on your leg. Do you understand?"

Fry nodded.

"We're looking for our friends. Two men, one black and one white. Where are they?"

Eddie Fry's upper body rocked back and forward, as if by doing so he could pump some of the pain from his leg. "They're in the woods," he said. "Last we heard, they were west of the inner road. We didn't see them. Our job was just to provide backup in case they made it through."

"They brought people with them. Two of them are dead at the bridge over there. What happened to the others?"

Fry was clearly reluctant to answer. The Detective turned to Jackie. "Jackie, step lightly on his foot."

"No!" Eddie Fry's hands were raised in supplication. "No, don't. They're dead. We didn't do it, but they're dead. I just work for Mr. Leehagen. I used to look after his cattle. I'm not a killer."

"You're trying to kill our friends, though."

Fry shook his head.

"We were told to keep them from leaving, but we weren't to hurt them. Please, my leg."

"We'll take care of it in a minute. Why weren't you supposed to kill them?"

Fry started to drift. The Detective slapped him sharply on the cheek.

"Answer me."

"Someone else." Fry's face was now contorted in agony, and sweat and rainwater mingled on his face. "It was someone else's job to kill them. That was the agreement."

"Whose job?"

"Bliss. Bliss is going to kill them."

"Who is Bliss?"

"I don't know! I swear to God I don't. I never even met him. He's in there, somewhere. He's going to hunt them down. Please, please, my leg . . ."

Willie Brew had joined them. He stood to one side, listening to what was being said, his face very white. Tony Fulci returned, carrying two Ziploc bags jammed with pharmaceuticals. He put them on the ground and began going through the blister packs and plastic bottles, examining the generic names and tossing aside those that he deemed of no use in the current situation.

"Bupirone: antianxiety," he said. "They never worked. Clozapine: antipsychotic. I don't even remember us taking those. Trazodone: antidepressant. Ziprasidone: 'nother antipsychotic.

Loxapine: antipsychotic. Man, it's like you can see a pattern . . ."

"You know, we don't have all day," said the Detective.

"I don't want to give him something that won't work," said Tony. He seemed, thought Willie, to be taking a certain amount of pride in his pharmaceutical knowledge.

"Tony, as far as I can tell, none of these things worked."

"Yeah, on *us.* He could be different. Here: flurazepam. That's a sedative, and there's some eszopiclone, too. Cocktail those." He produced a fifth of Jack Daniel's from his jacket pocket and handed it to the Detective along with four pills.

"That looks like a lot," said Jackie. "We don't want to kill him."

Willie looked at the dead men lying in the bloodstained cab, then back at Jackie.

"What?" said Jackie.

"Nothing," said Willie.

"It's not the same," said Jackie.

"What isn't?"

"Shooting someone, and poisoning him."

"I guess not," said Willie. He was now wishing he had never come. More blood, more bodies, a wounded man lying in agony on the grass. He had heard what Eddie Fry said: he wasn't a killer, he was just a farmhand pressed into service. Maybe Fry knew what others were trying to do, and for that he bore some responsibility, but he was out of his depth with men like the Detective. Fry and his friends were lambs to the slaughter. Willie hadn't expected it to be like this. He wasn't sure what he had expected, and he realized, once again, how naive he had been. He didn't belong in this situation any more than Fry did. Willie hadn't signed up to kill anyone, but men were dying now.

The Detective handed the tablets to Fry, then held the bottle steady so that he could wash them down with the Jack Daniel's. He left the bottle with the wounded man and walked over to the cab of the crashed truck. He opened the passenger door and removed the weapons, then found one of the radios. It appeared intact, but when he lifted it up the back came off and the ruined innards were exposed. He tossed it into the woods in disgust, then looked west.

"They're in there somewhere," he said. "The question is: how do we find them?"

CHAPTER TWENTY-FIVE

THE MAN LEANING ON the roof of the Ford Ranger was very wet. His name was Curtis Roundy, and if there was a stick being waved in his direction then five would get you twenty that Curtis would always find a way to grab the shitty end of it, or that was how it seemed to the man himself. No matter what lengths he went to in order to avoid getting himself into situations where his own personal comfort and satisfaction would have to be sacrificed for someone else's idea of the greater good, Curtis would inevitably end up holding a fork when soup fell from the sky, or experiencing the gentle trickle of urine down his back amid assurances that it was, in fact, rain. At least, he thought, as he stood with the binoculars pressed to his eyes and his feet squishing in his boots, this *was* just rain, and his poncho was keeping out some of it.

Nevertheless, it wasn't much consolation. He would have been a lot happier sitting in the cab instead of standing outside exposed to the elements, but Benton and Quinn weren't the sort of men who were open to reason or felt any great concern for the welfare of others. It didn't help that Curtis was younger than them by fifteen years and weighed a whole lot less than either of them, and was therefore pretty much their bitch in such situations. Of all the people that he might have been partnered with, Benton and Quinn were the worst. They were mean, petty, and unpredictable at the best of times, but Benton's experiences down in the city, and the reaction of Mr. Leehagen's son upon his return, had rendered him downright savage. He was popping pills for the pain in his shoulder and hand, and there had been an unpleasant confrontation with the man named Bliss, one that had resulted in Benton's being exiled to the hills, forced to take no further part in what was to come. Curtis had heard some of what was said, and had seen the way Bliss had looked at Benton once Benton had stormed out of the house. It wasn't over between them, not by a long distance, and Curtis, although he kept his opinion to himself, didn't rate Benton's chances of coming out best from any future encounter. Benton had been simmering about it ever since, and Curtis could almost hear him approaching the boil.

Edgar Roundy, Curtis's father, had worked in Mr. Leehagen's talc mine, and even though he had died riddled with tumors, he had never once blamed his employer for what had occurred. Mr.

Leehagen had put food on his table, a car in his drive, and a roof over his head. When the cancer took him, he put it down to bad luck. He wasn't a stupid man. He knew that working in a mine wasn't likely to lead to a long, happy life, didn't matter if it was talc, salt, or coal that was being dug out of the ground. When people started talking about suing Mr. Leehagen, Edgar Roundy would simply turn and walk away. He kept doing that until he could no longer walk at all, and then he died. In return for his loyalty, Mr. Leehagen had given Edgar's son a job that did not involve ingesting asbestos for a living. Edgar, were he still alive, would have been moved by the gesture.

Curtis was smart enough to know that he'd dodged a bullet when the mine closed and Mr. Leehagen had still seen fit to offer him some alternative form of employment. There were a lot of folk out there who had once worked for the Leehagens and were getting by on the kind of pensions that meant KFC family buckets and sawdust hamburgers were a dietary staple. He wasn't sure why fortune should have smiled on him and not on others, although one reason might have been the fact that old Mr. Leehagen, when his health was considerably better than it was now, had paid Mrs. Roundy an occasional recreational visit while her husband was sacrificing his life in the mine, cough by hacking cough, surrounded by filth and dust. Mr. Leehagen was lord of all that he surveyed, and he wasn't above invoking a version of *droit du seigneur,* that age-old perk of the ruling classes, if the mood struck him and there was an accommodating woman around. Curtis wasn't aware of Mr. Leehagen's former daytime visits, or had convinced himself that he wasn't, although men like Benton and Quinn weren't above bringing it up when they needed some amusement of their own. The first time they had done so, Curtis had responded to their goads by taking a swing at Benton, and had been beaten to within an inch of his life for his trouble. Strangely, Benton had respected him a little more as a consequence. He had told Curtis so, even as he was punching him repeatedly in the face.

Right now, Benton and Quinn were stink-ass drunk. Mr. Leehagen and his son wouldn't be pleased if they knew that they were drinking on the job. Michael Leehagen had stressed how important it was that the two men who were coming should be contained. Everyone needed to be alert, he had said, and everyone needed to follow orders. There would be bonuses all round once the job was done. Curtis didn't want to see his bonus jeopardized. Every cent mattered to him. He needed to get away from here: from the Leehagens, from men like Benton and Quinn, from the memory of his father withering away from the cancer yet refusing to listen when people criticized the man who chose to deny the reality of the disease that was killing him. Curtis had friends down in Florida who were making good money in roofing, helped by the fact that every hurricane season brought fresh calls for their services. They'd let him come in as a partner, just as long as he had some capital to bring to the table. Curtis had almost $4,000 saved, with another thousand owed to him by Mr. Leehagen, not counting any bonus that might come his way from the current job. He had set himself a target of $7,000: $6,000 to buy into the roofing business, and a thousand to cover his expenses once he got to Florida. He was close now, real close.

The sound of the rain on the hood of his poncho was starting to give him a headache. He removed the binoculars from his eyes to rest them, shifted position in a vain effort to find a more comfortable way to stand, then resumed his vigil.

There was movement at the edge of the woods to the south: two men. He rapped on the roof, alerting Quinn and Benton. The passenger window was rolled down, and Curtis could smell the booze and the cigarette smoke.

"What?" It was Benton.

"I see them."

"Where?"

"Not far from the Brooker place, moving west."

"I hate that old bastard, him and his wife and his freak son," said Benton. "Mr. Leehagen ought to have run them off his land a long time ago."

"The old man won't have helped them," said Curtis. "He knows better." Although he wasn't sure that was true. Mr. Brooker was ornery, and he kept himself and his family apart from the men who worked for Mr. Leehagen. Curtis wondered why Mr. Brooker didn't just sell up and leave, but he figured that was part of being ornery, too.

"Yeah," said Benton. "Old Brooker may be a pain in the ass, but he's no fool."

A hand emerged from the window. It held a bottle of homemade hooch and waved it at Curtis. This was Benton's own concoction. Quinn, who was an expert on such matters, had expressed the view that, as primitive grain alcohol went, it was as good as any that a man could buy in these parts, although that wasn't saying much. It didn't make you blind, or turn your piss red with blood, or any of the other unfortunate side effects that drinking homemade rotgut sometimes brought on, and that made it top-quality stuff in Quinn's estimation.

Curtis took it and raised it to his mouth. The smell made his head spin and seemed instantly to exacerbate the pain in his skull, but he drank anyway. He was cold and wet. The hooch couldn't make things worse. Unfortunately, it did. It was like swallowing hot fragments of glass that had spent too long in an old gasoline tank. He coughed most of it back up and spat it on the metal at his feet, where the rainwater did its best to dilute it and wash it away.

"Fuck this," said Benton. The engine started up. "Get in here, Curtis."

Curtis jumped down and opened the passenger door. Quinn was staring straight ahead, a cigarette hanging from his lips. He was just over six feet tall, four inches taller than Curtis, and had short black hair with the consistency of fuse wire. Quinn had been Benton's best buddy since grade school. He didn't say much, and most of what he did say was foul. Quinn seemed to have picked up his entire vocabulary from men's room walls. When he opened his mouth, he talked fast, his words emerging in an unbroken, unpunctuated stream of threats and obscenities. While Benton had been doing time in Ogdensburg Correctional, Quinn had been down the road in Ogdensburg Psychiatric. That was the difference between them. Benton was vicious, but Quinn was nuts. He scared the shit out of Curtis.

"Hey, move over," said Curtis. He climbed into the cab, expecting Quinn to scoot, but he didn't.

"Fuckyouthinkyoudoing?" said Quinn. It came out so quickly that it took Curtis a couple of seconds to comprehend what had been said.

"I'm trying to get in the cab."

"Sitinthedamnmiddlenotmovingsumbitch-kickyourass."

"Quit fooling, man," said Benton. "Let the kid through."

Quinn moved his knees a fraction to the left, allowing Curtis just enough room to squeeze past.

"Gotmeallwetmankickyourasskickyourass-good."

"Sorry," said Curtis.

"Betterbesorrymakeyousorrykickyourass-man."

Yeah, whatever, you whacko, thought Curtis. He briefly entertained visions of kicking Quinn's ass instead, but forced them from his mind when he turned and saw Quinn regarding him unblinkingly through light brown eyes flecked with points of black like tumors in his retinae. Curtis didn't believe Quinn was telepathic, but he wasn't about to take any chances.

"What are we going to do?" asked Curtis.

"What we should have done after we wrecked their car," said Benton. "We're going to take care of them."

Curtis shivered. He recalled the sight of the dead woman, and the weight of her in his arms as he and Quinn had placed her in the trunk, Benton and Quinn giggling at the little twist they had added to the job. Willis and Harding had done the killing during the night, and Benton had been left to bury the bodies, another punishment for his failures earlier in the week. Instead, he had decided to stuff them in the trunk of the car, and now Curtis couldn't seem to get the smell of the woman off his hands and clothes, even in the pouring rain.

"We were told not to get involved," said Curtis. "There were orders, orders from Mr. Leehagen's son."

"Yeah, well, nobody told those two assholes out there. Suppose Brooker did help them, or let them use his phone? Suppose there are people on their way up here right now? Hell, they might even have killed the old man and his family, and that'd be a regular tragedy. They're killers, ain't they? That's what these people do. While we wait around for some ghost to get here and do a job that we could have done for nothing, they're running free. Long as they end up dead on his land, Leehagen won't object."

Curtis wasn't sure that this was a good idea. He tended to take Mr. Leehagen at his word, even if that word usually came through his son now that Mr. Leehagen couldn't get around so good anymore, and it had been made clear to them that they were to restrain themselves when it came to the two men for whom they had been waiting. Confrontations—fatal ones, at least—were to be avoided. They just had to sit tight and wait. After the men had entered the Leehagen lands, they were to be contained there, and nothing more. All told, fifteen men had been entrusted with the task of ensuring that, once they entered the trap, they did not escape. Now Benton wanted to bend the rules. His pride had been hurt by recent events, Curtis knew. He wanted to make amends to the

Leehagens, and restore his own confidence along the way.

Benton drank some, it was true, but he was right more often than he was wrong, alcohol or no alcohol. The more Curtis thought about their situation, the more he saw Benton's point about not waiting around for Bliss to take care of the two men. But then Curtis always had been swayed by the voice that was nearest and loudest. If a backbone could be said to have chameleonesque qualities, changing to suit its moral environment, then Curtis's certainly qualified. His opinion could be swayed by a sneeze.

And so Quinn, Curtis, and Benton left the road and went in search of two killers who would soon be killing no more. They made one stop along the way, calling at the Brooker place to see what he could tell them. Curtis could see that Mr. Brooker thought as much of Benton as Benton thought of him, and even then Mr. Brooker's feelings toward Benton were probably pretty charitable compared to his wife's. She didn't even try to be civil, and the sight of their guns didn't seem to faze her at all. She was a tough old bitch, no doubt about it.

Their son, Luke, leaned against a wall, hardly blinking. Curtis didn't know if he could see out of his milky eye. Maybe he could, and the world looked as though it had been overlaid with a sheet of muslin, its streets populated with ghosts. Curtis couldn't ever recall hearing Mr. Brooker's son speak. He had never gone to school, not to any regular school, and the only time Curtis ever saw him away from the Brooker place was when he went into town with his father and the old man treated them both to ice cream at Tasker's ice cream parlor. As for the little girl, Curtis had no idea where she had come from. Maybe Luke had managed to get lucky, once upon a time, although it didn't seem likely. Screwing Luke Brooker would be like screwing a zombie.

Mr. Brooker showed them the guns that he had taken from the two men, and Benton's eyes lit up at the prospect of easy pickings. He slapped Brooker on the back and told him that he'd let Mr. Leehagen know how well he'd done.

When the three men had gone, Brooker sat silently at his kitchen table while his wife rolled dough behind him, and tried to ignore the waves of disapproval that were breaking upon his back.

Angel and Louis heard the truck before they saw it. They were in a trough between two raised patches of open ground, one of the grazing cuts, and it took them a moment to determine from which direction the sound was coming. Louis scaled the small incline and looked to the east to see the Ranger moving fast in their direction, following a dirt trail out of the forest from the direction of the old man's house. It was still too far away to identify the men inside, but Louis was pretty sure that they weren't friendly. Neither would Bliss be among their number. It wasn't his style. The rules had changed, it seemed. It was no longer a matter of containment. He wondered if Thomas had made a call, fearful of what the trespassers on his land might do even without guns. Perhaps the news that they were no longer armed had tilted the balance against them.

Louis sized up their options. The cover of the forest was lost to them. To the southwest, meanwhile, was what appeared to be an old barn, the raised, domed structure of an aged grain elevator beside it, with more forest behind. It was an unknown quantity.

Angel joined him.

"They're coming for us," said Louis.

"Which way do we go?"

Louis pointed at the barn.

"There. And fast."

Benton came to the top of a slight hill. Almost directly opposite them, and on the same level, their prey was running. One of them, the tall black guy, took a second to look back over at them. Benton slammed on the brakes and jumped from the cab, grabbing his Marlin hunting rifle from the rack behind his seat as he did so. He went down on one knee, aimed, and fired at the figure across from him, but the man was already disappearing over the rise, and the bullet hit nothing but air. By now, Quinn and Curtis were behind him, although neither had bothered to raise his weapon, Quinn because he had a shotgun and Curtis because he hadn't signed up to shoot at anybody, even though he'd brought along his father's old pistol, just as Mr. Leehagen's son had instructed him to do.

"Goddamn," said Benton, but he was laughing as he spoke. "Bet nobody in his family has moved that fast since someone waved a noose at them back in the old South."

"How'd you know he was Southern?" asked Curtis. It seemed like a reasonable question.

"A feeling I got," said Benton. "A Negro don't get into his trade unless he has a beef against someone from way back. That boy's looking for a way to strike back against the white man."

That sounded like bullshit to Curtis, but he didn't disagree. Maybe Benton was right, but even if he wasn't, it was good sense simply to nod along with him. Meanness ran through him like fat on marbled beef. It wouldn't be beyond him just to leave Curtis out here in the rain, and with a broken nose—again—or some busted ribs as a reminder to him to keep his mouth shut in future.

"Come on," said Benton, and led them back to the truck at a trot.

"Looks steep," said Curtis, as Benton drove down the slope at a sharp angle.

"Four-liter V6," said Benton. "Baby could do it on two wheels."

Curtis didn't reply. The Ranger was twelve years old, the treads were at 60 percent, and four liters didn't make it a monster. Curtis braced himself against the dashboard.

The Ranger might have made the climb on dry ground, but Benton hadn't reckoned with the rain that had soaked into the dirt at the base of the depression. It had turned the earth to mud, and when the Ranger hit bottom the wheels struggled to grip, even as they began to climb up the opposite side. Benton gunned the engine, and for a moment they lurched forward before stopping entirely, the wheels churning uselessly in the soft ground.

Quinn said something, from which Curtis could only rescue the words "shithead" and "eating dirt." Benton fired the Ranger again, and this time it made two more feet before sliding backward and losing its rear wheels in mud.

Benton slapped the dashboard in frustration and opened the door to inspect the damage. They were mired deep, the gloop almost touching the alloys.

"Shit," he said. "Well, I guess we go after them on foot."

"You sure that's a good idea?" asked Curtis.

"They're unarmed," said Benton. "You scared of unarmed men?"

"No," said Curtis, but he had the feeling that he had just lied to himself.

"Well, come on then. They ain't going to kill themselves."

Benton laughed at his own joke. Quinn joined in, contributing a combination of hyena sniggers interspersed with cuss words. Then they were off, their boots sinking into the mud as they climbed the slope.

With no other choice left to him, Curtis followed.

The barn loomed large against the dark sky, with the elevator on the left side of it. It was forty feet high, and not as modern as the one close to the cattle pens near Leehagen's house. There would be no breather bags, no molten glass fused to the steel sheets to allow an easy slide for the grain and guard against acids from fermented feeds, no pressure venting. This was a simple storage bin, and nothing more.

Louis's breath was coming in jagged rasps, and Angel was visibly struggling. They were both cold and wet, and they knew that they were running out of both strength and options. Louis took Angel by the arm and pulled him onward, looking behind him as he did so. The Ranger had not yet appeared over the lip of the slope. Both the incline and the decline had looked steep to him, perhaps too steep for the truck in this weather. A little time had been bought, but not much. The men would continue the pursuit on foot, and they were armed while he and Angel were not. If they caught them on the open ground, they could pick them off in their current tired state. Even if he and

Angel got to the barn, their problems would not end. They would be trapped inside, and if the pursuers called in others then it would all be over.

But Louis was anticipating that they would not call others. If what the old man at the farm had told him was true, then Bliss was coming, and Bliss worked alone. The ones who were now after them were acting on their own initiative. If they thought that he and Angel were still armed, the pursuers might have been more cautious once they reached the grain store, and caution would have given them pause, but Louis guessed that they had spoken to the old man before commencing the hunt. They knew now that they were dealing with unarmed men.

But one of the first lessons Louis had learned in his long apprenticeship as a bringer of death was that in every room there is a weapon, even if that weapon was only oneself. It was simply a question of identifying it and using it. He hadn't been in a grain store in many years, but his mind was already anticipating what lay within: tools, sacking, fire-fighting equipment . . .

His mind began making leaps.

Fire-fighting equipment.

Fire.

Grain.

He had the first of his weapons.

Quinn crested the rise ahead of the others, and thought that he saw one of the two men disappear behind the barn. There were two grain storage units on Leehagen's property. The main one was over by the new pens, close by the feed mill, while this one was a relic from the days when the herd was in its infancy, and had originally been a silage silo. Now it was used to hold grain in reserve, just in case anything should happen to the main store, or if snows came and separated the cattle. In fact, one of Benton's tasks, when he wasn't hunting down living things or intimidating those smaller than him, had been to monitor the secondary grain store, checking for damp, rodents, or other infestations. Nobody else bothered with it much, which made it a useful place for Benton to pursue his various hobbies, among them screwing some of the young foreign women, willing or not, who were occasionally transported through the farm from Canada.

Benton and Curtis joined him.

"You see where they went?" asked Benton.

Quinn pointed at the barn with his shotgun.

"It's empty fields beyond there," said Benton. "Ain't a tree for three, four hundred yards. If they try to run, we got 'em. If they stay put, we got 'em, too."

Benton had advised Mr. Leehagen to have the barn and the silo demolished, but the slaughter of the herd (a rich man's foolish indulgence from the start) had negated the need for any such action. The silo had been damaged by the fact that it was side-tapped for gravity unloading, causing one wall to collapse inward. A secondary outlet, created against Benton's advice, fed directly into the barn itself, an emergency measure in case it became necessary to house and feed the cattle there in winter. Benton was grateful that they had never had to use it. It was just like old Leehagen to cut corners in this way. Now it looked as if the barn might serve a final useful purpose after all, by trapping the men that they were hunting.

He slapped Curtis hard on the back.

"Come on, boy. We'll blood you yet!"

And, with his rifle held high, he led the three men toward the grain store.

The barn wasn't locked. Louis figured that nobody was going to cross Leehagen by stealing from him, and even the cleverest rat hadn't learned to open a door using the handle. He stepped inside. The barn was small, with makeshift cattle pens running parallel along its walls. It was lit through a trio of skylights in the ceiling, with a series of ventilation grills beneath them.

"Take a look around," he told Angel. "See if you can find oil, white spirits, anything that burns."

It was a small chance. While Angel searched, Louis examined the outlet that fed grain into the barn. It was little more than a metal pipe connecting the silo to the barn wall, with a valve at one end to release the grain. The outlet was ten feet off the ground, a portable metal chute to one side of it and a plastic storage bin beneath it. Louis climbed on to the bin and twisted the valve. It was slightly rusted, and he had to push hard against it to move it, but he watched with relief as grain began to pour onto the floor of the barn. He held some in his hands, rubbing it between his fingers. It was bone dry. He twisted the valve further, increasing the flow. Already, the air in the barn was filling with choking dust and grain particles.

After a minute or two, Angel appeared by his side.

"Nothing," he said.

"Doesn't matter. Go see how close they are."

Angel covered his nose and mouth with his coat and raced through the store until he reached the main sliding door at the front of the barn. There were dusty windows at either side. He glanced carefully through the glass and saw three shapes advancing through the rain. They were about two hundred feet away, and already spreading out. Two would go around the back while the other came in through the front. There would be no other way for them to search the barn safely while ensuring that their prey did not escape through the back door.

"Close," Angel shouted back. "Minutes." He coughed hard as some of the dust entered his lungs. Already, he could barely see Louis against the far wall.

"Let them get a look at you," said Louis.

"What?"

"Let them see you. Open the door, then close it again."

"Maybe I should put an apple on my head, too, or dress like a duck."

"Just do it."

Angel threw the bolt on the sliding door, then moved it back about five feet. Shots came. Quickly, Angel closed the door again and returned to Louis.

"Happy now?" he said, as he ran back to join Louis.

"Ecstatic. Time to go." Louis had some old grain sacks in his hand, and the spare clip for the Glock. He tied the sack around the clip, his Zippo held between his teeth.

"You still have yours?" he said, through the mouthful of brass.

Angel took the clip from his pocket and handed it over. Louis did the same again, adding more weight to the sack.

"Okay," he said. He gestured at the rear door. It opened to the left. They had just stepped outside when a young man appeared from around the corner to their right. He was small, and armed with a pistol. He stared at them, then raised his gun halfheartedly. It wavered in his hand.

"Don't move," he said, but Angel was already moving. He grabbed the gun, pushing it away to the left, and hit the man as hard as he could in the face with the crown of his head. The man collapsed, leaving Angel holding the gun. As he went down, Angel heard the sound of the double doors at the front of the barn opening.

Something flamed behind Angel. He turned to see Louis lighting the sack.

"Run," said Louis.

And Angel ran. Seconds later, Louis was beside him, his hand on Angel's aching back, pushing him down to the ground as Angel started to pray.

Benton and Quinn heard the shots as they moved into the barn. One end of the barn was heavy with dust, and they could not see the far wall. Quinn had already grabbed Benton by the shoulder and was forcing him back the way they had come when the burning bag came sailing through the double doors and into the dust-rich environment of the barn.

"Aw, hell," said Benton. "Aw—"

And then hell became a reality as the world turned to fire.

Jackie Garner was tired of being wet.

"We can't just stand here in the rain," he said. "We need to get going."

"We could split up," said Paulie, "take a road each and see what happens."

What happens if we do that is we end up dead, thought Willie. The Fulcis and their pal were clearly nuts, but at least they were armed and nuts. Five of them together had a better chance than two, or three.

"It's still a lot of ground to cover," said Jackie. "They could be anywhere."

At that moment, a hill to the south was suddenly altered by a plume of smoke and wood and dirt that soared into the gray sky, and their ears rang with the sound of the explosion.

"You know," said Jackie, "it's just a guess . . ."

Louis and Angel climbed to their feet. They were surrounded by debris: wood, sacking, burning grain. Louis's coat was on fire. He shrugged it off and tossed it to one side before he began to burn, too. Angel's hair was singed, and there was a bright-red scorch mark upon his left cheek. They surveyed the damage. Half of the barn was gone, and the grain store had collapsed. In the midst of the wreckage, Angel could make out the body of the young man who had, briefly, held a gun on them.

"At least we have one gun," he said.

Louis took it from him.

"I have a gun," he corrected. "Which would you rather have: you with a gun, or me with a gun at your side?"

"Me with a gun."

"Well, you can't have it."

Angel gazed beyond the remains of the barn.

"They're all gonna come now."

"I guess."

"At least they'll bring some more guns."

"I'll get you one when they do."

"Yeah?"

"Yeah."

"Thanks."

"Don't mention it."

"Bliss will come, too."

"Yes, he will."

"So we still going to see Leehagen?"

"We are."

"Good."

"That is good."

They began to walk.

"You know, my feet are wet," said Angel.

"But at least you're warm now . . ."

CHAPTER TWENTY-SIX

BLISS HEARD THE EXPLOSION, and knew that Louis was near. He had no concern that his target might be dead, for he knew in his heart that Louis's life was his to take. This reckoning was his due, after all that he had endured.

He had underestimated Gabriel's protégé, but then Gabriel had always been seeking the perfect Reaper, the one whom he could mold to do his bidding without question. Bliss had seen so many of them come and go, their dying bringing grief to Gabriel only because their failure was his failure. What he had not realized, but Bliss had, was that a man or woman who could be broken to Gabriel's will would be useless in the end. What made Bliss special—and, he had come grudgingly to acknowledge, what made Louis special, too—was that there was a streak of individuality to them both, perhaps even a kind of perversion of the spirit, that meant they would ultimately break free of the constraints placed upon them by Gabriel and by those who, in turn, used him to serve their own purposes. That was why they had stayed alive when so many others had not, but Bliss had been wise enough to know that such a situation could not go on forever. Eventually he would tire, and his thinking would slow. He would make a mistake, and pay the price; that, or he would attempt to slip quietly into anonymity, taking his secrets with him, but there would be some, Gabriel among them, perhaps, who might prefer if Bliss's secrets were buried with him, and sooner instead of later. So Bliss had taken a calculated risk: he had named a price, and it had been met. He had made one mistake: Louis had survived. Now it was time to rectify that error.

The explosion made the next part of his task easier. He knew Louis's location, even if it was farther southwest than he had expected. Curious, he thought, that Louis and his lover should be moving into the trap instead of trying to break out again. He knew from Leehagen's son that they had tried to find a way through the cordon and had been forced back into the woods. Had they persevered, they might well have broken through the line at another attempt. With luck, even to reach one of the bridges over the stream might not have been beyond them, although they would have managed to get no farther, for their movements had been tracked from the start. Their fate lay entirely in his hands, and he had written that they should die.

Moving in, not out. He thought about finding some way to warn Leehagen, then decided against it. The old thug could work out for himself what was happening, and if he couldn't then he didn't deserve to live. Despite all the obstacles that had been placed in his way, Louis was still coming for Leehagen. Bliss admired his dedication. He had always considered Louis impure, for no one had Bliss's purity, but something of his own tenacity lay buried deep in the younger man.

Quickly and steadily, Bliss began walking toward the site of the explosion.

Something moved in a ditch near the ruins of the barn. A pallet shifted, followed by a sheet of corrugated iron. Beneath it lay Benton. The left side of his face was charred and blackened, thin streaks of raw red flesh visible where the skin had broken like magma bursting through a volcanic crust, and he was now blind in that eye. The pain was excruciating.

He raised himself to a sitting position using the palms of his hands. The backs were burned and cracked, but the palms were unscathed. He looked down at himself. Part of his shirt had been burned away, and the skin beneath was covered in heat bubbles, and punctured by multiple fragments of wood. Beside him lay what was left of Quinn. When the barn had ignited, Quinn had taken the brunt of the explosion. His body had been lifted off the ground, striking Benton and inadvertently shielding him from the worst of what followed, assisted by a fortuitous accretion of debris.

He got to his feet and brushed red and black matter from his trousers. He suspected that some of it was part of Quinn, and felt a surge of indignation at the death of his friend. He put his hand to his head. His skull ached. There was a bare patch where hair used to be. His palm came back bloodied.

The pain in his eyeball was the worst because it was so specific and intense. His depth perception was gone, but he was aware of something protruding from the socket where his left eye used to be. Carefully, he raised his right hand and brought it closer to the eye. The palm of his hand brushed against a sliver of wood, and Benton yelled in shock. Tears fell from his right eye, and his vision blurred. He tried not to panic, forcing himself to stop taking short ragged breaths and instead draw air in deeply and slowly.

There was a splinter in his eye. He couldn't leave it there. You couldn't leave a splinter in your eye. It was just . . . wrong.

Benton held his hands before him and turned them sideways, one palm facing the other. He drew them toward him until they were almost touching his head, one at either side of his damaged eye. Then, slowly, he brought his index fingers together until they touched the splinter. The pain was still ferocious, but this time he had been expecting it. He tightened the tips of his fingers against the shard of wood, and pulled. It was buried deep, so there was some resistance, but Benton didn't stop. There was a noise like sirens in his head, high-pitched and intense, and it was only when the splinter had come free and something warm was trickling down his cheek that he realized it was the sound of his own screams.

He examined the splinter, holding it close to his left eye. It was almost two inches long, and nearly half of its length was coated in blood and ocular fluid. *Sons of bitches put a splinter in my eye,* he thought. He was going to get them for that.

Benton got to his feet. He found his rifle, half hidden beneath Quinn's remains, and picked it up. His brain didn't seem to be working the way it should. It wasn't sending the right messages to his limbs, causing him to stumble and drift as he walked. Still, he managed to leave behind the ruins of the barn while falling to his knees only once. He had already forgotten his burns and the remains of Quinn, and the fate of Roundy did not even impinge upon his shattered consciousness. All that mattered was the splinter that had blinded him in one eye. After all, what kind of men would blind another man? Men who didn't deserve to live, that was what kind.

Somewhere in the distance, he saw two shapes moving, one tall, the other shorter. He began following the men.

The Detective had gone only a short distance in the direction of the explosion when the first car appeared. It was a red Toyota Camry, moving away from them at speed. Willie's hand tightened on his gun, even as the Detective eased up on the gas, allowing the men to pull farther ahead. Behind them, Jackie Garner and the Fulcis also slowed down.

"You got any plans for when we get there?" asked Willie.

"The same plan as earlier: not dying."

Thick clouds of smoke were now drifting across the road. It made driving difficult, but it also meant that they would be hidden from the men before them. As it was, they almost drove into them as they reached the site of the explosion. The red car seemed to materialize out of nowhere, stopped with its front doors open, two men still sitting in the front seats. The Detective braked sharply and went right as soon as they came in sight and, behind them, Tony Fulci swung the wheel of his truck to the left, taking it around the Mustang and bringing it to a stop almost level with the men in the car.

Unable to open his door because of the proximity of the Fulcis' truck, the driver had simply decided to begin shooting, but because of the size of the truck he had to wind down his window and stick his hand out to hit anything. By the time he had managed to do all of that, Tony had fired four shots through the roof of the car, and the driver collapsed sideways, his left hand hanging uselessly from the half-open window, his gun lying on the ground beneath it.

The passenger, clearly wounded but still able to hold a gun, opened the door farthest from the Fulcis and tumbled out, coughing loudly, his eyes streaming from the smoke. The Detective hit the accelerator of the Mustang. The car shot forward, striking the gunman's lower body and cutting the door from the Toyota. The force of the impact doubled the passenger over at the waist and sent him sailing onto the hood of the Mustang. He fell off as the Detective swung the wheel to the right and stopped the car. The Detective opened his door and stepped out into the smoke and rain, Willie following.

Now there were two men running from the direction of the fire. Both wore yellow slickers and jeans, the slickers standing out even in the smoke, and both carried what looked like shotguns. Willie saw them before anyone else. He tried to speak, but the smoke entered his mouth, causing him to splutter instead. Jackie Garner and one of the Fulcis were still getting out of the truck, and Parker was kneeling beside the man on the ground.

Willie raised the Browning.

I don't want to do this. I believed that I could, but I was wrong. I thought that we'd be in and out, that we'd find Angel and Louis and get them away from here. I didn't believe that there would be all of this, this killing. I'm not a killer. I don't belong here. I'm not these men. I can never be.

The smoke drifted, carried by the breeze, and the figures in yellow disappeared from view for an instant.

Go away. Just turn back. Lose yourself in the smoke. Let this be the end of it.

And then they were back, closer now. He heard shots and saw muzzle flares in the smoke. Willie fired twice at the man on the left, aiming at his upper body. The man dropped to the ground and didn't move again. A fusillade of shots came from the direction of the Fulcis' truck, and the second man joined the first. Willie saw Jackie Garner and Tony Fulci move toward the fallen men, Tony covering Jackie as he removed their weapons and checked for any signs of life. The Detective was now looking at the driver of the car. Paulie Fulci joined him, and Willie heard the Detective tell Paulie that the driver was dead, and the other man soon would be. All four of them then began walking in the direction of the ruined barn, but Willie did not join them. He walked over to where the man whom he had killed lay spread-eagled on the ground. One shot had missed him entirely, the other had taken him in the chest. He looked to be in his forties, an overweight, balding figure wearing cheap denims and worn work boots.

Willie put his hands on his knees, leaned down, and tried not to throw up. Stars burst before his eyes. He felt anger, and grief, and shame. He moved upwind of the drifting smoke and sat beneath a lone tree. The rain was easing, and the tree didn't offer much shelter in any case, but Willie didn't trust his own body to hold him up. He leaned back against the bark, tossed the Browning aside, and closed his eyes.

He stayed that way until he heard footsteps. The Detective was approaching. His face was blackened with smoke. Willie guessed that he must have looked just the same.

"We have to keep moving," said the Detective. "There'll be others looking for them as well."

"Is it worth it?" asked Willie. "All of this, is it worth it?"

"I don't know," said the Detective. "I just know that they're my friends, and they're in trouble."

He reached out a hand. Willie took it.

"You'll need your gun," said the Detective.

Willie stared at the gun on the ground.

"Pick it up, Willie," said the Detective, and in that instant Willie hated him.

But he did as he was told. He picked up the gun, and joined the others.

• • •

Benton heard the gunfire behind him, but he didn't look back. It was all that he could do to keep moving forward. He was afraid that if he turned around, even for a moment, he would lose all sense of direction, and if he stopped he would surrender any possibility of further movement. All that he could do was to put one foot in front of the other, to maintain his grip on the rifle in his right hand, and eventually he would reach the men he was hunting. Slowly, the connections in his brain were dying, shorting out one by one like overloaded fuses. He could barely remember his own name, and had forgotten entirely the names of the men who had died in the inferno. All he knew was that those responsible for all of it, whatever it was, were ahead of him, and he needed to kill them. Once they were dead, he could stop moving, and then the pain would cease as well. Everything would cease. There would be no pain, no pleasure, no memories. There would be only blackness, like drowning in a warm sea at night.

CHAPTER TWENTY-SEVEN

IT WAS ANGEL WHO spotted Benton first. He was still some distance from them when Angel caught sight of his head appearing over the brow of a hill. He tapped Louis in warning, and together they turned to face the threat.

It was clear that the man was badly injured. He was shambling rather than walking, and he seemed to be drifting slightly to the left and then, realizing what he was doing, correcting himself. His head was low, and he held a rifle in his right hand. As he drew nearer, they could see the damage to his face and body caused by the fire, and they knew from whence he had come.

"Someone survived the explosion," said Angel. "He's hurt bad, though."

"He has a gun," said Louis.

"Doesn't look like it's going to be much good to him."

Louis raised his own gun and sighted along it as he moved toward the wounded man.

"No," he said, "I guess not."

• • •

Benton became aware that the men he was pursuing had stopped. It was time, so he stopped in turn, knowing that he would never go any farther, not here and not in this life. The landscape wavered, and the two men in the distance became blurred and misshapen. He tried to lift the rifle, but his arms would not respond. He tried to speak, but no words would come from his scorched throat. All was pain; pain, and the desire to avenge himself upon those who had caused it. His injuries had reduced him to the level of an animal. Disjointed memories of unconnected things appeared in his mind only to disappear before he was able to identify and understand them: a woman who might have been his mother; another who could have been a lover; a man dying in the rain, the blood like colors running in a painting . . .

The rifle was still in his hand. He knew that much. He concentrated hard, trying to focus on it. He managed to get the index finger of his right hand on the trigger, his left still gripping the stock. He pulled the trigger, firing uselessly into the ground. A tear fell from his eye. One of the figures was drawing nearer. He had to kill them, but now he couldn't remember why. He couldn't remember anything. All was lost to him.

His brain, understanding the imminence of its own oblivion, fired itself up for a final effort, and Benton's consciousness blazed for the last time, clearing his head of pain and anger and loss, allowing him to focus only on the man who was approaching. He raised his left arm, and it was steady. His vision cleared, and he sighted on the tall black figure. His finger tightened again on the trigger, and as he prepared to release his breath, he knew that everything was going to be fine after all.

The load was a 250-grain MatchKing bullet, which would have meant nothing to Benton even if it hadn't been the bullet that tore through the side of his head, entering just behind and beneath his remaining eye and exiting through his right ear, taking most of his skull with it.

From where he lay on the damp grass, Bliss watched as the target folded to the ground. He shifted position slightly, taking his eye from the sight so he could find the others. They were already running, ascending a slight rise and making for a copse of trees to the east. Even with the XL, they would soon be out of range. He intended to finish off Louis face-to-face, for he wanted him to know who was responsible for taking his life, but the other one, his partner, didn't matter. Bliss sighted slightly ahead of the smaller man, anticipating where the angle of his movement would take him, then breathed out slowly and squeezed the trigger.

"Shit!" said Angel, as his foot caught on a cleft in the ground and sent him stumbling forward and to his left. Louis was beside him, and paused momentarily, but Angel didn't fall. A spray of grass and dirt erupted from the ground slightly forward and to the right of where Angel now stood, even as he regained his balance and they continued running, their eyes now fixed only on the safety offered by the woods. Angel heard another shot, but the ground was sloping down and suddenly there were trees around him and he threw himself to the dirt and sheltered behind the nearest trunk. He huddled against it, his knees drawn into his chest, his mouth open as he gasped in air.

Angel looked to his left, but Louis wasn't there.

"Hey," he shouted. "You okay?"

There was no reply.

"Hey," he called again, frightened now. "Louis?"

But there was only silence. Angel didn't move. He had to find out where Louis was, but to do that would mean peering out from behind the tree, and if the shooter knew where he was, and was sighted on the tree, then he would end up dead. But he had to know what, if anything, had befallen his partner. He flattened himself as close to the ground as he could without exposing his legs to sight, began counting to three in his head, then at two decided to hell with it and risked a quick glance around the base of the tree.

Two things happened. The first was that he saw Louis lying on his side just beneath the lip of the small rise that descended toward the wood. He wasn't moving. The second thing that happened was a bullet striking the tree trunk and sending splinters into Angel's cheek, forcing him to retract his head quickly before another shot cured him of concerns about Louis, and splinters, and anything else in this life.

He was unarmed, the man who mattered most to him in the world was lying injured or dead and he couldn't reach him, and someone had him under his gun. Angel had a pretty good idea who that person was: Bliss. For the first time in many years, Angel began to despair.

It had been a lucky shot, but Bliss was not averse to taking such chances when they were offered. The natural movement of his weapon, combined with Louis's own momentum, had brought him into Bliss's sights, and he had taken the shot. He had seen the tall black figure's legs intertwine and had watched him fall, but then had lost him to view because of the incline of the land. He couldn't be sure where the shot had hit. He suspected it was the upper back, right side, away from the heart. Louis would be wounded, perhaps mortally, but he would not yet be dead.

He had to be sure. He had made two promises to Leehagen. The first was that Louis would die on his land, that his blood would soak into the old man's soil. The second was that he would bring him Louis's head as a trophy. The second promise had been made reluctantly. It smacked of excess to Bliss. It was curious that Hoyle had asked him to do the same with Kandic, the man who had been sent to kill him and whose eventual dispatch had been Bliss's first job after coming out of retirement. Decapitating him hadn't bothered Bliss particularly, although it was harder, and messier, than anticipated, and he had no desire to make a habit of it. He also recognized that a personal element had crept into all of his kills: he was now the mirror image of the man he had once been, no longer distant from those he dispatched. In one way, it added an edge to all that he did, even as it made him more vulnerable in another. The best killers were passionless, just as he himself had once been. Anything else was weakness.

But Bliss also realized that he was creating his own mythology. Kandic, Billy Boy, and now Louis—they would be his legacy. He was Bliss, the killer of killers, the most lethal of his kind. He would be remembered after he was gone. There would never be another like him.

But it was time to be done with the task at hand. Louis had been armed. Bliss had glimpsed the gun in his hands. He did not know about the other, the one called Angel, but he had seen no weapon. Bliss suspected that the smaller man would be reluctant to move for fear of taking a bullet. If he acted quickly, Bliss could cover much of the ground between them, move position to give him a better shot at Angel, and then finish off Louis.

Bliss shifted his weapon and closed in.

"So which way did they go?" asked Willie.

He and the Detective were standing upwind of the smoke. Behind them, the Fulcis were moving the Toyota so that the way would be clear for them if they decided to continue on their current road. Jackie Garner was admiring the destruction wrought upon the grain store. Jackie liked things that exploded.

"It would make sense for them to get as far away from here as possible," said the Detective. "But then we're talking about Angel and Louis, and sometimes what makes sense is not what they're inclined to do. They came here to kill Leehagen. It could be that none of this has changed their minds. Knowing them, it might have made them more determined. They'll stay off the roads for fear of being seen, so my guess is that they'll be heading for the main house."

At that moment, they heard the first shot.

"Over there!" shouted Jackie, pointing over Willie's shoulder. West, Willie thought, just like the man said.

Two more shots followed in close succession. The Detective was already running.

"Jackie, you and the brothers take the truck," he said. "Follow the road. Try to find a way to get there quickly. Willie and I will go on foot, in case you strike out."

He looked at Willie. "You okay with that?"

Willie nodded, although he wasn't sure what appealed to him less: the thought that he now had to run, or the possibility that he might have to use his gun again once he stopped running.

It was the damp that finally forced Angel to move. Such a small thing, such a minor discomfort in light of all that had befallen them that day, yet there it was. The dampness was causing him to itch and chafe. He shifted his lower body, trying to loosen his trousers, but it was no good.

"Louis?" he called again, but as before only silence greeted him. There was a warm sensation behind his eyes, and his throat burned. He was, he knew, already grieving, but if he were to allow grief to overcome him then all would be lost. He had to hold himself together. Louis might only be injured. There was still hope.

He considered his situation. There were two possibilities. The first was that Bliss had chosen to remain in place, hoping to get a clear shot at either Angel or Louis. But Louis was out of sight, and Louis, Angel knew, was Bliss's primary target. Angel only mattered insofar as he might interfere with Bliss's attempts to finish him off. From his original firing position, Bliss must have been unable to see Louis once he had fallen, otherwise he would have fired upon him again. He couldn't have been sure that the shot that hit him was a fatal one.

Which raised the second, and more likely, possibility: that Bliss was approaching, moving in on the two men to ensure that the job was completed to his satisfaction. If that was the case, then Angel might be able to break cover without being hit. It was a gamble, though, and while Angel had worked hard to cultivate a number of vices, gambling was not one of them. Even throwing away fifty bucks once at Sarasota Springs had plunged him into a depression that lasted a week. Then again, were he to lose his life now it was unlikely that he would have much time to regret his final decision, and if he stayed where he was then he, and Louis, would certainly die, if the latter was not dead already, and that was a prospect that Angel, for the present, refused to countenance.

He needed Louis's gun. If he could get to it, then they might have a chance against Bliss.

"Shit," said Angel. "Hell, hell, hell." He was experiencing a rising anger at Louis's selfishness. "Today, of all days, you had to get shot. Out here, in the middle of fucking nowhere, leaving me alone without a gun, without you." He felt his body tensing, the adrenaline coursing. "I told you I wanted that gun, but oh no, you had to have it. Mr. Big Shot needed his weapon, and now where has it left us? Screwed, that's where it's left us. *Screwed.*"

And at the height of his self-induced rage, Angel ran.

Bliss's advance had been made easier by the rise and fall of the land, making it harder for Louis's partner to trace his progress than it would have been if he was crossing level ground. The disadvantage was that, while he was in the slight depressions, he was unable to see the lower part of the woods in which Angel was hidden. He was also aware that Louis might have recovered sufficiently from his wound to enable him to look for cover, but while Bliss had maintained his vigil there had been no sign of movement over the small patch of clear ground between the place where Louis had fallen and the woods in which his lover cowered. Bliss anticipated that the fear of being shot would keep Angel in the woods, but in case he overcame that fear Bliss had quickly covered the ground between his original position and his targets, despite squatting and crawling much of the way. Now he was within touching distance of the rise overlooking the forest. He calculated that Louis lay perhaps ten feet to his right behind it.

Bliss put the Surgeon to one side. He would retrieve it once his work was done. Instead, he removed the little Beretta Tomcat from its holster beneath his arm. It was the perfect coup de grâce weapon, a comparatively cheap yet reliable .32 that could be disposed of quickly and without regret. Slowly and quietly, Bliss worked his way along the slope of the incline. Ten feet. Eight. Five.

He stilled his breathing. There was saliva in his mouth, but he did not swallow. He heard only birdsong, and the gentle shifting of the branches.

In one graceful movement, Bliss raised the gun and prepared to shoot.

Angel was halfway between the woods and the body of Louis when Bliss appeared. He was caught in the open, unarmed. He froze for an instant, then continued his run, even as Bliss altered the angle of his weapon to deal with the approaching man, the muzzle now centered on Angel's body.

Then two voices spoke. Both were familiar to Angel, and both said the same single word.

"Hey!"

The first voice came from behind Bliss. He swiveled to face the new threat, and saw a man kneeling in the grass, a gun leveled on him. Some distance behind him, and clearly struggling with the terrain, was an overweight man in overalls, also carrying a gun.

The second voice came from below Bliss. He looked down, and saw Louis lying on his back, a gun aimed at Bliss's chest.

Bliss almost smiled in admiration. *Such patience,* he thought, *such guile. You clever, clever boy.*

And then Bliss felt force and heat as the bullets entered his body, spinning him where he stood and sending him tumbling down the slope. The rain had stopped for a time, and the sky above him was a shard of clear blue as he died.

CHAPTER TWENTY-EIGHT

ANGEL NEEDED A MOMENT to take in what had happened. Once he had done so, his rage was no longer self-induced, and found an appropriate target in Louis.

"You asshole!" he shouted, once it was clear that his partner, lover, and now object of his ire was not dead. "You piece of shit." He kicked him hard in the ribs.

"I got shot!" said Louis. He pointed to a damp patch on his right arm where the bullet had grazed him, and the hole in his sleeve.

"Not shot enough. That's a scratch."

Angel's boot was poised for another kick, but Louis was already scrambling awkwardly to his feet.

"Why didn't you say something when I called to you?"

"Because I didn't know where Bliss was. If he heard me speak, or saw you react to something I said, he'd go for the long shot. I needed him to get close."

"You could have whispered! What the hell is wrong with you? I thought you were dead."

"Well, I'm not."

"Well, you should be."

"You could look pleased about the fact that I'm still alive. *I. Got. Shot.*"

"The hell with you."

Angel looked over Louis's shoulder and saw the Detective and Willie Brew standing on the top of the small hill, staring down at them. His brow furrowed. Louis turned. His brow did exactly the same.

"You two on vacation?" asked Angel.

"We came looking for you," said the Detective.

"Why?"

"Willie thought you might be in trouble."

"What gave you that idea?"

"You know, barns blowing up, that kind of thing."

"I got shot," said Louis.

"I heard."

"Yeah, well nobody seems too bothered by it."

"Except you."

"With reason, man. You two come alone?"

The Detective shifted awkwardly on his feet as he answered. "Not entirely."

"Aw no," said Angel, realization dawning. "You didn't bring them along."

"There was nobody else. I couldn't pick and choose."

"Jesus. Where are they?"

The Detective gestured vaguely. "Somewhere out there. They took the road. We came on foot."

"Maybe they'll get lost," said Angel. "Permanently."

"They came here because of you two. They worship you."

"They're psychotic."

"You say that like it's a bad thing." The Detective gestured at Bliss. "By the way, who was he?"

"His name was Bliss," said Louis. "He was a killer."

"Hired to kill you?"

"Looks like it. Think he might have taken the job for free anyway."

"Didn't work out so good for him."

"He was supposed to be the best, back in the day. Everybody thought he'd retired."

"I guess he should have stayed in Florida."

"Guess so."

They heard the sound of a vehicle to the east. Seconds later, the Fulcis' monster truck appeared over one of the rises, heading in their direction. Some of Angel's anger had begun to dissipate, and he had deigned to examine Louis's wound.

"You'll live," said Angel.

"You could sound pleased."

"Asshole," said Angel again.

The truck pulled up nearby, churning mud and grass as it did so, and the Fulcis emerged, followed closely by Jackie Garner. They looked at Bliss, then looked at Louis.

"Who was he?" asked Paulie.

"A killer," said the Detective.

"Uh-huh. Wow," said Paulie. He glanced shyly at Louis, but it was Tony who spoke first.

"You okay, sir?" he asked.

Willie saw the Detective trying to hide his amusement. There probably weren't a whole lot of people that the Fulcis called "sir." It made Tony sound like he was about nine years old.

"Yeah. I just got shot."

"Wow," he said, echoing his brother. Both of the Fulcis seemed awestruck.

"What now?" asked the Detective.

"We finish what we came here to do," said Louis. "You don't have to come if it doesn't sit easy with you," he added.

"I came this far. I'd hate to leave before the climax."

"What about us?" asked Tony.

"The two roads converge about a half mile from Leehagen's house," said Louis. "You stay there with Jackie and hold them, in case company comes."

The Detective walked over to where Willie was standing uncertainly. "You can stay with them or come with us, Willie," he said, and Willie thought that he saw sympathy in the Detective's eyes, but it was lost on him. Willie looked to the Fulcis and Jackie Garner. Jackie had taken some short cylinders from his rucksack and was trying to explain the difference between them to the Fulcis.

"This is smoke," he said, holding up a tube wrapped at either end with green tape. "It's green. And this one explodes," he said, holding up one wrapped in red tape. "This one is red."

Tony Fulci looked hard at both of the tubes. "That one's green," he said, pointing at the gas. "The other one is red."

"No," said Jackie, "you got it wrong."

"I don't. That one's red, and that one's green. Tell him, Paulie."

Paulie joined them. "No, Jackie's right. Green and red."

"Jesus, Tony," said Jackie. "You're color-blind. Did no one ever tell you?"

Tony shrugged. "I just figured lots of people liked red food."

"That's not normal," said Jackie, "although I guess it explains why you were always running red lights."

"Well, it don't matter now. So the green one is really red, and the red one is green?" said Tony.

"That's right," said Jackie.

"Which one explodes again?"

Reluctantly, Willie turned back to the Detective.

"I'll go with you," he said.

CHAPTER TWENTY-NINE

THEY APPROACHED LEEHAGEN'S HOUSE by the same route they had taken earlier that day, passing through the cattle pens. The car was still in the barn, the bodies of the Endalls still on the floor. The pens gave them more cover than they would have enjoyed had they approached by road although, as Angel pointed out, it also offered others more places in which to hide, yet they reached the rise overlooking the property without incident. Once again, Leehagen's house lay below them. It seemed almost to give off a sense of apprehension, as if it were waiting for the violent reprisal that must inevitably come the way of those inside. There was no sign of life: no shapes moving, no twitching of drapes, only stillness and wariness.

Angel lay on the grass as Louis scanned every inch of the property.

"Nothing," he said. His wound, although little more than a graze, was aching. The Fulcis had offered him some mild sedatives from their mobile drugstore, but the pain wasn't bad enough to justify dulling his senses before the task was complete.

"Lot of open ground between us and them," said Angel. "They'll see us coming."

"Let them," said Louis.

"Easy for you to say. You've already been shot once today."

"Uh-huh: a shot from an expert marksman at a moving target over open ground, and he still didn't make the kill. You think whoever's in there is going to do any better? This isn't a western. People are hard to hit unless they're up close."

Behind them knelt the Detective, and farther back was Willie Brew. He had said little since the killing at the ruined barn, and his eyes appeared to be looking inward, at something that only he could see, instead of out at the world through which he was moving. The Detective knew that Willie was in shock. Unlike Louis, he understood what Willie was going through. Deaths stayed with the Detective, and he knew that, in taking a life, you took on the burden of the victim's grief and pain. That was the price you paid, but nobody had explained that to Willie Brew. Now he would keep paying it until the day he died.

Louis looked to the sky. It was darkening again. More rain was coming after the brief hiatus. The Detective followed his gaze, and nodded.

"We wait," he said.

He turned to Willie Brew, offering him a final chance to absent himself from what was to come. "You want to stay here while we go in?"

Willie shook his head. "I'll go," he said. Willie felt as though the life were slowly seeping from his body, as though it was he who had been shot, not the man whom he had left dead on the ground. His hands wouldn't stop shaking. He didn't think he'd be able to hold the Browning steady, even if his life depended on it. The gun was back in the pocket of his overalls, and it could stay there. He wouldn't be using it again, not ever.

And so they remained as they were, unspeaking, until the rain again began to descend.

They moved fast, running in pairs. The rain had returned suddenly, falling hard, slanting slightly in the westerly breeze, aiding them in their task by hammering on the windows of Leehagen's house, masking their approach from those within. They reached the fence at the edge of the property, and then used the shrubs and trees in the yard for cover as they advanced on the main building itself. The house was surrounded by a porch on all four sides. The drapes were drawn on the first-floor windows, and the windows themselves were locked. A disabled access ramp ran parallel to the main steps below the front door, which was glassless and closed. They passed the nurse's little apartment, a single room with a bed and a small living area. There was nobody inside. She would have been sent away, Angel guessed. Leehagen would not have wanted her as a witness to what was planned.

They made their way to the back door, which was inset with eight glass panes behind which were lace drapes. Through the drapes they could see a large modern kitchen, and beyond it a dining room. An opening to the right of the dining room led into the hallway. It did not have a door, probably to make access easier for Leehagen and his wheelchair.

The back door was locked. Using the muzzle of Bliss's gun, Angel shattered a pane and reached in to turn the latch, his fingers moving quickly and nimbly, Angel conscious that he was briefly the most exposed among them. The latch shifted, and he yanked his hand from the gap and twisted the handle, pushing the door open at the same time as he drew himself flat against the wall of the house, anticipating gunfire. None came.

Louis entered first, staying low and moving left, cutting himself off from the sightline of anyone who might be tempted to open fire on them from the hallway. The Detective followed, and then there was the boom of a shotgun from inside the house and the glass above his head shattered. The Detective threw himself to the right and crawled along the floor as a shell was jacked and a second shot came, this one blasting a cupboard to pieces just inches from where his foot had been a moment before. Angel returned fire, allowing the Detective to move into the dining area while the shooter was pinned down, making for the door at the far end of the room. As soon as Angel paused to reload, he made his move. They heard shouts, and a scuffle. Angel and Willie rushed into the kitchen while Louis advanced down the hallway, Bliss's gun in his hand.

A young man lay on the timber floor, his scalp bleeding and his eyes rolled back in his head so that only the whites were visible. The Detective had struck him several times with the butt of his gun during the struggle instead of shooting him. It was clear why. He was no more than seventeen or eighteen, with blond hair and a tanned skin: another farmboy following orders.

"He's just a kid," said Willie.

"A kid with a shotgun," said Angel.

"Yeah, but still."

"They never thought that you'd get this far," said the Detective.

Louis looked into the dining room, where a chair faced the window, set apart from the table behind it. The Chandler rifle still stood upon the table, and the Hardigg case rested on the carpeted floor. He walked over and ran his fingers along the barrel of the gun, then rested his hand on the back of the chair. The Detective joined him.

"This was where he waited," said Louis.

"It was personal, wasn't it?" said the Detective.

"Yeah, real personal."

When they went back into the hall, they found that Willie had gently placed a cushion under the wounded boy's head.

"Why don't you stay with him?" said the Detective. "We need someone down here anyway, just in case."

Willie knew that he was being sidelined, but he didn't care. He was grateful for the chance to look after the boy. He'd get some water from the kitchen and clean out the wound in his scalp, make sure it didn't get infected and that he didn't go into convulsions. He didn't want to follow these men up the stairs, not unless he had to. Even if one of Leehagen's men popped up with a gun and pointed it in his face, Willie didn't think he'd be able to do much about it. He'd just close his eyes and let it come.

The Detective led the way up the stairs, Louis and Angel lagging behind until he gave them the all clear. There were five doors on the second floor, all closed but none, as it turned out, locked. They took them one at a time, Louis opening and covering to the right, Angel to the left, the Detective keeping his back to them and the other doors in view. Three were bedrooms, one of them filled with women's clothes, the other clearly a young man's, although their clothing was mixed in the man's room, and there was a box of Trojans on the nightstand. The fourth room was a large family bathroom that had been converted for Leehagen's use. There was an open wet room instead of a shower, with a plastic chair beneath the shower head, and a rubber cushion in the tub that could be inflated or deflated as needed. The shelves were packed with medication: liquids and pills and disposable plastic syringes. Underlying everything was a sickly, unpleasant smell: the scent of dying, of someone rotting from within.

A closed door connected the bathroom to what was, presumably, Leehagen's bedroom. Louis and Angel assumed positions at either side of it, while the Detective went into the hallway and prepared to enter through the bedroom door.

Louis looked at Angel and nodded. He took a step back, and kicked hard at the door just below the lock. The lock held, but at that moment the Detective entered the main bedroom. There was the sound of a shot, and then Louis kicked again. The lock splintered and the door flew open, revealing an overweight man in his forties holding a semiautomatic in his hand: Leehagen's son, Michael. Loretta Hoyle crouched at his feet, her head hidden in her arms. Between them and where Louis and Angel stood was a large hospital bed, upon which lay a withered old man with an oxygen mask over his mouth and nose.

For a moment, Michael Leehagen was distracted. He could not cover both doors at once, so he froze.

And Louis killed him. The bullet struck him in the chest, and he slid down the wall. Blood spread across the front of his white shirt, and he blinked at it in puzzlement as he sat heavily on the floor. Loretta Hoyle peered out of her cocoon, then wailed and reached for him, calling his name as she held his head between her hands. He tried to focus on her, but he could not. His body jerked once. His eyes closed, and he died. Loretta screamed, then buried her face in the nape of the dead man's neck and began to cry as Angel kicked away the fallen gun.

Arthur Leehagen's head moved on his pillow, and he regarded his dead son with rheumy eyes. A pale, thin hand reached for the mask, removing it from his mouth. He drew a rattling breath, then spoke.

"My boy," he said. His eyes filled with tears. They spilled over and flowed from the corners of his eyes, dropping soundlessly on the pillows.

Louis walked to the bed and stood over the old man.

"You brought this on yourself," he said.

Leehagen stared at him. He was nearly bald, only a few strands of thin white hair clinging to his skull like cobwebs. His skin was pale and bruised and looked cold to the touch, but his eyes shone all the brighter for being set in such an emaciated, dessicated frame. His body might have betrayed him, but his mind was still alert, burning with frustration as it found itself trapped in a physical form that would soon no longer be able to sustain it.

"You're the one," said Leehagen. "You killed my son, my Jon." He had to force each word out, taking a breath after every one.

"I did."

"Did you even ask why?"

Louis shook his head. "It didn't matter. And now you've lost your other son. Like I said, you brought it on yourself."

Leehagen's hand reached for the mask. He pressed it to his face, gasping in the precious oxygen. He stayed like that for a time until his breathing was under control once again, then moved the mask aside.

"You've left me with nothing," he said.

"You have your life."

Leehagen tried to laugh, but it came out as a kind of strangled cough.

"Life?" he said. "This is not life. This is merely a slow dying."

Louis stared down at him. "Why here?" he said. "Why bring us all the way up here to kill us?"

"I wanted you to bleed onto my land. I wanted your blood to seep into the place where Jon is buried. I wanted him to know that he had been avenged."

"And Hoyle?"

Leehagen swallowed drily. "A good friend. A loyal friend." The mention of Hoyle's name seemed to give him new energy, if only for a moment. "We'll hire others. It will never end. Never."

"You have no one left now," said Louis. "Soon, Hoyle won't either. It's over."

And something extinguished itself in Leehagen's eyes as he realized the truth of what had been said. He stared at his dead son, and remembered the one who had gone before him. With a last great effort, he lifted his head from the pillow. His left hand reached out and grasped the sleeve of Louis's jacket.

"Then kill me, too," he pleaded. "Please. Be . . . merciful."

His head sank back, but his eyes remained fixed on Louis, filled with hatred and grief and, most of all, need.

"Please," he repeated.

Louis gently released Leehagen's grip. Almost tenderly, he placed his hand over the old man's face, closing the nostrils tightly with his thumb and index finger, the palm pressed hard against the dry, wrinkled mouth. Leehagen nodded against the pillow, as if in silent agreement with what was about to pass. After a few seconds, he tried to draw a breath, but it would not come. He spasmed, his body shuddering and trembling. His fingers stretched themselves to their limit, his eyes opened wide, and then it was over. His body deflated, so that he seemed even smaller in death than in life.

There was a movement at the bedroom door. Willie Brew had entered during Leehagen's final moments, troubled by the silence that had followed the gunfire. There was desolation on his face as he approached the bed. Killing those who were armed was one thing, however terrible he considered it, but killing an old, frail man, snuffing the life from him between a finger and thumb as one might a candle flame, that was beyond Willie's comprehension. He knew now that his relationship with these men had come to an end. He could no longer tolerate their presence in his life, just as he would never be able to come to terms with the life that he had taken.

Louis removed his hand from Leehagen's face, pausing only to close his eyes. He turned to the Detective and began to speak, just as Loretta Hoyle lifted her head from her dead lover's shoulder and made her move. Her face had the feral quality of a rabid animal that has finally tipped over into madness. Her hand emerged from behind her lover's body holding a gun, her finger already on the trigger.

She raised it and fired.

It was Willie Brew who registered the movement, and Willie Brew who responded. There was nothing dramatic about what he did in response, nothing fast or spectacular. He simply stepped in front of Louis, as though he were nudging into line before him, and took the bullet. It hit him just below the hollow of his neck. He bucked at the impact, then backed into Louis, who reached instinctively beneath Willie's arms to break his fall. There were two more shots, but they came from Angel as Loretta Hoyle died.

Louis laid Willie on the carpet. He tried to loosen the shirt to get at the wound, but Willie pushed his hands away, shaking his head. There was too much blood. It gushed from the wound, drowning Willie in its tide. It bubbled from his mouth as his back arched, Angel and the Detective now beside him. Knowing he was dying, they took his hands, Angel the right and the Detective the left. Willie Brew's grip tightened. He looked at them and tried to speak. The Detective leaned down, his ear so close to Willie's lips that blood sprayed upon his face as the mechanic tried to say his final words.

"It's okay, Willie," he said. "It's okay."

Willie struggled to draw breath, but it was denied him. His face darkened with the effort, and his features contorted in his distress.

"Let it come, Willie," whispered the Detective. "It's nearly over now."

Willie's body slowly grew limp in Louis's arms, and the life left him at last.

CHAPTER THIRTY

THEY WRAPPED WILLIE BREW's body in a white sheet and placed it in the bed of a truck that was parked at the back of the house. Angel drove, the Detective beside him, while Louis kept vigil beside Willie. They followed the road to where the Fulcis and Jackie Garner were waiting. They saw the body in the back of the truck, the sheet stained with blood, but they said nothing.

"Nobody came," said Jackie. "We waited, but nobody came."

Then vehicles appeared in the distance: three black vans and a pair of black Explorers, approaching fast. The Fulcis grew tense and hefted their guns in anticipation.

"No," said Louis simply.

The convoy came to a halt a short distance from where they stood. The passenger door of the lead Explorer opened, and a man in a long black overcoat stepped forward, placing a gray homburg hat on his head to protect him from the rain. Louis climbed down from the bed of the truck and walked to meet him.

"Looks like you've had quite the morning," said Milton.

Louis regarded him without expression. The distance between the two men was only a couple of feet, but a chasm yawned there.

"Why are you here?" said Louis.

"There'll be questions asked. You don't just declare war on someone like Arthur Leehagen and expect no one to notice. Is he dead?"

"He's dead. So is his son, and Nicholas Hoyle's daughter."

"I would have expected no less of you," said Milton.

"Bliss, too."

Milton blinked once, but said nothing in response.

"You didn't answer my question," said Louis. "Why are you here?"

"A guilty conscience, perhaps."

"You don't have one."

Milton inclined his head gently in acknowledgment of the truth of Louis's statement. "Then call it what you will: professional courtesy, a tying up of loose ends. It doesn't matter."

"Did you order the killing of Jon Leehagen?" said Louis.

"Yes."

"Did Ballantine work for you?"

"On that occasion, yes. He was just one more layer of deniability, a buffer between us and you."

"Did Gabriel know?"

"I am sure that he suspected, but it wouldn't have done for him to have asked. It would have been unwise."

Milton looked over Louis's shoulder, in the direction of Leehagen's house, and his eyes were far away for a moment.

"I have bad news for you," he said. "Gabriel died during the night. I'm sorry."

The two men stared at each other. Neither broke.

"So, what now?" asked Louis.

"You walk away."

"What's the cover story?"

"Gang warfare. Leehagen crossed the wrong people. He was engaged in illegal activity: drugs, people trafficking. We can say the Russians did it. We hear you know all about them. I'm sure that you'll agree it's entirely plausible."

"What about the survivors?"

"They'll keep quiet. We're good at making people hold their tongues."

Milton turned and waved to the clean-up teams. Two of the vans headed for Leehagen's house.

"I have one more question," said Louis.

"I think I've answered enough questions for now. In fact, I've answered all of the questions I'm going to answer from you."

He began to walk back to the Explorer. Louis ignored what Milton had said.

"Did you want Arthur Leehagen dead?" asked Louis.

Milton paused. He was smiling when he looked back.

"If you hadn't done it, we'd have been forced to take care of him ourselves. People trafficking is a risky business. There are terrorists out there willing to exploit every loophole. The Leehagens weren't as particular as they should have been about who they dealt with. They made mistakes, and we had to clean up after them. Now we're going to clean up after you instead. That's why you're walking away, you and your friends. It looks like you did one last job for us after all."

He turned and signaled to the remaining black van. The side doors opened, and two men stepped out: the Harrys.

"The local cops picked them up," said Milton, "probably on Leehagen's orders. Best thing that could have happened to them, under the circumstances. Take them home, Louis, the dead and the living. We're finished here."

With that, Milton climbed in the Explorer and followed the clean-up crew to the Leehagen house. Louis stood in the pouring rain. He raised his face to the sky and closed his eyes, as though the water could wash him clean of all that he had done.

EPILOGUE

I
Am found.
O let him
Scald me and drown
Me in his world's wound.

—DYLAN THOMAS (1914–53), "VISION AND PRAYER"

IF NICHOLAS HOYLE WAS concerned for his safety after what had occurred, then he gave no sign of it. His daughter was buried in a cemetery in New Jersey, but Hoyle did not attend the funeral, and neither did any of the men whom Louis and Angel had encountered at Hoyle's penthouse, the enigmatic Simeon included. It appeared that Simeon had an apartment of his own somewhere in the Hoyle building, because when he did leave the penthouse he always returned before dark, and he was never alone on his sojourns. None of this concerned Angel and Louis, who were content merely to watch and wait. Over the course of six weeks they, and others, kept vigil from a rented apartment overlooking Hoyle's building, noting all that went on, keeping track of delivery companies, office cleaners, and the other outside services that kept the building running. In all that time, they saw no sign of Hoyle himself beyond the doors of his apartment. He was sequestered in his fortress, unassailable.

On the day after Loretta Hoyle was buried in New Jersey, Willie Brew was laid to rest in Queens. The Detective, Angel, and Louis were there, as was Willie's ex-wife and all of his friends. It was a well-attended affair. The mechanic would have been proud.

After the funeral, a small group retired to Nate's to remember Willie. Angel and Louis sat in a corner alone, and nobody bothered them, not until an hour had passed and Arno arrived at Nate's door. His absence until that point had been noted, but nobody knew where he was or what he was doing. He made his way through the crowd, ignoring outstretched hands, words of condolence, offers of drinks. He paused briefly in front of the Detective and said: "You should have looked out for him."

The Detective nodded, but said nothing.

Arno moved on to where Angel and Louis were sitting. He reached into the inside pocket of the only suit that he owned and withdrew a white envelope, which he handed to Louis.

"What is it?" said Louis, taking the envelope.

"Open it and see."

Louis did so. It contained a bank draft.

"It's for twenty-two thousand three hundred and eighty-five dollars," said Arno. "It's all the money that Willie owed you on your loan."

Louis placed the draft back in the envelope and tried to hand it to Arno. Around them, the bar had gone quiet.

"I don't want it," said Louis.

"I don't care," said Arno. "You take it. It's money that was owed to you. Now the debt is paid. We're all square. I don't want Willie lying in the ground owing something. He's done now. We're done. In return, I'd appreciate it if you'd stay away from our place of business in the future."

"Our" place of business. Willie's and his. That was the way it had always been, and that was the way it would stay. Willie's name would remain above the door, and Arno would continue to service the cars that came his way, overcharging only slightly.

With that, Arno turned his back on them and left the bar. He walked down the street to the auto shop and entered through the side door. He hit the lights and breathed in deeply, before walking to the little office and taking the bottle of Maker's Mark from the filing cabinet. He poured what was left into Willie's mug, headed out onto the floor, pulled Willie's favorite stool from a corner, and sat down.

Then Arno, now truly alone, began to weep.

The pool cleaners arrived at the Hoyle building, as always, at 7:00 P.M. after Hoyle had just finished his evening swim. Maintenance checks were always performed in the evening, while Hoyle prepared for dinner, so as not to disturb his routine. The cleaners were met in the outer lobby by Simeon and another guard named Aristede, and there they were wanded and frisked. The two men who arrived on this particular evening were not the usual cleaners. Simeon knew them all by sight and name, but these guys he had never seen before. They were a pair of Asians: Japanese, he thought. He called the owner of the pool company at home and she confirmed that yes, they were her men. Two of the regular cleaners were sick, and the others were tied up with jobs all over the place, but the Japanese guys were good workers, she said. At least, she thought they were Japanese. To be honest, she wasn't quite certain either. Simeon hung up, gave the cleaners a final pat-down just to be safe, checked their tool kits and chemical containers for weapons, then admitted them to Hoyle's inner sanctum.

Nicholas Hoyle's pool was state-of-the-art, the most technically advanced that money could buy. At the touch of a button, a river effect could be created giving the sensation of swimming against the current, variable according to the exercise level required. It had a UV sterilizing system, complete with auto-chlorine dosing to maintain the chlorine levels, an automatic backwash filter, and an automatic pH controller. A Dolphin 3001 pool cleaner took care of routine brushing and vacuuming, and the entire system was overseen by a control panel enclosed in a small ventilated cabin next to Hoyle's private sauna. Although it was all environmentally costly, Hoyle had made some provisions for power saving and privacy. The lights came on upon entry and turned themselves off when Hoyle exited. Once he was inside the pool area, an internal palm-print-activated lock made it virtually impregnable.

But, as with all such advanced systems, routine maintenance was essential. The pH electrodes needed to be cleaned and calibrated, and the chlorine and pH adjusting solutions replenished, so the two Asians had brought all the necessary fluids and test equipment with them. Simeon watched as the cleaners performed the usual routines, chatting animatedly as they did so. When they were done, he signed off on their work and they departed, bowing slightly to him as they thanked him and entered the elevator.

"Polite little fellas, ain't they?" said Aristede, who had worked for Hoyle for almost as long as Simeon.

"I guess," said Simeon.

"My old man never trusted them, not after Pearl Harbor. I liked those ones, though. He'd probably have liked them, too."

Simeon didn't comment. Regardless of race or creed, he tended to keep his feelings about others to himself.

The woman who owned the pool company was named Eve Fielder. She had taken over the running of it after her father died and had built it into a well-regarded concern catering to upscale clients and private health clubs. Right now, she was staring at the receiver that she had just replaced in its cradle and wondering for just how much longer her company would be of any concern at all.

"Happy?" she asked the man seated across from her.

The man wore a ski mask. He was short, and she was sure that he was white. His colleague, who was tall and, judging by the flashes of skin that she could see beneath the mask, black, was sitting quietly at the kitchen table. He had tuned her satellite radio to some godawful country-and-western station, which suggested a degree of sadism to those who were currently holding her hostage. Alone. For the first time in years, she wished that she was not divorced.

"Contented," said the small man. "It's the best we can hope for in life."

"So what do we do now?"

He checked his watch.

"We wait."

"For how long?"

"Until the morning. Then we'll be on our way."

"And Mr. Hoyle?"

"He'll have a very clean pool."

Fielder sighed.

"I get the feeling this is going to be bad for my business."

"Probably."

She sighed again.

"Any chance we could turn off that hick music?" she asked.

"I don't think so, but he'll be gone soon."

"It really sucks."

"I know," he said. He sounded sincere. "If it's any consolation, you're only going to have to listen to it for an hour. Me, I got a life sentence with that as the sound track."

Hoyle worked in his private office until shortly after 9:00 A.M. He was an early riser, but he liked to break up his morning with exercise. He spent an hour on the stairmaster in his personal gym before stripping down to his trunks and entering the pool area. He stood at the side of the pool, his toes hanging over the edge. He put on his goggles, took a deep breath, then dived into the deep end, his body barely making a splash as it broke the water, his arms outstretched, bubbles of air emerging from his nostrils and floating upward. He stayed under the water for half the length of the pool, then kicked powerfully for the surface.

The dosing system had been altered during the maintenance check, making the water slightly acidic, and sodium cyanide had been added to the chlorine dosing system. When the door lock was activated, and the internal lights came on, the cyanide solution was released rapidly into the acidified water, resulting in the release of hydrogen cyanide.

Hoyle's pool area had just become a gas chamber.

Hoyle was already feeling dizzy by the end of the second lap, and his sense of direction seemed to have deserted him because he had finished his lap against the side of the pool, not the end. He was having trouble breathing and, despite his exertions, his heartbeat was slowing. His eyes began to itch and burn. There was a pungent taste in his mouth, and he vomited into the water. His lips were hurting, too, and then the pain was all over his body. He started to kick for the ladder, but he could barely lift his feet. He tried to shout for help, but the water had entered his mouth, and now his tongue and throat were burning, too.

Hoyle panicked. He could no longer move sufficiently to keep himself afloat. He sank below the surface and thought he could hear shouting, but he could see nothing because he was already blind. His mouth opened and he started to drown, the water seeming to scald his insides.

Within seconds, he was dead.

By the time Simeon realized what was happening, it was too late for him to save his employer. He managed to override the security system, but the instant that he smelled the air in the pool he was forced to seal it off once again. As an additional precaution, he evacuated the penthouse until the area had vented, then went back in alone. He stared at Hoyle's body, suspended in the water.

Simeon's cellphone rang. The caller display told him that the call was coming from a private number.

"Simeon," said a man's voice.

"Who is this?"

"I think you know who it is." Simeon recognized Louis's deep tones.

"Was this your doing?"

"Yes. I didn't notice you leaping in to save him."

Simeon instinctively looked around, staring at the tall buildings that surrounded the pool, their windows gazing back at him, impassive and unblinking.

"He was my employer. I was hired to protect him."

"But not to die for him. You did your best. You can't protect a man from himself."

"I could come after you. I have my reputation to consider."

"You're a bodyguard, not a virgin. I think your reputation will recover. If you come after me, your health won't. I suggest you walk away from this. I don't believe that you knew everything of what passed between Hoyle and Leehagen. You don't strike me as the kind of man who would comfortably set up another. Or maybe I'm wrong. Maybe you'd like to contradict me."

Simeon didn't speak for a time.

"Okay," he said. "I walk."

"Good. Don't stay in the city. Don't even stay in the country. I'm sure a gentleman of your abilities won't find it hard to pick up work somewhere else, far away from here. A good soldier can always find a convenient war."

"And if I don't?"

"Then our paths might cross again. Someone once told me to avoid leaving witnesses. I wouldn't want to start thinking of you in that way."

Simeon ended the call. He put the cellphone and his security pass by the side of the pool and left Hoyle's penthouse. He traveled down to the lobby and walked quickly but casually from the building, facing the great skyscrapers that dominated the skyline, their windows reflecting the late fall sun and the white clouds that scudded across the sky. He did not doubt for one minute that he was fortunate to be alive. He felt only a slight twinge of shame at the fact that he was running away. Still, it was enough to make him pause in an effort to reassert his dignity. He stopped and looked up at the buildings around him, his eyes moving from window to window, frame to frame. After a time, he nodded, both to himself and at the man who he knew was following his progress:

Louis, the killer, the burning man.

Louis, the last of the Reapers.

ACKNOWLEDGMENTS

A NUMBER OF BOOKS proved particularly useful during the writing of this novel. They were: *Sundown Towns: A Hidden Dimension of American Racism* by James W. Loewen (Touchstone, 2005); *The Adirondacks: A History of America's First Wilderness* by Paul Schneider (Owl Books, 1997); and *On Killing: The Psychological Cost of Learning to Kill in War and Society* by Dave Grossman (Back Bay Books, 1996).

I am grateful for the kind assistance provided by Joe Long and Keith Long while researching the Queens sections of the book; and to Geoff Ridyard who, in another life, would have made a very good assassin indeed. Thanks also to my U.K. editor, Sue Fletcher, and everyone at Hodder & Stoughton; Emily Bestler, my U.S. editor, and all at Atria Books and Pocket Books; and to my agent, Darley Anderson, and his wonderful staff. Finally, Jennie, Cameron, and Alistair put up with a lot, as always. Love and thanks to you all.

Atria Books
Proudly Presents

THE LOVERS
John Connolly

Available in hardcover June 2009
from Atria Books

I

I hate and I love. Perhaps you ask why I do so. I do not know, but I feel it happen and I am tormented.

Catullus, *Carmina,* 85

CHAPTER ONE

The Faraday boy had been missing for three days.

On the first day, nothing was done. After all, he was twenty-one, and young men of that age no longer had to abide by curfews and parental rules. Still, his behavior was out of character for him. Bobby Faraday was trustworthy. He was a college student, although he had taken a year off before deciding on the direction of his graduate studies in engineering, with talk of going abroad for a couple of months, or working for his uncle in San Diego. Instead, he had stayed in his hometown, saving money by living with his parents and banking as much of what he earned as he could, which was a little less than the previous year as he could now drink with impunity, and was maybe indulging that newfound liberty with more enthusiasm than might have been considered entirely wise. He'd had a couple of killer hangovers over New Year's, that was for sure, and his old man had advised him to ease up before his liver started crying out for mercy, but Bobby was young, he was immortal, and he was in love, or had been until recently. Perhaps it would be truer to say that Bobby Faraday was still in love, but the object of his affection had moved on, leaving Bobby mired in his own emotions. The girl was why he had opted to remain in town instead of seeing a little more of the world, a decision that had been met with mixed feelings by his parents: gratitude on the part of his mother, disappointment on that of his father. There had been some arguments about it at the start, but now, as with two reluctant armies on the verge of an unwanted battle, a truce of kinds had been declared between father and son, although each side continued to watch the other warily to see which one might blink first. Meanwhile, Bobby drank, and his father fumed, but remained silent in the hope that the ending of the relationship might lead his son to broaden his horizons until college resumed in the fall.

Despite his occasional overindulgences, Bobby was never late for work at the auto shop and gas station, and usually left a little later than he had to, because there was always something to be done, some task that he did not wish to abandon uncompleted, even if it could be finished quickly and easily in the morning. It was one of the reasons why his father, whatever their disagreements, didn't worry too much about his son's future prospects: Bobby was too conscientious to leave the beaten track for long. He liked order, and always had. He'd never been one of those messy teenagers, either in appearance or approach. It just wasn't in his nature.

But he hadn't come home the night before, and he hadn't called to tell his parents where he might be, and that in itself was unusual. Then he didn't make it to work the following morning, which was so out of character that Ron Nevill, who owned the gas station, called the Faraday house to check on the boy and make sure that he wasn't ailing. His mother expressed surprise that her son wasn't already at work. She'd simply assumed that he'd come home late and left early. She checked his bedroom, which lay just off the basement den. His bed had not been slept in, and there was no indication that he'd spent the night on the couch instead.

When there was no word by 3:00 p.m., she called her husband at work. Together they checked with Bobby's friends, casual acquaintances, and his ex-girlfriend, Emily Kindler. That last call had been delicate, as she and Bobby had broken up only a couple of weeks before. His father suspected that this was the reason his son was drinking more than he should have, but he wouldn't have been the first man who tried to drown love's sorrows in a batch of alcohol. The trouble was that frustrated love was buoyant in booze: the more you tried to force it to the bottom, the more it insisted on bobbing right back up to the top.

Nobody had heard from Bobby, or had seen him, since the previous day. When 7:00 p.m. came and went, they called the police. The chief was skeptical. He was new in town, but familiar with the ways of young people. Nevertheless, he accepted that this was not typical behavior for Bobby

Faraday, and that twenty-four hours had now gone by since he left the gas station, for Bobby had not hit any of the local bars after work, and Ron Nevill seemed to be the last person who had seen him. The chief put together a description of the boy at the Faraday house, borrowed a photograph that had been taken the previous summer, and informed local law enforcement and the state police of a possible missing person. None of the other agencies responded with any great urgency, for they were almost as cynical about the behavior of young males as the chief was, and in the case of one going missing, they tended to wait for seventy-two hours before assuming that there might be more to the disappearance than a simple case of booze, hormones, or domestic difficulties.

On the second day, his parents, and their friends, began an informal canvass of the town and its environs, with no result. When it began to grow dark, his mother and father returned home, but they did not sleep that night, just as they had not slept the night before. His mother lay in bed, her face turned toward the window, straining to hear the sound of approaching footsteps, the familiar tread of her only son returning to her at last. She stirred only slightly when she heard her husband rise and put on his robe.

"What is it?" she asked.

"Nothing," he said. "I'm going to make some tea, sit up for a time." He paused. "You want some?"

But she knew that he was asking only out of politeness, that he would prefer it if she stayed where she was. He did not want them to sit at the kitchen table in silence, together but apart, the fears of one feeding those of the other. He wanted to be alone. So she let him go, and when the bedroom door closed softly behind him, she began to cry.

On the third day, the formal search began.

THE GOLDEN HOST MOVED as one, countless shapes bending obediently in unison at the gentle touch of the late-winter breeze, like a congregation at church bowing in accordance with the progress of the service, awaiting the moment of consecration that is to come.

They whispered to themselves, a soft, low susurration that might have been the crashing of distant waves were such an alien noise not unknown in this landlocked place. The paleness of them was dappled in spots by small flowers of red and orange and blue, a scattering of petals upon an ocean of seed and stem.

The host had been spared the reaping, and had grown tall, too tall, even as its crop decayed. A season's grain had gone to waste, for the old man upon whose land the host was gathered had died the previous summer, and his relatives were fighting over the sale of the property and how the proceeds would be divided. While they fought, the host had stretched skyward, a sea of dull gold in the depths of winter, speaking in hushed tones of what lay, rush hemmed and undiscovered, nearby.

And yet the host, it seemed, was at peace.

Suddenly, the breeze dropped for an instant and the host stood erect, as though troubled by the change, sensing that all was not as it had been, and then the wind rose again, more tempestuous now, transforming into smaller, dispersed gusts that divided the host with ripples and eddies, their caresses less delicate than what had gone before. Unity was replaced by confusion. Scattered fragments were caught in the sunlight before they fell to the ground. The whispering grew louder, drowning the calling of a solitary bird with rumors of approach.

A black shape appeared upon the horizon, like a great insect hovering over the stalks. It grew in stature, becoming the head, shoulders, and body of a man, passing between the rows of wheat while, ahead of him, a smaller form cleaved invisibly through the stalks, sniffing and yelping as it went, the first intruders upon the host's territory since the old man had died.

A second figure came into view, heavier than the first. This one seemed to be struggling with the terrain and with the unaccustomed exercise that his participation in the search had forced upon him. In the distance, but farther to the east, the two men could see other searchers. Somehow, they had drifted away from the main pack, although that itself had diminished as the day wore on. Already the light was fading. Soon it would be time to call a halt, and there would be fewer of them to search in the days that followed.

THEY HAD BEGUN THAT morning, immediately after Sunday services. The searchers had congregated at the Catholic church, St. Jude's, since that had the largest yard and, curiously, the smallest congregation, a contradiction that Peyton Carmichael, the man with the dog, had never quite understood. Perhaps, he figured, they were expecting a mass conversion at some point in the future, which made him wonder if Catholics were just more optimistic than other folk.

The chief of police and his men had divided the township into grids, and the townspeople themselves into groups, and had assigned each group an area to search. Sandwiches, potato chips, and sodas in brown bags had been provided by the various churches, although most people had brought food and water of their own, just in case. In a break with Sunday tradition, none had dressed up in the usual finery. Instead, they wore loose shirts and old pants, and battered boots or comfortable sneakers. Some carried sticks, others garden rakes to search in the undergrowth. There was an air of subdued expectation, a kind of excitement despite the task before them. They shared rides, and drove out to their assigned areas. As each area was searched, and nothing found, another was suggested either by the cops who were coordinating the efforts on the ground, or by contacting the base of operations that had been set up in the hall behind the church.

It had been unseasonably warm when they began, a curious false thaw that would soon end, and the difficulty of coping with soft ground and melting snow had sapped the strength of many before they took a break for lunch at about one or one-thirty. Some of the older people had returned home at that stage, content that they had made some effort for the Faradays, but the rest continued with the search. After all, the next day was Monday. There would be work to do, obligations to be met. This day was the only one that they could spare to look for the boy, and the best would have to be made of it. But as the light had grown dim, so too the day had grown colder, and Peyton was grateful that he had not left his Timberland jacket in the car but had chosen to tie it around his waist until it was needed.

He whistled at his dog, a three-year-old spaniel named Molly, and waited, once again, for his companion to catch up. Artie Hoyt: of all the people with whom he had to end up. Relations between the two men had been cool for the last year or more, ever since Artie had caught Peyton eyeing his daughter's ass at church. It didn't matter to Artie that he hadn't seen exactly what he thought he'd seen. Yes, Peyton had been looking at his daughter's ass, but not out of any feelings of lust or attraction. Not that he was above such base impulses: at times, the pastor's sermons were so dull that the only thing keeping Peyton awake was the sight of young, lithe female forms draped in their Sunday best. Peyton was long past the age when he might have been troubled by the potential implications for his immortal soul of such carnal thoughts in church. He figured that God had better things to worry about than whether Peyton Carmichael, sixty-four, widower, was paying more attention to objects of female beauty than he was to the old blowhard at the pulpit, a man who, in

Peyton's opinion, possessed less Christian charity than the average alligator. As Peyton's doctor liked to tell him, live a life of wine, women, and song, all in moderation but always of the proper vintage. Peyton's wife had died three years earlier, taken by breast cancer, and although there were plenty of women in town of the correct vintage who might have been prepared to offer Peyton some comfort on a winter's evening, he just wasn't interested. He had loved his wife. Occasionally he was still lonely, although less often than before, but those feelings of loneliness were specific, not general: he missed his wife, not female company, and he viewed the occasional pleasure that he took in the sight of a young, good-looking woman merely as a sign that he was not entirely dead below the waist. God, having taken his wife from him, could allow him that small indulgence. If God was going to make a big deal of it, then, well, Peyton would have a few words for Him too, when eventually they met.

The problem with Artie Hoyt's daughter was that, although she was young, she was by no means good looking. Neither was she lithe. In fact, she was the opposite of lithe and, come to think of it, the opposite of light too. She'd never been what you might call svelte, but then she had left town and gone to live in Baltimore, and by the time she came back she'd piled on the pounds. Now, when she walked into church, Peyton was sure that he felt the floor tremble slightly beneath her feet. If she were any bigger, she'd have to enter sideways; that, or they'd be forced to widen the aisles.

And so, the first Sunday after she'd returned to

the parental home, she had entered the chapel with her mom and dad and Peyton had found himself staring in appalled fascination at her ass, jiggling under a red and white floral dress like an earthquake in a snow-covered rose garden. His jaw might even have been hanging open when he turned to find Artie Hoyt glaring at him, and after that, well, things had never been quite the same between them. They hadn't been close before the incident, but at least they'd been civil when their paths had crossed. Now they rarely exchanged even a nod of greeting, and they hadn't spoken to each other until fate, and the missing Faraday boy, had forced them together. They'd been part of a group of eight that had started out in the morning, quickly falling to six after old Blackwell and his wife seemed set to pass out and had, reluctantly, turned back for home, then five, four, three, until now it was just Artie and him.

Peyton didn't understand at first why Artie didn't just give up and go home himself. Even the modest pace that Peyton and Molly were setting seemed too much for him, and they had been forced to stop repeatedly to allow Artie to catch his breath and gulp water from the bottle that he was carrying in his rucksack. It had taken Peyton a while to figure out that Artie wasn't going to give him the satisfaction of knowing that he'd kept searching while Artie had faded, even if the other man were to die in the attempt. With that in mind, Peyton had taken a malicious pleasure in forcing the pace for a time, until he acknowledged that his needless cruelty was rendering null and void his earlier efforts at worship and penitence, the occasional glance at young women notwithstanding.

They were nearing the boundary fence between this property and the next, a field of fallow, overgrown land with a small pond at its center sheltered by trees and rushes. Peyton had only a little water left, and Molly was thirsty. He figured he could water her at the pond, then call it a day. He couldn't see Artie objecting, just as long as it was Peyton who suggested quitting, and not him.

"Let's head into the field there and check it out," said Peyton. "I need to get water for the dog anyway. After that, we can cut back onto the road and take an easy walk back to the cars. Okay with you?"

Artie nodded. He walked to the fence, rested his hands upon it, and tried to hoist himself up and over. He got one foot off the ground, but the other wouldn't join it. He simply didn't have the strength to continue. Peyton thought he looked like he wanted to lie down and die, but he didn't. There was something admirable about his refusal to give up, even if it had less to do with any concerns about Bobby Faraday than his anger at Peyton Carmichael. Eventually, though, he was forced to admit defeat, and landed back down on the same side on which he'd started.

"Goddammit," he said.

"Hold up," said Peyton. "I'll boost you over."

"I can do it," said Artie. "Just give me a minute to catch my breath."

"Come on. Neither of us is as young as he was.

I'll help you over, and then you can give me a hand up from the other side. No sense in both of us killing ourselves just to prove a point."

Artie considered the arrangement, and nodded his agreement. Peyton tied Molly's leash to the fence, in case she caught a scent and decided to make a break for freedom, then leaned down and cupped his hands so that Artie could put one booted foot into his grip. When the boot was in place, and Artie's hold on the fence seemed secure, Peyton pushed up. Either he was stronger than he thought, which was possible, or Artie was lighter than he looked, which seemed unlikely, but, either way, Peyton ended up almost catapulting Artie over the fence. Only the judicious hooking of his left leg and right arm on the slats saved Artie from an awkward landing on the other side.

"The hell was that?" asked Artie once he had climbed down and had both feet on firm ground once again.

"Sorry," said Peyton. He was trying not to laugh, and only partially succeeding.

"Yeah, well, I don't know what you're eating, but I could sure do with some of it."

Peyton began climbing the fence. He was in good condition for a man of his age, a fact that gave him no little pleasure. Artie reached a hand up to steady him and, although Peyton didn't need it, he took it anyway.

"Funny," said Peyton, as he stepped down from the fence, "but I don't eat so much anymore. I used to have a hell of an appetite, but now some breakfast and a snack in the evening does me just fine. I even had to make an extra hole in my belt to stop my damn pants from falling down."

There was an unreadable expression on Artie Hoyt's face as he glanced down at his own belly and reddened slightly. Peyton winced.

"I didn't mean anything by that, Artie," he said quietly. "When Rina was alive, I weighed thirty pounds more than I do now. She fed me up like she was going to slaughter me for Christmas. Without her . . ."

He trailed off and looked away.

"Don't talk to me about it," said Artie after a moment had passed. He appeared anxious to keep the conversation going, now that the long silence between them had at last been broken. "My wife doesn't believe it's food unless it's deep fried, or comes in a bun. I think she'd deep-fry candy if she could."

"They do that somewhere in Europe," Peyton said.

"You don't say?" Artie looked mildly disgusted. "Jesus, don't tell her that. Chocolate's the closest that she gets to health food as it is."

They began walking toward the pond. Peyton let Molly off the leash. He knew that she had sensed the presence of water, and he didn't want to torment her by forcing her to walk at their pace. The dog raced ahead, a streak of brown and white, and soon was lost from sight in the tall grass.

"Nice dog," said Artie.

"Thank you," said Peyton. "She's a good girl. She's like a child to me, I guess."

"Yeah," said Artie. He knew that Peyton and his wife had not been blessed with children.

"Look, Artie," said Peyton, "there's something I've been meaning to say for a while."

He paused as he tried to find the right words, then took a deep breath and plowed right in.

"In church, that time, after Lydia had come home, I— Well, I wanted to apologize for staring at her, you know, her . . ."

"Ass," finished Artie.

"Yeah, that. I'm sorry, is all I wanted to say. It wasn't right. Especially in church. Wasn't Christian. It wasn't what you might think, though."

Suddenly, Peyton realized that he had wandered onto marshy ground, conversationally speaking. He now faced the possibility of being forced to explain both what he believed Artie might have thought Peyton was thinking, and what, in fact, he, Peyton, *had* been thinking, which was that Artie Hoyt's daughter looked like the *Hindenburg* just before it burned.

"She's a big girl," said Artie sadly, saving Peyton from further embarrassment. "It's not her fault. Her marriage broke up, and the doctors gave her pills for depression, and she suddenly started to put on all this weight. Doesn't help that she eats enough for two, but that's part of it, you know, the eating. She gets sad, she eats more, she gets sadder, she eats even more. It's a vicious cycle. I don't blame you for staring at her. Hell, she wasn't my daughter, I'd stare at her that way too. In fact, sometimes, it shames me to say, I do stare at her that way."

"Anyway, I'm sorry," said Peyton. "It wasn't . . . kind."

"Apology accepted," said Artie. "Buy me a drink next time we're in Dean's."

He put his hand out, and the two men shook. Peyton patted Artie on the back. He felt his eyes water slightly, and blamed it on his exertions.

"How about I buy you a beer when we're done here? I could do with something to toast the end of a long day."

"Agreed. Let's water your dog and get the—"

He stopped. They were within sight of the sheltered pond. It had been a popular trysting spot, once upon a time, when both Artie and Peyton were both much younger men, until the land changed hands and the new owner, the God-fearing man whose estate was now being fought over by his godless relatives, let it be known that he didn't want any adolescent voyages of sexual discovery being embarked upon in the vicinity of his pond. A large beech tree overhung the water, its branches almost touching the surface. Molly was standing a small distance from it. She had not drunk the water. She had, in fact, stopped several feet from the bank. Now, she was waiting, one paw raised, her tail wagging uncertainly. Through the rushes, something blue was visible to the approaching men.

Bobby Faraday was kneeling by the water's edge, his upper body at a slight angle, as though he were trying to glimpse his reflection in the pool. There was a rope around his neck, attached to the trunk of the tree. He was swollen with gas, his face a reddish-purple, his features almost unrecognizable.

"Ah, hell," said Peyton.

He wavered slightly, and Artie reached up and put his arm around his companion's shoulder as the sun set behind them, and the wind blew, and the host bowed low in mourning.

THE REAPERS

is now available on CD
and for download!

Also available from John Connolly
on CD and for download:

THE UNQUIET

Coming in June 2009:

THE LOVERS

Listen to free excerpts from
John Connolly's audiobooks at:

WWW.AUDIO.SIMONANDSCHUSTER.COM

SIMON & SCHUSTER
AUDIO

PRAISE FOR JOHN CONNOLLY AND HIS THRILLING TALES OF BLOOD AND DARKNESS

**"Connolly writes like a poet about terrible horrors. . . .
His words sing."**

—Houston Chronicle

THE REAPERS

"Powerful, disturbing prose. . . . New fans will be searching Connolly's backlist to find out more."

—*Omaha World-Herald*

"As dark and convoluted as his previous novels and just as enjoyable. . . ."

—*Library Journal*

"The past comes back with a vengeance in bestseller Connolly's unsettling eighth novel to feature ex–NYPD detective turned disgraced PI Charlie 'Bird' Parker. . . . Rich prose and compelling plot. . . ."

—*Publishers Weekly*

"One of the most darkly intriguing books this reviewer has encountered. . . . Veteran crime fans will want to savor every note-perfect word."

—*Booklist* (starred review)

THE UNQUIET

"The haunting creepiness . . . will guarantee late-night goose bumps."

—*Richmond Times-Dispatch*

"Hard to put down, harder to forget."

—*The Observer* (London)

***The Reapers* is also available as an eBook**

"Connolly is a master of suggestion, creating mood and suspense with ease, and unflinchingly presents a hard-eyed look at the horrors that can lurk in quiet, rustic settings."

—*Publishers Weekly*

"You can't put down a book in this series once you've begun it."

—*Kingston Observer*

"Superbly mesmerizing dialogue. You'll be running shards of it through your mind after the book is finished. . . ."

—*The Irish Times*

"This frightening work of darkness and beauty, written by one of the true masters in the thriller and horror genres, is not to be missed."

—Bookreporter.com

"Offer[s] the thought-provoking philosophical and theological depths that are missing from most of the genre."

—*The Sacramento Bee*

THE BOOK OF LOST THINGS

"Deliciously twisted."

—*Richmond Times-Dispatch*

THE BLACK ANGEL

"Stylishly literate gore and terror."

—*Kirkus Reviews*

BAD MEN

"Connolly has quickly and decisively established himself as a unique voice."

—Michael Connelly

"Terrifying. . . . Think Thomas Harris by way of Stephen King. . . . Not for the faint of heart."

—*Publishers Weekly*

THE WHITE ROAD

"Darkly brilliant, spellbinding, and disturbing."

—Harlan Coben

"The malevolence here is almost palpable."

—*Publishers Weekly* (starred review)

THE KILLING KIND

"Unfolds with the force and logic of a nightmare."

—*The Washington Post*

"Connolly has that rare ability to hit you head-on with a great crime story while giving you goose bumps in the process."

—*Clarion Ledger* (Jackson, MS)

DARK HOLLOW

"Grim, hard-edged, and compulsively readable."

—*Publishers Weekly*

"A frightening, disturbing, and brutal tale interspersed with moments of dark humor."

—*Yorkshire Evening Press* (UK)

EVERY DEAD THING

"Speeds us through a harrowing plot to a riveting climax."

—Jeffery Deaver, *New York Times* bestselling author

"A spellbinding book. . . . Holds the reader fast in a comfortless stranglehold."

—*The Los Angeles Times*

ALSO BY JOHN CONNOLLY

Every Dead Thing

Dark Hollow

The Killing Kind

The White Road

Bad Men

Nocturnes

The Black Angel

The Book of Lost Things

The Unquiet

Contents

Internet links

Throughout this book we have recommended websites where you can find out more about dinosaurs and fossil discoveries around the world. To visit the sites, go to the Usborne Quicklinks Website where you will find links to all the sites.

1. Go to **www.usborne-quicklinks.com**
2. Type the keywords for this book: **atlas of dinosaurs**
3. Type the page number of the links you want to visit.
4. Click on the links to go to the recommended sites.

Site availability

The links in Usborne Quicklinks are regularly reviewed and updated. If any sites become unavailable, we will, if possible, replace them with suitable alternatives. Sometimes we add extra links too, if we think they are useful. So when you visit Usborne Quicklinks, the links may be slightly different from those described in your book.

Internet link

For links to all the websites described in this book, go to **www.usborne-quicklinks.com** and enter the keywords "atlas of dinosaurs".

Help

For general help and advice on using the Internet, go to the Usborne Quicklinks Website and click on "Net Help".

To find out more about using your web browser, click on your browser's Help menu and choose "Contents and Index". You'll find a searchable dictionary containing tips on how to find your way around the Internet easily.

What you need

The websites described in this book can be accessed using a standard home computer and a web browser (the software that enables you to display information from the Internet). Here's a list of the basic requirements:

- A PC with Microsoft® Windows® 98 or a later version, or a Macintosh computer with System 9.0 or later
- 64Mb RAM
- A web browser such as Microsoft® Internet Explorer 5, or Netscape® Navigator 6, or later versions
- Connection to the Internet via a modem (preferably 56kbps) or a faster digital or cable line
- An account with an Internet Service Provider (ISP)
- A sound card to hear sound files

Computer viruses

A computer virus is a program that can damage your computer. A virus can get into your computer when you download programs from the Internet, or in an attachment (an extra file) that arrives with an email. We strongly recommend that you buy anti-virus software to protect your computer and that you update the software regularly. You can buy anti-virus software at computer stores or download it from the Internet. To find out more about viruses, go to Usborne Quicklinks and click on "Net Help".

Extras

Some websites need additional programs, called plug-ins, to play sounds, or to show videos, animations or 3-D images. If you go to a site and you do not have the necessary plug-in, a message should come up on the screen.

There is usually a button on the site that you can click on to download the plug-in. Alternatively, go to Usborne Quicklinks and click on "Net Help". There you can find links to download plug-ins. Here is a list of plug-ins that you might need:

- QuickTime – lets you play video clips.
- RealOne Player® – lets you play video clips and sound files.
- Flash™ – lets you play animations.
- Shockwave® – lets you play animations and enjoy interactive sites.

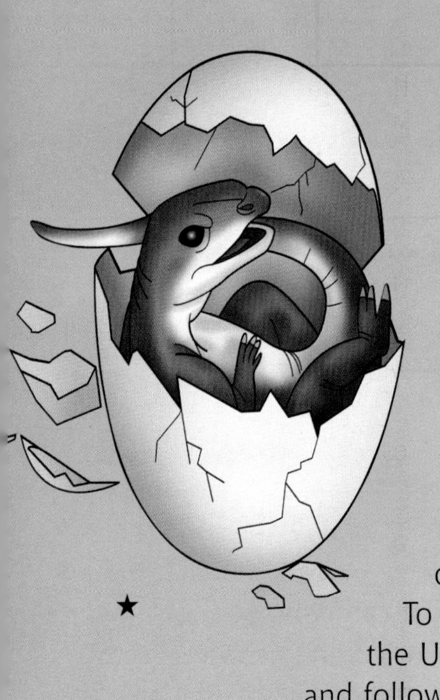

Downloadable pictures

Pictures in this book marked with a ★ symbol can be downloaded from the Usborne Quicklinks Website for your own personal use. The pictures are the copyright of Usborne Publishing and may not be used for any commercial or profit-related purpose. To download a picture, go to the Usborne Quicklinks Website and follow the instructions there.

Saying dinosaur names

For a pronunciation guide to dinosaur names, and the names of other prehistoric animals, go to the Usborne Quicklinks Website and follow the instructions there.

Internet safety

- Ask your parent's or guardian's permission before you connect to the Internet. They can then stay nearby if they think they should do so. If you are using someone else's computer, always check first that it is all right for you to connect to the Internet.
- If you write a message in a website guest book or on a website message board, do not include your email address, real name, address or telephone number.
- If a website asks you to log in or register by typing your name or email address, ask the permission of an adult first.
- If you receive email from someone you don't know, tell an adult and do not reply to the email.
- Never arrange to meet anyone you have talked to on the Internet.

Note for parents

The websites described in this book are regularly checked and reviewed by Usborne editors and the links in Usborne Quicklinks are updated. However, the content of a website may change at any time and Usborne Publishing is not responsible for the content of any website other than its own.

We recommend that children are supervised while on the Internet, that they do not use Internet chat rooms, and that you use Internet filtering software to block unsuitable material.

Please ensure that your children read and follow the safety guidelines above. For more information, go to the Net Help area on the Usborne Quicklinks Website at **www.usborne-quicklinks.com**

Macintosh and QuickTime are trademarks of Apple computer, Inc., registered in the USA and other countries.

RealOne Player is a trademark of RealNetworks, Inc., registered in the USA and other countries.

Flash and Shockwave are trademarks of Macromedia, Inc., registered in the USA and other countries.

Incredible animals

Around 240 million years ago, long before people existed, a new group of animals appeared on Earth. They were the dinosaurs. They included some of the largest ever land animals and some of the deadliest predators. No one has ever seen a live dinosaur, as they all died out 65 million years ago.

Reptiles with a difference

Dinosaurs were reptiles. Like other reptiles, such as crocodiles and lizards, dinosaurs laid eggs and had scaly, waterproof skin. Most reptiles have legs that stick out sideways from their bodies, but dinosaurs' legs supported their bodies from underneath. This meant dinosaurs' legs were stronger than other reptiles'.

Dinosaur variety

There were many different kinds, or species, of dinosaurs. Some were no bigger than a hen, while others grew to more than ten times the size of an elephant. Meat-eating dinosaurs had razor-sharp teeth whereas some plant-eating dinosaurs had toothless beaks. There were dinosaurs with horns on their faces, crests on their heads and some even had frills around their necks.

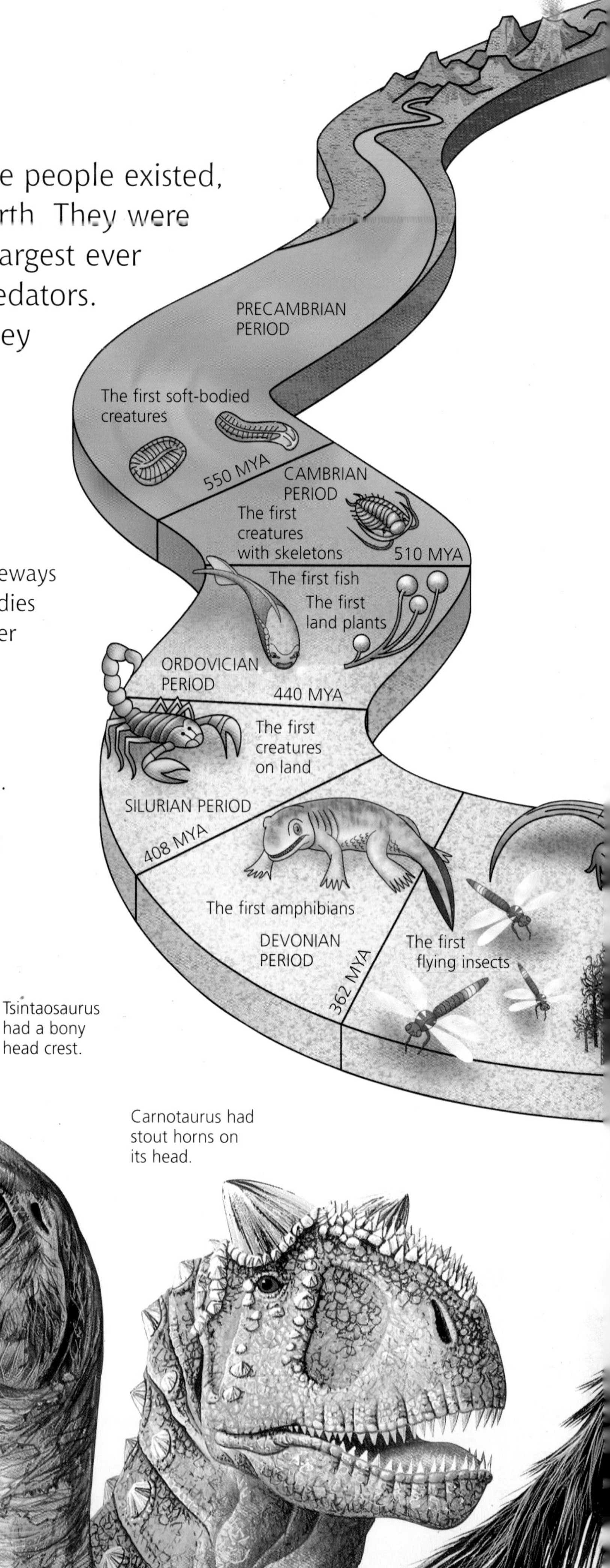

Tsintaosaurus had a bony head crest.

Carnotaurus had stout horns on its head.

Gallimimus had a toothless beak.

When did they live?

Dinosaurs lived in a time known as the Mesozoic era, which lasted from 250 to 65 million years ago. The Mesozoic era is divided into three periods: the Triassic (when the first dinosaurs appeared), the Jurassic and the Cretaceous. Each dinosaur species lived for a few million years and new species developed all the time. Dinosaurs dominated the Earth for 175 million years and were one of the most successful animal groups of all time.

Internet link

For links to websites where you can watch video clips of dinosaurs and test your knowledge with a quiz, go to **www.usborne-quicklinks.com**

This timeline shows the history of the Earth from the first plants and animals to the present day. The letters MYA stand for "Million Years Ago".

Velociraptor was covered in feathers.

Dividing up dinosaurs

So far, more than 900 different kinds of dinosaurs have been discovered. To work out how all the different dinosaurs are related to each other, scientists divide them into groups, according to the features they shared.

Lizard and bird hips

Dinosaurs are divided into two main groups: saurischian dinosaurs and ornithischian dinosaurs. Saurischians had hipbones that were similar in shape to modern lizards' hipbones. Ornithischians had hipbones similar to modern birds' hipbones.

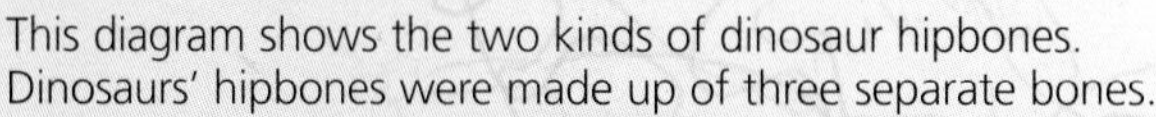

This diagram shows the two kinds of dinosaur hipbones. Dinosaurs' hipbones were made up of three separate bones.

The biggest group

Ornithischians made up the largest group of dinosaurs. They were all herbivores and many of them lived in herds. Ornithischians are divided into five main groups: stegosaurs, pachycephalosaurs, ornithopods, ceratopsians and ankylosaurs.

Ornithopods were the most common type of ornithischian. They ranged from the smallest of the hypsilophodontids, which were only around 1m (3ft) long, to the larger iguanodontids and hadrosaurs, which grew up to 15m (49ft) long.

Internet link

For links to websites with panoramic movies of lizard- and bird-hipped dinosaurs, and a clickable chart of dinosaur groups, go to **www.usborne-quicklinks.com**

Stegosaurs had bony plates on their bodies. The plates were not very strong and may have been used for display.

Pachycephalosaurs had thick, domed skulls. They were fast-moving and walked on two legs.

Hypsilophodon was an ornithopod dinosaur. Ornithopods had strong teeth for chewing vegetation. They walked on two or four legs and foraged for food on all fours.

Like most ceratopsians, Triceratops had bony frills at the back of its skull and sharp horns on its face for scaring off enemies.

Ankylosaurs were the best-protected ornithischians. Their bodies were covered in thick, bony spikes and plates.

Theropods' sharp claws helped them to catch their prey.

Like many theropods, Tyrannosaurus had sharp, serrated teeth for ripping chunks of meat off other animals.

Plant-eaters and predators

Saurischian dinosaurs are divided into sauropodomorphs and theropods. Most sauropodomorphs were herbivores. They walked on four legs most of the time and had long necks and tails. Sauropodomorphs included the largest and heaviest dinosaurs.

Theropods were the killers of the dinosaur world. They were fast-moving animals that walked on two legs. Most of them were carnivores and many had sharp teeth and claws that were well-suited to catching and eating prey.

Tyrannosaurus walked on two powerful back legs.

Theropods had four toes but only walked on three. The first toe was held just above the ground.

Changing climate

The Cretaceous climate was warm, with wet and dry seasons. Tropical seas stretched as far north as London and New York, and temperatures never fell below freezing. Then, at the very end of the Cretaceous period, there were some dramatic climate changes. Sea levels dropped, temperatures changed and there were lots of volcanic eruptions. These changes could be part of the reason why dinosaurs became extinct.

The first flowers

The biggest change between the Jurassic and Cretaceous period was the appearance of flowering plants. By the middle of the Cretaceous period, they had begun to spread across the world and had developed into many different species. Bees, wasps and butterflies, which fed on the flowering plants, also appeared for the first time.

Different dinosaurs

There were more dinosaur species in the late Cretaceous period than at any other time. Sauropods remained some of the most abundant plant-eaters, but ornithopod dinosaurs, such as the hadrosaurs, were diversifying into lots of new species.

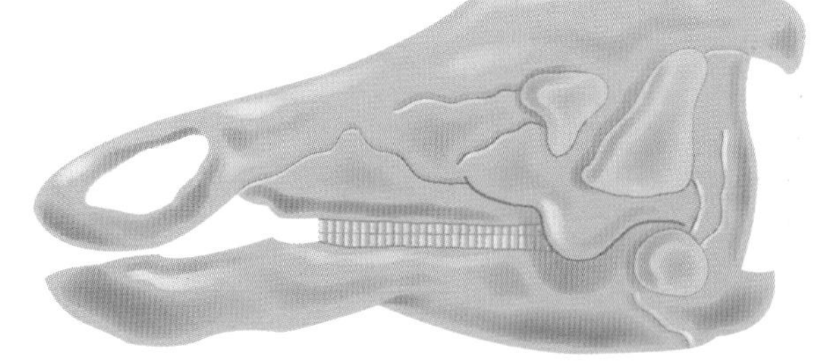

Hadrosaurs were such successful plant-eaters because of their hundreds of grinding teeth. In this diagram, you can see the teeth at the back of the jaw.

There was also a greater diversity of theropod dinosaurs, including the horned abelisaurs in the southern continents, the giant tyrannosaurs in the north and the fast-paced dromaeosaurs.

This is a skeleton of Dromaeosaurus, a fast-moving predator that was about the size of a small pony. The name "Dromaeosaurus" means "running lizard".

Internet link

For links to websites with facts about the Cretaceous world and an interactive guide to dinosaurs of the Cretaceous period, go to **www.usborne-quicklinks.com**

Evolution

Most scientists believe that living things gradually change over time. This idea is called the theory of evolution. Scientists use the theory of evolution to try to work out where dinosaurs came from and why they developed the way they did.

500 million years ago, the first fish evolved. They had thick skin and no jaws. There were no land animals at this time.

375 million years ago, some water-dwelling creatures began to leave the water, possibly to escape from predators. They were the first amphibians.

The fossil record

All the fossils found so far are together known as the fossil record. The fossil record shows us how plants and animals have changed over time. According to the fossil record, the first living things were bacteria, which first existed over 3,500 million years ago. Over the course of millions of years, these living things developed to become the first plants and animals.

300 million years ago, the first reptiles appeared. Their bodies were suited to life on land. They had dry, scaly skin to protect them from the Sun.

★

Around 240 million years ago, some reptiles evolved legs that supported their bodies from underneath. These were the first dinosaurs.

These are fossils of trilobites, which were among the first animals to have skeletons. They are around 550 million years old.

Internet link

For links to websites with online activities about evolution and how different species evolved, go to www.usborne-quicklinks.com

A changing world

Living things change over time because environments change. Animals that are suited to the changes survive, while others die. The surviving animals pass on their useful qualities to their offspring. This is known as natural selection. Evidence for this also comes from animals alive today. Many types of animals that live in cold climates, for example, have adapted to their environment by evolving thick fur coats to help keep them warm.

Polar bears live in the freezing Arctic. They have evolved thick fur coats to help them survive in icy waters.

Shapes and sizes

The movement of the continents affected how dinosaurs evolved. During the Triassic period, when the continents were joined together as Pangaea, dinosaurs looked very similar worldwide. As the continents broke up, dinosaurs gradually developed different shapes and sizes to suit their new environments.

Evolving features

Some dinosaur features evolved in response to other animals in the environment. Ankylosaurs, for example, gradually evolved bony plates and spikes as protection against meat-eating dinosaurs. Scientists think dinosaurs also evolved certain features to help them reproduce. Horned dinosaurs, such as Pentaceratops and Chasmosaurus, may have evolved the horns on their heads to help them attract mates.

This fossilized skeleton of the ankylosaur Gastonia shows its defensive bony plates and spikes. Some of its spikes grew up to 1m (3ft) long.

Mass extinction

At the end of the Cretaceous period, there was a mass extinction of life on Earth. On land, all animals over 2m (7ft) long died out, and 70% of marine life became extinct. No dinosaurs survived the extinction. Scientists are still trying to work out why this happened.

Internet link

For links to websites where you can watch animations of extinction theories and find out the reasoning behind them, go to **www.usborne-quicklinks.com**

This volcano in Hawaii is erupting runny lava capable of spreading for miles. Eruptions like this at the end of the Cretaceous period would have caused widespread devastation.

Mesozoic mystery

Little evidence remains to show what really happened 65 million years ago. Most scientists think that an asteroid impact killed the dinosaurs, although others argue that climate change or volcanic eruptions may have wiped them out.

The evidence

To discover more about what caused the mass extinction, scientists study rocks that date from the time between the end of the Cretaceous period, 65 million years ago, and the beginning of the Tertiary period. As "K" is the symbol for the Cretaceous period and "T" is the symbol for the Tertiary period, these rocks are said to form the K–T boundary.

Lava floods

At the end of the Cretaceous period, there was an increase in volcanic activity around the world. In India, for example, massive volcanoes were spewing out floods of lava. The lava floods hardened into rock, and can be seen today at the K–T boundary known as the Deccan Traps.

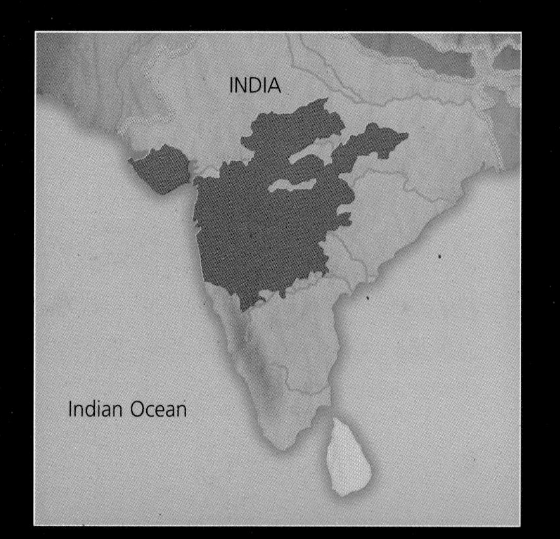

The Deccan Traps (shaded in red) cover an area of nearly 500,000 sq km (195,000 sq miles) in western India.

Death by volcanoes

The floods of lava would have destroyed dinosaur habitats, as well as killing any dinosaurs in their path. The poisonous gases belched out by the volcanoes were even more dangerous. They may even have affected baby dinosaurs growing in their eggs. Gases from volcanoes can also alter the climate. Scientists think the gases may have made the climate either too warm or too cold for some dinosaur species to survive.

This shows how the asteroid may have looked as it collided with Earth. It would have burned up as it plummeted through the Earth's atmosphere, creating a fiery glow.

Disaster strikes

Around the time the dinosaurs died out, a huge asteroid, 10km (6 miles) wide, collided with the Earth. Scientists think they have found the giant crater it made at Chicxulub, in Mexico. Further evidence of an asteroid impact comes from particles of the metal iridium in K–T rocks around the world. Iridium is very rare on Earth, but is commonly found in asteroids.

Deadly impact

The effects of a large asteroid impact would have been deadly enough to kill the dinosaurs. The impact would have scattered molten debris across the planet's surface, starting global fires. It could also have set off a chain of devastating earthquakes and volcanic eruptions. Clouds of dust would have blocked out the sunlight, bringing global darkness and freezing conditions for many years.

This shows the destruction caused by the Mount St. Helens volcanic eruption in 1980. The survivors of the K–T extinction may have lived in a world very similar to this.

The survivors

Not all life was wiped out by the K–T mass extinction. Small lizards, birds, insects, mammals and snakes survived whatever it was that killed the dinosaurs. Scientists are still unsure why some animals survived and others did not.

Animals alive in the Mesozoic	K–T boundary	Surviving animals
Dinosaurs		
Pterosaurs		
Plesiosaurs		
Ammonites		
Mammals		
Crocodiles		
Lizards and snakes		
Turtles		
Amphibians		
Sharks and fishes		
Insects		
Birds		

This chart shows some of the animal groups that became extinct at the end of the Mesozoic era and some that survived.

Small survivors

Scientists think one of the reasons smaller animals may have survived the mass extinction was because of their feeding habits. Smaller animals tend to eat a variety of food, whereas larger animals often rely on one specific food source. If that food source is wiped out, then the animals are faced with extinction.

Mesozoic mammals fed on a variety of food, such as insects, nuts or seeds. This helped them to survive.

Large, meat-eating dinosaurs only fed on plant-eating dinosaurs. As soon as that food source was wiped out, the meat-eaters became extinct.

New life

Every mass extinction of life on Earth has been followed by a major burst of evolution. The Permian period, which preceded the Mesozoic era, ended in the mass extinction of up to 95% of all species. This extinction led to the evolution of the dinosaurs. The death of the dinosaurs left room for other animal groups to take over. This time mammals and birds spread over the world and developed into many different species.

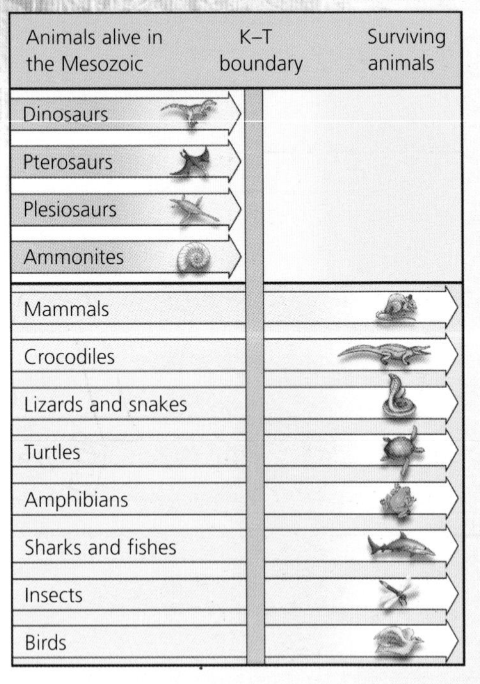

Megazostrodon lived around 180 million years ago and was typical of early mammals. It was only around 10cm (4in) long and probably fed on insects.

Mesozoic mammals

Mammals first appeared around 203 million years ago, but they were dwarfed by the dinosaurs. The first mammals were able to survive because they were small and came out mainly at night. Unlike the dinosaurs, mammals changed very little during the Mesozoic era and for more than 100 million years they stayed very small.

Rise of the mammals

After the death of the dinosaurs, mammals gradually evolved to occupy almost every habitat. One group of insect-eaters evolved into bats, developing flaps of skin between their long fingers, which enabled them to fly. Some land mammals moved into the oceans and developed streamlined bodies suited to life in the water. Mammals also took advantage of the different food sources available. Some mammals remained insect-eaters, while others adapted to feed on plants or other animals.

Human beings

One group of mammals, called primates, lived in trees. Over millions of years the primates evolved into apes, and then into human beings. Human beings have now been around for 2.3 million years. Compared to dinosaurs, which lived for 175 million years, humans have been on Earth for a very short period of time.

This baby chimpanzee is swinging through the branches using its superbly adapted hands and feet. Chimpanzees are part of the ape family, which first appeared on this planet around 30 million years ago.

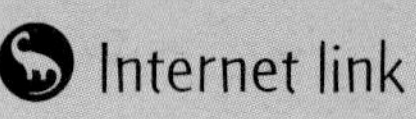

For a link to a website where you can see amazing images of prehistoric animals, go to **www.usborne-quicklinks.com**

Digging dinosaurs

Heterodontosaurus may have slept in burrows during the hottest part of the year.

Heterodontosaurus was another small, fast-moving dinosaur from the Karoo. It had three different kinds of teeth, for biting, tearing and grinding food. It also had long fingers and toes, and sharp, powerful claws, which meant that it was good at digging. Like many desert animals today, Heterodontosaurus may have sheltered from the Sun's heat by digging burrows in the sand.

King of the Karoo

At around 4m (13ft) long, the prosauropod Massospondylus was the largest dinosaur from the Karoo. However, most of its length was in its neck and tail, and its body was only about the size of a small pony. Massospondylus had especially large hands and feet, which would have helped it to dig for plants and roots, as well as any water underground.

Massospondylus had extremely large claws, which would have helped it to tear roots from the ground.

Cracks in the Karoo

The Karoo Basin once straddled the boundary between the African and the Antarctic plate. When Pangaea began to break up 190 million years ago, the two plates pulled apart and cracks appeared in the Karoo. Burning hot molten rock, or lava, rose up through the cracks, flooding 2 million sq km (0.8 million sq miles) of land. Most dinosaurs and other animals would have managed to escape the flooding and flee to other areas, but the lava would have destroyed their habitats and made it impossible for animals to live in the Karoo for many years.

The largest expedition

One of the biggest dinosaur expeditions ever was to Tendaguru, a remote hill in Tanzania, East Africa. The expedition lasted from 1909 until 1913 and involved around 900 people. Ten different kinds of dinosaurs, all from the late Jurassic period, were discovered there.

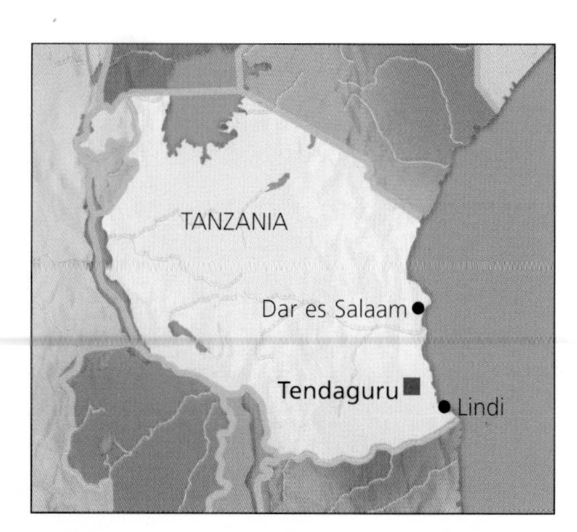

Tendaguru is in the south of Tanzania. All the dinosaur bones were shipped to Germany from Lindi, the nearest port.

Tons of bones

The Tendaguru expedition was organized by a team of German scientists. They employed local people to dig pits all over Tendaguru. The locals had to carry the bones to a nearby port, a four-day walk away, so they could be shipped to Germany. Over four years, 250 tonnes (275 tons) of bone were removed and nearly 5,000 trips were made between the site and the port.

Similar sites

Many of the different types of dinosaurs from Tendaguru have also been found at Dinosaur National Monument in Utah, North America. Africa and North America were joined in the late Jurassic period, so dinosaurs could spread between them. The theropods Allosaurus and Ceratosaurus, for example, are known from both sites. Only a few Ceratosaurus teeth were found at Tendaguru, but their size suggests they belonged to one of the largest species of Ceratosaurus.

Male ceratosaurs had sharp horns on their heads. Two rival males would fight by trying to butt each other with their horns.

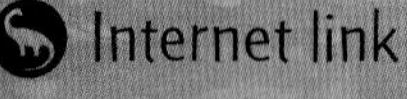

Internet link

For links to websites where you can find out more about brachiosaurs and other dinosaurs from Tanzania, go to **www.usborne-quicklinks.com**

Death by drowning

Numerous bones of the stegosaur Kentrosaurus were found at Tendaguru. One ancient riverbed alone contained more than 70 Kentrosaurus thighbones, which may be from a herd drowned by a flash flood. Kentrosaurus was one of the spikiest stegosaurs, with seven tail spikes and another pair of spikes on its shoulders. It probably used its tail spikes to defend itself against large theropods, such as Ceratosaurus.

Tallest dinosaur

Five different kinds of sauropods were discovered at the site: Barosaurus, Dicraeosaurus, Janenschia, Tendaguria and Brachiosaurus. Brachiosaurus was the tallest dinosaur. Unlike other sauropods, it had front legs that were much longer than its hind legs. These raised its neck and shoulders high above the ground, enabling it to feed on leaves that no other dinosaurs could reach.

A Brachiosaurus could eat a lot of leaves in one mouthful. Their mouths were wide enough to swallow a human whole.

Amazing skeleton

The remains of several brachiosaurs were found at Tendaguru. By combining the bones of different individuals, scientists were able to put together a whole skeleton, which is now on display at the Humboldt Museum, in Berlin, Germany. It stands nearly 25m (82ft) long and 12m (39ft) high, and is the largest complete dinosaur skeleton in the world.

Surviving winter

Most of the dinosaurs from Dinosaur Cove were small ornithopods, such as Leaellynasaura and Qantassaurus. Scientists are not sure how they survived the long, dark winters. Small animals generally do not migrate far, as it uses up too much of their energy, so it seems likely they stayed in the area. They may have grown plump during the summer, and in the winter their extra body fat would have then kept them warm. It would also have provided them with energy when there wasn't enough food.

Leaellynasauras lived together in groups. They had stiffened tails to help them balance on two legs.

Predators at the pole

Fragments of bone from various theropod dinosaurs have been found at Dinosaur Cove. These include a shin bone, which scientists think may belong to an ornithomimosaur, and an anklebone, which is thought to belong to a dinosaur that was part of the same group of theropods as Allosaurus. These predators probably preyed on the small ornithopod dinosaurs during the summer and migrated away from Dinosaur Cove during the winter.

Antarctica

Until 1986, no dinosaurs had ever been found in Antarctica. But since then, the fossilized remains of several different species have been discovered, including a theropod that has not been found anywhere else in the world.

Internet link

For a link to a website where you can find out about the different fossils discovered in Antarctica by paleontologist William Hammer, go to **www.usborne-quicklinks.com**

This map of Antarctica shows the dinosaurs found there so far. Most of the remains were just fragments, so the dinosaurs have not yet been named.

Cretaceous finds

The fossilized remains of three ankylosaurs and a hypsilophodontid dinosaur, all from the late Cretaceous period, have been found on James Ross Island, in northwest Antarctica. When these dinosaurs lived, it was much warmer in Antarctica than it is today, but there would still have been times of the year when it was very cold. Dinosaurs living in Antarctica may have migrated to warmer areas during the cold seasons.

Ankylosaurs ate low-lying plants, such as ferns. Their spikes helped them to defend themselves.

Bridging the gap

On Vega Island, in northwest Antarctica, paleontologists have found a hadrosaur tooth. Hadrosaurs first appeared around 80 million years ago, by which time Antarctica had already separated from America and Asia. The hadrosaur find indicates that there must have been a land bridge joining South America to Antarctica when hadrosaurs were alive.

Unique theropod

Theropod Cryolophosaurus was discovered in Antarctica in 1991. Bones from three individuals were found 3,660m (12,010ft) up the side of Mount Kilpatrick. Cryolophosaurus was about 7m (23ft) long, walked on two legs and probably looked similar to Allosaurus. It had a 20cm (8in) forward-facing crest on its head. No other theropod found so far had a forward-facing crest.

Male cryolophosaurs may have used their crests to attract mates.

Choked to death

Fossilized prosauropod bones were found alongside the Cryolophosaurus remains. Some of the prosauropod's bones were found in the throat of a Cryolophosaurus. One explanation for this is that the Cryolophosaurus had attacked and killed the prosauropod and was eating it when it died itself. It may even have choked to death on a bone.

Difficult terrain

One of the reasons why so few dinosaurs have been found in Antarctica is that 98% of the land there is covered in ice. Although there is some exposed Mesozoic rock, most of it is buried beneath ice up to 5km (3 miles) thick. High winds and an average temperature of -50°C (-58°F) also make expeditions to the region difficult and dangerous.

This is the camp where paleontologist William Hammer and his team were based during the excavation of Cryolophosaurus.

Egg and nest sites

The first dinosaur eggs ever found belonged to the sauropod Hypselosaurus. They were discovered in France, in 1859. The first dinosaur nests were found much later, in 1923, in the Gobi Desert. Since then, scientists have uncovered many spectacular egg and nest sites around the world.

Internet link

For links to websites where you can hunt for dinosaur eggs around the world and see reconstructions of eggs and nests, go to **www.usborne-quicklinks.com**

Some of the world's main dinosaur egg sites are marked on this map. All these sites date from the Cretaceous period.

Nest design

Some dinosaur eggs have been found just lying on the ground, but scientists believe that most dinosaurs made nests to keep their eggs safe. These nests consisted of a hollow scraped out of the ground or a muddy rim built to keep the eggs in place. Dinosaurs squatted over their nests to lay eggs, perhaps moving around their nests as they laid each one.

Saltasaurs made nests close to each other, though they had to leave enough space to move between them without knocking the eggs.

Egg shape and size

As many as 30 eggs have been found together in some dinosaur nests, often arranged in lines or arcs. Dinosaur eggs are either round or long and thin, and have a rough, wrinkled surface. The biggest egg found is 45cm (18in) long, and was discovered in eastern China. It probably belonged to a therizinosaur.

The Oviraptor eggs on the left form a circle. The mother may have moved them into this neat position after laying them.

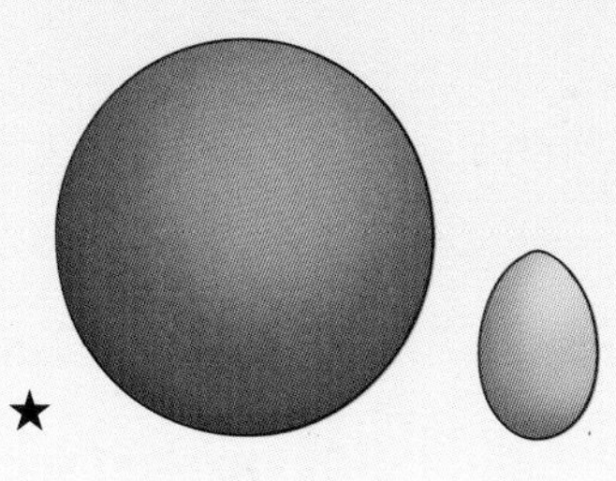

★ This shows the size of a typical dinosaur's egg compared with a hen's egg. Considering the size of most adult dinosaurs, their eggs are very small.

Amazing egg finds

In 1995, scientists visiting a village near Green Dragon Mountain, in China, discovered hundreds of dinosaur eggs embedded in streets and sticking out of cliffs. They even found an egg in the wall of a building, where it had been used instead of a stone. A similar find was made in Tremp, in Spain, where many rocks are so full of egg fragments that scientists named the stone "eggshell sandstone".

Nesting together

Scientists have found large dinosaur nest sites in Montana, USA, and Auca Mahuevo, Argentina. Each site has around 20 nests, built close together. This indicates that some dinosaurs bred in a group, probably as protection against predators. Scientists at the Montana site, known as Egg Mountain, also uncovered older nests underneath. This suggests that dinosaurs returned to the same place year after year to lay eggs.

After laying their eggs, many dinosaurs piled vegetation on top to keep them warm.

Dinosaur babies

This model shows an oviraptor baby inside its egg.

Scientists have discovered few remains of baby dinosaurs. This is because the bones of very young dinosaurs were so soft and fragile that they rarely fossilized well. Even those that have been preserved cannot easily be identified.

Inside the egg

A dinosaur baby developed inside its egg for about three or four weeks before hatching out. Tiny pores in the shell allowed it to breathe, and a yolk provided it with all the nutrients it needed to grow. However, it was quite likely that the baby dinosaur would be eaten by a hungry predator before it had grown enough to hatch out, as eggs were an easy target for dinosaurs and small mammals.

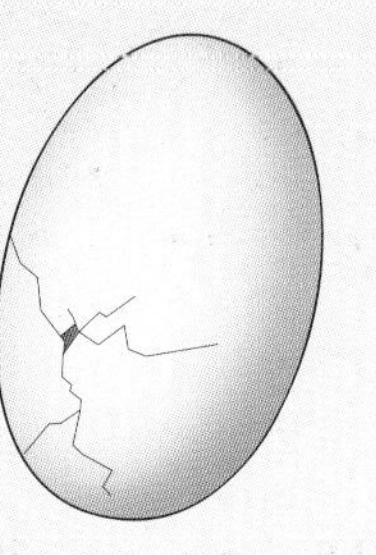

This shows how a baby dinosaur would have begun to hatch.

The baby chipped all the way around the egg to get out.

When hatching, a baby dinosaur used a sharp tooth on its snout to break through the shell. After leaving the egg, the baby had to eat very soon, or it would die.

Preserved in mud

Some of the best-preserved dinosaur babies were found in the 1990s at Auca Mahuevo, in Argentina. The site contained thousands of titanosaur eggs, many of which had babies fossilized inside. When studying these remains, scientists found tiny teeth, skulls and even a piece of skin, which was scaly, like a lizard's. These eggs were so well preserved because they had been buried in mud flows, which prevented them from decaying or being eaten.

This reconstruction of a Maiasaura nest shows babies emerging from their eggs. The babies were about 25cm (10 in) long when they first hatched.

Egg protectors

Until recently, scientists thought that all dinosaurs abandoned their eggs after laying them. This is almost certainly true of large sauropods, which would have risked crushing their eggs underfoot if they stayed nearby. But scientists now know that a few dinosaurs incubated their eggs like birds do. For example, fossilized oviraptors have been found huddled on top of nests in bird-like brooding positions.

This oviraptor from the Gobi Desert was fossilized sitting on its eggs. Its forelimbs can be seen stretched out to the sides, encircling and protecting the eggs.

Internet link

For links to websites where you can find out more about baby dinosaurs and examine a dinosaur embryo online, go to **www.usborne-quicklinks.com**

Caring parents

A few dinosaurs may have cared for their young. Scientists think this because some dinosaur babies, such as hadrosaurs, had poorly-developed limbs at birth, so they probably relied on adults for food and protection. At Egg Mountain, in Montana, USA, the remains of a hadrosaur group were found. The hadrosaurs ranged from very young to fully-grown, which suggests that parents looked after their offspring. It prompted scientists to name this type of hadrosaur Maiasaura, which means "good mother reptile".

Maiasauras probably protected their young from predators such as small, fierce troodons. Hadrosaur babies took about ten years to reach full size, so they were very vulnerable to attack.

Location: India
Description: Predator that walked on two legs. It had a snout and might have had bony ridges above its eyes.

INGENIA ("for Ingeni")
Group: saurischians, theropods, coelurosaurs
Period: Late Cretaceous
Size and weight: 1.5m (5ft) long, 5kg (11lb)
Location: Mongolia
Description: Toothless dinosaur with a head shaped like a parrot's head. It walked on two legs and was either a herbivore or an omnivore.

IRRITATOR ("Irritator")
Group: saurischians, theropods, spinosaurs
Period: Early Cretaceous
Size and weight: 6m (20ft) long, 600kg (1,320lb)
Location: Brazil
Description: Predator with a narrow skull like a crocodile's skull. It had a low crest above its eyes and walked on two legs.

ISANOSAURUS ("Isan lizard")
Group: saurischians, sauropodomorphs, sauropods
Period: Late Triassic
Size and weight: 12m (39ft) long, 6 tonnes (6.6 tons)
Location: Thailand
Description: Primitive herbivore that walked on four legs. It had column-like legs and a long neck.

ITEMIRUS ("of Itemir")
Group: saurischians, theropods, coelurosaurs
Period: Late Cretaceous
Size and weight: 4m (13ft) long, 180kg (395lb)
Location: Mongolia
Description: Dinosaur known only from a partial skull. It might have been similar to tyrannosaurs.

JANENSCHIA ("for Janensch")
Group: saurischians, sauropodomorphs, sauropods
Period: Late Jurassic
Size and weight: 18m (59ft) long, 14 tonnes (15 tons)
Location: eastern Africa
Description: Large herbivore with sturdy legs and a long neck. It walked on four legs.

JAXARTOSAURUS ("Jaxartes lizard")
Group: ornithischians, ornithopods, iguanodonts
Period: Late Cretaceous
Size and weight: 9m (30ft) long, 4 tonnes (4.5 tons)
Location: Kazakhstan
Description: Herbivore with a beak shaped like a duck's beak. It probably had a plate-like crest on its skull and it could walk on two or four legs.

JEHOLOSAURUS ("Jehol lizard")
Group: ornithischians
Period: Early Cretaceous
Size and weight: 80cm (32in) long, 3kg (6.6lb)
Location: China
Description: Herbivore with a beak, and leaf-shaped teeth. It walked on two legs.

JIANGSHANOSAURUS ("Jiangshan lizard")
Group: saurischians, sauropodomorphs, sauropods
Period: Early Cretaceous
Size and weight: 20m (66ft) long, 12 tonnes (13 tons)
Location: China
Description: Long-necked herbivore with slim legs. It walked on four legs and might have been similar to Alamosaurus.

JINGSHANOSAURUS ("Jingshan lizard")
Group: saurischians, sauropodomorphs, prosauropods
Period: Early Jurassic
Size and weight: 10m (33ft) long, 3 tonnes (3.3 tons)
Location: China
Description: Long-necked herbivore with a sturdy body and a sloping snout. It walked on four legs.

JINZHOUSAURUS ("Jinzhou lizard")
Group: ornithischians, ornithopods, iguanodonts
Period: Early Cretaceous
Size and weight: 7m (23ft) long, 1.5 tonnes (1.7 tons)
Location: China
Description: Herbivore with grinding teeth. It could walk on two or four legs.

JOBARIA ("for Jobar")
Group: saurischians, sauropodomorphs, sauropods
Period: Early Cretaceous
Size and weight: 18m (59ft) long, 20 tonnes (22 tons)
Location: western Africa
Description: Long-necked herbivore with huge nostrils. It walked on four legs.

KAIJIANGOSAURUS ("Kai River lizard")
Group: saurischians, theropods and possibly coelurosaurs
Period: Middle Jurassic
Size and weight: 7m (23ft) long, 1 tonne (1.1 tons)
Location: China
Description: Large predator that walked on two legs. It might have been similar to Gasosaurus.

KAKURU ("ancestral servant")
Group: saurischians, theropods, coelurosaurs
Period: Late Cretaceous
Size and weight: 2.5m (8ft) long, 23kg (50lb)
Location: Australia
Description: Predator that walked on two legs. It's known only from its slim back leg bones.

KELMAYISAURUS ("Karamay lizard")
Group: saurischians, theropods and possibly allosaurs
Period: Early Cretaceous
Size and weight: 7m (23ft) long, 1 tonne (1.1 tons)
Location: China
Description: Large predator that walked on two legs. It might have been similar to Allosaurus.

KENTROSAURUS ("sharp-point lizard")
Group: ornithischians, thyreophorans, stegosaurs
Period: Late Jurassic
Size and weight: 4m (13ft) long, 320kg (705lb)
Location: eastern Africa
Description: Herbivore with plates sticking up from its neck, back and tail. It walked on four legs.

KHAAN ("ruler")
Group: saurischians, theropods, coelurosaurs
Period: Late Cretaceous
Size and weight: 1m (3ft) long, 4kg (8.8lb)
Location: Mongolia
Description: Toothless omnivore with a short skull shaped like a parrot's skull. It had long arms and a short tail, and it walked on two legs.

KLAMELISAURUS ("Klameli lizard")
Group: saurischians, sauropodomorphs, sauropods
Period: Middle Jurassic
Size and weight: 17m (56ft) long, 15 tonnes (17 tons)
Location: China
Description: Long-necked herbivore that walked on four legs. It had spoon-shaped teeth and might have had a ridge along its back.

KOPARION ("scalpel")
Group: saurischians, theropods, coelurosaurs
Period: Late Jurassic
Size and weight: 1m (3ft) long, 6kg (13lb)
Location: USA
Description: Small predator known only from fossilized teeth. It walked on two legs and might have been similar to Troodon.

KOTASAURUS ("Kota lizard")
Group: saurischians, sauropodomorphs, sauropods
Period: Early Jurassic
Size and weight: 18m (59ft) long, 8.5 tonnes (9.4 tons)
Location: India
Description: Primitive herbivore that walked on four legs. It had a long neck and spoon-shaped teeth.

KRITOSAURUS ("separated lizard")
Group: ornithischians, ornithopods, iguanodonts
Period: Late Cretaceous
Size and weight: 6.5m (21ft) long, 1.9 tonnes (2.1 tons)
Location: USA
Description: Herbivore with a bump on its nose, and a beak shaped like a duck's beak. It could walk on two or four legs.

KULCERATOPS ("lake horned face")
Group: ornithischians, marginocephalians, ceratopsians
Period: Early Cretaceous
Size and weight: 2m (7ft) long, 50kg (110lb)
Location: Uzbekistan
Description: Herbivore with horns on its face, a neck frill and teeth well-suited to shearing through vegetation. It walked on four legs.

LABOCANIA ("for La Bocana")
Group: saurischians, theropods and possibly coelurosaurs
Period: Late Cretaceous
Size and weight: 8m (26ft) long, 1.5 tonnes (1.7 tons)
Location: Mexico
Description: Predator with a large, heavy skull. It walked on two legs. Not much is known about it.

LAEVISUCHUS ("light crocodile")
Group: saurischians, theropods, neoceratosaurs
Period: Late Cretaceous
Size and weight: 1m (3ft) long, 4kg (8.8lb)
Location: India
Description: Small predator that walked on two legs. It might have been similar to Noasaurus and probably had slim limbs.

LAMBEOSAURUS ("Lambe's lizard")
Group: ornithischians, ornithopods, iguanodonts
Period: Late Cretaceous
Size and weight: 9m (30ft) long, 4.5 tonnes (5 tons)
Location: Canada and Mexico
Description: Large herbivore with a beak and a head crest. It could walk on two or four legs.

LAMETASAURUS ("Lameta lizard")
Group: saurischians, theropods, neoceratosaurs
Period: Late Cretaceous
Size and weight: 7.5m (25ft) long, 1 tonne (1.1 tons)
Location: India
Description: Predator that walked on two legs. It might have had bony ridges above its eyes.

LANASAURUS ("woolly lizard")
Group: ornithischians, heterodontosaurids
Period: Early Jurassic
Size and weight: 1m (3ft) long, 5kg (11lb)
Location: South Africa
Description: Small omnivore with fang-like front teeth. It could walk on two or four legs.

LAOSAURUS ("fossil lizard")
Group: ornithischians, ornithopods, hypsilophodontids
Period: Late Jurassic
Size and weight: 1.5m (5ft) long, 9kg (20lb)
Location: USA and Canada
Description: Small herbivore with a beak, short hands and long legs. It walked on two legs and was similar to Hypsilophodon.

LAPLATASAURUS ("La Plata lizard")
Group: saurischians, sauropodomorphs, sauropods
Period: Late Cretaceous
Size and weight: 18m (59ft) long, 11 tonnes (12 tons)
Location: Argentina and Uruguay
Description: Long-necked herbivore with column-like legs and plates on its back. It walked on four legs.

LAPPARENTOSAURUS ("Lapparent's lizard")
Group: saurischians, sauropodomorphs, sauropods
Period: Middle Jurassic
Size and weight: 16m (53ft) long, 20 tonnes (22 tons)
Location: Madagascar
Description: Large herbivore with column-like legs and a long neck. It walked on four legs.

LEAELLYNASAURA ("Leaellyn's lizard")
Group: ornithischians, ornithopods, hypsilophodontids
Period: Early Cretaceous
Size and weight: 1.5m (5ft) long, 9kg (20lb)
Location: Australia
Description: Small herbivore with long limbs and a beak. It had large eyes and walked on two legs.

LEPTOCERATOPS ("small horned face")
Group: ornithischians, marginocephalians, ceratopsians
Period: Late Cretaceous
Size and weight: 2.5m (8ft) long, 120kg (265lb)
Location: USA and Canada
Description: Herbivore with a short tail, a beak and a huge head. It walked on four legs.

LESOTHOSAURUS ("Lesotho lizard")
Group: ornithischians
Period: Early Jurassic
Size and weight: 1m (3ft) long, 4kg (8.8lb)
Location: southern Africa
Description: Dinosaur with a beak and a long snout. It was either a herbivore or an omnivore, and had slim hind legs. It walked on two legs.

LESSEMSAURUS ("Lessem's lizard")
Group: saurischians, sauropodomorphs, prosauropods
Period: Late Triassic
Size and weight: 10m (33ft) long, 3 tonnes (3.3 tons)
Location: Argentina
Description: Large herbivore with column-like hind legs, a long neck and a ridge along its back. It walked on four legs.

LEXOVISAURUS ("Lexovian lizard")
Group: ornithischians, thyreophorans, stegosaurs
Period: Middle and Late Jurassic
Size and weight: 5m (16ft) long, 1.1 tonnes (1.2 tons)
Location: England and France
Description: Herbivore with tough plates sticking up from its neck, back and tail. It had spikes along its tail and on its shoulders, and it walked on four legs.

LIAOCERATOPS ("Liaoning horned face")
Group: ornithischians, marginocephalians, ceratopsians
Period: Early Cretaceous
Size and weight: 90cm (35in) long, 5kg (11lb)
Location: China
Description: Small herbivore with a short neck frill and narrow beak. It probably walked on two legs.

LIAONINGOSAURUS ("Liaoning lizard")
Group: ornithischians, thyreophorans, ankylosaurs
Period: Early Cretaceous
Size and weight: 34cm (13in) long, 1kg (2lb)
Location: China
Description: Small, plated herbivore known only from one skeleton that belonged to a young animal. It walked on four legs.

LIGABUEINO ("Ligabue's little one")
Group: saurischians, theropods, neoceratosaurs
Period: Early Cretaceous
Size and weight: 1m (3ft) long, 4kg (8.8lb)
Location: Argentina
Description: Small predator that probably had slim limbs and a straight neck. It walked on two legs and might have been similar to Noasaurus.

LILIENSTERNUS ("for Lilienstern")
Group: saurischians, theropods, coelophysoids
Period: Late Triassic
Size and weight: 5m (16ft) long, 130kg (290lb)
Location: Germany
Description: Predator with a slim body and a skull similar to Coelophysis' skull. It walked on two legs.

LIRAINOSAURUS ("slender lizard")
Group: saurischians, sauropodomorphs, sauropods
Period: Late Cretaceous
Size and weight: 12m (39ft) long, 6 tonnes (6.6 tons)
Location: Spain
Description: Large herbivore with a long neck and plates on its back. It walked on four legs.

LOPHORHOTHON ("crested nose")
Group: ornithischians, ornithopods, iguanodonts
Period: Late Cretaceous
Size and weight: 8m (26ft) long, 3.2 tonnes (3.5 tons)
Location: USA
Description: Herbivore with a beak and a bump on its snout. It walked on two or four legs.

LOSILLASAURUS ("Losilla lizard")
Group: saurischians, sauropodomorphs, sauropods
Period: Early Cretaceous
Size and weight: 23m (75ft) long, 16 tonnes (18 tons)
Location: Spain
Description: Herbivore with a long neck and tail. It walked on four legs and was similar to Diplodocus.

LOURINHANOSAURUS ("Lourinhã lizard")
Group: saurischians, theropods, allosaurs
Period: Late Jurassic
Size and weight: 4m (13ft) long, 180kg (395lb)
Location: Portugal
Description: Predator that walked on two legs. It might have been similar to Sinraptor or Allosaurus.

LOURINHASAURUS ("Lourinhã lizard")
Group: saurischians, sauropodomorphs, sauropods
Period: Late Jurassic
Size and weight: 17m (56ft) long, 16 tonnes (18 tons)
Location: Portugal
Description: Long-necked herbivore that might have been similar to Camarasaurus. It walked on four legs.

LUCIANOSAURUS ("Lucian lizard")
Group: ornithischians
Period: Late Jurassic
Size and weight: 1m (3ft) long, 4kg (8.8lb)
Location: USA
Description: Dinosaur known only from its teeth. It was either a herbivore or an omnivore and might have been similar to Lesothosaurus. It walked on two legs.

LUFENGOSAURUS ("Lufeng lizard")
Group: saurischians, sauropodomorphs, prosauropods
Period: Late Triassic
Size and weight: 6m (20ft) long, 1 tonne (1.1 tons)
Location: China
Description: Long-necked herbivore with a long tail. It could walk on two or four legs.

LURDUSAURUS ("heavy lizard")
Group: ornithischians, ornithopods, iguanodonts
Period: Early Cretaceous
Size and weight: 9m (30ft) long, 5 tonnes (5.5 tons)
Location: western Africa
Description: Herbivore with a large body, stout limbs, a beak and spike-shaped thumbs. It could walk on two or four legs.

LYCORHINUS ("wolf snout")
Group: ornithischians, heterodontosaurids
Period: Early Jurassic
Size and weight: 1m (3ft) long, 5kg (11lb)
Location: South Africa
Description: Small omnivore with fang-like teeth at the front of its jaws. It could walk on two or four legs.

MACRUROSAURUS ("long-tailed lizard")
Group: saurischians, sauropodomorphs, sauropods
Period: Early Cretaceous
Size and weight: 18m (59ft) long, 11 tonnes (12 tons)
Location: England
Description: Long-necked herbivore with column-like legs. It walked on four legs.

MAGNOSAURUS ("large lizard")
Group: saurischians, theropods, and possibly spinosaurs
Period: Middle Jurassic
Size and weight: 5m (16ft) long, 220kg (485lb)
Location: England
Description: Predator that probably had short arms and a long skull. It walked on two legs.

MAGYAROSAURUS ("Magyar lizard")
Group: saurischians, sauropodomorphs, sauropods
Period: Late Cretaceous
Size and weight: 5m (16ft) long, 1 tonne (1.1 tons)
Location: eastern Europe
Description: Herbivore with a long neck and protective plates on its back. It walked on four legs.

MAIASAURA ("good mother lizard")
Group: ornithischians, ornithopods, iguanodonts
Period: Late Cretaceous
Size and weight: 9m (30ft) long, 4.5 tonnes (5 tons)
Location: USA
Description: Herbivore with a beak shaped like a duck's beak, and a crest above its eyes. It could walk on two or four legs.

MAJUNGATHOLUS ("Majunga dome")
Group: saurischians, theropods, neoceratosaurs
Period: Late Cretaceous
Size and weight: 8m (26ft) long, 1.1 tonnes (1.2 tons)
Location: Madagascar
Description: Long-limbed predator with a horn on its forehead. It walked on two legs.

MALAWISAURUS ("Malawi lizard")
Group: saurischians, sauropodomorphs, sauropods
Period: Early Cretaceous
Size and weight: 18m (59ft) long, 11 tonnes (12 tons)
Location: eastern Africa
Description: Large, long-necked herbivore with a small head and tough plates on its back. It walked on four legs.

MALEEVUS ("for Maleev")
Group: ornithischians, thyreophorans, ankylosaurs
Period: Late Cretaceous
Size and weight: 5m (16ft) long, 700kg (1,540lb)
Location: Mongolia
Description: Plated herbivore that walked on four legs. It had a box-shaped skull and a club at the end of its tail.

MAMENCHISAURUS ("Mamenchi lizard")
Group: saurischians, sauropodomorphs, sauropods
Period: Late Jurassic
Size and weight: 20m (66ft) long, 14 tonnes (15 tons)
Location: China
Description: Herbivore with an unusually long neck. It had long legs, a small, box-shaped head and it walked on four legs.

MARSHOSAURUS ("Marsh's lizard")
Group: saurischians, theropods, and possibly allosaurs
Period: Late Jurassic
Size and weight: 5m (16ft) long, 280kg (620lb)
Location: USA
Description: Predator with short, powerful arms. It walked on two legs and might have been similar to Allosaurus.

MASIAKASAURUS ("Masiaka lizard")
Group: saurischians, theropods, neoceratosaurs
Period: Late Cretaceous
Size and weight: 2m (7ft) long, 12kg (26lb)
Location: Madagascar
Description: Small predator with long front teeth that stuck out horizontally. It walked on two legs.

MASSOSPONDYLUS ("elongated vertebra")
Group: saurischians, sauropodomorphs, prosauropods
Period: Late Triassic
Size and weight: 4m (13ft) long, 130kg (290lb)
Location: southern Africa, Argentina and the USA
Description: Long-necked omnivore with large, curved thumb claws and a small head. It could walk on two or four legs.

MEGALOSAURUS ("great lizard")
Group: saurischians, theropods, spinosaurs
Period: Middle Jurassic
Size and weight: 7m (23ft) long, 1 tonne (1.1 tons)
Location: England
Description: Predator with short arms and backward-curving teeth. It walked on two legs.

MEGARAPTOR ("large thief")
Group: saurischians, theropods, coelurosaurs
Period: Late Cretaceous
Size and weight: 8m (26ft) long, 600kg (1,320lb)
Location: Argentina
Description: Predator with a large curved claw on each second toe. It walked on two legs.

MELANOROSAURUS ("Black Mountain lizard")
Group: saurischians, sauropodomorphs, prosauropods
Period: Late Triassic
Size and weight: 12m (39ft) long, 6 tonnes (6.6 tons)
Location: South Africa
Description: Large herbivore with a long neck and column-like hind legs. It walked on four legs.

METRIACANTHOSAURUS ("moderately spined lizard")
Group: saurischians, theropods, spinosaurs
Period: Late Jurassic
Size and weight: 7m (23ft) long, 1 tonne (1.1 tons)
Location: England
Description: Predator with short arms and a tall ridge along its back. It walked on two legs.

MICROCERATOPS ("small horned face")
Group: ornithischians, marginocephalians, ceratopsians

Period: Late Cretaceous
Size and weight: 75cm (30in) long, 2kg (4.4lb)
Location: China
Description: Herbivore with a beak, a short neck frill and wide cheeks. It was small and slim and could walk on two or four legs.

MICROPACHYCEPHALOSAURUS ("small thick-headed lizard")
Group: ornithischians, marginocephalians, pachycephalosaurs
Period: Late Cretaceous
Size and weight: 60cm (24in) long, 2kg (4.4lb)
Location: China
Description: Tiny herbivore with a broad body and a skull with a thick, flat top. It walked on two legs.

MICRORAPTOR ("small thief")
Group: saurischians, theropods, coelurosaurs
Period: Early Cretaceous
Size and weight: 30cm (12in) long, 350g (0.8lb)
Location: China
Description: Tiny bird-like predator with long arms, a stiff tail and curved foot claws. It walked on two legs.

MICROVENATOR ("small thief")
Group: saurischians, theropods, coelurosaurs
Period: Early Cretaceous
Size and weight: 1.5m (5ft) long, 11kg (24lb)
Location: USA
Description: Short-tailed dinosaur that was either a herbivore or an omnivore. It walked on two legs.

MINMI ("Minmi")
Group: ornithischians, thyreophorans, ankylosaurs
Period: Early Cretaceous
Size and weight: 3m (10ft) long, 60kg (130lb)
Location: Australia
Description: Herbivore with a beak, and plates on its belly, back and tail. It walked on four legs.

MONKONOSAURUS ("Monko lizard")
Group: ornithischians, thyreophorans, stegosaurs
Period: Late Jurassic and Early Cretaceous
Size and weight: 4.5m (15ft) long, 650kg (1,430lb)
Location: Tibet
Description: Herbivore with plates and spikes along its neck, back and tail. It walked on four legs.

MONOCLONIUS ("single sprout")
Group: ornithischians, marginocephalians, ceratopsians
Period: Late Cretaceous
Size and weight: 5m (16ft) long, 1.1 tonnes (1.2 tons)
Location: USA and Canada
Description: Herbivore with a beak, a long nose horn and a short neck frill. It walked on four legs.

MONOLOPHOSAURUS ("single crested lizard")
Group: saurischians, theropods, allosaurs
Period: Middle Jurassic
Size and weight: 6m (20ft) long, 600kg (1,320lb)
Location: China
Description: Predator with a hollow head crest and sharp teeth. It walked on two legs.

MONONYKUS ("one claw")
Group: saurischians, theropods, coelurosaurs
Period: Late Cretaceous
Size and weight: 1m (3ft) long, 3kg (6.6lb)
Location: Mongolia
Description: Feathered predator with a head shaped like a bird's head and short arms. It was an omnivore and it walked on two legs.

MONTANOCERATOPS ("Montana horned face")
Group: ornithischians, marginocephalians, ceratopsians
Period: Late Cretaceous
Size and weight: 1.8m (6ft) long, 50kg (110lb)
Location: USA
Description: Herbivore with a beak, a short neck frill and a small nose horn. It walked on four legs.

MUSSAURUS ("mouse lizard")
Group: saurischians, sauropodomorphs, prosauropods
Period: Late Triassic
Size and weight: Possibly 3m (10ft) long, 85kg (190lb)
Location: Argentina
Description: Long-necked herbivore known only from its eggs and tiny babies. It could walk on two or four legs.

MUTTABURRASAURUS ("Muttaburra lizard")
Group: ornithischians, ornithopods, iguanodonts
Period: Late Cretaceous
Size and weight: 9m (30ft) long, 4.1 tonnes (4.5 tons)
Location: Australia
Description: Herbivore with a toothless beak and grinding teeth. It had a thick crest on its snout and it could walk on two or four legs.

MYMOORAPELTA ("Mygatt and Moore's shield")
Group: ornithischians, thyreophorans, ankylosaurs
Period: Late Jurassic
Size and weight: 3m (10ft) long, 430kg (960lb)
Location: USA
Description: Herbivore with spikes on its tail and plates on its back and sides. It walked on four legs.

NAASHOIBITOSAURUS ("Naashoibito lizard")
Group: ornithischians, ornithopods, iguanodonts
Period: Late Cretaceous
Size and weight: 6.5m (21ft) long, 1.9 tonnes (2.1 tons)
Location: USA
Description: Herbivore with a beak shaped like a duck's beak, and a bump on its nose. It could walk on two or four legs.

NANOSAURUS ("pygmy lizard")
Group: ornithischians, ornithopods, hypsilophodontids
Period: Late Jurassic
Size and weight: 90cm (35in) long, 4kg (8.8lb)
Location: USA
Description: Tiny herbivore with a beak, short hands and long legs. It was similar to Hypsilophodon and walked on two legs.

NANSHIUNGOSAURUS ("Nanxiong lizard")
Group: saurischians, theropods, coelurosaurs
Period: Late Cretaceous
Size and weight: 6m (20ft) long, 300kg (660lb)
Location: China
Description: Omnivore with long hand claws, a broad belly and a short tail. It was similar to Erlikosaurus and walked on two legs.

NANYANGOSAURUS ("Nanyang lizard")
Group: ornithischians, ornithopods, iguanodonts
Period: Early Cretaceous
Size and weight: 4.5m (15ft) long, 260kg (570lb)
Location: China
Description: Herbivore with grinding teeth and a toothless beak shaped like a duck's beak. It could walk on two or four legs.

NEDCOLBERTIA ("for Ned Colbert")
Group: saurischians, theropods, coelurosaurs
Period: Early Cretaceous
Size and weight: 3m (10ft) long, 40kg (88lb)
Location: USA
Description: Predator with long, slim hind legs and sharp claws on its hands. It walked on two legs.

NEIMONGOSAURUS ("Nei Mongol lizard")
Group: saurischians, theropods, coelurosaurs
Period: Late Cretaceous
Size and weight: 2.5m (8ft) long, 100kg (220lb)
Location: China
Description: Long-necked dinosaur with long arms and leaf-shaped teeth. It was either a herbivore or an omnivore and walked on two legs.

NEMEGTOSAURUS ("Nemegt lizard")
Group: saurischians, sauropodomorphs, sauropods
Period: Late Cretaceous
Size and weight: 12m (39ft) long, 10 tonnes (11 tons)
Location: Mongolia
Description: Large, long-necked herbivore with pencil-like teeth and a wide mouth. It walked on four legs.

NEOVENATOR ("new hunter")
Group: saurischians, theropods, allosaurs
Period: Early Cretaceous
Size and weight: 7.5m (25ft) long, 1 tonne (1.1 tons)
Location: England
Description: Predator with a ridged skull. It was similar to Allosaurus and walked on two legs.

NEUQUENSAURUS ("Neuquén lizard")
Group: saurischians, sauropodomorphs, sauropods
Period: Late Cretaceous
Size and weight: 12m (39ft) long, 6 tonnes (6.6 tons)
Location: Argentina
Description: Herbivore with column-like legs and a long neck. It walked on four legs and probably had protective plates on its body.

NIGERSAURUS ("Niger lizard")
Group: saurischians, sauropodomorphs, sauropods
Period: Early Cretaceous
Size and weight: 15m (49ft) long, 7 tonnes (7.7 tons)
Location: Niger
Description: Long-necked herbivore that walked on four legs. Its mouth was wider than the rest of its head and was filled with around 600 thin teeth.

NIOBRARASAURUS ("Niobrara lizard")
Group: ornithischians, thyreophorans, ankylosaurs
Period: Late Cretaceous
Size and weight: 6m (20ft) long, 1.2 tonnes (1.3 tons)
Location: USA
Description: Herbivore with protective plates, a long flexible tail, wide hips and short legs. It walked on four legs.

NIPPONOSAURUS ("Japanese lizard")
Group: ornithischians, ornithopods, iguanodonts
Period: Late Cretaceous
Size and weight: 5m (16ft) long, 1.1 tonnes (1.2 tons)
Location: Russia
Description: Herbivore with grinding teeth and a beak shaped like a duck's beak. It could walk on two or four legs.

NOASAURUS ("northwestern Argentina lizard")
Group: saurischians, theropods, neoceratosaurs
Period: Late Cretaceous
Size and weight: 2m (7ft) long, 15kg (33lb)
Location: Argentina
Description: Small predator with a raised claw on each foot and a rather straight neck. It walked on two legs.

NODOCEPHALOSAURUS ("knob-headed lizard")
Group: ornithischians, thyreophorans, ankylosaurs
Period: Late Cretaceous
Size and weight: 6m (20ft) long, 1.2 tonnes (1.3 tons)
Location: USA
Description: Herbivore known only from its broad, plate-covered skull. It had a beak, and walked on four legs.

NODOSAURUS ("knob lizard")
Group: ornithischians, thyreophorans, ankylosaurs
Period: Late Cretaceous
Size and weight: 6m (20ft) long, 1.2 tonnes (1.3 tons)
Location: USA
Description: Plated herbivore with a short neck and legs and a long, flexible tail. It had a narrow head with a pointed snout. It walked on four legs and had broad hips.

NOMINGIA ("for Nomingiin")
Group: saurischians, theropods, coelurosaurs
Period: Late Cretaceous
Size and weight: 2.5m (8ft) long, 30kg (66lb)
Location: Mongolia
Description: Dinosaur that was either a herbivore or an omnivore and walked on two legs. It was similar to Oviraptor, but it had tail bones that were fused together.

NOTHRONYCHUS ("slothful claw")
Group: saurischians, theropods, coelurosaurs
Period: Late Cretaceous
Size and weight: 5m (16ft) long, 180kg (400lb)
Location: USA
Description: Omnivore that was similar to Erlikosaurus. It had long claws on its hands, a broad belly and a short tail. It walked on two legs.

NOTOHYPSILOPHODON ("southern Hypsilophus tooth")
Group: ornithischians, ornithopods, hypsilophodontids
Period: Late Cretaceous
Size and weight: 1.5m (5ft) long, 9kg (20lb)
Location: Argentina
Description: Herbivore with a beak, slim hind legs and short arms. It walked on two legs.

NQWEBASAURUS ("Kirkwood lizard")
Group: saurischians, theropods, coelurosaurs
Period: Early Cretaceous
Size and weight: 1m (3ft) long, 4kg (8.8lb)
Location: South Africa
Description: Predator with three fingers on each hand and slim, curved claws. It walked on two legs.

NUTHETES ("monitor")
Group: saurischians, theropods, coelurosaurs
Period: Early Cretaceous
Size and weight: 1m (3ft) long, 3kg (6.6lb)
Location: England
Description: Small predator known only from its teeth. It walked on two legs and probably had long arms and a stiff tail.

OHMDENOSAURUS ("Ohmden lizard")
Group: saurischians, sauropodomorphs, sauropods
Period: Early Jurassic
Size and weight: 4m (13ft) long, 150kg (330lb)
Location: Germany
Description: Long-necked herbivore that might have been similar to Vulcanodon. It walked on four legs.

OMEISAURUS ("Emei lizard")
Group: saurischians, sauropodomorphs, sauropods
Period: Late Jurassic
Size and weight: 18m (59ft) long, 8.5 tonnes (9.4 tons)
Location: China
Description: Herbivore with a very long neck, a box-shaped skull and long legs. It walked on four legs.

OPISTHOCOELICAUDIA ("tail cupped behind")
Group: saurischians, sauropodomorphs, sauropods
Period: Late Cretaceous
Size and weight: 12m (39ft) long, 10 tonnes (11 tons)
Location: Mongolia
Description: Long-necked herbivore that walked on four legs. The shape of its tail bones suggests it could rear up on its hind legs, using its tail for support.

ORNATOTHOLUS ("decorated dome")
Group: ornithischians, marginocephalians, pachycephalosaurs
Period: Late Cretaceous
Size and weight: 2.5m (8ft) long, 60kg (130lb)
Location: Canada
Description: Herbivore with a beak, a wide body and short arms. It walked on two legs.

ORNITHODESMUS ("bird link")
Group: saurischians, theropods, coelurosaurs
Period: Early Cretaceous
Size and weight: 1.5m (5ft) long, 5kg (11lb)
Location: England
Description: Predator known only from its hipbones. It walked on two legs and might have been similar to Velociraptor.

ORNITHOLESTES ("bird thief")
Group: saurischians, theropods, coelurosaurs
Period: Late Jurassic
Size and weight: 2m (7ft) long, 13kg (29lb)
Location: USA
Description: Small predator with three long fingers on each hand, a small skull and a long tail. It walked on two legs.

ORNITHOMIMUS ("bird mimic")
Group: saurischians, theropods, coelurosaurs
Period: Late Cretaceous
Size and weight: 3m (10ft) long, 110kg (240lb)
Location: USA and Canada
Description: Fast-running omnivore with a toothless beak and long hands. It walked on two legs.

ORODROMEUS ("mountain runner")
Group: ornithischians, ornithopods, hypsilophodontids
Period: Late Cretaceous
Size and weight: 2m (7ft) long, 13kg (29lb)
Location: USA
Description: Herbivore with a beak, a stiff tail, short arms and five fingers on each hand. It walked on two legs.

OTHNIELIA ("for Othniel")
Group: ornithischians, ornithopods, hypsilophodontids
Period: Late Jurassic
Size and weight: 3m (10ft) long, 16kg (35lb)
Location: USA
Description: Dinosaur that was either a herbivore or an omnivore. It had a beak, and walked on two legs.

OURANOSAURUS ("fearless lizard")
Group: ornithischians, ornithopods, iguanodonts
Period: Early Cretaceous
Size and weight: 6m (20ft) long, 1.1 tonnes (1.2 tons)
Location: northern Africa
Description: Herbivore with a beak like a duck's and a sail on its back. It could walk on two or four legs.

OVIRAPTOR ("egg thief")
Group: saurischians, theropods, coelurosaurs
Period: Late Cretaceous
Size and weight: 2.5m (8ft) long, 35kg (77lb)
Location: Mongolia
Description: Toothless omnivore with long arms and a skull shaped like a parrot's skull. It had a short tail and walked on two legs.

OZRAPTOR ("Australian thief")
Group: saurischians, theropods
Period: Middle Jurassic
Size and weight: 2.5m (8ft) long, 20kg (44lb)
Location: Australia
Description: Predator known only from a partial leg bone. It walked on two legs.

PACHYCEPHALOSAURUS ("thick-headed lizard")
Group: ornithischians, marginocephalians, pachycephalosaurs
Period: Late Cretaceous
Size and weight: 5m (16ft) long, 300kg (660lb)
Location: USA
Description: Herbivore with a beak, and lumps and spikes on its thick skull. It walked on two legs.

PACHYRHINOSAURUS ("thick nose lizard")
Group: ornithischians, marginocephalians, ceratopsians
Period: Late Cretaceous
Size and weight: 6m (20ft) long, 1.5 tonnes (1.6 tons)
Location: Canada
Description: Herbivore with a beak, a neck frill and a thick, bony pad on its nose. It walked on four legs.

PANOPLOSAURUS ("completely shielded lizard")
Group: ornithischians, thyreophorans, ankylosaurs
Period: Late Cretaceous
Size and weight: 7m (23ft) long, 1.5 tonnes (1.6 tons)
Location: USA and Canada
Description: Plated herbivore with forward-pointing shoulder spikes. It walked on four legs.

PARALITITAN ("tidal giant")
Group: saurischians, sauropodomorphs, sauropods
Period: Late Cretaceous
Size and weight: 27m (89ft) long, 78 tonnes (86 tons)
Location: Egypt
Description: Giant, long-necked herbivore with long, column-like legs. It walked on four legs.

PARANTHODON ("near flower tooth")
Group: ornithischians, thyreophorans, stegosaurs
Period: Early Cretaceous
Size and weight: 4.5m (15ft) long, 650kg (1,430lb)
Location: southern Africa
Description: Herbivore with plates and spikes sticking up from its neck, back and tail. It walked on four legs.

PARARHABDODON ("near fluted tooth")
Group: ornithischians, ornithopods, iguanodonts
Period: Late Cretaceous
Size and weight: 5m (16ft) long, 1 tonne (1.1 tons)
Location: Spain
Description: Herbivore with a beak shaped like a duck's beak and grinding teeth. It could walk on two or four legs.

PARASAUROLOPHUS ("near crested lizard")
Group: ornithischians, ornithopods, iguanodonts
Period: Late Cretaceous
Size and weight: 9m (30ft) long, 5 tonnes (5.5 tons)
Location: USA and Canada
Description: Herbivore with a beak and a curved, tube-like head crest. It could walk on two or four legs.

PARIVCURSOR ("small runner")
Group: saurischians, theropods, coelurosaurs
Period: Late Cretaceous
Size and weight: 1m (3ft) long, 3kg (6.6lb)
Location: Mongolia
Description: Feathered omnivore with a head shaped like a bird's head. It walked on two legs.

PARKSOSAURUS ("Parks' lizard")
Group: ornithischians, ornithopods, hypsilophodontids
Period: Late Cretaceous
Size and weight: 2.5m (8ft) long, 60kg (132lb)
Location: Canada
Description: Herbivore with a beak, slim hind legs, short arms and leaf-shaped teeth. It walked on two legs.

PATAGONYKUS ("Patagonian claw")
Group: saurischians, theropods, coelurosaurs
Period: Late Cretaceous
Size and weight: 2m (7ft) long, 6kg (13lb)
Location: Argentina
Description: Feathered omnivore with a head shaped like a bird's head and short arms. It was an omnivore and walked on two legs.

PATAGOSAURUS ("Patagonian lizard")
Group: saurischians, sauropodomorphs, sauropods
Period: Middle Jurassic
Size and weight: 15m (49ft) long, 9 tonnes (10 tons)
Location: Argentina
Description: Long-necked herbivore with spoon-shaped teeth. It was similar to Cetiosaurus and walked on four legs.

PAWPAWSAURUS ("Paw Paw lizard")
Group: ornithischians, thyreophorans, ankylosaurs
Period: Early Cretaceous
Size and weight: 5m (16ft) long, 700kg (1,545lb)
Location: USA
Description: Herbivore with blunt horns and a plated skull. It walked on four legs.

PEKINOSAURUS ("Pekin lizard")
Group: ornithischians
Period: Late Jurassic
Size and weight: 1m (3ft) long, 4kg (8.8lb)
Location: USA
Description: Dinosaur known only from its distinctive teeth. It was either a herbivore or an omnivore and it was probably similar to Lesothosaurus. It walked on two legs.

PELECANIMIMUS ("pelican mimic")
Group: saurischians, theropods, coelurosaurs
Period: Early Cretaceous
Size and weight: 2.5m (8ft) long, 25kg (55lb)
Location: Spain
Description: Omnivore with a long skull and around 200 small teeth. It had long arms and it walked on two legs.

PELLEGRINISAURUS ("Pellegrini lizard")
Group: saurischians, sauropodomorphs, sauropods
Period: Late Cretaceous
Size and weight: 25m (82ft) long, 20 tonnes (22 tons)
Location: Argentina
Description: Huge, long-necked herbivore with a long, flexible tail and a broad body. It walked on four legs.

PELOROSAURUS ("colossal lizard")
Group: saurischians, sauropodomorphs, sauropods
Period: Early Cretaceous
Size and weight: 16m (53ft) long, 20 tonnes (22 tons)
Location: England, Portugal and France
Description: Long-necked herbivore with very long, slim front legs. It walked on four legs.

PENTACERATOPS ("five-horned face")
Group: ornithischians, marginocephalians, ceratopsians
Period: Late Cretaceous
Size and weight: 7.5m (25ft) long, 2.2 tonnes (2.4 tons)
Location: USA
Description: Large herbivore with a frill, three very long horns and a beak. It walked on four legs.

PHAEDROLOSAURUS ("nimble dragon")
Group: saurischians, theropods, coelurosaurs
Period: Early Cretaceous
Size and weight: 2m (7ft) long, 15kg (33lb)
Location: China
Description: Bird-like predator with long arms and large claws on its feet. It walked on two legs.

PHUWIANGOSAURUS ("Phu Wiang lizard")
Group: saurischians, sauropodomorphs, sauropods
Period: Early Cretaceous
Size and weight: 15m (49ft) long, 14 tonnes (15 tons)
Location: Thailand
Description: Large herbivore with a long, broad neck and wide body. It walked on four legs.

PHYLLODON ("leaf tooth")
Group: ornithischians, ornithopods, hypsilophodontids
Period: Late Jurassic
Size and weight: 90cm (35in) long, 4kg (8.8lb)
Location: Portugal
Description: Tiny herbivore known only from its leaf-shaped teeth. It walked on two legs and was probably similar to Hypsilophodon.

PIATNITZKYSAURUS ("Piatnitzky's lizard")
Group: saurischians, theropods, spinosaurs
Period: Middle Jurassic
Size and weight: 5m (16ft) long, 280kg (620lb)
Location: Argentina
Description: Predator with three fingers on each hand and horns above its eyes. It walked on two legs.

PINACOSAURUS ("plank lizard")
Group: ornithischians, thyreophorans, ankylosaurs
Period: Late Cretaceous
Size and weight: 5m (16ft) long, 700kg (1,545lb)
Location: China and Mongolia
Description: Plated herbivore with a box-shaped skull and a clubbed tail. It walked on four legs.

PISANOSAURUS ("Pisano's lizard")
Group: ornithischians
Period: Late Triassic
Size and weight: 1m (3ft) long, 7kg (15lb)
Location: Argentina
Description: Primitive herbivore with a beak and short arms. It walked on two legs.

PIVETEAUSAURUS ("Piveteau's lizard")
Group: saurischians, theropods, and possibly spinosaurs
Period: Middle Jurassic
Size and weight: 10m (33ft) long, 2 tonnes (2.2 tons)
Location: France
Description: Large predator that might have been similar to Megalosaurus. It walked on two legs. Not much is known about it.

PLANICOXA ("flat hip")
Group: ornithischians, ornithopods, iguanodonts
Period: Early Cretaceous
Size and weight: 7m (23ft) long, 1.5 tonnes (1.7 tons)
Location: USA
Description: Herbivore that could walk on two or four legs.

PLATEOSAURUS ("broad lizard")
Group: saurischians, sauropodomorphs, prosauropods
Period: Late Triassic
Size and weight: 7m (23ft) long, 800kg (1,765lb)
Location: Germany, Switzerland and France
Description: Long-necked herbivore with large thumb claws and a long tail. It could walk on two or four legs.

PLEUROCOELUS ("hollow-sided")
Group: saurischians, sauropodomorphs, sauropods
Period: Early Cretaceous
Size and weight: 13m (43ft) long, 7 tonnes (7.7 tons)
Location: USA
Description: Long-necked herbivore that walked on four legs. It had long, slim front legs.

POEKILOPLEURON ("varied ribs")
Group: saurischians, theropods, spinosaurs
Period: Middle Jurassic
Size and weight: 9m (30ft) long, 1 tonne (1.1 tons)
Location: France
Description: Predator with short arms and backward-curving teeth. It walked on two legs.

POLACANTHUS ("many spines")
Group: ornithischians, thyreophorans, ankylosaurs
Period: Early Cretaceous
Size and weight: 5m (16ft) long, 800kg (1,765lb)
Location: England and Spain
Description: Herbivore with triangular spikes on its tail, and plates on its back and sides. It walked on four legs.

PRENOCEPHALE ("sloping head")
Group: ornithischians, marginocephalians, pachycephalosaurs
Period: Late Cretaceous
Size and weight: 2m (7ft) long, 35kg (77lb)
Location: Mongolia
Description: Dinosaur with a dome-shaped skull and short arms. It was either a herbivore or an omnivore and walked on two legs.

PROBACTROSAURUS ("before club lizard")
Group: ornithischians, ornithopods, iguanodonts
Period: Late Cretaceous
Size and weight: 3.5m (11ft) long, 180kg (400lb)
Location: Mongolia
Description: Herbivore with a toothless beak shaped like a duck's beak, and grinding teeth. It walked on two or four legs.

PROCERATOSAURUS ("before horned lizard")
Group: saurischians, theropods, coelurosaurs
Period: Middle Jurassic
Size and weight: 1.5m (5ft) long, 5kg (11lb)
Location: England
Description: Predator with a narrow skull, a nose horn and curved, serrated teeth. It walked on two legs. It is one of the oldest-known coelurosaurs.

PROCOMPSOGNATHUS ("before elegant jaw")
Group: saurischians, theropods, coelophysoids
Period: Late Triassic
Size and weight: 1.2m (4ft) long, 2kg (4.4lb)
Location: Germany
Description: Small, slim predator with a long skull, sharp teeth and short arms. It walked on two legs.

PROSAUROLOPHUS ("before crested lizard")
Group: ornithischians, ornithopods, iguanodonts
Period: Late Cretaceous
Size and weight: 8m (26ft) long, 3.2 tonnes (3.5 tons)
Location: Canada and USA
Description: Herbivore with a beak shaped like a duck's beak. It could walk on two or four legs.

PROTARCHAEOPTERYX ("before ancient wing")
Group: saurischians, theropods, coelurosaurs
Period: Early Cretaceous
Size and weight: 1m (3ft) long, 4kg (8.8lb)
Location: China
Description: Small, feathered dinosaur with a short, skull, a beak and a short tail. It was either a herbivore or an omnivore and it walked on four legs.

PROTOCERATOPS ("first horned face")
Group: ornithischians, marginocephalians, ceratopsians
Period: Late Cretaceous
Size and weight: 1.4m (4.6ft) long, 24kg (53lb)
Location: Mongolia
Description: Herbivore with a narrow beak and a large neck frill. It walked on four legs.

PROTOGNATHOSAURUS ("first jaw lizard")
Group: saurischians, sauropodomorphs, sauropods
Period: Early Jurassic
Size and weight: 15m (49ft) long, 12 tonnes (13 tons)
Location: China
Description: Long-necked herbivore that might have been similar to Cetiosaurus. It walked on four legs.

PROTOHADROS ("first hadrosaur")
Group: ornithischians, ornithopods, iguanodonts
Period: Late Cretaceous
Size and weight: 7m (23ft) long, 2.2 tonnes (2.4 tons)
Location: USA
Description: Herbivore with a beak shaped like a duck's beak, and grinding teeth. It could walk on two or four legs.

PSITTACOSAURUS ("parrot lizard")
Group: ornithischians, marginocephalians, ceratopsians
Period: Late Cretaceous
Size and weight: 1.5m (5ft) long, 12kg (26lb)
Location: Mongolia, China and Thailand
Description: Herbivore with a skull shaped like a parrot's skull, and pointed cheeks. It could walk on two or four legs.

PUKYONGOSAURUS ("Pukyong lizard")
Group: saurischians, sauropodomorphs, sauropods
Period: Early Cretaceous
Size and weight: 10m (33ft) long, 8.5 tonnes (9.4 tons)
Location: South Korea
Description: Long-necked herbivore that probably had a blunt snout and slender legs. It walked on four legs. Not much is known about it.

PYRORAPTOR ("fire thief")
Group: saurischians, theropods, coelurosaurs
Period: Late Cretaceous
Size and weight: 2m (7ft) long, 15kg (33lb)
Location: France
Description: Bird-like predator with long arms and a large claw on each foot. It walked on two legs.

QANTASSAURUS ("Qantas lizard")
Group: ornithischians, ornithopods, hypsilophodontids
Period: Early Cretaceous
Size and weight: 1.5m (5ft) long, 10kg (22lb)
Location: Australia
Description: Herbivore with a beak, short arms, long hind legs and a long tail. It walked on two legs and had a shorter skull than other hypsilophodontids.

QINLINGOSAURUS ("Qin Ling lizard")
Group: saurischians, sauropodomorphs, sauropods
Period: Late Cretaceous
Size and weight: 15m (49ft) long, 12 tonnes (13 tons)
Location: China
Description: Long-necked herbivore known only from hipbones. It walked on four legs.

QUAESITOSAURUS ("extraordinary lizard")
Group: saurischians, sauropodomorphs, sauropods
Period: Late Cretaceous
Size and weight: 12m (39ft) long, 10 tonnes (11 tons)
Location: Mongolia
Description: Large, long-necked herbivore known only from its skull. It had pencil-shaped teeth and it walked on four legs.

QUILMESAURUS ("Quilmes lizard")
Group: saurischians, theropods, and possibly neoceratosaurs
Period: Late Cretaceous
Size and weight: 7.5m (25ft) long, 1 tonne (1.1 tons)
Location: Argentina
Description: Predator known only from leg bones. It walked on two legs and might have been similar to Abelisaurus.

RAPATOR ("plunderer")
Group: saurischians, theropods, coelurosaurs
Period: Early Cretaceous
Size and weight: 4m (13ft) long, 140kg (310lb)
Location: Australia
Description: Predator known only from one hand bone. It walked on two legs and might have been a giant relative of Mononykus.

RAPETOSAURUS ("Rapeto lizard")
Group: saurischians, sauropodomorphs, sauropods
Period: Late Cretaceous
Size and weight: 10m (33ft) long, 8 tonnes (8.8 tons)
Location: Madagascar
Description: Long-necked herbivore with a wide body and pencil-shaped teeth. It walked on four legs.

RAYOSOSAURUS ("Rayoso lizard")
Group: saurischians, sauropodomorphs, sauropods
Period: Late Cretaceous
Size and weight: 20m (66ft) long, 14 tonnes (15 tons)
Location: Argentina
Description: Herbivore with pencil-shaped teeth, a long neck and slim legs. It walked on four legs.

REBBACHISAURUS ("Rebbach lizard")
Group: saurischians, sauropodomorphs, sauropods
Period: Early Cretaceous
Size and weight: 20m (66ft) long, 14 tonnes (15 tons)
Location: northern Africa
Description: Large, long-necked herbivore with a long tail and a tall sail on its back. It walked on four legs.